KU-543-953

We hope you enjoy this book. Please return or renew it by the due date.

You can renew it at www.norfolk.gov.uk/libraries or by using our free library app.

Otherwise you can phone 0344 800 8020 - please have your library card and PIN ready.

You can sign up for email reminders too.

NORFOLK ITEM

30129 088 545 430

NORFOLK COUNTY COUNCIL
LIBRARY AND INFORMATION SERVICE

ALSO BY TIM SULLIVAN

The Dentist
The Cyclist

The
Patient

TIM
A **DS CROSS** THRILLER
SULLIVAN

HEAD
ZEUS

An Aries Book

Typeset by Siliconchips Services Ltd UK

Printed and bound in Great Britain by
CPI Group (UK) Ltd, Croydon CR0 4YY

Head of Zeus
5–8 Hardwick Street
London EC1R 4RG

WWW.HEADOFZEUS.COM

For Roger Michell
with thanks for a lifetime of friendship and wise counsel

Chapter 1

Cross was unlocking his bike in the shelter outside the Major Crime Unit in Bristol when he heard a noise behind him. He turned, expecting to see maybe a stray cat or dog, but instead found a woman crouching in the corner of the racks, eating a sandwich. He'd seen this woman before. She had been sitting in the reception of the MCU for the past three days. On one occasion he'd seen her talking to the desk sergeant. She had seemed quite calm, gently spoken, as if whatever it was she was there for was being dealt with. She was well dressed in a middle-class, fairly affluent way. She didn't seem to be creating a fuss or making a nuisance of herself.

After three days of walking past her, Cross had determined to talk to her and find out what the issue was. But she wasn't in reception as he left that day, so he assumed that it had been dealt with. Her presence in the bike shelter obviously contradicted this. She had left the building, yes, but she hadn't left, per se. His previous curiosity was now doubled by her apparent dogged determination not to leave. She was bedraggled, her hair and clothes wet from the incessant rain they'd had that afternoon. 'Wet rain' was how his work partner DS Josie Ottey had once described it. When he'd

1

asked her whether rain was not, by its very nature, always wet, she explained that she meant the kind of rain that fell in large voluminous drops. Drops so large they were almost impossible to avoid, as if there was a giant leaky tap in the sky.

The woman's dishevelled appearance wasn't helped by the fact that she had tied the plastic carrier bag in which she had brought her lunch round her head as a makeshift rainproof scarf. She had brought her lunch with her every day for the past few days. She'd planned her visits and was organised; obviously anticipating a lengthy wait, he remembered thinking. He had also noticed that she made her sandwiches with baguettes, not sliced white bread. He took this as a further sign of her being middle class, though he was sure that Ottey would call him a snob for such an observation. She looked like she was in her late sixties.

He stopped unlocking his bike when he saw her. She said nothing; nor did he. He was never very good at initiating conversation unless he was conducting an interview, in which case he realised it was a fundamental requirement. However, it occurred to him that as he had been intending to talk to this woman when she was inside anyway, he probably shouldn't wait for her to speak first.

'What are you doing in here?' he asked.

'Keeping out of the rain,' she replied, quietly.

'Wouldn't that have been more efficiently achieved if you'd stayed inside?' It wasn't an unreasonable question, he thought.

'They asked me to leave,' she said.

'Why?'

'Because they obviously think I'm a nuisance and don't want to have to deal with me.'

'Well, that would be because this isn't actually a police station. A police station has to deal with everyone. I can tell you where the nearest one is,' he replied.

'I've already been there. I've been to all the local police stations and they sent me here. Now they've sent me away as well.'

'Why?' he asked.

'"Why" what?'

'Have you been to all the neighbouring police stations?'

'And who are you, exactly?' she asked.

Cross thought this a perfectly legitimate question. 'I'm DS George Cross of the Major Crime Unit,' he replied.

'Oh good. You're just the person I need to talk to then. My name is Sandra Wilson and my daughter has been murdered,' she said matter-of-factly.

Why this had been of no interest to all the desk sergeants in the area was exactly what intrigued Cross and led to him inviting her back into the building to his office. It was possible she had mental health issues, he thought; though if she had, she was hiding them well.

As they walked into the MCU reception police staffer Alice Mackenzie was leaving, her day finished. 'Goodnight, DS Cross,' she said politely.

'Towel,' he replied.

Mackenzie stopped in her tracks, swivelled round and said to his disappearing back, 'What?'

'Towel,' Cross repeated.

She looked at the woman walking up the stairs with Cross and saw that she was soaking wet. She sighed and went back into the building in search of a towel. She had become used to his often peremptory-sounding instructions by now and didn't take offence – most of the time. She couldn't help smiling, though, as she heard the desk sergeant calling after Cross futilely. He was presumably wondering what Cross was doing taking the woman who'd been sitting in reception for the last three days, and who he himself had escorted off the premises at lunchtime, back into the building. This was classic Cross. He was Marmite to most of his colleagues at the MCU. They either liked him or loathed him. There was no in-between. He often came across as rude, difficult or plain obtuse. But it wasn't intentional. George Cross was on the spectrum, which sometimes made him a little challenging to work with. But it was also his gift. It was what made him an extraordinary detective.

Cross took his time going through the slim file of documents Sandra Wilson had given him. Mackenzie had decided to invite herself to the meeting, if indeed that was what it was, as she'd said that it might make Sandra feel 'more comfortable'. Cross wasn't entirely sure why this was but was too tired to take her up on it. For her part Mackenzie had quietly congratulated herself on being a little more assertive with Cross recently, and proving her value to him. She'd joined the force the year before and, despite her initial qualms, she was loving the job more and more each day. She was also beginning to see where she could be of use to Cross, which helped; making others at their ease with him was one of those occasions – unless, of course, she had determined that a degree of discomfort was what Cross wanted for his interlocutor. She made small talk with Sandra as Cross concentrated on the file. He finally looked up and cut across their conversation completely, as if it wasn't even taking place.

'The coroner has determined that your daughter died

on the seventeenth of June this year from an accidental overdose. There was a post-mortem, and the toxicology report clearly confirms his finding. Your daughter Felicity—'

'Flick,' Sandra interrupted. 'We called her Flick.'

'Your daughter Flick had a long, troubled history of drug abuse. Several unsuccessful stays in rehab. There's a detailed statement from her psychologist...'

'Dr Sutton,' Sandra volunteered.

'...saying that she had been a suicide risk in the past. It all points to a tragic death, Mrs Wilson – self-inflicted, whether deliberately or not. Anyone reading this report would come to the same, inevitable conclusion. Which is, I imagine, the reaction you received from the various police stations you've visited.'

'She did not kill herself, deliberately or otherwise,' Sandra said.

'Sometimes these things are hard to accept, particularly for a mother,' said Mackenzie.

'I'm telling you, she didn't kill herself. She was murdered,' Sandra reiterated.

Cross wondered about this woman's conviction for a moment. She was obviously determined, as evidenced by her presence in their reception for the last three days, as well as her apparent refusal to take the verdict of the coroner and the subsequent reactions of the police as final. 'Why would anyone want to murder your daughter?' he asked.

'I have no idea,' she replied.

Cross went back to the report, turning the pages slowly.

'Nothing was taken; there was no evidence of there being a break-in. Indeed, there is no evidence of anyone else having been with your daughter at the time of, or immediately prior to, her death. What makes you so convinced, in complete contradiction to the facts, such as they are, that she was murdered?'

'I knew my daughter,' was the reply.

Cross said nothing. He'd heard this kind of intuitive, emotionally based statement thousands of times before from relatives, friends, family who couldn't accept what they were being told: that their son was a killer, a rapist, a thief or, as in this case, dead. A refusal to believe what was evident and right in front of them was understandable but, in his opinion, equally frustrating. Sandra was an obvious case of this. He regretted having brought her back into the building. The facts were plain to him. Suicide or accident.

'Many people think they know those close to them, only to find out that something was being hidden from them all those years. Do you know anyone who might have wished your daughter harm?' he asked.

'I knew everything about my daughter. Everything. And I am telling you. She was killed,' she said, ignoring his question.

Cross was never impressed by people's instinctive convictions about things. He dealt in evidence. Facts. There was nothing in this situation that made him think that the grief-stricken woman in front of him was right about her daughter. He went back to the coroner's report to ensure that he hadn't missed anything. He read it again. Twice. This took a further twenty minutes, during which he didn't look up.

Mackenzie filled the silence by making small talk with Sandra once more. She was pleased she'd stayed, because even though Cross may not have valued her presence there, she was sure Sandra derived some comfort from it and it might be of use in the long run. She had discovered in her time at the MCU that she could be useful sometimes as a point of contact for people during an enquiry. She thought of herself as a conduit between them and Cross.

Cross looked up, pushed the file across his desk back to Sandra and stood up, hoping to indicate that the meeting was over.

'Mrs Wilson, there is really nothing I can add to the information you have been provided with. It seems quite clear to me that your daughter died from an overdose, accidental or otherwise. Nothing in there indicates any other possibility.' He looked at her with a neutral expression which he hoped would go some way to persuading her that he was telling the truth. He then remembered what Ottey had told him to say in such circumstances and so added, 'I'm sorry for your loss.'

The woman got up, obviously very disappointed, but she smiled in a dignified manner and put the file back into her handbag. She then said, 'Thank you for your time, Detective Sergeant.'

'I'll show you out,' said Mackenzie. 'Where are you off to now? Do you need transport?'

'No, you're very kind. I'll take the bus. I'm picking up my granddaughter from a neighbour who's been looking after her.'

'How old is she?' Mackenzie asked.

'Just two; she's Flick's child,' Sandra replied as Mackenzie closed the door behind them.

Cross thought for a moment then immediately strode over and reopened the door.

'Your daughter had a small child?' he asked.

Mackenzie and Sandra stopped and turned.

'Yes – Daisy,' Sandra said.

Cross did not speak for a moment but was thinking as he stared at the carpet.

'Where was this child when your daughter overdosed?' he asked.

'In the flat with her. In her bedroom,' Sandra replied.

'The child was in the flat?' he asked again.

'Yes. Flick would've just put her down for the night. She was very big on routine. Daisy went to bed at seven every night, tears or not.'

Cross thought about this.

'So she puts the child down and then injects herself,' he said slowly, as if asking himself.

Mackenzie thought she detected a tone of disbelief in his voice, but with him it was always so difficult to know.

'Exactly,' said Sandra.

Mackenzie showed Sandra out of the building ten minutes later. Sandra was happy to leave, as Cross had promised to look into a couple of things. She, in return, had promised not to come back to the MCU until he'd called her with some more information.

Mackenzie went back to Cross's office but he'd gone. He often did this, she had noticed, when he didn't want to discuss something, or wanted to avoid confrontation. Sometimes it was when he simply wanted to have time to think on his own. He would then leave the office by the back stairs, and have to walk round the entire building, on this occasion in the rain, to get to his bike. She toyed with the idea of running down and intercepting him, but decided against it.

What she didn't know was that it wasn't her Cross was

avoiding. It was his boss, DCI Ben Carson, who he knew was still in the building, as he'd seen his car outside in its parking bay when he'd gone to get his bike. He knew that Carson would have been informed by the desk sergeant, who didn't like Cross and had no time for his 'weirdness', that the woman Carson had asked to be removed from reception had now been taken back into the building by DS Cross. Cross had neither the time nor the patience for issuing unnecessary explanations to his superior that night.

His interest in Flick's death had been piqued by the obvious lack of logic in the process of her overdose. He found it hard to believe that Flick, either about to relapse or kill herself, would not make arrangements for her child. Her infant. If she had been wanting another drug-induced trance – which he thought unlikely in the context of her recent behaviour – or wanted to kill herself, she surely wouldn't have done it with the child in the next room. That seemed out of place to him. What alerted him even more was the fact that the child hadn't featured at all in the inquest. That indicated a lack of thoroughness to Cross, and more often than not such an approach led to a mistake. He'd give it more thought in the morning. Right now, he needed his bed.

Chapter 2

'DS Cross,' he announced, holding up his warrant card as he entered the pathology lab.

Clare Hawkins looked up and waited for him to explain his presence there. She didn't have any of his cases on her docket.

'I was wondering if you could do me a favour?' Cross elaborated, carefully repeating the words Ottey had told him to use to approach this conversation.

'Oh, I didn't realise we'd moved on to favour-exchanging terms now,' she replied wryly.

This completely threw Cross. 'I beg your pardon?'

'Oh, forget it,' she said. 'It was just a joke. What do you want?'

'Could you explain? The joke?'

'It was a joke about the progress of familiarity in our relationship, or lack thereof,' she explained.

'There is no familiarity,' Cross replied.

'That's the joke,' she said.

He thought for a moment, concluding that he would have to take her word for it and move on.

'Could you look at this coroner's report, particularly the toxicology findings, and report back to me?'

She flicked through the folder.

'Overdose; in all probability accidental, but possibly suicide. What am I looking for?' she asked.

'If I knew that I wouldn't be asking.' He thought this reply was not unreasonable.

'What's the issue?' Clare asked.

'Her mother thinks she was murdered. Not an uncommon emotional reaction to such a finding, but there is something out of place in this situation.'

'What?'

'She had a child. A two-year-old who was in the next room when the fatal dose was administered. That, together with the mother's description of her daughter's recent behaviour and demeanour, seems to cast some doubt on the coroner's findings. I think something has been missed and I'd like you to find it. Something is wrong and it's in there.'

This was key to Cross's reaction in this particular case. He simply couldn't tolerate things being wrong, or out of place. Clare liked this about him. The fact that he never acted on instinct but only on the evidence as presented to him. She had learnt that if he had a doubt about something seemingly as straightforward as this coroner's report, it was definitely worth looking into.

'What do you think happened?' she asked.

'Well, obviously I don't as yet know, but hopefully you'll find something erroneous which will encourage us to look into it further.' He then just stood there expectantly. When she looked up he said, 'I'll wait.'

'No, I'd rather you didn't. I have an autopsy report to finish then I'll have a look,' she said.

'So when shall I come back?' He looked at his watch.

'I'll call you.'

'When?' he insisted.

'The minute I've looked at it,' she said, laughing at his persistence.

He sensed there was no point in trying to make her more specific time-wise, so left without a word of thanks or valediction.

She smiled. She was getting to like him the more she knew him. Maybe 'like' was the wrong word, but she was definitely starting to find his directness and his way of working refreshing.

'Bye!' she called after him, as had become her habit. Not to upbraid him for his lack of manners, but to amuse herself a little.

Chapter 3

Cross had successfully avoided DCI Carson the night before, so knew his boss would be hot on his heels the moment he set foot in the open-plan area of the department on the way to his own office. Cross was the only one who had a separate office, not because of any seniority – he didn't have any – but because he couldn't function with all the attendant noise of others at work, making calls, tapping on their keyboards, talking. The open area was much busier during an investigation, even with budgets being slashed the way they were. It would be populated by at least fifteen people, from other detectives to police staff. The scientific team were housed in another building but often dropped in for meetings or discussions about their findings, or lack of, over a cup of coffee. For Cross the most important members of any investigating team were the office manager and the exhibits officer. But he had a chequered career with office managers. They were not, as their name might suggest, in charge of desks and pencil sharpeners. They were themselves detectives who ran the incident room. This involved issuing and staying on top of all the actions an investigation required. These actions were written in a duplicate book with detachable pages. A little archaic, maybe, but incredibly efficient. A copy was then given to the relevant team member and would be checked off in the book when the action was completed or no longer deemed necessary. The problem was that Cross loved this system so much that if the manager wasn't around, he would put actions in the book himself and hand out the dockets. This inevitably caused friction. One attempt to solve the problem had been to make Cross the office manager himself on a case. He actually quite enjoyed this, despite the number of people he seemed to upset in the process. But the team was far less successful in solving cases with him back in the office and not applying his prodigious detecting skills in the field. An exception was then made for him – another in an ever-increasing list of allowances some detectives thought – he was allowed access to the actions book. Cross being made a special case again caused yet more resentment to which he was oblivious.

He hadn't taken more than a few steps into the open area when he heard the familiar sound of Carson's door opening and his name being called. Cross just continued to his office, opened the door and waited for the DCI to follow him. This wasn't before Carson had bellowed his name again. Ottey, who was watching from her desk, wondered why Carson hadn't learnt by now that Cross didn't respond to people shouting at him. He would always ignore them, thinking that shouting was unpleasant and unnecessary, and that whatever the shouter wanted to impart would soon be divulged in closer proximity without the need for a raised voice.

Cross also applied this rule to himself. He never shouted to get someone's attention or to ask for something to be done. He would go over to the person he wanted something from and talk to them in a normal way. His view was that shouting was warranted only occasionally in their job; for example, in a chase or if they were trying to prevent something happening from a distance. He waited for Carson to come into his office as he put down his backpack and took off his bike gear, putting everything in its habitual, proper place.

'Would you mind telling me why you invited Sandra Wilson back into the building yesterday?' Carson began.

'She is convinced her daughter was murdered and that the coroner's verdict is wrong,' Cross said.

Ottey had now joined them from her desk.

'The poor woman is beside herself with grief and can't accept the facts,' Carson went on. 'This is tragic, but none of our concern, which is why she was asked to leave the premises yesterday.'

'Unless of course she's right,' said Cross.

'It is not our job to uncover crime, George.' There was a silence as the three of them tried to process what Carson had just said. 'What I meant was, where there is none. Crime, that is,' he said awkwardly.

'No, but it is our job to uncover crime nonetheless,' Ottey pointed out.

'I have reason to believe that this woman was murdered,' Cross said.

'That's a bit of a stretch, even for you. You're saying that the original investigating officer, the medical examiner and the coroner were all wrong in this case?' Carson asked.

'That's a very precise summation of my position, except for the fact that the original investigating officer seemed to do very little,' he said, then added for clarification, '"investigating".'

'Who was the original SIO?' Carson asked.

'Campbell,' said Ottey.

'Oh, you're joking. Is that why you're doing this?' sighed

Carson. The fact was that DI Johnny Campbell disliked Cross, not because of the way he was, but because he had an uncanny knack of uncovering deficiencies in Campbell's investigations.

'I don't understand the question,' said Cross.

'Well, I'm sorry, but I think your time would be better spent on crimes that have actually been committed. For example, the body in the river. Let's get to the bottom of that murder before we indulge bereaved and, most likely, unhinged mothers,' said Carson.

Mackenzie arrived in the open area for the start of her day and saw Carson and Ottey in Cross's office. She wandered over to listen, not out of nosiness, but from the need to be ahead of whatever she might be asked to do. Also, going over there reminded them that she existed and was there to be asked to do things.

'Josh Trent, aged twenty-three, had been on a drinking binge with two of his friends the night of his death in a pub half a mile upriver from where his body was found,' Cross said. 'They were fairly inebriated, according to the manager of the first pub they were drinking in, the King William IV. He'd had to eject them after Trent became involved in a fight. Hence the bruising to his face, which had not occurred at the time of his going into the river, but at least three hours prior. On leaving the second pub he went to the side of the river to urinate into it and fell. His friends noticed he'd gone but were so drunk themselves they thought nothing of it – assuming that he'd simply wandered off. It wasn't till they heard the news the following morning that they realised what had happened and came forward.' Cross paused for a moment to make sure he'd left nothing out.

'How can you be so sure he went for a piss and that no one else was involved?' asked Carson.

'The protuberance of the deceased's penis from his open fly,' said Cross neutrally, causing Mackenzie to stifle a giggle. Ottey would normally have shot her a warning look, but she was too busy trying not to laugh herself. 'I also walked half a mile upriver and found marks in the mud where he'd slid into the river. He was wearing a large overcoat and boots, which would have impeded his efforts to swim. Though those efforts would have been fairly fruitless.'

'And why is that?' Carson asked.

'Because Josh Trent could not swim. All of this is in my report, which you presumably haven't had a chance to read. Frankly, had uniform done their job properly, there would have been no reason for us to be involved.'

'And where is this report?' Carson asked.

'I put it on your desk yesterday afternoon,' said Mackenzie.

Carson didn't have a ready rejoinder for this, so when Cross's phone started to buzz he suggested the detective answer it, hoping it might distract from his embarrassment. It was Clare, the pathologist.

'I've looked over the report and it all seems fairly straightforward to me. Overdose,' she said.

'You're missing something,' Cross replied.

'Well, I can only go on what I'm reading,' she said, smiling to herself at his bluntness.

'Excellent point. I can rectify that,' Cross replied.

'How so?' she asked.

'I'll send you Felicity's body,' he replied.

Carson now realised what was going on. 'Who are you talking to?'

'Clare, the pathologist. I asked her to go over the coroner's report.'

'And what is her conclusion?'

'She can't find anything wrong,' Cross replied.

'Well then, there you are. Point proven. A tragic occurrence which the mother needs to come to terms with. Please leave well alone.'

'Clare would like to examine the body,' Cross went on.

'I said no such thing!' protested Clare on the other end of the phone, laughing, despite herself, at the man's gall.

'Her mother had the prescience not to have a funeral, so the body is still available to us.' Cross looked at Carson expectantly. 'But of course Clare will need your authority to go ahead.'

Carson hated situations like this with Cross. If it had been anyone else, he would simply have ordered them to move on and leave it. But no one else would have put him in such a position. He wasn't sure what was worse: having to immediately climb down from his order for Cross to desist and suffer the – admittedly quite small – humiliation that came with that, or stick to his guns and repeat his instruction. The problem with the latter was that Cross would never give up, particularly when he was told to. He was like a terrier snapping at your heels; once he'd got hold of your trouser leg, he would stubbornly refuse to let go, even if you spun him round in circles. He would just grimly hold on with his teeth, flying through the air.

Cross also had an extraordinary capacity, bearing in mind his outwardly awkward manner, to persuade people like Clare to do things under the radar. When he did so, he was invariably proved right, which was even more humiliating for

Carson, although if the case was successful and came to the attention of 'upstairs' he would ensure that he, Carson, took full credit.

'Fine. Do it, but you'd better be right,' said Carson.

'Oh, I hope not. Or do you think that would be better for her mother? To find out that her daughter had been murdered?' Cross asked.

Carson couldn't figure out whether Cross was being sarcastic, although of course he should've known he wasn't, so just stared at him.

'Oh, I think so,' volunteered Mackenzie. There was a pause. She felt like a child at an adults' cocktail party, giving an opinion which was neither expected nor welcome. 'I mean, don't you think it would be better to be proved right and know that your daughter hadn't killed herself, intentionally or otherwise?'

Cross thought for a moment. 'She may well be right,' he said.

Carson left the room quickly, shaking his head as if he was exasperated that he had to work with such a bunch of fools.

'Can your department make arrangements for Felicity's transport?' Cross asked Clare who was still on the phone.

'Of course. I'll come back to you as soon as I have something.'

'Don't you mean "if" you have something?' Cross asked.

'Something tells me your instincts are right on this one,' she said.

'It has nothing to do with instincts,' he replied. 'The child being in the room next door is an incontrovertible and denotative fact.' He cut off the call.

★

'I love him when he's like this,' said Mackenzie, as she and Ottey returned to their desks.

'Like what?' Ottey asked.

'When his autistic dander is up,' Mackenzie replied. Ottey shot her a look. 'Brother's autistic, remember? Gives me special privileges,' she went on. Then, sensing Ottey's continued disapproval, she added, 'Point taken. I will be careful in future.'

Chapter 4

'DS Cross,' he said, warrant card held up high for Clare to see.

'I left a message for you to *call* me. You didn't have to come all the way over,' she said. He didn't reply, but she knew why he was actually there. To see the body for himself. To double check her work. She sighed, turned to one of the assistants and said, 'Could you bring in Miss Wilson?'

Cross thought this encapsulated her attitude to the dead. She always accorded them a formal courtesy. To her they weren't bodies, cadavers, stiffs, corpses. They were still people, albeit dead, who should be given the same respect they would've been given if alive.

'So what can you tell me about Miss Wilson?' he asked.

'Cause of death, overdose. Only one puncture wound, in the crook of her arm where the hypodermic had been left, and a bruise on her forehead. It's impossible to tell whether it was caused at the time of death or was something that was incurred prior because of the length of time since her death,' she said.

'So possibly irrelevant?'

'Nothing is irrelevant at this stage, Sergeant,' she reminded him.

'This is very true,' he replied.

It was three weeks since Cross had asked Clare to look at Flick. This interval was because she had decided to run the toxicology tests again.

'There is something odd here, though. Flick died from an overdose of diamorphine,' she continued.

'Why is that odd?' Cross asked.

'Because in this case, taking into account the presentation of the death scene and the victim's past history of drug use, I'd expected it to be heroin. Heroin is a synthetic form of diamorphine. People assume they're the same, but they're not. Heroin breaks down in the body in a different way to diamorphine. They share the same breakdown product, a substance called 6-MAM. But street heroin is not a clean drug. There would also normally be adulterants present – codeine, noscapine and papaverine. None of them are there.'

'So what are your conclusions?' he asked.

'Flick died from an overdose of medical morphine, which raises a lot of questions. Questions that should have been looked into previously. If she had wanted a fix, which I doubt, or wanted to end it all, you would expect it to be by virtue of heroin, street heroin. Where would she have got medical morphine from?'

'What are you saying, exactly?'

'You asked me to look for the out of place, the not normal, the out of the ordinary, and this is it. In my opinion it lends credence to her mother's claim that she was murdered. I'll admit it asks more questions than it answers. But I suppose that's your job,' she said.

Cross was thinking this through. It was exactly this kind of kink in the facts of a case that others often overlooked

– as indeed in this situation – or hadn't seen, that led him to believe a crime had been committed.

'One other thing they also failed to do was a hair test. If she had taken heroin in recent months there would have been traces left in her hair. A residue. This woman had been clean for at least eighteen months,' she concluded.

At this point a body covered by a sheet was wheeled into the room by the assistant. Cross turned and started to leave.

'Don't you want to look at the body?' she asked.

'No need. You've found the un-obvious, as I was sure you would, given your application to your work.' So saying, he left.

'Bye!' she said into the air. The mortuary assistant turned to her.

'Did he just pay you a compliment?' he asked.

'If he did, he definitely wasn't aware of it,' she replied.

Chapter 5

Cross was about to brief Ottey with Clare's findings back in his office when Mackenzie appeared at the door.

'You're wanted in Carson's office,' she said. They both got up. 'Just DS Cross.'

Ottey stopped; she was about to exchange a look with Cross but he'd already gone, so she was talking to his back. She followed him out and looked across at Carson's office, where she saw the boss talking to someone else. The back of that balding, shaved head was unmistakable. It was Campbell.

'DI Campbell is unhappy about you reopening the Wilson case,' Carson started off by saying to the standing Cross.

'He's not reopening it. There was no case. Is no case,' spat Campbell.

'Felicity Wilson died from an overdose—' Cross began.

'We know that,' interrupted Campbell.

'Of medical morphine, not heroin,' said Cross.

Campbell went quiet, probably because he was actually trying to work out what the implications of this were.

'Which obviously raises certain questions,' Cross continued.

'So she died from an overdose of medical morphine. What about it? She was an addict,' said Campbell.

'A recovering addict...' Cross said.

Campbell snorted. 'Oh, don't give me that crap. Once an addict always an addict.'

'Indeed, which is why I believe they are referred to as "recovering addicts". Flick Wilson was clean, which you would've known had her hair been tested, which it wasn't, because you were too quick to write this off as a suicide or accidental overdose.'

Campbell tried to interrupt, but Cross just continued with an ever so slight increase in volume and authority. 'If you'd done your job thoroughly – no, let me rephrase that – *properly*, you would've tested her hair, because as you know, certain drugs remain in the hair and indicate the precise time they were ingested. Felicity had been drug-free for at least eighteen months. There wasn't a trace of anything in her hair. Something else you would've known had you listened to the mother and followed through.'

'In my opinion there was nothing to follow up on, and that still remains the case. She killed herself, tragic accident or tragic suicide,' said Campbell.

'Even in the light of what I've just told you?' asked Cross.

'Particularly in light of what you've just told me,' Campbell replied.

Cross thought for a moment in case he hadn't heard Campbell correctly. Realising he had, he looked up.

'Really? Then perhaps you could explain, as I don't understand.' He turned to Carson. 'Do you understand how he can still reach the same conclusion in light of the new evidence, or rather the old evidence which he didn't actually look for?'

'You want to watch your tone, Sergeant,' said Campbell.

'I am well aware of your superior rank, DI Campbell, but it doesn't mean you're any better at doing the job than I am. In fact, in your case, as we seem to have clashed on many occasions and almost always because of your lack of ability, it would seem to imply exactly the opposite,' said Cross, with no side to it.

Carson nearly laughed but realised, just in time, that as the senior officer, that wouldn't be appropriate. 'So you're saying Felicity Wilson was murdered?' he said.

'I am not,' Cross replied.

'Then what's all the fuss about?' asked Campbell.

'What I am saying is that it is at the very least suspicious and warrants investigation. We don't have any information to categorically say she was murdered, or indeed, at this point in time, whether a third party was involved,' Cross said. 'A conclusion we could've come to some weeks ago had DI Campbell not been in his usual rush to wrap things up without properly examining the evidence right in front of him.'

'That's it; I've had enough,' said Campbell. 'I'm not going to sit here and listen to this crap. You let him get away with way too much. I'm making an official complaint.'

'On what grounds, Johnny?' asked Carson.

'His lack of respect, total disregard for the chain of command and a personal vendetta against me,' said Campbell.

'Vendetta implies a need for revenge. I'm curious – what have you done that I need to avenge, DI Campbell?' asked Cross.

'Do you want a slap?' said Campbell.

'I think you'll find threatening another officer is a breach of the code. I'm not entirely certain, but if you put it in your complaint I'm sure someone will be able to clear that up,' said Cross, who had nevertheless taken a step back.

Campbell looked at Carson.

'George, that's enough, thank you,' said Carson. 'Johnny, you are perfectly entitled to make a complaint. I would suggest you go straight through to Human Resources. Having said that, you might want to think about it for a minute, and after you've calmed down decide whether it's your best course of action.'

'Well, it would be pretty pointless sending it to my superior officer now, wouldn't it?' Campbell said.

'And what exactly is that supposed to mean?' asked Carson.

'I've wasted enough time here. I'll leave you with your pet,' Campbell said and turned on his heels as Ottey appeared at the door.

'Sandra Wilson is here,' she said.

'Oh good,' said Cross. 'Perhaps DI Campbell would like to take the opportunity to apologise to her. I know the force is big on relations with the public at this present time.'

Campbell paused for a second, then continued on his way out. Carson and Ottey shared a smile.

'DI Campbell is making a complaint about me,' said Cross, as he and Ottey walked towards the Voluntary Assistance suite.

'I'm surprised it's taken him so long,' she replied.

'You think I have something to answer for? That he's justified?'

'No, not at all. If he was half as good at his job as he

thinks he is, you wouldn't be able to constantly highlight his shortcomings.'

'Oh dear,' said Cross.

'I wouldn't worry about him,' she said reassuringly.

'I wasn't. I was just thinking of all the other officers in the department whose shortcomings I might have drawn attention to, deliberately or otherwise. Will they all be making complaints?'

'Maybe. Hey, they could do a kind of class action. A load of complaints in one,' she said.

He frowned. 'I think you're joking, but even if you're not, it's not in the least bit helpful.'

Ottey laughed. It was a full twelve months since she'd become his partner and although it had taken some time to get used to him she had come to respect and understand him. As a single mother of two daughters she often found herself applying her domestic experience to deal with her idiosyncratic work partner. She realised that if she gave him the kind of latitude she often dispensed at home, they could rub along quite nicely. In many ways she had become Cross's apologist in the department; his interpreter. She confessed to friends that she might have been less understanding had he not been such an irritatingly brilliant cop. He had the highest conviction rate in the force. By far. Having said that, there were times when she would happily have thrown him off Clifton suspension bridge.

Chapter 6

Sandra Wilson looked a lot more together than when Cross had last seen her. This wasn't only because she was dry and well dressed, but there was something about her which seemed calmer. Cross wondered whether the mere fact that he had taken her seriously had relieved her of some stress. She reminded him of the Scottish actress Elizabeth Sellars, with beautifully coiffed blonde hair, elegant, chiselled cheekbones and dark, piercing eyes. Obviously a beauty in her youth, she wouldn't have looked out of place herself on a movie poster from the 1950s. Mackenzie had already made her a cup of tea and was discussing the pleasure and pain of bringing up a two-year-old toddler in your late sixties.

'Mrs Wilson, we've had a further look at both the autopsy report and the coroner's report,' Cross began. 'We've done more tests, which have taken a few weeks to complete, and we've asked you in to present our findings to you.'

'Was she murdered?' Sandra asked quickly.

'That we cannot say categorically,' said Cross. He noticed that her shoulders slumped a little with disappointment. 'However, something came up which I think warrants further investigation. Your daughter Felicity died from an overdose of diamorphine, not heroin.'

Her blank look seemed to indicate that she wasn't aware of the difference. Her daughter had died from an overdose; what was new about this information?

'Diamorphine is a medically prescribed opioid. Heroin is made from diamorphine and is sometimes referred to as such but it's not actually the same thing,' he said.

'I'm sorry. I'm not sure I completely follow,' said Sandra.

Cross looked over at Ottey for help, as was his habit when people didn't understand him.

'What we're saying, Sandra, is that your instincts that something wasn't quite right about Flick's death would seem to be correct and we'd like to look into it further,' said Ottey.

'Oh, I see. Yes of course. I'm so glad – relieved, actually. I've thought maybe I was going mad and that my friends who were telling me I just couldn't accept Flick's passing were right. Is that awful? To feel relieved?' she asked.

'It's a very confusing time. It's fine to feel whatever you feel,' said Ottey.

'You're just trying to do your best for her,' said Mackenzie.

Cross noticed how this seemed to pick Sandra up a little. He'd seen this happen with Mackenzie quite a lot recently. She appeared to have the skill of saying the right thing to people exactly when it was needed; a facility he was aware he did not possess in any measure.

'So although we cannot as yet say that Felicity was murdered, we will nevertheless conduct our enquiries as if this was a murder enquiry,' he said, looking over at Ottey.

She knew this signal well by now. Cross had made the judgement that it might be better if she conducted this initial interview. He thought that she would glean more out of

Sandra than he would. He would just listen and take notes. He often did this when Ottey conducted an interview, but unlike other officers he used quite a large pad rather than a small notebook. His notes often took a diagrammatic form, with arrows and boxes, all drawn with different coloured pens. She wondered if it was a pictorial representation of how his mind worked.

'So Daisy is two and she's now in your custody. Who's the father?' Ottey began.

'Her boyfriend, well, ex-boyfriend currently, well, obviously not her boyfriend at all now…' Sandra faltered.

'So, an on-off relationship?' Ottey asked.

'More off than on before her death,' Sandra replied.

'What was his name? Is his name?' Ottey said.

'Simon, Simon Aston.'

'How did they meet?' Ottey asked.

'Backpacking. A few years ago now. That's where it all began, the drug-taking. When it became an all-consuming problem. They did their first stint of rehab together then both relapsed at the same time. It was like they fell off the wagon with twice the force than if they'd been on their own, if you know what I mean. They were so bad for each other. Truth is, I don't know who was worse. Who was to blame. It could've been Flick, I just don't know.'

'And where is he now?' Ottey asked.

'Back in a rehab facility.'

'I'm sorry to hear that. So he was still using while she was clean. Was that why they split up?' Ottey went on.

'He was struggling. Flick had become totally sober. No alcohol, obviously no drugs. She even gave up caffeine for a while. But he kept relapsing. She said she couldn't have him around her or the baby if he was still using. Then there was the dealing. Nothing major. But he dealt to make money for his habit. He tried to give her money for the baby but she wouldn't take it. Dirty money, she called it. Daisy was the reason she got sober and she wasn't going to let anything jeopardise that.'

'Was it becoming a mother that made her sort herself out?' Ottey asked.

'Yes, but not in the way you're thinking. Daisy was born dependent. She was so ill. Flick was devastated when she saw her. I didn't know Flick was pregnant till right at the end of the pregnancy.'

'Why was that?' asked Ottey.

'I'd had enough. Reached the end of my tether. Isn't that terrible?' said Sandra.

'It's understandable, I think,' said Ottey.

'All the lies and promises. She stole from me. It was awful. I didn't know who she was in the end. I didn't throw her out, though I was close to it. But she left and I never even bothered to find out where she'd gone. Then she got in touch. She said she needed her mother. They were living in such squalor. I couldn't believe it when I saw it, and on top of that she was heavily pregnant.'

'Was she still using?'

'Yes. But I could tell she was done. She was admitted straight into hospital. They weaned her off the drugs. But Daisy. Have you ever seen a baby in heroin withdrawal? They call it neonatal abstinence syndrome. She had it for over a week. I could see in Flick's eyes that it was over. It had to be. She couldn't believe what she'd done to this innocent baby. Daisy was so ill it was hard to watch.'

'Was Simon in rehab at the time of your daughter's death?' asked Cross.

'No. We'd taken him in a month earlier. Flick had come with me. She insisted on bringing Daisy so he could see what he was risking losing as he went in. He wanted to be part of their lives. I really believed that. But she wouldn't have him around them, as much for her sake as for the baby's. She knew her sobriety was fragile.' She looked up immediately, regretting having said that. 'I don't mean that she thought she was in danger of a relapse. It's just that that is what it's like. It's fragile. A day at a time, as they say.'

'Was she a member of any support groups like AA or NA?' Ottey asked.

Sandra shook her head. 'No. That wasn't for her,' she said. All that talk of a "higher power". She didn't like it. She was in therapy, though, and had been in rehab several times. She called herself a "professional patient".' She smiled at the memory.

'So what happened with Simon and rehab that time?' asked Ottey.

'He came out after five days, claiming he could do it on his own this time. Of course he couldn't. So she ended it. For good. She didn't want to offer him false hope, or a false promise, as she put it. There would be no life for the three of them together,' she said quietly.

'How did he react to that?' asked Ottey.

'He was devastated, angry, beside himself. In the end we had to take out a restraining order. Flick didn't need much persuading. Hundreds of texts a day, most of them incomprehensible. Sleeping rough in the shop doorway opposite her flat. It was awful.'

'Had he seen her since the restraining order?' asked Ottey.

'Not as far as I know, no.'

'When did he go back into rehab?' asked Cross.

'A few days after her death. He begged me to take him. He even asked me to try and get him sectioned. Poor boy. I called his parents. Like me, they were out of touch with their child. Didn't even know about Daisy – she's two! They were shocked about Flick. They came down straight away. I think maybe they thought, "there but for the grace of God".' She stopped, then looked up as if the last few sentences had knocked the wind out of her. 'Could we have a little break?' she asked, as if not wanting to cause anyone any trouble.

'Of course,' said Ottey. 'Alice, could you make Sandra another cup of tea, please?'

'Of course,' replied Mackenzie.

'Cake,' said Cross.

'You want some cake?' asked Mackenzie.

'Obviously not. For Mrs Wilson. Sweet cake. Some sugar will do her good. Ask DCI Carson. He often has cake secreted about his office.'

'Of course,' said Mackenzie again, smiling at this titbit of information.

'Mrs Wilson, did you take any pictures of Flick?' Cross asked.

'How do you mean?' asked Sandra.

Ottey looked horrified. Surely he wasn't asking…

'Post-mortem. In situ. At her flat,' he stated blankly.

Ottey was lost for words. How on earth could he think a grieving mother would do such a thing, and how could he think about asking her in this way? She couldn't help but think of Carla and Debbie, her own daughters, and realised she had no idea how she would have reacted had she been in Sandra's shoes, so it wasn't for her to judge.

'Oh, I'm so glad you asked,' said Sandra, getting out her phone. 'I felt a little ghoulish and people were giving me very odd looks, but I could tell that the detective who was there had already made his mind up.'

'DI Campbell?' Cross asked.

'Yes, that was him. So I wanted to record everything in case someone needed to look at it later. I'm afraid I got carried away. I took well over fifty.' She gave him her phone.

Later, back in his office, Ottey asked him, 'What made you think a mother who had just lost her daughter in tragic circumstances would photograph the scene?'

'Logic. I knew she thought the police had come to the most obvious conclusion almost immediately, as well as having the feeling that all was not as it seemed. The logical thing to do was photograph the way everything appeared so that it could be examined at a later date, because she wasn't about to give up on her,' he said as the photographs sprang up on his desktop.

There were indeed dozens of them. The room itself, the body, close-ups of the syringe in Flick's arm. Close-ups of things on the table next to the armchair she was sitting in. Everything was documented in extraordinary detail. It was the kind of thing that made Cross's day.

'Blimey,' said Ottey. 'She could have a career in forensics.'

'No, she's way too old,' said Cross with complete seriousness.

Chapter 7

Flick had lived in a first-floor flat in Southville which had been bought for her by her mother. Sandra had used money from her and her late husband's pension pot to finance the purchase. Flick had lived with her mother in Clifton for a while after Daisy's birth. Then after they were both confident she could cope on her own, she moved into the flat. It was in the nearest area to Sandra's house that they could afford. So near, in fact, that it was known as 'Lower Clifton', or 'Clifton Lite' as Flick had called it. It was a trendy little area now with the old Wills Tobacco factory at its centre. Sandra had left everything exactly as it was when her daughter passed away. When Cross discovered this he wanted to visit the flat. Something had occurred to him while looking at Sandra's photos of her daughter's death scene, but he didn't share it with anyone and Ottey didn't ask, so he hadn't told her. But she had noted it.

In the car on the way to Flick's flat she turned to him to ask:

'What was it about the photographs? What did you see?' She instantly regretted her question as she knew no answer would be forthcoming and of course she was right. 'You're so annoying,' she continued. 'What's more annoying is you don't even know how annoying you are.'

They drove on for a while in silence.

'Why don't you ever share?' she persisted.

'Share what?'

'What you're thinking about on a case. You think of something. Everyone can see it but you don't share, leaving everyone, well, mostly me, trying to figure out what it is you're thinking about.'

'If it's something I'm not sure about I don't like to mention it until I'm certain.'

'Why?'

'Because I've learnt from experience that my reputation for solving cases is such that if I mention a potential line of enquiry or possible lead everyone will act on it despite any instructions to the contrary. If I'm wrong it's then an unnecessary waste of people's time and resources. Therefore I am circumspect in what I, as you put it, share.'

She laughed. Coming out of anyone else's mouth this would be pure arrogance.

'Bullshit. You just don't want to be seen to be wrong. That's all it is. Pride.'

'I can assure you it's no such thing and that my reasoning is entirely correct, while your conjecture is just that. Conjecture,' he replied.

This was a typical example of the constant reminders for Ottey that working with Cross was, and possibly always would be, different to anything she had ever experienced in the force. As well as banter, she missed the element of teasing that existed between colleagues. It so often lightened the tension or was a way to get a tricky point across to a colleague without causing offence. None of this was possible with Cross.

Ottey had tried to convince Sandra not to come with them back to the flat – she hadn't been back there since the coroner had removed the body – but she was insistent. She made no scene when they entered, indeed, she actually showed them around with all the ease of a landlord showing it to a prospective client she liked. She then sat on the sofa with Mackenzie. Cross watched as Sandra delicately moved a strand of hair to reveal Mackenzie's pierced ear and complimented her on her studs. He reflected that she was a kindly woman and how unfortunate it was that any of this had befallen her.

The flat was very organised, clean and tidy. It had two bedrooms, a small one used as a nursery, and Flick's bedroom. There was a light bohemian feel to the way Flick had decorated it, Ottey thought, with pieces of material draped over lamps, South American rugs on the floor, scented candles everywhere. She noticed that all the child's clothes were still there.

'I took what I could, but there was so much other stuff to take. I bought whatever else I needed,' Sandra explained.

'Why don't we pack up all the stuff you need for Daisy and then I could help you take it back to yours?' suggested Mackenzie.

'Would you? That would be so kind,' said Sandra.

'Perhaps you could wait till DS Cross and I have finished,' said Ottey.

'What exactly are you after?' asked Sandra.

But before Ottey was able to answer, Cross strode back into the room purposefully. He had concentrated his search on the floor around the chair Flick was found on – in fact the whole of the sitting room floor – then the kitchen and the bathroom. He hadn't found what he was looking for.

'Alice, do you have the original police report and the coroner's report with you?' he asked.

'Yes, you asked me to bring them.' She handed them to him.

He sat for a moment and scanned the documents quickly. Then he got up, handed them back to Mackenzie, walked to the front door of the flat and opened it.

'George, where are you going?' asked Ottey.

'Back to the MCU. Are you coming? I need you to drive me.'

'Are we done here?' she asked.

'Yes.'

'The reason being?'

'I have all I need,' he replied, getting a little impatient.

'For what?' said Ottey.

'To determine that Mrs Wilson is indeed correct in her conviction that her daughter was murdered,' he said.

There was a pause as both Ottey and Mackenzie tried to figure out how he had come to this conclusion. Sandra herself looked momentarily shell-shocked before breaking down in shuddering tears. Mackenzie put her arms around her.

Cross was confused. This woman was convinced that her daughter had been murdered, had been frustrated and angry that the police wouldn't listen to her, and now he had formed the conclusion that she was right, she became upset.

He was sent out by Ottey to get some fresh milk so they could make tea. Even he knew it was just a pretext to get him out of there so they could comfort Sandra without him.

There was a small mini-market on the corner of Flick's road, about a hundred yards from her flat. The road itself was a terrace of small Victorian two-up two-down houses, some of which were divided into flats. The shop seemed a little out of character with the rest of the road. Cross thought it was in all probability one of a succession of buildings which had filled a space left by a Second World War bombing raid. Bristol had been subjected to a six-month bombing blitz as the Germans tried to knock out the harbour. Southville was just south of the harbour and suffered a lot of collateral damage from bombs missing their target.

The outside of the shop was clad in scaffolding as some work was being done to the roof and the front of the building was being repainted. Cross was pleased to see that it was still independently owned. He felt that the large supermarket chains which were moving into this smaller sector, with their so-called 'local' branches, would have no loyalty to the area or their customers as soon as the economy got tough again. They would be out of these areas as soon as the figures no longer stacked up.

He returned the girl at the till's greeting and headed for the fridge at the back of the shop. It was at this point that he realised he didn't know what kind of milk they needed. He thought about going back to the flat for a moment, but that would surely defeat the object of him going to get milk in the first place; namely to get rid of him. There was only one thing for it. He took three cartons out of the fridge.

When he'd come into the shop, Cross had noticed the smell of Indian food being cooked. There was something about it that had a real authenticity. He wasn't sure what it was, but he knew that if he had gone into an Indian restaurant and smelt that as he got to his table, he would think he was in good hands. He took the milk over to the till.

'Are you a detective?' she asked.

'I am. How do you know?'

'I saw you going into Flick's flat. Is there a problem?' she asked.

'A girl is dead.'

'I know; killed herself, poor thing,' she said. Cross said nothing. 'You don't think she killed herself?' she said, picking up on his silence.

'That is correct,' Cross replied.

'Was she murdered?' the girl asked, falteringly.

'I think so, yes,' he said.

'But who would want to murder her?' she asked.

'Good question. Have you seen anyone suspicious in the area lately?'

'No. Just her ex making a nuisance of himself.'

'Simon?' asked Cross. 'Had he been around recently?'

'Yes. She had a restraining order but he started sleeping in the shop doorway.'

'Did he attempt to make contact with her?' Cross asked.

'I don't know. The owners would know. They became quite friendly with her.'

'Can you remember if he was here the day of her death?'

'Yeah. I opened up that day. I had a right go at him. Told him Anil and Sunetra would call the police if he kept coming round.'

'Anil and Sunetra?'

'The owners.'

Cross paid her and left. As the bell above the door signalled his departure the young shop assistant was thinking a 'thank you' wouldn't have been out of place.

*

He returned to the flat with the cartons of milk – full fat, semi-skimmed and skimmed.

'Why did you get so much milk?' Ottey asked as she took over making the tea from him.

'You didn't specify which milk,' he said.

'I'm so sorry about just now,' said Sandra, who had recovered somewhat.

'Yes, it was confusing,' said Cross.

'What he means is that it's perfectly all right and quite understandable,' said Mackenzie, shooting him a look.

Ottey smiled: at last an ally to keep him in check. Maybe they could work as one. A tag team.

'What makes you so sure she was murdered?' Sandra continued. Mackenzie was relieved she'd asked this as she couldn't figure it out herself and didn't want to look stupid by asking.

'I couldn't see it in your comprehensive and immensely useful photographs, so when you said the flat had lain undisturbed since Flick's...' he stopped himself quickly from being so matter-of-fact, not wanting to instigate another, to him, incomprehensible display of grief, 'passing, I wanted to check for myself. Something's missing.'

'What?' asked Ottey, throwing the tea bags into the sink which made Cross grimace.

'The vessel,' he said.

'What?' asked Mackenzie.

'Speak English,' said Ottey, immediately regretting it when she saw his look of confusion as he tried to process that comment and then decided just to move on.

'The diamorphine had to have come in some sort of container. A small container, labelled, no doubt. But it's not here,' he said.

'What does that mean?' asked Sandra.

'It means that someone had to have taken it,' said Mackenzie.

'Exactly,' confirmed Cross.

'Could it have been the coroner or the police?' Sandra asked.

'There is no mention of it in either report,' said Cross. 'It's been removed from the scene. A mistake. The killer left the scene as carefully as they could to give the impression of self-administration, leaving the tourniquet on the arm, the needle in the elbow.'

'The diamorphine could have already been in the syringe,' suggested Ottey.

'Highly unlikely. It comes in a bottle. A sealed bottle with a serial number which would've given away the source. Where it had been obtained. The killer realised he couldn't leave it, but in not leaving it, inadvertently proved to us that there was a third party involved. The fact that the container is not here and the fact that it was diamorphine and not heroin is sufficient for me to believe that your daughter didn't take her own life, Mrs Wilson. Someone else did.'

'Thank you,' she replied.

'I'm not sure that's what you mean, but I think I understand what you do mean,' he replied. 'We need to interview Simon,' he continued.

'Oh, I don't think that's such a good idea,' Sandra replied.

'He slept in the shopfront door the day of her death. He was here,' Cross said.

'I don't believe for a minute he would have hurt her,' Sandra said.

Cross then noticed a row of neatly labelled journals with dates on them. On closer inspection they were diaries. He picked one up without asking permission and started going through it.

'She kept diaries,' he observed. The pages were crammed with close, well-formed handwriting, together with the odd relevant ticket stub or receipt.

'Ever since she was small. The ones from when she was a child are back at mine in a box for safe keeping,' Sandra replied.

'Very detailed and very regular.'

'Yes, it was slightly obsessive. Even when she was at her worst with the drug use she still kept a journal. Not that the entries made a huge amount of sense some of the time. She used to read them back to remind herself of the state she got herself into.'

Cross put the journal back then looked at the date of the last one on the shelf. He looked around the room.

'Do you know where this year's journal is?'

'I don't. It should be here somewhere.'

But despite them all looking, it couldn't be found.

'It's not at your house?' Ottey asked.

'No. It was always here. Normally on the table. She'd write in it at all times of the day. It should be here.'

'That's odd,' said Ottey. A further search by all four of them didn't turn it up. As they left Sandra to gather up some of Daisy's clothes and equipment, Cross turned to her and asked, 'Downstairs. Who lives there?'

'Brian.'

They knocked on his door. There was no response. They went back to the flat upstairs.

'There's no one in,' Ottey told her.

'He's probably at work,' Sandra told them.

'What does he do?' asked Cross.

'He's a nurse at the BRI. He works in ITU,' she went on.

Ottey looked at Cross who was thinking the same as her – he had regular access to drugs which would, without question, include morphine.

'Were they close?' asked Ottey.

'Practically lived in each other's pockets. She was grateful for the company but I think he had a bit of a soft spot for her, to be honest.'

Chapter 8

Mackenzie stayed behind to help Sandra with Daisy's things and drive her home. Meanwhile, Cross and Ottey drove to the rehab centre where Simon was staying.

'That was strange,' said Cross.

'No it wasn't,' replied Ottey. 'You were so wrapped up in what you were doing, as usual, you forgot to tell poor Sandra what you were thinking. You needed to sit down and tell her quietly or, better still, tell me in the next room so I could tell her. You can't just drop it in passing.'

'Okay,' he said and started writing in his notebook.

'What are you doing?'

'Just making a note for future reference,' he answered. Then he continued, a little puzzled, 'But she got the answer she was looking for. At last someone was taking her seriously and had proved her right. Why was she so upset?'

'It was the bald, brutal fact of it. Hearing it out loud. That someone had ended her daughter's life. It must be upsetting and hard to take in, even if you suspected it was the truth. She's her mother. Her child has been taken away from her.'

'She knew her child had been taken away from her already,' he persisted.

'I know, and in some ways maybe it's better that someone else had ended her life. Better than the fact that she'd done it herself, accidentally or deliberately, that is. But then the fact that someone else actually did do it has other emotional connotations. It's a violent act – even if no actual violence was used – unnecessary, brutal,' she said.

'Her conviction was admirable. She wasn't to be swayed and she was right,' he added.

'She was Flick's mother. It's an unbreakable bond, mother–child – with mother and daughter maybe even stronger. I certainly feel that with my girls.'

'Not in my experience,' he said, immediately regretting it. He spoke again quickly to prevent her taking him up on this comment. 'But a mother's instinct isn't always infallible, is it? In similar cases to this I'm sure it's often the case of unwillingness by the mother to accept the facts. There was something about her preternatural calmness when claiming her daughter had been killed that was quite compelling. At the same time as not knowing the why. Why would someone kill her daughter?'

'Why, who and how?' added Ottey.

'And does the bruise signify a material blow to the head?' he asked.

'It has to, otherwise I just can't figure out how it happened.'

'It is an intriguing set of circumstances,' said Cross.

'What about the journal? Do you think whoever killed her took it?'

'It seems more than likely, given that it's probable she knew her killer.'

Ottey's phone buzzed. She handed it to Cross.

'Carson. He wants us back at base for an update,' he said reading the text.

'What a waste of time.' She sighed, then said loudly and authoritatively, 'Call Carson!'

Cross was slightly surprised by her tone. 'Certainly,' he replied, but as he did so a ringing tone sounded through the car stereo.

'I was talking to the car!' Ottey exclaimed, laughing.

They were put through to Carson.

'Hi, it's Josie. Could we do this on the phone as we're on our way to see the ex-boyfriend? You're on speaker with me and George.'

'Sure. So I'm getting questions from upstairs asking why we're devoting resources to a death which the coroner has already ruled an accidental overdose or suicide,' Carson said.

'This is thanks to Campbell, I assume,' Ottey said.

'You know how thick he is with the super. They're in the same five-a-side football team,' said Carson.

'She was murdered,' said Cross.

'What? How?'

'Overdose,' said Cross.

'Explain. She could've administered the diamorphine herself.'

'It's possible, but it doesn't fit with her recent behaviour,' said Cross.

'Who knows how the mind of an addict works? Do you? I certainly don't,' said Carson.

'She also had a child,' Cross went on.

'We know all this.'

'In the room next door to where her body was found,' said Cross.

Ottey looked at him. It was as if he was teasing their boss, but he wasn't. He was laying the facts out in the order he'd come across them. He always did this, repeating the pattern and process of their discovery. It was a mantra which prepared him for the interview room. He wanted their discovery and the timeline to be second nature to him by the time he entered that room, because in their process there was a narrative which at this point he wasn't aware of. But once he was, remembering the process helped him construct that narrative more effectively.

'I'm going to need more than that, George. They know all of this. It's nothing new,' sighed Carson. But the fact was that he knew Cross well enough by now. The detective never followed a hunch or gut instinct. He only worked with and reacted to facts. That was why Carson let him have more leeway than others in the unit, much to the annoyance of some people – like Campbell.

'There was no container for the morphine discovered at the scene and it isn't there now,' said Cross.

'Which means?' said Carson, trying to give the impression of thinking out loud.

'It means a third party had to be involved. Someone who then took it away with them,' said Cross.

'Okay, I understand. Good work. It raises more questions than it answers, though.'

'Isn't that true with most of the cases we work?' Cross asked.

Chapter 9

The Hopewell Clinic was in a nondescript house in Bedminster, situated among residential houses. There had been a shipbuilding yard there in the nineteenth century as the river Malago ran through – a tributary of the River Avon. Cross liked the fact that its two main streets, East and West Street, were also indications that it was probably an early Roman settlement. It, like neighbouring Southville, had suffered much damage during the war. Not quite as much damage, aesthetically, thought Cross, as the post-war planners had managed to wreak upon the area in the following decades. Inside the clinic it was very functional; not clinical, but slightly institutional. Cross wondered whether there was a balance to be reached in the way the interior came across to the residents. Not too forbidding and uncomfortable, with an element of encouragement for them to stay there for the duration. But not so comfortable that it detracted from the fact that they were there for a serious business – recovery.

There was a small receptionist's desk. Its occupant disappeared into the front office to get the manager, who didn't look at all happy that there were two police officers in her reception when she appeared. Her name was Billie Williams.

'Simon can't have any visitors at the moment,' she started by saying.

'I'm afraid we need to interview him as a matter of urgency,' said Ottey.

'Like I said, that's just not possible at the moment,' the manager insisted.

'We can get a warrant if you'd prefer,' said Ottey. 'But once we've done that we would take him down to the station for questioning and keep him for at least twenty-four hours. Surely a conversation with him here, in familiar surroundings, would be preferable and better for his recovery?'

'Can't it wait? It's not as if he's going anywhere, and I'm more than happy to let you know when he's due to leave.'

'This is a murder enquiry. It can't wait,' said Cross.

'Murder? Is he a suspect?' she asked, slightly alarmed.

'We can only tell you that we need to speak to him,' Ottey said.

'Did you know Felicity Wilson?' asked Cross.

'Yes. She was a patient here. Did her final recovery here...' The words faded as if she was thinking that in the circumstances of Flick's death, perhaps that wasn't the most appropriate word.

'"Final"? So she'd been with you a few times?'

'Yes, the first couple weren't successful. She called herself a frequent flyer and thought we should have a loyalty card scheme. She was funny, an easy patient.'

'This is an enquiry into her death and we need to speak to Simon,' said Cross. 'I would argue that as her mother seems to think her death was in some way a catalyst for this particular spell in rehab for him, he might be more than glad to help.'

'Let me speak to him,' she replied, disappearing.

A few minutes later they were sitting with Simon in the meeting room. It was a little odd, as there was a horseshoe of chairs facing each other, which they sat in to talk. It was like being in an AA meeting, Ottey imagined – albeit a badly attended one.

Simon was nervy, dressed in navy tracksuit bottoms and a white T-shirt. He looked like he was in some sort of young offenders' institutional clothing. He stared at the floor, constantly jogging his legs and up down quickly, while he twiddled a piece of paper between his fingers into a straw shape. He was difficult to read for Cross, as there were so many things going on in this young man's life. Fragile from recent withdrawal; traumatised, presumably, by the death of his girlfriend. It transpired that he was troubled by the fact of now being a single father and worried that his current situation might mean his child would go into care.

'How are you doing, Simon?' Ottey asked.

'Yeah, okay. They think I'm doing okay,' he replied, staccato-like.

'Good. I was thinking more in terms of Flick, though. How are you coping?' she said.

'Yeah. Okay. Sad. Really sad. But okay,' he muttered.

'What do you think about her dying like that?' she asked.

'Sad. Terrible.'

'Were you surprised?' she said.

'Doesn't make any sense. She wouldn't see me because I was using. Took out a restraining order. Wouldn't let me see my daughter and then she does that.' He shook his head as if hearing it out loud somehow made it worse.

'Does what?' Ottey prodded gently.

'Kills herself.'

'You think she killed herself?'

'Well, that's what they're saying.'

'Is that what you think happened?'

'I don't know. What else could it be? But it doesn't make any sense.'

'You keep saying that.' Cross spoke for the first time.

Simon looked at him as if he'd forgotten he was in the room. 'She was clean,' he remonstrated. 'She was happy. The only thing that made her unhappy was me; let's face it. And now I'm in here trying to get straight and it's all too late.'

'Why did she take out a restraining order?' asked Cross.

'Why d'you think? She didn't want me around. Didn't want to see me. Didn't want me to see Daisy,' he said, as if pointing out the obvious to someone who wasn't paying attention.

'But why a restraining order? Why did she have to go to court?' Cross insisted.

'I was always stoned. Messed up. I wouldn't listen,' Simon said.

'Did you see her the day she died?' asked Cross.

'No,' he replied quietly.

'But you were there. You slept in the shop doorway opposite the night before.'

'No. I mean yes, I was, but no, I didn't.'

'Are you sure about that?' Ottey jumped in. 'Because here's what I think happened. You went in to see her and you persuaded her to shoot up with you. It was a tragic accident.'

'What? No! Why would she take drugs with me? Why would I want her to do that?' he asked.

'Because you couldn't stop,' said Ottey.

'But she had. She'd done it. Do you have any idea how difficult that is? Look at me. I'm not stupid. I know how I look. Like a mess. Like I'm barely keeping it together in here. Why would I want to take that away from her? I loved her.'

'Okay, let me ask you another question. Were you in possession of any drugs the day she died? Truth now,' Ottey said.

'Of course I was.'

'What, exactly?' she asked.

'Bit of grass and smack – heroin,' he replied. 'Did I give her any? No. Anyway, I didn't have enough to kill her.'

'Heroin?' asked Ottey.

'Yeah. Why did you say "shoot up"?'

'Sorry, I meant inject,' she replied.

'Oh right, but that wasn't our thing. We always smoked or chased. Never did needles.' He suddenly shook, as if he was shaking off a shiver that had enveloped him.

'Really? Never?' asked Cross.

'Swear to God,' he said, pulling up his sleeves to show his arms and make his point. 'None of this makes any sense. Ask Billie, the lady who let you in. She worked with Flick for months. Her doing this doesn't make any sense,' he repeated.

Ottey now looked at Cross. He knew what this meant. She wanted to move this on and tell Simon that this was a murder enquiry. He nodded. Bombshells like this were generally handled with more finesse by Ottey than by him; he was still prone to making the odd mistake now and then. It also gave him the opportunity to observe Simon's reaction.

'Simon, there is no easy way of saying this, but we no longer think Flick killed herself,' she said quietly.

'That would make more sense,' he said, nodding his head gently in agreement. Then he looked up quickly. 'Wait a minute, if she didn't...'

'This is now a murder enquiry,' said Cross bluntly.

Ottey looked at him. She hadn't finished. Seriously. Why did he always do this? Why didn't he ever learn?

This really upset the young man. He grasped his head tightly with both hands and started swaying in his chair. Then he got up and began pacing around the room. He suddenly stopped and turned to face them.

'Is that why you're here? You think I did it? Do you think I did it?' he asked.

In situations like this detectives never give anything away, in part because at this stage they don't actually know what they think. But even if they had concluded that Simon was a suspect, they would still say nothing, so that he didn't put up his guard. Things changed in an interview when someone thought the police suspected them. It was often better not to let them think or know that, so they were a little more free with what they said.

'Why would I do that?' Simon continued. 'I wanted her back. I wanted us to be a family, the three of us. Why would I do that? *How* would I do that? Was she attacked?'

'Why would you think she might've been attacked?' asked Cross.

'Because she would never have allowed someone to... How did it happen?'

'That, we don't know,' said Ottey.

'This is so messed up. Someone killed her? Who would want to kill her? Why?' he said.

'All pertinent questions,' said Cross.

'Do you know anyone who would want to kill her?' Ottey asked.

'No, of course not,' he protested.

'Did she owe anyone money? Her dealer perhaps?' asked Ottey.

'No, man, she was clean. Our dealer from back then is in the nick.'

He suddenly looked really pained, as if a thought had crossed his mind with searing ferocity.

'If I'd got clean, if I'd stayed clean, none of this would've happened. She'd still be here,' he said.

'What makes you say that?' asked Ottey.

'Because I would've been there, wouldn't I? Whoever did it wouldn't have been able to. I'd have stopped them.' He stood up and started hitting the sides of his head with the base of his hands, really hard, with resounding, sickening thuds. 'You idiot, you fucking idiot!' he kept repeating.

The door opened and Billie, the manager, walked in quickly, with no drama and not so much as a look in the direction of the two detectives. She grabbed Simon's hands.

'Stop this now, Simon. Please stop this,' she said firmly.

She managed to pull his hands down to his sides. Cross expected her to ask them to leave but instead, when she had calmed Simon and sat him back down, she turned and left the room. Cross and Ottey sat there for a while in silence.

'Sandra said someone had done this but I didn't believe her. It just didn't seem possible. I thought she was just upset. How did she take it when you told her?' Simon asked.

Cross thought this was interesting. That in his emotional turmoil this boy – because he was a boy really – could think about someone else's feelings.

'She was upset, obviously,' said Ottey.

'None of this makes any sense,' Simon said again.

'So you keep saying,' said Cross. 'And at the moment none of it does. But it will. We will find out what happened here, however senseless.'

'Do you know Brian?' asked Ottey.

'Of course I do.'

'What do you mean by that?'

'I couldn't get to her without going through him. He's a pain in the arse. I swear he used to sit behind the curtains in his window, waiting for me to turn up so he could come out of his flat and tell me to piss off.'

'So you didn't get along?' Ottey asked.

'Anyone would think he was her boyfriend, not me. He was so, what's the word... possessive.'

'But you weren't her boyfriend anymore, were you?' Cross pointed out.

'That's true, but he didn't help. Kept telling her she needed to get me out of her life for good. But that was never going to happen.'

'What do you mean by that?'

'Daisy.'

'So Flick didn't want you out of her life?' Ottey asked.

'No, she wanted me to get clean so I could be a proper father.'

'Then you and Flick could get back together,' Cross suggested.

'No chance.' He ruminated over this for a few seconds

when something suddenly occurred to him. 'You don't think it could be him, do you? Have you spoken to Brian?'

'Not yet.'

'He's a nurse at the Infirmary, you know? Intensive care. You don't think…' He thought for a moment before he continued. 'She trusted him. You don't think he could've done it, do you? But why would he?' he said, answering his own question. He seemed to get energised by this line of thinking. 'Maybe he was trying to help, you know? She was so stressed by this tribunal thing.'

'And you,' Cross pointed out.

'And me,' he agreed quietly. 'But maybe he tried to help and killed her by mistake.'

Ottey started the car and reversed. 'What did you think? Of him?'

'I think he's an emotional and physical mess at present,' said Cross.

'Do you think he might have done it?' she asked, knowing full well he wouldn't answer such a question. But she couldn't help it. It was almost as if she just wanted to hear herself ask it out loud. 'He was very distraught. If it was an act, it was very convincing.'

'He's an addict,' Cross replied. 'They're always convincing, in my experience. It comes with practice. We need to find this Brian.'

'I thought we weren't allowed to state the obvious.'

Cross didn't reply, which made Ottey feel a little mean. But he wasn't offended in the least. He was already going back over their interview with Simon, word by word.

Chapter 10

Sandra was quiet as Mackenzie drove her back to her house in Clifton. Mackenzie was just coming up to her twenty-fifth birthday. She was the same age as Flick – their birthdays were in the same month, with Flick being three days older. She knew this because one of her first jobs in new cases was to trawl through the victim's social media. She was familiar with Flick's circle of friends, small as it was, and of course her child, Daisy. She also knew that the woman sitting in the car next to her was fiercely resistant to having photographs of herself posted on Facebook or Instagram. There were several captions that read along the lines of 'Daisy with her cropped-out, camera-shy Granny' and 'Daisy being held by invisible Granny'. But there was nothing in Flick's social media that suggested she was troubled or suicidal. There was a significant gap in her history of about two years, which Mackenzie thought might have been when she was at the height of her addiction.

Sandra directed her to a Georgian house in a quiet, tucked-away square, the front of which was draped in a prolific-looking wisteria.

'How long has that wisteria been there?' said Mackenzie as she unloaded the baby things out of her car.

'Longer than us, and we've, well, I've lived here for over forty years – since the end of the seventies,' said Sandra.

'Must be wonderful when it's in flower.'

'Yes, it's quite something. It's white.'

They carried the things into the house. Mackenzie was quite surprised by the interior. To her mind older people's houses, particularly when they lived on their own, had an air of gentle decay. A sense of the past, as if life had been lived there years before, but no longer was. There was no real future. She hated that dismal, depressing air. Her parents had many friends, mostly from academia and past political movements, who had naturally got old. Their homes often had the musty smells of old campaigns and decaying sun-dried, yellowing pamphlets and leaflets, with fading 'Support the miners' stickers on the home-made pine bookcases, imbuing an atmosphere of political anachronism.

Sandra's house was nothing like that. It was fresh, light, clean and airy. Mackenzie noticed a couple of scent diffusers in the rooms giving out a sense of welcome and optimism – if that was possible. The kitchen was large, well fitted and modern, with a sitting and dining area. A large TV screen was attached to the wall opposite an inviting sofa, which looked so plump you could probably sit down and disappear into the cushions. There were some framed black and white photographs of Flick and Daisy on the walls. They were poster size and obviously professionally taken, capturing the intimacy and joy of a young mother with her new child.

'Wow, this looks amazing. It could be in a magazine,' Mackenzie said.

'I had it remodelled last year,' Sandra replied. 'The old kitchen was falling apart. Flick was terribly upset at first. She thought I'd demolished part of her childhood. But she came round to it. I think part of her thought, why bother? That I'm at such an advanced age where I should make do with what I have. But I've never been like that, I'm afraid. I like change. I need to have things to look forward to. Well, we all do, don't we? After my husband died I decided I wouldn't just live out the rest of my life, I'd live it to the full. I love this kitchen.'

'Well, good for you. It's gorgeous.'

'And weirdly practical for a bumptious two-year-old. Would you like tea?' Sandra offered.

'Yes, thank you. But only if you're having some.'

'Sure. It's the least I can do after all your help,' said Sandra.

Mackenzie was studying the photographs on the walls.

'I love these photographs. They really capture something special,' she said, immediately thinking that maybe it had come out a little crassly.

'Don't they? I'm so pleased we did them. We almost didn't. Flick wasn't feeling great that day. But I knew she'd love having them in the end. And she did, thank goodness.'

'They're professional, obviously,' Mackenzie added.

'Yes, a woman who specialises in that kind of thing. She had them at their ease so quickly, it was kind of extraordinary. Like she had a gift.'

'A child whisperer,' volunteered Mackenzie.

'Yes,' said Sandra, laughing.

'Tell me about her. Flick,' asked Mackenzie. Sandra paused for a moment and Mackenzie wondered whether she'd overstepped the mark.

'She was really happy being a mother. It was her salvation really; certainly our salvation. I was unsure about it at first, when I found out she was pregnant. Was it just another of her screw-ups? She'd been a nightmare for a few years. I was so pleased her father wasn't here to witness it. It would've broken his heart. He worshipped her. But in the end the pregnancy was the best thing that happened to her. She came home. It wasn't easy getting clean, but it was like the pregnancy had made her utterly determined.'

'She wanted a healthy baby,' Mackenzie added.

'Well, that was the plan, but she'd left it a little late, unfortunately. She'd been home before, to get clean. But it had never worked back then. I became the gaoler. The gatekeeper. The devil.'

'How did her drug habit start?'

'I have no idea. Everything was fine,' Sandra said quietly. 'No issues at school. Boyfriend problems, all that kind of thing obviously. Nothing serious, though. But I remember thinking after she went to university at Sussex that we'd done quite well with her. Little did I know. She left Sussex, didn't really have an idea of what she wanted to do, so she went travelling. She met Simon in South America, and to be honest it nose-dived from there.'

'Do you blame Simon?'

'I don't know. I mean, yes, I suppose so. But she had to be a willing participant, didn't she? So she had to take responsibility. She learnt that in her last stay at rehab.'

'And yet you helped Simon. Put him back in rehab.'

'Well, we both did that,' Sandra replied.

'But even after Flick died,' Mackenzie pointed out.

'Well, yes...'

'Why?'

Sandra thought for a moment. 'I just knew it was what she would've wanted me to do. And he is Daisy's father. I didn't want her growing up knowing her mother had died from an overdose and not knowing her father, because he was a drug addict. Not a great start in life. So I did it as much for Daisy as I did it for him.'

'Are his parents around?' Mackenzie asked.

'They are now. They're delighted about Daisy and want to have her in their lives. That encouraged them to get involved in this stint in rehab,' Sandra said.

'Had they been estranged?'

'Yes, a bit like me – they'd become frustrated with Simon. Hadn't been in contact for well over a year. Went down the "tough love" route. Cut them off. Throw them out. But it's also the selfish, easiest route. It's an excuse just to wash your hands of them and the problem.'

'Sounds a little harsh,' Mackenzie commented.

'Don't give them money so they can use, by all means. Don't be the enabler. Don't let them into your house so they can't steal from you. Saying that even now takes my breath away. That your child, who you've loved and nurtured to the best of your ability, comes to your house and steals cash, jewellery – anything they can get their hands on. It's beyond comprehension. In retrospect I should've made it possible for him to see her in other ways – just not in the house, and so remove the temptation. There had to be other ways to deal with it. I just never found out what they were.'

'At least she got clean,' said Mackenzie.

'Yes.'

'Did she work at all, or was she a full-time mum?'

'That's a bit of a sore point, to be honest with you,' Sandra replied. 'She started working when Daisy was about one. She wanted to. It was her idea. Nothing too vexing. Her counsellor, therapist really, found her a part-time job at a dry cleaner's. Turned out to be a terrible mistake. Dr Sutton is beside himself with remorse.'

'Dr Sutton? Her therapist, presumably?' Mackenzie asked.

'Yes, that's right.'

'Why was it such a mistake? What happened?'

'She was fired,' Sandra replied.

'I see.'

But at this point the childminder arrived with Daisy and Sandra treated her as an excuse to end the conversation there. Mackenzie didn't push it. She thought Sandra was tired and had probably found the afternoon emotionally draining. She'd phone her and follow up tomorrow.

As Sandra lifted her granddaughter up for a kiss, Mackenzie felt a pang of sadness in the pit of her stomach at the situation this family found themselves in. How important it was to find answers, not just for Sandra but for Daisy later, when she'd grown up. The fact that Cross had determined that Flick was killed by a third party made it all the more tragic and, for a better word, grotesquely unfair.

Chapter 11

Cross went to see his father, Raymond, that night. He had been seeing a lot more of him recently. Most nights of the week, in fact, rather than their usual prearranged twice-weekly meetings. This was because Raymond had had a fall at home the previous month and fractured his hip. He'd had an operation to insert some pins and rods into the joint, as it had been quite a complex break. Cross had been both concerned and annoyed by the fall. In his opinion his father's flat was a health hazard for the old man. It was only a matter of time before Raymond's obsessive hoarding would result in an accident, and so it had.

Cross had been nagging his father for years about culling the collection, but was always met with a blank refusal to do so. Raymond had relented one weekend a couple of years before and they made an attempt to start clearing the flat out. It had lasted a full half an hour, until Cross found a deflated forty-year-old Space Hopper. It had a huge puncture in it but Raymond categorically refused to let Cross dispose of it, as he intended to repair it with an old bicycle puncture kit he had saved somewhere, and sell it on eBay. At one point there was even a half-hearted tug of war over it and Raymond won, partly because Cross had decided clearing out the flat was a futile exercise.

This had become Raymond's 'one size fits all' excuse for not getting rid of anything of late – the possibility of making money on eBay, with the implication that in the end they could be talking a small fortune. Piles of ancient, dust-collecting, sun-faded magazines could be worth something to someone. Unfashionable pieces of furniture could be worth something to the right collector with a little restoration. So the clear-out project had been a total failure.

But things had now been taken out of Raymond's hands. The home situation could no longer go on unaddressed, as social services had become involved. The nurses had picked up on Cross's conversation with his father, in which he referred to his hip as 'an accident waiting to happen'. They asked him about it and Cross had no compunction in describing his father's flat as a death-trap. The hospital was under an obligation not to discharge someone of Raymond's age, living on his own, until they were happy with his living arrangements and the provision of care for him afterwards. Social services had visited the flat with Cross and rapidly concurred with his opinion that his father's living conditions were unsuitable. He couldn't go home till someone had given the flat an extensive clear-out which, luckily for him as they pointed out, his son was willing to do.

Raymond reluctantly agreed to this, but Cross's satisfaction was short-lived as the hospital then promptly told them that they needed Raymond's bed. So Cross had gone to the hospital that night to discuss the situation with Raymond and the rehabilitation team. Cross had taken the time to think about the alternatives and had decided that the only solution was for his father to come and live with him.

He was surprised by Ottey's reaction when he informed her that he was thinking of making this altruistic gesture. She wasn't at all sure it was sensible. She tiptoed round the reasons, but he knew why she was saying it. She thought he wouldn't be able to deal with living with someone, let alone his father. It just made him all the more determined to go through with it, if only to prove to her that he was capable of thinking of and looking after others.

'It's quite simple,' he told the team at the hospital. 'He will come and live with me until he is fully recovered and his flat has been made suitable.'

'You know that's not realistic, George,' said Raymond, who was surprised and at the same time touched by his son's suggestion.

'I don't see why not. What are your objections? Specifically?' Cross countered.

'It's a one-bedroomed flat,' said Raymond.

'In point of fact it is a two-bedroomed flat,' said Cross.

'Okay, but you use one of them for your study. There is no bed in there.'

'I'll buy a sofa bed.'

'A complete waste of money,' his father said.

'Come to think of it, I wouldn't be surprised if I found one hidden away somewhere in your flat,' Cross went on. 'Anyway, it might come in useful in the future when I have people round to stay.'

Raymond suppressed a laugh at this point. As so often with parents, he was capable of upsetting his son or offending him unintentionally in a way that no one else could. Such a laugh at this moment in time would be a dagger in Cross's pride. So he trod carefully.

'George, no one, except me, has ever set foot in your flat. He won't even have a cleaner,' he told the team, as if to prove his point.

'I don't need one. I happen to like cleaning. It gives me a sense of satisfaction,' Cross replied.

'Well, you're welcome to come round to my house and clean anytime you like,' joked the ward sister.

'I'm afraid I already have a full-time job,' Cross replied seriously. Then, remembering what Ottey had told him about being polite, he added, 'But thank you for the offer.'

'You live on the first floor, George. I won't be able to manage the steps,' said Raymond.

'We'll carry you up,' replied Cross.

Raymond turned to the team. 'He's a policeman. A very good one, as it happens. Best conviction rate in the force. If you're murdered, he's your man. But he's always at work. His hours are completely unpredictable.'

'We will, of course, be arranging carers to visit you,' said one of the team.

Raymond couldn't help but smile as he saw George flinch at this.

'What exactly do you mean by "carers"?' Cross asked.

'People who come into the flat to care for me, George,' said Raymond matter-of-factly, but with a hint of triumph.

There was a moment's pause as Cross considered this.

'That won't be possible, I'm afraid.'

'Why not?' asked the sister.

'I can't have strange people in my flat,' he stated baldly.

'Well, that settles it then.' Raymond smiled broadly.

'Fine, well, if you could give us ten minutes we'll go and discuss the alternatives,' the sister said. She gave Cross a slightly disapproving look, which went straight over his head.

'George, I need to go to the lavatory. Why don't you pop down to the canteen for ten minutes?' Raymond suggested.

Cross did as he was told and went to the hospital café. He bought a bottle of water and sat at a table, drinking it ruminatively. Some people wrongly assumed, because of his demeanour and behaviour, and the way he reacted to certain situations, that Cross had no feelings. It was true that, to an extent, he was lacking in empathy, as some people with Asperger's were. But he often had feelings. He just didn't know what to do with them and so, more often than not, simply ignored them; avoided them wherever possible. It was by far the easiest solution.

He never had intuitive reactions to people, but after a while, a period of observation, he would form an opinion of them. He was perfectly capable of liking or disliking people. It just took him longer than most people to figure it out. His feeling at this precise moment, as he fiddled obsessively with the top of his water bottle, was that he was being selfish about the carers. These were exceptional circumstances. His father had broken his hip and he should therefore make an exception about the way he lived to care for him. It was, after all, only temporary. 'Get over yourself' was how Mackenzie would have described what he had to do.

'My response,' Cross looked at his watch, 'seventeen minutes ago, was unreasonable. Of course my father must come and stay with me while he is recuperating and carers must visit. I shall make the necessary arrangements. How many carers are we talking about?'

'Three a day,' replied one of the team.

'I shall need their details, names, addresses,' Cross said.

'Why?' asked the sister.

'So I can do a criminal background check,' he informed them.

'That won't be possible, DS Cross,' said the sister.

Cross thought about this for a moment then replied, 'Very well. I'm sure the agencies employing them will have done the requisite DBS checks. We'll just have to put our trust in them.'

'DBS checks?' Raymond asked wearily.

'Disclosure and Barring Service.'

Raymond was by now quite uncomfortable at the prospect. He knew the reality was going to be impossibly stressful for both of them.

'I really don't think this is the best solution,' he volunteered.

'Nonsense,' said Cross, who then excused himself. He would be in touch at the end of the week to make all the arrangements for Raymond's transfer to his flat.

He reflected as he left that his father looked far from happy. This confused him, as he was under the impression that he was making a great sacrifice for his father by taking him in, which Raymond surely had to be aware of. It was yet another occasion where he recognised that understanding the workings of family relationships was more intricate and complex than he'd realised.

Chapter 12

Cross and Ottey drove down to the Bristol Royal Infirmary the next day. Brian, Flick's neighbour, was not at the hospital. He was on a week's leave; his second time since her death – he'd taken a sudden, unexpected leave of absence immediately afterwards. They spoke to various colleagues, doctors, nurses and an ITU consultant who were pretty unanimous in their opinion of Brian – hard-working, compassionate and highly rated as an ITU nurse.

'It takes a special kind of person to work here. They encounter death on a weekly basis, are dealing with patients who, for the most part, they cannot communicate with. It truly is a vocation and Brian is one of our very best,' said the impossibly young consultant they spoke to. A couple of the nurses mentioned Flick's death and that it had really hit him hard. Other than his grief, though, nothing in his behaviour had seemed out of the ordinary. Flick's death was undoubtedly the reason for him taking the first break. This second period of leave seemed to have concerned a couple of them. It was as though he really wasn't over it. He was due back at work the following week but a couple of them wondered whether he would return at all. Was his disappearance a result of grief or something altogether darker? wondered Ottey.

'What are you thinking?' she asked, on their way back.

'That we should interview him as soon as he's back,' Cross replied.

'If he comes back.'

'It is predicated on his return, yes.'

Mackenzie had told them about her conversation with Sandra at the house. Flick having been fired from her job interested Cross, obviously. Other than her past addiction it was the only negative, adverse factor in her recent, brief life. When they looked into it further they discovered that Flick hadn't accepted it without a fight. She was taking her former employer, one Daniel Stokes, to an employment tribunal. She had taken on a solicitor at a big Bristol firm, even though her mother wasn't at all sure that it was an advisable course of action. It wasn't that Sandra didn't think Flick had a case – she knew the dismissal was grossly unfair – but she thought it might put an impossible emotional strain on her daughter. Flick was also alleging sexual harassment. She claimed that her former employer had made unwelcome sexual advances to her and that she had been sacked because she had rejected them.

Cross was taken by Flick's obvious determination to see it through, not just for herself, but also to prevent the ex-employer from subjecting others to the same treatment. According to her mother, she was well aware of the fact that the employer's lawyers would have dwelled on Flick's drug history in the tribunal and portrayed her as an unreliable witness. But she was undeterred, even with the prospect of a savage character assassination in court. Sandra went on to say that instead of it being a source of stress and worry, Flick seemed to gain strength and a sense of purpose from it.

'Are you really sure it's such a good idea?' said Ottey, predictably he thought, as they drove to meet Flick's employment lawyer. He had just told her of his decision to have his father stay with him during his rehabilitation.

'I am,' he retorted. 'Why do you ask? There's a definite tone of doubt in your voice.'

'Because I'm not sure you'll be happy with someone living with you,' she replied.

'He's my father.'

'Because he's your father,' she said.

'Compromises will obviously have to be made.'

'George, let's be honest, compromise and you are not happy bedfellows,' she replied.

'I concede you may have a point. But my father has brought me up, on his own, since I was five. He has devoted his life to aeronautical engineering and me. It's now time to repay that debt,' said Cross.

'It's not a debt, George,' she pointed out.

'Then it's my duty. I have to take responsibility, which I am doing. He is to come and live with me,' Cross said emphatically.

Ottey said nothing, sensing that this was a one-sided discussion. He had made up his mind.

He went on, 'I have to say I'm a little surprised by your attitude. I thought, fancifully as it turns out, that you would have considered it to be the right and proper course of action for me to take, and possibly one which you would have expected of me.'

'Both of those things are true,' she replied. 'What does Raymond think about it?'

Cross hesitated. She knew immediately what this meant.

'He doesn't think it's a good idea either, does he? Because he knows it's going to cause you an enormous amount of stress,' she said.

'He's going to have carers,' Cross said, as if this answered her concern. But it just gave her more ammunition.

'What? You're going to have strange people coming into your flat every day? My case rests.'

'Good, because I really don't think it appropriate for us to be talking about this on police time.'

This was Cross's by now familiar reply in such situations. He had taken to saying it quite frequently of late to avoid conversations of a personal nature. He was unused to such talks and was still a little reluctant to involve himself in them. He'd noticed that conversations like this with Ottey had been occurring with increasing frequency recently, either in the car or the office. He was beginning to think that maybe his partner was nosy. He didn't realise it was actually an indication of a growing friendship – friendship being something of an alien concept to him.

This was a genuinely contradictory thing about Cross. Had he observed this behaviour between two people in a case he was working, he would undoubtedly have concluded that the increasing interest of one of the people in the personal affairs of the other would have indeed indicated a developing friendship between the two. He just couldn't see it when the identical thing was applied to himself.

Ottey and Cross arrived at the offices of West and West solicitors, which was off St Augustine's Parade. Most people referred to this as the city centre these days. It used to form part of Bristol's docks, but as they became busier in the late nineteenth century more adjacent space was needed to deal with the trade, and so the River Frome was covered over. Later it had been called the Tramway Centre when Bristol ran trams. Cross had always liked this area but felt that it had lost some of its character since the further changes made to it in the 1990s. Broad Quay was so broad that its modern pedestrianisation had made it a bit of a bland desert. It felt purposeless somehow. A vast emptiness surrounded by a disconnect of various chains – more 'local' branches of national supermarkets, ubiquitous coffee shops – to service the office blocks that dwarfed them. From a bustling city centre it had turned into a place that people didn't dwell in; they simply passed through.

Tammy Smith was a young associate at this large firm. Probably in her late twenties, Ottey felt she exuded ambition and would no doubt navigate her way up the corporate ladder with stealthy ease. Like so many law firms that had once been approachable, if never exactly inviting, West and West had amalgamated and merged with several other firms over the years and was now a corporate behemoth. One of the ways Tammy was trying to be noticed by the corner offices was by doing pro-bono cases, specifically for women in employment tribunals. She had something of the crusader about her, Cross thought. A little too earnest – nothing wrong with that, but it was the whiff of self-righteousness surrounding her that he didn't warm to.

'How did Flick's case first come to your attention?' asked Ottey, who as usual began the interview to prevent Cross from inadvertently getting them off on the wrong footing.

'Through another client,' Tammy replied.

She had a trainee lawyer with her who made notes on a large yellow pad. What, thought Cross, is he writing down? Tammy already knows her own answer to the question. Cross thought this was more of a reflection on Tammy than the young assistant – in that he was worried that if he didn't make a note of everything he would be in trouble.

'Could you be more specific?' said Ottey.

'Another woman who was thinking about taking similar action against Stokes,' Tammy replied.

'Stokes, the former employer?' Ottey confirmed.

'That's correct.'

'Could you elaborate on the details of Flick's case for us?' Ottey went on.

'I'm afraid that's confidential,' replied the young lawyer.

A rookie mistake, thought Ottey, but not before Cross had joined the conversation.

'She's dead,' he said bluntly.

'I'm well aware of that,' said Tammy. Her tone suggested she'd taken an instant dislike to Cross.

'And with her died her right to confidentiality,' Cross went on.

'I'm not actually sure that's the case,' she retorted.

'Miss Smith, this is a murder investigation,' said Cross.

This threw the young lawyer.

'I see. I wasn't aware of that,' she said, still taking it in. 'She was claiming unfair dismissal and sexual harassment.'

'He made advances to her which she rebuffed?' said Ottey.

'Yes. Persistent advances,' added Tammy.

'Did you believe her?' asked Cross.

'Yes, why wouldn't I?'

'She was a drug addict,' Cross said.

'A recovering addict,' Tammy reminded him.

'Quite so. Thank you for the correction.'

She didn't seem sure whether this was sarcasm on his part or not.

'What was the employer's response?' asked Ottey.

'It didn't get to the tribunal before she died.'

'We know, but you must've met with the other side to see if the issue could be resolved. Whether there was any chance of it settling,' said Ottey.

'Oh my God, do you think he had something to do with her death?' said Tammy. She was suddenly quite shocked and a little panicked by the thought, observed Cross.

'We're investigating all possibilities,' Ottey assured her.

'What evidence did you have of the harassment?' asked Cross.

'Witnesses, but they had all subsequently lost their jobs so could be portrayed as disgruntled ex-employees with a grudge.'

'But establishing a pattern,' said Cross.

Tammy nodded. 'Hopefully. We had explicit and bullying texts he'd sent her. He also had form.'

'There were others?' asked Ottey.

'Several, but two of them had settled and a couple of others had sunk back into their habits, sadly.'

'He employed other addicts?' asked Cross.

'Oh, that's his thing. Taking in addicts. Helping them in their recovery but in truth preying on the vulnerable. It's really shocking.'

'Where do they come from? I mean, how do they end up working for him?' asked Ottey.

'He had a regular supply from a rehab clinic. He's on the board... well, was,' Tammy replied.

'Hopewell,' Cross suggested.

'That's right. He had to resign and they've stopped sending clients to him. Largely thanks to Flick. Something else he had to resent her for.'

'Why didn't he try and settle with Flick? He was obviously open to that,' said Ottey.

'Oh he did, but Flick refused.'

'Why?' asked Cross.

'Because it involved a non-disclosure agreement, as they always do. For her that was tantamount to his getting away with it, which she couldn't accept.'

'A brave girl,' Ottey observed.

'A dead girl,' Cross found himself saying out loud. He often did that – said something everyone was thinking but keeping to themselves. 'So she was taking him to a tribunal, despite his efforts to settle. Had him removed from the Hopewell board and had his supply of vulnerable women dry up,' he observed.

'Yes, but more than that. She was actively trying to organise the other girls to join her in taking him to the tribunal. She had at least five who were talking to her, and he was aware of that.'

'And they've backed off since her death?' said Cross.

'Yep. Three of them are settling and two of them are working for him but in another location, so not within his immediate grasp,' Tammy said with an air of defeat.

'I'd like their details,' said Cross.

Tammy hesitated for a moment, but then saw a determination in Cross that changed her mind.

'Do you think he killed her?' she asked as she showed them out.

'I don't think anything.'

Ottey turned to the lawyer. 'George will never give an opinion. It's not how he works. He follows the facts. But we will be paying Mr Stokes a visit,' she explained.

'Do you have any email correspondence from Flick that we could look at?' Cross asked.

'Sure, but don't you have her laptop?'

'Good point. It would certainly save you the trouble,' Cross replied.

'No, I'm sorry. Of course I'll forward them to you. I have something else which might be helpful.' She left the office, returning a few minutes later. 'I've made a copy for you,' she said, handing them a plastic file which contained three sheets of paper.

'They're copies of pages from her journal where she wrote about Stokes.'

Cross flicked through them quickly.

'You don't happen to have the journal, do you?' Cross asked.

'No, we just copied the relevant pages. It should be in her flat, though. She was never without it. Making notes in meetings, times of appointments.' She then gave Ottey a card.

'Please get in touch if you need anything else.'

'We will,' replied Ottey.

'One other thing,' said the young lawyer. 'If there's any way you can encourage the girls to rethink not taking him to the tribunal, I'd be really grateful. It's just that I seem to have come to the end of my persuasive powers.'

'Sure, I'll see what I can do,' said Ottey.

'It would be a fitting memorial to Flick, don't you think? Taking him down?' Tammy said.

Ottey smiled as she left. She had warmed to the young lawyer over the course of the meeting. She had a humane side to her and had obviously formed an emotional attachment to Flick.

Chapter 13

Danny's Dry Cleaner's was at the start of the Bath Road, near Bristol Temple Meads station. It was garishly coloured – bright pink, with pink delivery vans parked outside. According to Danny Stokes, he'd had an epiphany when visiting Hollywood and using Milt & Edie's dry cleaning service in Burbank. Efficient, big, friendly, and with six service points, there was nothing like this in the south-west of England, if indeed in England at all. He had basically copied the American one.

Danny regaled the two detectives with this story as soon as they came in. 'I should have paid Milt and Edie something. Do I feel guilty? Hell no! Under-promise and over-deliver is our motto here,' he said, spouting a well-honed patter and routine. He was a short man, maybe just over five feet tall. 'What I lack in height, I make up for in personality. Is it true that our counters are a good six inches shorter than the normal? No. I use a box!'

He was wearing sharply pressed suit trousers with an open white shirt. His neck was weighed down with gold jewellery, chains, his initials and a pair of glasses on a gold chain. His wrists were similarly adorned, together with a gold Rolex. His hair had that artificial look favoured by ageing rock stars, who dyed their locks an improbably dark shade of black in a desperate attempt to hang onto their youth. Stokes's hair was also incredibly fine and had been subjected to the kind of tight perm that had been fashionable in the sixties with churchgoing women of a certain age.

The front of the shop had a long counter with six customer-service points. No one had to wait long to be served. As soon as a new customer entered the shop a light went on above one of the stations. The customer was politely asked to go to it over a loudspeaker. Then the number of the station was announced and someone miraculously dropped whatever they were doing and came to serve. Behind the counter, suspended from the ceiling, was a moving carousel from which hung polythene-covered laundry. This fascinated Cross.

They followed Danny up to an old man of similar stature to him, busily doing alterations at a worktable. He wore an old editor's shade with a green see-through peak. He didn't look up as they approached, but carried on with his work diligently.

'This is my father. He used to own the business, till I bought him out. He's still a little pissed off about it,' Danny said, laughing.

'I think he is,' observed Cross.

'No, he's not. That was a joke, Detective. He had to sell to look after my mother,' Danny said defiantly.

'Well, I'm not surprised he has an air of resentment about him. Firstly that he had to sell and secondly that he has to work for his son, who takes delight in pointing out to any strangers who pass by that he employs his father,' said Cross matter-of-factly.

Danny's tone shifted audibly. 'This way,' he muttered.

But Cross had spotted something that interested him.

'Do you mind if I have a look at the shirt-pressing system?'

Danny was naturally taken aback.

'Sure, of course. You too?' he said to Ottey.

'No, I'm good. Is there somewhere we can talk?' she said.

'Let's go to my office.' Danny watched as Cross walked over to the pressing machine, then indicated that Ottey should follow him upstairs.

Danny's office was on a mezzanine level and overlooked the work floor. It had slanted windows that were one-way mirrors. He could see everything going on on the shop floor, but no-one could see back into his domain. The walls of the office were covered with photographs of celebrities, mostly minor TV and radio personalities. All were signed with grateful messages to 'Danny'. He himself was in quite a few of them, one arm around the celebrity proprietorially. There were also dozens of pictures of him with different beautiful young women, most of whom dwarfed him in height. He had a large desk with an even larger leather chair, which he sank into as Ottey sat opposite him.

'Terrible news about Flick,' he said immediately. 'I'm not surprised, just sad really.'

'What aren't you surprised about?' asked Ottey.

'That she started using again. Such a terrible thing, addiction,' he said ruefully.

'What makes you think she started using again?'

'I only know what I read in the papers. We had our differences but I wished her all the best.'

'Differences?' said Ottey. 'She was suing you for wrongful dismissal.'

'I was just trying to be respectful, Detective. Poor girl. I bear no grudges,' he said.

Ottey took a breath. She was annoyed by the man, but didn't want to show it.

'Wrongful dismissal and sexual harassment.'

'Yeah, yeah, yeah,' sighed Danny.

'That sounds fairly dismissive.'

'Because I am. It's all fiction. Made up. Sure, there were a couple of misunderstandings, but it happens here all the time. Far too often,' he said.

'Well, aren't you the one who could put a stop to it?' said Ottey.

'What? I didn't do anything. It's always the same and I'm beginning to lose patience.'

'With what?' asked Ottey.

His tone became indignant. 'Trying to help. Who else would take these girls on and give them a chance? Most of them have criminal records. Where are they going to get a job? I'm trying to put them back on track and this is what I get in return.'

'What?' asked Ottey.

'False accusations. Fabrications. Thinking I'm fair game. They make it all up and I'm getting to the point where I've had enough.'

'But you've settled with,' Ottey consulted her notes, unnecessarily, 'five of them. Why? If you had nothing to hide?'

'Because I'm a businessman. I don't have time for these distractions. It's easier just to make them go away.'

'But Flick Wilson wouldn't go away.'

'No, she wouldn't. Not that it matters anymore,' he said. 'Sorry, that came out wrong. Why are you here? You haven't told me why you're here.'

'I haven't had a chance,' said Ottey.

'Yeah, sorry about that. Once a salesman always a salesman, I suppose. Tell me something. Is it true that plain-clothes police always have a change of clothes in their offices? Clean shirts and the like in case they work overnight?'

Once more, Ottey didn't have time to answer before he went on, 'So here's what I was thinking. A shirt service for you guys at the office. I could do a pick-up once or twice a week, twenty-four-hour turnaround. You'd never be short of clean laundry. We could leave you each with a bag; you wouldn't have to do a thing – just put it in the bag. Here,' he handed her a card, 'that's my mobile there. You can call me direct if there are any problems.'

'The reason we're here—' Ottey began.

'Think about it,' the dry cleaner interrupted, looking at his business card, which had remained on the desk. 'No rush, but we are the best shirt service in Bristol. No one else comes close. And of course we can offer you a special discount.'

'Mr Stokes, we're here on a serious matter,' Ottey pointed out.

'So it would seem,' was his reply, as he watched Cross on the floor below, examining the shirt presses as carefully as he might a crime scene.

There were three separate presses, operated by a young man and two women. The first was an undulating press where they did the collars and cuffs, two shirts at a time. This was followed by two cylinders over which the operators draped the sleeves, and they were then pressed. Finally came a machine which looked like a flat shirt cut out of metal. The shirt was placed over this and pressed.

Cross was always fascinated by machines like this, probably something he'd inherited from his father, a retired engineer. He was intrigued by the carousel delivery system when he discovered that it was controlled by a computer. The assistant took the customer's receipt and scanned it, and the carousel spun round and presented the corresponding piece of laundry. If more than one assistant was using it, it would automatically place them in a queue. Cross loved the efficiency of it, and the truth was that he was an obsessive ironer. He ironed everything, even his bed sheets. But it was the ironing of his shirts that filled him with immense satisfaction.

It wasn't long before he was asking the young laundry workers whether they used starch on the collars or whether there was no need with this wondrous machine. Did they need to dampen the shirts first? They thought he was making fun of them initially, but when it became clear he was genuinely interested, they replied with enthusiasm. It seemed that Cross had, quite unintentionally, made their day by taking an interest in their work. The highlight for them was when he took his coat off and asked if he could have a go. Much to his satisfaction, he pressed a white shirt perfectly. He was really pleased, but they couldn't tell, as his face was a picture of intense concentration.

During this exercise he had noticed that one of the young girls was made nervous by his presence. She hadn't joined in with the good-humoured laughter of the others at his shirt-pressing efforts. She was extremely thin, like an underfed sparrow, with dark shadows under her eyes. She smiled with strained politeness, averting her eyes to the floor when he thanked her for showing him her part in the process. Just before he left the shop floor he turned his back to Danny's office and, making sure that no one else was looking, presented her with his card. She looked at it, then back up at him, but he said nothing. She quickly snatched the card from him and stuffed it in the pocket of her jeans.

'Flick Wilson was murdered,' said Ottey.

'What? I thought she overdosed,' said Danny.

'She did. But it wasn't self-administered.'

Danny thought for a moment then began shaking his head.

'No, no, you've got this all wrong,' he protested. 'She was an addict. She fell off the wagon. Where'd you come up with this? How is that even possible? Unless there was a struggle. Was there a struggle?'

'I can't divulge that information,' Ottey replied.

'Look, it's tragic, but you guys are barking up the wrong tree. Is it the mother? Is she the one who wound you up? She's a right nutter, that one.'

Ottey thought this was interesting, because no one could fairly describe Sandra as a 'nutter'. In all their dealings with her, even when no one was listening, she maintained her equanimity and dignity.

'Where were you on the night of Tuesday the seventeenth of June?' Ottey asked.

There was a pause, then he laughed. But before he could reply, Cross walked in.

'Quite the operation you have here, Mr Stokes. Very impressive,' he said.

Danny looked at him, unsure how to react. Was the

detective taking the piss? Was he trying to get him off guard? He just couldn't work it out. He opened his computer and looked at his calendar.

'I was working, obviously. I always work. Some people call me a workaholic, but what can you do if you happen to love what you do?'

'June the seventeenth,' Ottey reiterated.

'I don't know. At home probably,' he said.

'Is there a Mrs Stokes?' Ottey asked.

'Nope. Never been married. Never wanted kids. Bit of a ladies' man, if truth be told.' He winked at her.

'In the circumstances I'd call that an unwise description, Mr Stokes,' said Cross.

'It's just a bit of harmless fun.'

'Is that what you told the girls who were taking you to the tribunal for harassment?' Cross continued.

'There was only one girl taking me to a tribunal,' Danny said.

'Who is now dead,' said Cross. 'Quite convenient, some might say.'

'Like I said – she had no case.'

'Not according to her lawyer,' said Ottey.

'Even if she had a case, which she didn't, it was an employment tribunal. Who in their right mind would kill someone to prevent that happening? It's not worth it,' he said.

'That could imply that you've thought about it. Weighed up the odds,' said Cross.

'I have never thought about killing anyone. I'm a dry cleaner, for God's sake.'

'A dry cleaner with no alibi for the night of the murder,' said Ottey.

'True, but I don't need one because I didn't do it,' he said.

'Everyone needs an alibi in a murder case, Mr Stokes. I wouldn't underestimate the importance of that if I were you,' said Cross.

Back in the car Ottey turned to Cross.

'So what did you learn?' she asked.

'That a domestic iron is never going to be a match for an industrial shirt press, no matter how hard you try,' Cross said.

'From the employees,' she said.

'Oh, nothing,' he replied.

This puzzled her, as she couldn't figure out whether he was holding something back. She thought it must mean that on this occasion he actually had been interested in the mechanics of the dry cleaning operation. He really was a puzzle at times.

Chapter 14

Unless the photocopies had been scaled down, Flick's journal was A5 sized. There were six photocopied journal pages, set side by side on A4 paper. The relevant material stopped towards the bottom of the fifth journal page, with the sixth page opposite on the sheet pretty much illegible as the ink from the seventh page had bled through the paper for some reason. The legible five pages consisted of notes of the other girls, their accounts of the various assaults and the dates, together with the likelihood of their taking part in the tribunal case against Stokes. His abusive behaviour followed a pattern. From unwanted attempted kisses, to unwelcome hugs where he pressed his obviously aroused member against the girl's thigh. Playing with himself behind his desk, then asking the girl if she wanted to have a look. If, through fear of the consequences of not doing so, they walked forward to see his engorged penis, he would ask if they wanted to 'give him a hand'. He really was a loathsome individual, thought Cross, taking advantage of vulnerable young women who he purported to the outside world to be helping.

He then took the pages out to Edwin the exhibits officer. He liked Edwin. They had a lot in common, these two, as they were sticklers for detail and procedure. The exhibits officer had to be as he or she was responsible for the chain of evidence. Any break in that chain, any potential for contamination, could make a case collapse in court. Edwin was very particular, almost obsessive in his job. His labelling system was legendary in the force not just for its detail and the way it enabled him to put his hands on anything requested at a moment's notice, but because his indexing of the evidence was comprehensive and comprehensible. In short he was fantastic at it. Some years before, Edwin had overhauled the evidence-indexing system in the department, for his own convenience really. He found the existing system, 'if you could call it that,' he'd said, was confusing and overly-complex. His system was quickly seen to be more coherent, comprehensible and user-friendly. It wasn't long before it had been adopted across the entire force. Cross was envious not only of the obvious efficacy of the system but the fact that it had become universally known as the 'Edwin index'. Ottey often found herself thinking that Edwin was more pedantic than her partner which amused her. Edwin surveyed the photocopies in the plastic folder. They then had the kind of conversation which their colleagues loved to eavesdrop on.

'They're copies,' he said.

'Facsimiles, yes,' Cross replied.

'So I suppose the question is – are they strictly speaking evidence?'

'A good question and one to which I gave some consideration,' replied Cross. 'Strictly speaking I am not sure of their admissibility in court as evidence but they are of evidential relevance to the case.'

'Ah, I take your point.'

'Good, then I leave them under your care.'

'Hmm,' replied Edwin. 'The question is how to index them accurately.'

'Indeed,' replied Cross as he gave this conundrum some thought. Edwin did what he always did when confronting an indexing puzzle. He picked up his pipe, his tamper, his matches and his tobacco pouch and headed for the fire escape. Cross was quite envious of this routine and would have taken up pipe smoking himself were it not for the obvious health risks.

Carson eventually got his way and a meeting was convened at the Major Crime Unit. It was a very small meeting, as not many resources had been assigned to the case. Ottey thought this was because Carson was, as yet, unconvinced of Cross's determination that it was murder. He was being cautious so that if Cross was wrong he, Carson, would attract less flak from upstairs. What had really annoyed Ottey – and it didn't take much when it came to Carson – was the fact that he was behaving as if he was doing them all a favour by letting them look into Flick's case in the first place. It was as if he was indulging them. But it was a murder. So why on earth was he behaving in this way? She concluded that, as usual, it simply fed his enormous appetite for feeling superior.

'So where are we at?' Carson began. An inane, nonsensical question in Cross's opinion, but on this occasion he managed, with some effort, to bite his lip.

'Nowhere much,' replied Ottey.

As far as Cross was concerned, this was actually true. He was convinced it was murder, but they had nothing to go on. True, there was no container, but that being the leading fact was also the major complication – there was no evidence. The missing drug container was their only lead, as frustrating as that was.

'We have determined to our satisfaction, if not to that of the higher-ups—' Ottey continued.

'Sorry to interrupt but what exactly makes you say that?' asked Carson.

'Well, you only have to look at the number of people in this room to get your answer,' she said.

Cross didn't get involved in this exchange, not because he didn't believe she had a point – he very much did – but because he had observed over time that this little dance between his partner and their superior officer seemed to be a ritual they needed to perform before they were able to put their heads together on a case.

'Flick Wilson was killed by a dose of diamorphine. The absence of the container containing the drug makes us believe that it was administered by a third party,' she said.

'Our killer,' said Carson.

'Our killer, yes. A search of the flat and the surrounding area has not revealed the container, which means the killer probably took it with them. But it remains our main clue,' she went on.

'So, our only clue is non-existent,' Carson commented.

'A clue nevertheless,' Cross said.

'Who in her circle had access to such drugs and had a reason to kill her?' Ottey finished.

'Next step?' Carson asked.

'Well, just before you called this meeting we were on our way to interview Flick's neighbour in the downstairs flat. Brian Stott,' she replied.

'Why hasn't he been interviewed before?' asked Carson.

'He's been out of the country. He phoned in this morning,

voluntarily, having been told we'd been to his place of work asking about him,' she replied.

'And why is he of particular interest?'

'Because he's a nurse who works in ITU at the BRI,' said Ottey.

'The Bristol Royal Infirmary,' added Cross helpfully.

Carson looked impatient. 'I know what the BRI means, George, thank you.'

'Then you will also know that his job means he must have regular access to a range of powerful drugs in dealing with people close to death – including diamorphine,' Cross continued.

Mackenzie now spoke for the first time. 'According to Sandra, Flick's mother, Brian had something of a soft spot for Flick. But while she was fond of him, romantic feelings were not reciprocated. We don't know how he felt about that as yet.' She had become more confident about contributing to meetings, feeling that she knew when it was useful and welcome.

'Daisy's father, Flick Wilson's ex, says Brian was obsessed with her. They had a few run-ins,' interjected Ottey.

'Why would he want to kill her if he was obsessed with her?' asked Carson.

'Because she wasn't interested in him,' replied Ottey.

'Excellent. Then what are we waiting for? Let's go over there and see what he has to say for himself,' he said, clapping his hands together.

'I loved her, Detective,' said the young man sitting on the sofa opposite the two police officers. He was in his late thirties and had a series of colourful, childlike tattoos on his arms. Pictures of teddy bears, penguins, Aardman-like figures of sheep and penguins. Together with vast swathes of vibrant colours filling the spaces in between. He was in his nurse's scrubs, having just done a night shift. One side of his head was shaved to a stubble. There was then an extravagant, thick mane of hair swept over to the other side of his head from where there might have been a parting. It was dark black and incredibly shiny. Cross found himself thinking that a hair advertisement would probably describe it as having a 'lustre' to it. He had a thick Liverpudlian accent.

'I think she was resistant to us being a thing because all the men in her life had turned out to be unreliable or just wanted to take advantage of her,' Brian said.

'Unless she just didn't love you,' Cross pointed out.

'Maybe. But I think we could have been happy, the three of us. I love Daisy as well. She's a gorgeous child. But Flick wouldn't have it and I didn't want to become a nuisance like Simon. I decided it was better to have her as a friend than not have her in my life at all.'

'Where were you immediately after her death? You took two weeks' sudden leave,' Cross asked.

'I needed to get away. I was upset and I live below her…'

'And last week?'

'I was in Liverpool visiting my parents. My father is unwell. I wanted to give my Mum a break.'

'I'm sorry to hear that,' said Ottey.

'Thanks.'

'Did you see a lot of Flick when she was alive?' asked Cross.

'Are you kidding? We were in and out of each other's flats when I wasn't at work,' he said. 'We ate together a couple of nights a week. I'd cook. We'd have the baby monitor on with Daisy upstairs. We had movie nights. It was great. I'd babysit for her when she wanted to go out with Sandra for dinner and be alone with her mum.'

'You sound like a good friend,' said Ottey.

'Thank you,' he said.

'Was it enough?' asked Cross.

'For me? Um, not to start with, if I'm honest. Then I thought I might win her round with quiet persistence. But by the end we'd become such good friends that the idea of it going any further had become a bit too weird.'

'Did she talk much about things?' asked Ottey.

'You're joking, right? Of course she did. That's all we ever did. Talk, talk, talk. Till the early hours of the morning sometimes, which was completely unfair,' he laughed.

'Why?' asked Ottey.

'Because she was obviously stone cold sober and I got more and more pissed as the night wore on. Then the next day she'd make out that I'd told her all sorts of personal stuff about myself, which I couldn't remember, and she wouldn't then tell me what it was. Complete lies, of course,' he said, still smiling at the thought.

'You sound like you were really close,' said Ottey.

'She was really fun,' he said, getting lost in the memory. 'You're here because Sandra thinks someone killed her.'

'We're here because *we* think someone killed her,' said Cross.

'It's just inconceivable. I mean, isn't it? We're talking murder, right?' he said.

'We generally are when someone has been killed deliberately,' said Cross.

'You work in ITU,' said Ottey, changing the subject.

'I do, yes.'

'That must be tough,' she went on.

'Sure, but you get used to it.'

'I have to say I'm full of admiration for you. Both my parents were in ITU. In your hospital as it happens. I was really impressed with the doctors and nursing staff,' she said.

'I think it's something you feel you want to do,' he said. 'It's not for everyone.'

'You must see a lot of death,' she said.

'We do. But also a lot of recovery.'

'As a nurse, do you have access to all the drugs used in ITU?' asked Cross.

'As a senior nurse, yes. Why?' he asked.

'Would that include diamorphine?' Cross went on.

'Of course, among others. We're dealing with the very edge of life, DS Cross. The margins between life and death can be very small.'

'I can't imagine,' said Cross and left it there.

'What makes you so sure it's murder, not an accidental overdose or suicide?' Brian asked.

'Let me ask you a question. Do you think that Flick could have fallen off the wagon, or wanted to kill herself?' said Ottey.

'No. Neither. I get your point. It's odd. But surely that's not enough for you guys, is it?' he asked.

'She was killed by an overdose of diamorphine,' said Cross.

Brian thought about this for a moment.

'How is that possible? Where did she get it from?' The detectives said nothing. 'Oh I see. That's why you're here,' he said, putting two and two together.

'It sounds like you'd do anything for her, Brian. You said it yourself – you were quite smitten,' Ottey said.

'What are you suggesting?'

'That maybe it was an accident. She asked you for the drugs. You supplied them. Then you found her dead and disposed of the container before you called the ambulance,' said Ottey.

'You know what? It's such a stupid idea that I'm not even going to get angry. You obviously don't know anything about Flick. She would never have asked me to get drugs for her. She knew I would've disapproved. Anyway, wouldn't she have gone to Simon rather than me? Have you talked to him?'

'We have. He said you were obsessed with her,' Ottey said.

'Well, he would, wouldn't he? He hated the fact that I saw so much of her and Daisy. Much more than him. Couldn't stand it. Anyway, it's nonsense. Flick was well and truly into her recovery. She was strong. I don't believe for a minute she was complicit. Nor do you. Which is why you're here. You think she was killed.'

'But you do have access to diamorphine,' said Cross.

'I do. On a daily basis. But you obviously haven't a clue about the strict drug protocols in a place like ITU. Everything is logged in and out. Signed for. The stock is constantly monitored. If it was diamorphine it won't have come from any hospital ITU in this country.'

'So just to be sure, you're saying it wasn't you?' said Cross.

'Wasn't me what? Who gave her the diamorphine? Were you listening? Why would I want to risk losing my job? Why would I want to turn someone I had feelings for back into a junkie? What would there be in that for me? I worked in

A&E when I first started out as a nurse, and I dare say I had more experience with drug overdoses and clearing up after them with charcoal and stomach pumps than you've had in your entire police career.'

'So you'd have no objection if we had a look around your flat?' asked Cross. He was looking directly at Brian in the way that some people took as being challenging. It wasn't. He was just waiting for an answer.

'I not only don't mind,' said the young man, 'I insist you do. I'll make coffee.'

Ottey took note of this answer. There was something about Brian's body language, getting up to make the coffee before he'd finished speaking, which told her that he not only had nothing to hide, he wanted them to get this part of it, and him as a suspect, out of the way so they could concentrate on looking for the real murderer. For Cross, the offer of coffee meant that the young nurse wanted to talk more to the two police officers about the case before they left.

Twenty minutes later the police officers were drinking their coffee. Well, Ottey was. They had, as Cross suspected, found nothing. He noticed that Brian had gone very quiet. Initially he thought that he was just reflecting on the loss of his dear friend, but then something about the way he seemed to be agitatedly bouncing his knee up and down made Cross wonder whether this actually meant he was judging whether to tell them something.

'What is it?' Cross asked.

'Simon,' said Brian.

'What about him?'

'Look, I don't think he could've done this, but then sometimes he's so high, so out of it, who knows what he might do? Thing is, he and I had a fight the day Flick died. I'm just wondering, but it doesn't make any sense,' he said.

'Why don't you let us decide that?' said Ottey.

'You don't think that had anything to do with it, do you? You don't think that if we hadn't had a fight she'd still be alive?' he asked.

'That's a lot of "ifs", Brian,' said Ottey.

'What happened that morning?' asked Cross.

'I wouldn't let him in. Flick had told him to go away over the intercom, but he wouldn't leave. He then tried to get past me when I went to work. We had a scrap and I threw him out. Flick was watching from upstairs. I called her and told her not to let him in.'

'You didn't see him come back?' asked Ottey.

'No, like I said; I was on my way to work.'

'What can you tell us about him?' asked Cross.

'He was always hanging around. But she had a really soft spot for him,' he said.

Cross reflected that this was the exact expression Sandra had used to describe Brian's feelings for her daughter.

'Were you jealous of him?'

'I suppose I was, yes. I think if he'd been clean she would've taken him back. They had a permanent bond, after all.'

'Daisy?' Cross confirmed.

'Exactly. But I didn't want to be him. He was a mess. Is a mess.'

'He's back in rehab,' said Ottey.

'Well, that's good. Mind you, he has been there before. Several times,' said Brian.

'I get the feeling there's no love lost here,' said Ottey.

'He just caused her so much grief, you know? So much

worry. She never knew when he was going to come round and yell at her. He threatened to kill himself once. She told me he'd said one time that they would be better off if none of them were around anymore,' he went on.

'You mean, if they were all dead? Daisy as well?' asked Ottey.

'Yep, but according to her he was always trashed when he said it. It didn't worry her. Just annoyed her. That's why she took out the restraining order.'

'Do you think he could've hurt her? Wanted to hurt her? When he was high?' asked Ottey.

'Maybe, I don't know,' he replied.

'Did he ever offer her drugs, to your knowledge?' Cross asked.

'Oh, yeah. Frequently. It was so stupid. He couldn't see it just drove more of a wedge between them. I think, in a perverse kind of way, he just wanted things to go back to what they'd been before, with both of them completely out of it all of the time. That's why she didn't want him around. She didn't need that.'

'Need what?' asked Cross.

'The pressure to use again. The temptation. Whatever you want to call it,' he said.

'You must have been thinking about what happened to Flick a lot,' said Cross.

'Can't get it out of my mind.'

'Do you think Simon could have given her the diamorphine?' asked Cross.

'Look, it wouldn't surprise me if he tried to give it to her. But what would surprise me was if she took it. She was so strong-willed. I find that hard to believe.'

'It wouldn't be the first time a recovering addict disappointed and surprised those who loved her,' said Ottey.

'That's true. Fact is, I have so many conflicting emotions about this. I can't... I don't want to believe she took drugs with him. But at the same time the idea of someone killing her deliberately or otherwise seems so unreal,' he said.

Something in what he said made Cross pause momentarily.

'She kept a journal.'

'She did. Religiously.' Brian suddenly looked up as something occurred to him. 'There might well be a clue in there. She wrote everything in there, and I mean everything – from what she ate that day, how she felt about people. Everything. Have you looked?'

'We can't locate it at the moment,' Cross replied.

'It'll be in her flat. On the table. That's where it always was. I should know. I was always trying to look and see what she'd written about me. She didn't like that. She'd go schizo and she wasn't messing about.'

'It's not there.'

Brian thought for a moment. 'That's well weird,' he concluded. Cross walked over to the door to let himself out.

'Thanks for your time,' said Ottey, realising the meeting was up.

'I really hope you find out what happened. It just keeps on going round in my head. It's driving me crazy,' Brian said. He let them out. 'Would you like my mobile number?'

'Sure,' replied Ottey.

'It's just that I'm thinking of moving. I don't think I can live here anymore.'

'That's understandable,' said Ottey as she put his number into her phone.

Chapter 15

Cross tasked Mackenzie to look deeper into Simon the ex-boyfriend's background. She was pleased to be doing something pertinent to the case even though it was office-bound.

Later that afternoon he wanted to go to the hospital and make final arrangements, date and time, for Raymond's release into his care. As Ottey was dropping him off there, she decided she would come in and visit Cross's father with him. Cross initially said no, as this wasn't a social visit but a practical one. She had retorted that there was no such thing, and even if there had been she was sure you could do both. He didn't argue the point, as he thought she might be a useful distraction for his father, while he made the arrangements for him to come and stay. He waited patiently as Ottey visited the hospital shop to get a gift. This was completely unnecessary in his view.

'Soft fudge,' she said, holding up a little plastic bag with a ribbon tied round it. 'Always a safe bet with the elderly. Soft enough to chew or suck, with or without teeth. Not sticky enough to remove bridges or dentures.'

Armed with this, he had to admit, useful information, they made their way up to Raymond's ward. But he wasn't there.

Not in a 'just popped to the loo' kind of way but in a 'he's no longer in the hospital' way. Cross was confused.

'What do you mean, he's been discharged? I haven't bought a sofa bed yet,' he said to the now equally confused nurse.

The ward sister came to her rescue.

'Raymond wasn't happy about the arrangement you suggested and asked for us to look into some alternatives. He decided to go into a nursing home until he's completed his rehabilitation and you've made his flat safe enough for him to return,' she said.

'A nursing home?' Cross asked in disbelief.

'Yes. We had to move quickly, as a bed became available in an NHS care home. It's not ideal, but any bed is like gold dust at the moment, and as it's only temporary everyone was happy with it.'

'What do you mean, "not ideal"?' Cross asked.

'Well, it mainly deals with dementia patients, but they're happy to help out with respite care whenever they can.'

Cross frowned. 'Why wasn't I consulted?'

'You don't have power of attorney. Do you remember, we discussed it?' she asked with a practised smile. She was one of those people who believed that anything delivered with a smile made it more palatable.

'Of course I do,' retorted Cross. 'Don't patronise me. This is unacceptable.'

'Could you give us the address of the care home?' Ottey interceded politely.

'Of course,' replied the sister.

Ottey could see that Cross was completely taken aback by this turn of events. He was clearly confused about what to do next, so she decided to take charge. She didn't make the mistake of telling him this, as that would inevitably have involved them in fifteen minutes of discussion. She simply assumed control.

As they got into her car she turned to her colleague.

'What is it exactly that you're upset about?' she asked.

'I'm not upset. It isn't what we arranged. We made an arrangement. This isn't what we arranged,' he said, and kept repeating it over and over again.

Ottey decided to leave him be and started the car.

After about five minutes of driving he turned to her and asked, 'Where are we going?'

'To do what we set out to do earlier. Visit Raymond,' she replied.

Cross looked at his watch. 'But I have organ practice in an hour.'

'You practise on your own, don't you?' she said.

'What has that got to do with it? The fact is I practise at seven.'

'Well, you can be a little late tonight. No one's expecting you, are they?'

'That's not the point,' he insisted.

'You practise at seven every Thursday,' she said, as if this was what he was about to say himself.

'It used to be Wednesday but we had to change,' Cross went on.

'Because of Raymond's work at the air museum,' she said.

'His voluntary work.' He seemed to need to point this out, though she had no idea why. Possibly he felt it lessened its importance somehow.

'What if something in a case came up which meant you couldn't make it to practice?' she asked.

'Work would take precedence, obviously.'

'So why is this any different?'

'Because it's not work,' he said.

'But things other than work can take precedence over practice, surely?'

'No,' he replied firmly.

'Why ever not?'

'Because that would confuse things. If everything was flexible it would all be out of order and suffer accordingly. You wouldn't understand,' he said, a little dismissively.

'Oh, I do understand,' she replied. 'But you try being a single mother of two and not being flexible. See how far that gets you.'

'It's not the same,' he said.

Truth be told, he always needed to have the last word in a discussion. Ottey would admit, if pushed, that she also liked to have the last word in any given conversation. But if you tried that with Cross the conversation would go on for hours, literally, so determined was he to win. She'd tried it and learnt quite quickly that she couldn't win. It was like a verbal staring competition and she always blinked first.

They both disliked the care home the minute they set foot in it. It was depressingly institutional and worn down.

It was the stuff of Ottey's nightmares. She'd always been terrified of getting old, and this was one of the reasons why. She couldn't bear ending up in a place like this where the armchairs were not chosen for their comfort, design or aesthetic but for the ease of being wiped down. She would rather be dead. The heating was up ridiculously high. Ottey thought this was probably to keep the residents soporific. Judging by the number of them asleep in their chairs lined up along the walls of the sitting room their policy was working.

A television set blared in the background, broadcasting a quiz featuring so-called celebrities all happy to display their ignorance for the sake of a few minutes' more pointless media exposure. The majority of patients here, as the sister had told them back at the hospital, were dementia sufferers. The few that were awake seemed pitifully far gone down that awful road. Ottey thought that the prospect of staying with his son was obviously so appalling to Raymond that he considered this to be a better alternative.

Raymond was playing a game of chess by himself when they found him. He seemed in quite good spirits, but it was obvious that part of him was thinking that he hadn't quite thought this through.

'Why? Why did you do this?' his son asked without so much as a greeting.

Ottey gave Raymond a kiss and sat next to him holding his hand.

'This is better all round, son. For all of us,' said Raymond.

Cross looked round him as if to make sure he hadn't made a rash judgement of the place as he walked through, then asked, 'Why is this better than living with me?'

'You know why, George,' said his father.

'If I knew why, I wouldn't be asking,' he retorted, but he now needed to leave. Urgently. He felt an unfamiliar panic in his chest, which he didn't understand. So he turned on his heels and left Ottey with his father. She gave him the bag of fudge.

'Oh, contraband! Thank you!' Raymond said excitedly.

'Are you not allowed it?' she asked.

'Yes, of course we are. I'm just joking,' he said. 'Don't worry about George. I knew he'd be like this. It wasn't what he'd been expecting and he'd made an arrangement with me which I didn't stick to.'

'Shall I go after him?' she asked.

'Did you bring him in your car?'

'I did.'

'Then I wouldn't bother. He'll be needing a lift and will wait for you rather than ordering a cab and travelling home with a stranger,' he said.

'What if he takes the bus?'

'Oh, he won't. They're too unreliable for him. He can't wait for one not knowing exactly when it's going to appear.'

Ottey made a mental note to show Cross the app her elder daughter used for the buses.

'George is a problem-solver and I have now given him a new problem to solve,' Raymond continued. 'He likes problems and projects. Because I'm here, in this place, he now knows – even though he won't accept it – that I'll go to any lengths to avoid moving into his flat. Had I moved into an all right home, he would still have insisted on me moving in with him. Instead, me being in a home designed for the care of dementia patients has given him a problem he must solve immediately. He'll set about finding somewhere else for me – with no further mention of his flat,' he said.

Ottey left with a smile on her face. Raymond was obviously a wily old fox when it came to dealing with his son. She felt she could probably learn a lot from him about how to deal with her partner at work.

'I thought I'd ask Alice to look into alternative care homes in the Bath and Bristol area,' she said to Cross as they drove out of the home's car park. 'For Raymond.'

'That would be a completely inappropriate use of police time and resources. I am quite capable of finding my father suitable accommodation,' he replied.

'What about your flat?' she asked mischievously.

'Not an option.'

If Cross didn't want to discuss something or wanted to bring a conversation with Ottey to an end in the car, he would stare, fixedly, out of the passenger window. That day he turned his head so far away from her that the tendons in his neck stood out. He remained like this all the way to the church – Ottey was dropping him off for his organ practice. When they arrived he got out of the car, closed the door and simply walked away without a word. Normally, when he did this, Ottey would give him a ticking off. But this time she gave him a pass as she knew that he was preoccupied with what had just happened with Raymond. She decided to ask Mackenzie for help, despite what he'd said.

She was completely wrong about Cross's state of mind, however. At some point in the car journey his thoughts had moved away from his father to Flick's murder and how, at present, there didn't seem to be any clear way forward. For many detectives this point in an investigation was hugely frustrating, but not for Cross. He loved it. He loved puzzles, and with crime he knew the answer probably lay with what they already had directly in front of them. It just required a bit of tangential thinking and exploration.

His feeling was that if there were pertinent facts to be found hidden away in what was already in front of them they, more often than not, made themselves apparent in this way. Besides, what else was he supposed to do? Sit in his office bemoaning the fact that they had nothing to go on? His colleagues often became confused by his process at this time, as his lines of investigation went in all sorts of seemingly random directions. Ottey initially dismissed them as just fishing expeditions, and she was right to an extent. They were. Except that Cross was an expert in bait, understanding the undercurrents of a crime scenario and which particular spot to cast his line. But, above all, he had infinite patience.

Chapter 16

Cross often played the organ to clear his head during a case, or in this situation, when clarity wasn't the issue, to just think it through calmly. He found that hearing what he was playing echoing around the empty church and the effort to coordinate his hands and feet induced a preternatural state of concentration in him.

As he worked his way through César Franck's Chorale No. 3 in A minor, he started thinking about the diamorphine in Flick's murder. This was central to their making further progress in the case, while at the same time being the major sticking point. It was a question of who obtained it and where it had been obtained. Pretty obvious and basic questions, but the only starting point they had. The fact was, it had to have been provided by someone she knew and trusted. There had been no sign of a break-in and no signs of any struggle or disturbance, except of course for the bruise, which Clare had been unsure was relevant. She thought it might have occurred prior to the death. Nothing was out of place; there was nothing out of the ordinary. The only clue – the container or bottle – was missing. Its absence in itself was the only indication they had that someone else had been involved.

The answer, therefore, had to be in the small circle of people in Flick's life. For now it made sense to narrow down the investigation to the ex, Simon, and the former employer, Danny Stokes. He needed to look into them and their backgrounds further. The answer might lie therein, somewhere. He wasn't in the least bit sure either of them had killed Flick, but they were the only avenues the investigation could go down at present. Something would come up. It usually did.

As he finished his practice he found Stephen, the priest, waiting for him in the middle of the empty pews.

'Good evening, George. That was the perfect tonic for a weary man of God, after a particularly vexing day,' he said.

'César Franck,' Cross informed him.

'Yes, I've heard you play it before. It's beautiful. Is it part of your intended programme?' Stephen asked.

He had finally persuaded Cross, after a concerted six-month campaign with some helpful pressure from what he called the 'recital committee' – no such thing, in fact, just a group of harmless old ladies who constantly accosted Cross whenever they saw him – to give an organ recital for a small number of congregants, as he refused on principle to play in any religious services, being an atheist. The recital would raise money for some essential church maintenance, namely the provision of a new boiler. Cross had thought that, by agreeing, he might get the priest off his back. (Although, to his consternation, Ottey had pointed out when he told her this that perhaps it wasn't the best expression to be used in this day and age.)

'It is part of my proposed programme, yes. Here, I've drawn it up for you,' Cross replied, handing over an Excel spreadsheet with the composers' names, the works to be performed and the date they had been written, together with a series of asterisks.

'Gosh, George, this is very detailed. What do the asterisks signify?' Stephen asked.

'Well, I've put together a programme of popular pieces that the audience should be familiar with, may be familiar with and possibly won't be familiar with at all. Five stars, for example, against the Widor Toccata indicates that they should be familiar with that from weddings or possibly minor public schools,' Cross informed him.

'This one doesn't have a star at all.' Stephen pointed to the sheet.

'Because absolutely no one will have heard Wilhelm Middelschulte,' Cross said confidently.

'It's quite extensive, George. How long are you expecting it to last? Exactly?' Stephen asked.

'Exactly? One hundred and three minutes and twenty-seven seconds,' Cross replied.

'I see. Gosh, that really is good value for money.'

'How much are you charging?' Cross asked.

'A tenner a head, and we'll be selling wine and some canapés Mrs Williams is making. Which should add a little to the profit. It'll also give you an opportunity to answer any questions they have,' he said.

'I don't think so,' Cross said quickly.

'No?' Stephen asked uncertainly.

'No,' came the firm reply.

Stephen sensed that George was in no mood for compromise or discussion that night. He obviously had something on his mind. Probably work. A case he was working on. He'd told the priest he did this occasionally. So Stephen decided to readdress the matter of the Q&A at some other time when Cross was more amenable.

'Well, a hundred and three minutes,' said Stephen.

'And twenty-seven seconds,' Cross reminded him.

'Indeed. Now I'm thinking maybe that's a little long for old bones on cold wooden pews,' said Stephen carefully.

'Put the heating on.'

'We are actually raising money for a faulty boiler, George,' the priest pointed out.

'Fair point,' Cross replied.

'So with that I mind, I think it might be a good thing to maybe reduce the length, perhaps?' he said.

'I see.'

'So why don't we just take out these longer pieces?' Stephen pointed to the piece of paper.

'No,' Cross said abruptly. 'We can't do that!'

'We can't?'

'There's a structure here. A musical narrative. There are all sorts of factors that have gone into the construction of this,' said Cross.

Stephen thought for a second that he might be joking. Then he remembered he was talking to George Cross.

'I see. Yes, of course. Well, can I suggest that we treat this like a first draft of a play?' This completely threw Cross. 'What I'm suggesting is that we take this beautifully curated list as a preliminary proposal and that you go away and with due sympathetic consideration possibly bring the duration down a little?'

Cross looked at the sheet for a second. He knew he needed to be reasonable here. Yes, it would take a little work, but he could probably take out ten or fifteen minutes without damaging the musical integrity of the concert. So what Stephen said next came as something of a shock.

'Could we perhaps think of making it around fifty minutes? Just under an hour? I don't know why but I think that keeping things under an hour makes them a more attractive proposition. Like pricing something for 99p instead of a pound.'

Cross didn't understand this at all. By making it as long as he had he thought he was being generous – he'd even had to learn two entirely new pieces.

'It seems hardly worth all the effort for just fifty minutes,' he replied.

'Well, maybe we could divide it into two?' suggested Stephen.

'Oh, I see – and have an interval, you mean?' said Cross.

'No. Two separate recitals,' said the priest, maybe pushing his luck a bit. The prospect of this was doubly intolerable to Cross. One recital was bad enough, but two didn't really bear thinking about. So he quickly conceded to the abridged fifty minute recital and immediately made his way out of the church before he found himself agreeing to anything else. He stopped to put his habitual five pounds in the collection box despite Stephen constantly telling him it really wasn't necessary.

Chapter 17

At the office the next morning Mackenzie gave Cross a list of well-reviewed care homes in the Bristol and Bath area. Everything was reviewed on the internet these days. Even care homes, it seemed. Cross wasn't at all sure whether this was a useful thing or not, but thought on the whole that anyone with any sense could weed out the 'revenge' reviews, as he believed they were called, and be guided by the honest ones.

'I looked them up last night at home; I wasn't on police time. It was my personal time,' Mackenzie said.

'I see.' He was a little flummoxed, because his natural reaction to something like this was to find an objection to it but none was forthcoming. 'I'll have a look through them,' he said and walked away towards his office.

'Thank you!' shouted Ottey from the other side of the open area.

He stopped, momentarily irritated by being shouted at, then turned to Mackenzie. 'Thank you,' he said quietly.

'A pleasure,' she replied. 'Let me know if there's anything else I can do.'

*

Later that afternoon Ottey and Cross drove to Sandra Wilson's house. They were in fact ten minutes early, but Cross had insisted they park up in the road till the precise appointed time. He always did this. He was, therefore, always prompt for any appointment or meeting, something he not only thought was important in life, but he took great pride in.

Sandra was not alone when they arrived. She was sitting in the kitchen with an elegant, distinguished-looking man in his sixties. He was wearing an immaculate three-piece suit with a broad, prominent chalk pinstripe which begged for attention. He had a matching pink silk square and tie. As they walked into the kitchen he checked his pocket watch, suspended from his waistcoat by a chain and said, 'I should be getting off, Sandra.'

He smiled politely at the two detectives.

'Of course. This is Dr Sutton,' she told them.

'How do you do?' said Ottey as she shook his hand and introduced herself and Cross.

Cross thought this was an uncharacteristically formal greeting from his colleague and wondered whether it was the suit, the fact that he was a doctor or perhaps the pocket watch which had affected her.

'How do you do?' Sutton replied and then offered his hand to Cross, who ignored it.

'GP?' Cross asked instead.

'No, psychotherapist. I was a GP in a previous life but not any longer. That is to say, I still have my licence but no longer practise,' he replied.

'He was Flick's shrink,' said Sandra, smiling mischievously. 'He hates me saying that.'

Ottey smiled. 'Nice to meet you. I'm sorry for your loss.'

'Thank you,' he replied.

Cross was momentarily baffled, thinking it a coincidence that the doctor too had lost someone, and that possibly he and Sandra were deriving some mutual support from each other. 'Who's died?' he asked.

There was a silence.

'He was Flick's doctor,' said Ottey.

'I know that,' Cross replied tetchily.

'Which is why I'm expressing my sympathies,' she explained.

'I see. I wasn't aware that courtesy applied to professional relationships.'

'Well, now you are,' she said.

'Indeed I am.' He became aware that Ottey was now staring at him expectantly. 'Ah,' he said. 'My condolences to you, also, Doctor.'

'Thank you, Sergeant, and for what it's worth I completely understand your confusion. Why should such a courtesy be extended when the loss occurs in a professional relationship? I think it's possibly optional,' Sutton said with complete charm.

'Why don't you stay, Benedict?' said Sandra.

'Would you like me to?' he replied, then immediately turned to the two police officers. 'I suppose I really ought to be addressing that question to you.'

'We're happy if Sandra would like you to stay,' said Ottey.

They sat at the table, having refused the customary offer of a cup of tea – they were 'all tea-ed out', as Ottey had put it.

'Did Flick keep a file on her case with Stokes?' Ottey began.

'Yes, I think it's still at the flat,' Sandra said.

'Is it all right if we have someone go over and pick it up?' Ottey asked.

'Yes. Alice has a key. I gave it to her in case you needed to go back, and she knows her way around,' Sandra said.

'Do you think Stokes might have been involved?' asked Sutton.

'He's a person of interest, obviously, because of the action she was taking against him,' replied Ottey.

'It just seems so unlikely,' Sutton went on.

'Murder is, more often than not, unlikely,' replied Cross.

Sutton smiled at this. He seemed to have taken a particular interest in Cross, from the moment he refused to shake hands.

'What did Flick tell you about Stokes?' Ottey asked Sandra.

'She spared me the details. Didn't want to upset me. But I now know she wasn't the first or indeed the last he tried to get his filthy hands on. This habit of exposing himself to women when he didn't get his way happened quite regularly.

'Did he ever threaten her?' asked Ottey.

'She started receiving threatening texts after she'd taken on lawyers,' said Sandra. 'Before that he bombarded her with lewd and obscene texts suggesting all sorts of things he wanted to do to her. It was quite disgusting. She erased the first few, but then started keeping them as proof when she could see where this might be going.'

'Do we have that phone?' asked Ottey.

'No. I'll get it for you. You will be careful with it, won't you?' said Sandra, anxiously. 'It has so many photos and other things on it. I'd hate to lose it.'

'We'll back it up before we do anything,' Ottey assured her.

Sandra got up to go and find the phone. 'Before she died she started getting menacing texts from an unknown number,' she said.

'Probably Stokes on a burner phone,' said Ottey, making a note to look at them. Sandra left the room.

'What is your opinion of the manner of her death, Doctor?' Cross asked.

'My immediate reaction was suicide,' he said. 'But it didn't make any sense.'

'Does suicide ever make sense?' Cross asked.

'An excellent question, and one which requires a longer answer than I think you have time for right now. Suicide is always shocking but not always surprising. With Flick it was both,' said Sutton.

'Despite her history?' Cross said.

'Actually, precisely because of her history. Because of what she'd been through. She was in an unexpectedly good place,' Sutton said.

'Unexpected by whom?' Cross went on.

'Another good question, Sergeant. Unexpected by her and her mother,' the doctor said.

'But not by you?' asked Cross.

'I myself try not to have any expectations, good or bad, with my patients. I find it unconstructive and an obstacle to my treatment of them,' he answered.

'How so?'

'Well, if I might be so bold as to compare my work with yours, I deal only with what is in front of me,' Sutton replied. 'Every appointment with a particular patient is different from their last and their next. I, of course, track their progress, but not in such a way that would tempt me to make an unfounded prediction as to what may happen in the future or have any expectations thereof. These could simply lead me down the wrong avenue of treatment. You may work the same way,

Sergeant. In any given case you probably deal with what's in front of you and make your decisions how to proceed based on those facts, not assumptions. Assumptions can lead to so much time wasting. Don't you think?'

'That's very perceptive of you, Dr Sutton. I do indeed,' replied Cross.

'It's part of my job,' said the doctor.

'What is?' asked Cross.

'Analysing what or who is in front of me.' Sutton looked directly at Cross as if that was exactly what he was doing at that very moment. Analysing him. 'Do you have any leads thus far?'

'We do not,' replied Cross.

'But what about the diamorphine? Surely that's a lead,' Sutton went on.

'A lead which currently leads precisely nowhere,' said Cross.

'Does the bottle not have information on the label? It should be traceable.'

'There was no bottle,' said Cross.

'Ah. Which is why you've come to the conclusion someone else was involved, presumably. Is that why you've concluded it's murder?' the doctor asked.

'What else could it be?' asked Ottey.

'Assisted suicide, perhaps,' said Sutton.

'Two things would seem to rule that out,' said Cross. 'The fact that she made no arrangements for her daughter, and the absence of a suicide note. She was very close to her mother and her child, and had she committed suicide, I believe she would have left a note to explain herself in some way. If she had been organised and clear-headed enough to get a third party to help, she would surely have made arrangements for her daughter, rather than leaving her on her own in the flat. She couldn't have known when she would be missed and her daughter thereby discovered.'

'That does have a certain logic to it. I find myself taking some comfort from it, while at the same time feeling quite horrified at the fact that someone would want to kill her,' said Sutton.

'She also, according to people who knew her, such as yourself, showed no signs of wanting or needing to end her own life,' said Cross.

'But it's not at all easy to get hold of diamorphine,' said Sutton.

'It is not,' said Cross.

Sandra now came back into the room with Flick's mobile phone.

'Well, if I can be of any assistance – any – here's my card. Please do get in touch,' said Sutton.

Cross leant forward and took the card. Sandra then handed Ottey the phone as if it was some sort of holy relic.

'We'll take very good care of it, Sandra. Don't worry,' said Ottey.

Chapter 18

A few days later they were still not much further on with the case when Cross received a call from a woman named Karen. She turned out to be the tiny little bird of a girl Cross had spoken to at Danny Stokes's dry cleaner's. She wanted to meet. At first Cross thought Ottey should go, as Karen might be more relaxed with her, but Ottey disagreed. Karen had reached out to Cross; she would be expecting him. He should go and take Mackenzie with him.

They met her at a small café near Temple Meads station. She was just as nervous as when Cross had first seen her. Her nails were bitten to the quick. She had dark bags under her eyes and was way too skinny for it to be healthy. Cross volunteered to get the beverages to give Karen a chance to talk to Mackenzie alone. When he returned he noticed that she only looked at Mackenzie when she spoke.

'Are you an addict, Karen?' Mackenzie asked.

'Yes. Recovering addict,' she said, by way of correction.

'I'm sorry, "recovering". Are any other employees at the dry cleaner's?' Mackenzie asked.

'Yes. He always has a few working for him. It's his thing. He pretends, makes out, it's his way of giving back, but it's all about him trying to take whatever he can,' Karen said quietly.

'How did you get the gig?' asked Mackenzie.

'Through Hopewell, but they've stopped sending girls now.'

'Why?' asked Mackenzie.

'Because Flick told them what was going on. Then when she decided to go to the tribunal, obviously they had to stop.'

'Did you know Flick when she worked there?' Mackenzie asked.

'Yes. Then after she left she often came over with Daisy at the end of the shift to talk to us.'

'What did Stokes think about that?' asked Cross.

'He hated it. Would always come out and tell her to go away. Even called you lot out once,' said Karen. 'Then her lawyers told her she should stop coming round as it could be made to look bad in court.'

'Has Stokes made any sexual advances towards you?' Cross asked.

There was a momentary pause. Cross thought she was weighing up how much to tell them. She wanted to talk, obviously, as she'd called them. But when it actually came down to it she was unsure of how much to impart.

'Yes,' she said quietly.

'What happened?' Mackenzie asked gently.

'He asked me to work late. Earn some overtime. I thought it was odd I was the only one there, but I needed the money and didn't want to piss him off,' she began. 'He came down to where I was working and started talking to me in a really friendly way. Said he'd had his eye on me since I'd arrived. He started touching himself through his trousers. You know, on his crotch, and saying stuff. I asked him to stop, but he wouldn't. So I said I'd leave. He carried on for a bit and then I suppose he gave up, but he didn't touch me that time.'

'What do you mean, "that time"?' asked Mackenzie.

'He's always doing it. You're asked up to his office and…' Her voice faded. 'But I need the job. What else can I do? I got nicked for solicitation a couple of years back. I'm not proud of it. It was needs must. So who's going to give me a job now? It's like a vicious circle. Now I'm clean and I need a wage,' she went on.

'That's understandable,' Mackenzie tried to reassure her.

'Because he knows I was on the game – for only two months, mind you; that doesn't make me a prostitute, does it? – he keeps asking for a freebie. Then when I say no he gets angry. I really want to get out of there.'

'What's the worst thing he's done to you?' asked Mackenzie.

'He gets his knob out in the office when he talks to you. Just looks at you and rubs it. It's disgusting.'

'Why did you want to talk to us?' asked Cross, who was convinced she was holding the worst of it back.

'Is it true someone killed Flick?' she asked.

'Yes,' said Cross.

'And you think he did it?'

'He's certainly a person of interest,' was as much as Cross would say.

'Well, what if it was him?' she asked.

'Why would you think he killed her?' asked Cross.

'We're still working for him. What if he did it again?' she said, not answering the question.

'Firstly, we don't know it was him, but you're right to be concerned. However, I think it unlikely, and I hope this may be of some comfort, that he would be stupid enough to do it again to an employee or ex-employee, as he would be drawing attention to himself. But again – why do you think it might have been him?' Cross persisted.

'Because he's always offering us drugs. He knows why we were at Hopewell. It's disgusting. He employs us to give us another chance, he says, then he tries to get us to use. He offers us drugs to have sex with him. I don't know which is worse. Using again or doing it with him.'

'Did he offer you drugs?' Cross asked.

'After I'd said no a few times, yes,' she said.

'Kudos for not taking them, Karen. That must've been really hard,' said Mackenzie.

'Not really. I saw what happened to Angie. She couldn't resist it in the end. Then when he'd had enough of her, he sacked her. Said she was using again and had become unreliable. Which was true, but whose fault was that? He said he had a strict no drugs policy. It's a joke.'

'Do you think Angie would talk to us?' Mackenzie asked.

'Probably not. But I can ask her.'

'You still see her?' Cross asked.

'Now and again. She comes round because she wants money. Screams through the window at Stokes. He gives her money sometimes, which is stupid, because she only comes back for more.'

'Do you know where she lives?' asked Mackenzie.

'Not anymore. She got kicked out,' she said sadly.

Mackenzie gave her a card and wrote her mobile number on it. 'Call me if she comes back to your work, will you?'

'Do you think that's what he did with Flick? Gave her drugs?' Karen asked.

'Difficult to say,' said Mackenzie.

'The old man's lovely – it doesn't make any sense he had a bastard kid like him. I reckon he knows what's going on and doesn't like it.'

'Why do you think that?' asked Cross.

'They have big rows up in the office. All the time. And it's not about the business.'

'She's not telling us everything,' said Cross, once he and Mackenzie were back in the car.

'Yeah, I thought so too, but if we pressed she might clam up altogether,' she replied.

'Correct,' Cross affirmed.

Chapter 19

The following Wednesday, as was his routine prior to Raymond's admission to hospital, Cross bought a Chinese takeaway from his regular spot, Xiao Bao's, and took it to share with his father. The fact that Raymond was in a care home with a restaurant made no difference to him. The additional fact that Xiao Bao's takeaway was convenient for Raymond's flat, but completely out of the way for the care home, also made no difference to him. It was their routine.

Xiao Bao now did deliveries and was more than happy to lend Cross one of the thermal delivery bags his riders used. He also told Cross that he would be delighted to deliver to the care home despite the fact that it was outside his area, if that would make things easier. Unsurprisingly, Cross declined this thoughtful offer. He found comfort in the routine of it all even though it was, for the time being, a little more protracted.

Cross had moved his father from the NHS dementia care home into one that was more suitable, as Raymond had predicted he would. Privately funded, of course, and Cross paid in advance. There had been no further mention of the father living in the son's flat during his period of recovery. This was a relief to both of them.

Raymond was secretly touched by his son's speedy

rearrangement of his rehabilitation accommodation, but knew better than to say that to him. This kind of problem-solving was the closest his son ever came to a demonstration of emotion or a sentimental gesture to his father, and Raymond was happy with that. He also didn't dispute Cross's paying. Most people in this situation would make the offer, knowing it would be rebuffed but taken as a gesture of gratitude. Cross would not see it this way, and so a long and unnecessary discussion would have ensued, which would only have come to an end after he'd managed to convince himself that this was, as he'd thought all along, the right course of action for both of them. The implied gesture would have gone completely over his head.

The care home was purpose-built and located in Stoke Bishop just off the Downs. There were a number of halls of residence for Bristol University in the area and several sports fields. The population of the area seemed to vary according to whether it was term time or not. Cross hadn't selected it by simply trawling the internet. He had narrowed Mackenzie's list down to a shortlist of five. He then visited and inspected them. He discovered that care homes had moved on a lot since the squalid institution his grandmother had had to endure for the last months of her life.

This was not so much a philanthropic shift, he thought. It was more to do with medical advances resulting in an increasingly large elderly population, which in turn resulted in an increased demand for senior care. As people realised this, homes proliferated across the country so the private care sector had become very competitive.

He'd decided on the one Raymond was in for a few reasons. Firstly, he was dealt with by the manager and not an 'account services manager'. Secondly, the manager had asked him questions about his father: who he was; what he'd done before retirement; what his interests were. All of these things were important to her, it seemed, even though Raymond's stay would be for less than a month. There were no such questions from the others.

The home he chose was more like a four-star hotel in a respected national chain than a care home. There were sofas in the capacious reception for the residents and their guests to relax in and enjoy coffee from the 'straight from the bean to cup' coffee machine. Cross thought Raymond would be comfortable here, and the residents seemed a little younger and more alert than in some of the other homes.

'I hope you haven't eaten,' said Cross, as he walked into Raymond's room.

'It's Wednesday – of course I haven't. I told them you'd be in at seven and it's…' but Raymond wasn't wearing his watch.

'Seven oh two,' answered Cross, as he took the food out of the insulating bag and laid it out.

'Did you buy that bag?' asked his father.

'No, it's Xiao Bao's.'

'That was kind of him. Can I see?' said Raymond. Cross passed it over and Raymond examined it inside and out. 'Excellent quality, and look how the rice is still steaming. Did you know there are three main types of foam insulation for bags like this?'

'I did not,' answered Cross.

'Polyvinyl chloride, which is a type of thermoplastic polymer known more commonly as PVC. Polyurethane – or PU – and Polyester. Terribly clever stuff.'

'Interesting,' commented Cross.

'Isn't it?' Raymond continued enthusiastically. 'Revolutionised the food delivery industry. Everyone mistakenly thinks it was the internet, but the fundamental shift occurred thanks to polymers and polyethers. No point in being able to order food on your computer if it arrives cold.'

'Unless it's a salad,' said Cross.

'Yes, that's true,' Raymond conceded.

This was typical of the conversations these two men enjoyed together. They then watched television and ate in silence. They did this often, but tonight the truth was that they were doing it to avoid the conversation neither of them wanted to have – about the clearance of Raymond's flat to facilitate his return home. Cross had in fact come up with a solution. A good one, he thought, but not one he was going to mention to his father, as he knew that any compromise he suggested would never be good enough. The best thing for him to do was just get on with it.

Cross got up to leave as soon as he had swallowed the last mouthful of his egg fried rice. He packed away the takeaway containers in the insulating bag then threw away the paper plates and plastic knives and forks he'd brought with him.

'There's a retired policewoman here. Before your time, I think. In her late eighties. What's her name...? Moffatt,' said Raymond.

'Don't know the name.'

'You should pop in and say hello,' suggested Raymond.

'No, I don't think so,' said Cross as he left.

Chapter 20

Cross discovered quite a lot about Stokes the next day. Stokes senior, that is. He hadn't set out to, as such, but what he came across interested him. It turned out he was a quietly wealthy man with a portfolio of properties in the Bristol area. They were all commercial except for his own modest house and a couple of flats in the Bristol docks. It appeared that, far from his son buying him out of the business, Gerry Stokes had simply handed over the day-to-day running of it to his son some years before, when his wife became ill. She had been ill for many years and had finally passed the year before. The father and son were so different. Why did he let Danny parade around, pretending not only that he owned the business, but that he'd bought his father out?

One property stood out in Gerry's portfolio. He owned the freehold of the building occupied by the Hopewell Clinic and had been on the board of the clinic for several years. It transpired that Danny Stokes had inherited his place on the board when his father stood down to look after his wife. Things were starting to connect.

He decided to lay out the little information they had in the case and see if they'd missed anything. It didn't take him long to find something and he castigated himself for not having done it earlier. But it wasn't about Danny Stokes. It was to do with Simon the ex-boyfriend.

While Cross was going through everything they knew about Simon, he came across his previous criminal convictions again. One was for attempted burglary, presumably to fund his drug habit. The other two were drug offences, and Cross decided to delve into these a little deeper. He pulled up Simon's file on the database. The first drug offence was possession – of cannabis. He was given a warning and a fine. The next was for possession of a Class A drug for which he received a six-month prison sentence. But it was the drug itself which stood out to Cross. Not heroin, but diamorphine. They would need to question him again, and their opportunity came at Flick's funeral.

The three of them went, Cross, Ottey and Mackenzie. It was quite a good turnout, with a lot of young people. School friends, gleaned Cross, most of whom, it seemed, had no idea of her problems; hadn't been in touch for a long time; felt guilt about it all. As usual with younger people, whether they meant it or not, quite a few of them seemed to be making the death of a friend they were not in touch with about themselves rather than the recently deceased, Cross thought. But to be fair, the death of a contemporary hit the young hard. It was incomprehensible, to an extent; not part of the plan. There was a lot of hugging and crying, in small groups, mostly young women with young men standing on the periphery not entirely sure how they should be behaving. Sandra was surrounded by supportive friends. Cross noticed Tammy Smith, Dr Sutton, and, at the back of the church, rather surprisingly, he thought, Gerry Stokes.

Poems were read, memories shared. Brian gave an address which was both funny and moving. There was the obligatory religious element but it was kept to a minimum; Flick wasn't the religious sort, but maybe Sandra was. There was no organ music, which Cross found a little disappointing.

Afterwards, as the crowd gathered, Cross noticed Gerry walking swiftly towards his car. Simon was standing off from the queue that had formed for the mourners to give Sandra their condolences. Cross heard a few of them saying how hard they'd found it to accept the idea that Flick might have committed suicide. As Cross walked over to Simon he saw the young man's face drop, but was that fear that the policeman had discovered something further, or simply that he had nothing else to say and so the prospect of talking to the police held little attraction?

Simon was wearing an ill-fitting suit with a shirt and tie. Everything was too big. There was a large gap between the shirt collar and his Adam's apple. He looked like he was dressed in clothes he'd reluctantly borrowed from his dad for a last-minute interview for a job he had no prospect of getting. When Cross reached him, Billie Williams appeared protectively at his side.

'I need to ask you a few more questions,' Cross said, straight out of the gate.

'Can this not wait till the end of his treatment? He only has a couple of weeks left,' said Billie.

'Ms Williams, we've already had a conversation similar to this where I informed you that this is a murder enquiry. Perhaps you'd like to ask Flick's mother over there, if she would be happy to wait for two weeks,' Cross replied.

'What more do you want to know?' Simon asked.

'I can elaborate down at the Major Crime Unit,' said Cross.

'Are you arresting me?' asked Simon.

'I am not. I simply have further questions to ask.'

They were now joined by an older couple.

'Is everything all right?' asked the man.

'Everything's fine. Why would you even ask that?' insisted Simon. It was obvious from the irritable tone of the reply, together with the resentful sigh, that these were Simon's parents, thought Cross.

'This is the detective investigating Flick's death,' said Billie.

'Murder,' said Cross, correcting her.

'He wants to ask Simon some more questions,' Billie went on.

'I see. Do we need a lawyer?' asked the father.

'Why would you need a lawyer?' asked Cross.

'What? I meant Simon, of course,' the father replied.

'I don't know. Do you need a lawyer, Simon?' Cross asked.

Simon wasn't able to answer before his father spoke again.

'I'd like to sit in on his interview.'

'That won't be possible,' said Cross. 'Shall we go?' he said to Simon.

'Now?' Simon asked.

'Would be ideal,' replied Cross.

'But we're going back to the house,' said Simon's mother, looking over at Sandra.

'Of course you are,' replied Cross. 'Afterwards is acceptable.'

Simon saw someone approach behind Cross and hastily moved away. He was followed by his parents, but not before Cross noticed his mother casting a disdainful look to whoever was joining them.

'Detective Sergeant,' a voice said behind him.

Cross turned to see Dr Sutton.

'Billie,' the doctor then said by way of a greeting, as she'd stayed back with Cross.

'Benedict,' she replied.

'Have you made any progress?' Sutton asked Cross.

'No.'

'None at all?' Sutton asked.

'That would be correct.'

'That is disappointing,' said Sutton.

'That would depend on your expectations,' said Cross.

'I suppose it would.' Sutton looked at the detective for a moment. Cross looked directly back. 'I must say I'm slightly surprised you haven't been in touch,' said the doctor.

'And why is that?' asked Cross.

'Well, I thought I might have been of some use,' Sutton replied.

'If that becomes the case I will come and see you,' said Cross and wandered off to find Ottey.

Ottey was with Mackenzie who had been talking to some of Flick's friends. Cross had noticed how warmly Sandra had embraced Mackenzie before the service. People warmed to Mackenzie and opened up to her in a completely different way to either him or Ottey. He was aware that in his case this came as no surprise. He knew people thought him odd. Not difficult; odd. He thought it was probably because of Mackenzie's youth, but also because she wasn't actually a police officer. (For others, though, her youth was the very reason they wouldn't talk to her.) She was able to elicit more from the relatives, particularly, than he was. He wondered whether this was because he could be so concentrated and blinkered in his line of questioning and that her way was so much more conversational. Unexpected and really useful bits of information often came out of her chats with people.

Sutton had been watching Cross and turned to Billie.

'I think our friend there may be on the spectrum,' observed Sutton as Cross was walking away.

'Gosh, Ben, you always amaze me with your dazzling diagnostic skills,' said Billie waspishly.

Chapter 21

Simon arrived at the MCU a little after four that afternoon with both his parents and Billie Williams in tow. He had the look of a schoolboy called to the head's office, with his parents also receiving a summons, and who thought the whole inquest a waste of his time. His father's expression seemed to say that he knew as soon as they let their son back into their lives this would be the kind of place they'd inevitably end up in. At a police station.

'Simon's parents are here, Ms Williams. So why are you?' Cross asked the head of the Hopewell Clinic.

'I want to make sure that Simon comes back to Hopewell afterwards,' she replied.

'You're that confident that this interview won't result in his arrest?' Cross asked innocently.

'Simon didn't kill Flick, accidentally or otherwise,' she said.

'You know him that well?'

'I knew Flick that well,' she replied firmly.

An interesting distinction, thought Cross.

Simon slumped into the armless sofa of the Voluntary Assistance suite next to the large indoor plant which had somehow found its way in there at some time in the past weeks. From the long roots dangling down it looked like it might have conceivably crawled in there on its own. The sofa was impossible to sit on comfortably or to strike an attitude in. Somehow its design made the occupant perch a little indignantly. Quite a useful characteristic for it, Cross thought.

'Do I need a lawyer?' Simon began.

'Why do you keep asking that question when we've answered it several times already today?' replied Cross.

'Then why am I here?'

'We have a few questions,' Ottey replied. 'When we saw you at the clinic you said you didn't see Flick the day she died.'

'Because I didn't,' said Simon.

'But that's not entirely true, is it?' she asked.

'It is.'

'All right, let me put it another way. Were you in Flick's building the day she died?' Ottey asked.

Simon offered no reply.

'Well, let me help you out. You did go there that morning and had an altercation with her downstairs neighbour, Brian,' said Ottey. 'Why didn't you tell us that?'

'Well, obviously, because I was in breach of the restraining order and you're the police,' he said in his best effort at a patronising monotone.

'What was the fight about?' Ottey persisted.

'It was more handbags than a fight, let's be honest. He's such a loser, that guy.'

'Why do you say that?' asked Ottey.

'Because he has a hard-on, *had* a hard-on, for Flick.'

'So you had something in common. Does that also make you a loser?' asked Ottey.

'She wasn't interested. That makes him the loser, not me,' he said.

'Except that he wasn't the one with the restraining order,' Ottey pointed out.

'Whatever,' Simon muttered.

'Were you jealous of him?' she asked.

'Like I said, she wasn't interested in him.'

'But they spent a lot of time together. She even left your daughter alone with him when she went to see her mother,' Ottey went on.

'How sweet,' he spat.

'Bet that pissed you off,' she said. He didn't answer. 'Playing happy families, the three of them. Exactly what you were so desperate for. Did you try to go back to the flat after Brian had left for work that day?'

'No,' he said.

'Tell me about Dr Sutton,' Cross said, entering the conversation for the first time.

'He's a creep,' said Simon.

'What makes you say that?' Cross asked.

'He just is. Loves himself. Just look at the way he dresses. Thinks he's a god to addicts and behaves like it.'

'Go on,' said Cross.

'You don't have an appointment with him. It's more like a bloody audience,' Simon continued.

'You don't like him,' said Cross.

'No. Whatever gave you that idea?' he replied sarcastically.

'It seemed a little more than that when you ran off at the church,' Cross observed.

'No. Like you said, I just don't like him.'

'Why? Was it because he told Flick to stay away from you?' he asked.

'If that was the case I wouldn't have anyone left to like,' said Simon.

Cross said nothing further. But he sensed that Simon wanted to say more, now that he had the opportunity.

'He was all over her,' Simon continued. 'I told her to be careful of him. But she was taken in. There's a word for it. A Svengali, isn't it? It's like a cult the way he deals with his patients. I'd have said he had a thing for Flick, but Billie says that's how he is with all of them. You either sign up for it or you don't. Flick did. You should talk to him. He must have an opinion about what happened to her. He has an opinion about just about everything else.'

'Have you ever had a session with him?' Cross asked.

'No. He "selects" his patients carefully. Only deals with the ones he thinks he can help, he says,' said Simon.

'He thought you were a bad influence on her, presumably,' said Cross.

'He signed a supporting letter for the restraining order. So what does that tell you?'

'Wasn't he just doing that to protect her?' said Cross.

Simon said nothing for a moment then looked up. 'I didn't see her the day she died. Did I try? Yes. Brian stopped me. We had a scrap then I went into town and scored.'

'Diamorphine?' Cross asked.

'No!' Simon said.

'But you have scored it before,' said Cross, then without waiting for an answer, 'Why did you tell us you don't inject?'

'Because I don't.'

'But you have in the past,' Cross went on.

'Says who?'

Cross didn't reply.

'You must've known we'd look at your record, Simon,' said Ottey. 'You were convicted of possessing a Class A drug. Namely, diamorphine.'

'That was a long time ago,' Simon said.

'So?' she said.

'So I haven't done it since because I haven't needed to.'

'But look at it from our perspective,' she went on. 'Flick died from a diamorphine overdose and you have a past conviction for possession of diamorphine.'

'Sure, but this wasn't me. How am I supposed to make you believe that?' Simon protested.

'By helping us,' she said.

'I've told you I'll do anything to help. Do you have any idea how frustrating it is to know you're wasting your time talking to me, when I know I didn't do it and you could be looking for who really did it?' he said miserably.

Cross thought his body language looked sincere.

'So you want to help?' asked Ottey.

'Of course. Someone killed my girlfriend,' he said.

'*Ex*-girlfriend,' Cross pointed out, not to be cruel, but accurate.

They pushed Simon for a further couple of hours. What Cross wanted to know was where Simon had obtained the diamorphine from all those years before. Was it readily available on the street?

'Sometimes. Sometimes not,' Simon replied.

'Where did you get it from?' Cross asked again.

'I can't tell you that.'

'Can't or won't?' asked Ottey.

'What's the difference? The end result is the same,' he said.

Ottey had become fed up with Cross's circling. His dogged

persistence wasn't getting them anywhere. She was bored, was the truth of it. Interviews like this often became interminably boring, particularly if you were in the room with Cross, who could go along with the same monotonal line of questioning for hours. At times it was enough to make her want to bash her brains out against the wall. Cross was about to repeat the question when she stepped in.

'So here's what's going to happen in the next five minutes if you don't tell us. I'm going to arrest you on suspicion of the murder of Flick. You'll spend the night partly in the cells, but mostly in here with another detective who works nights and who will take over from us and ask you the same single question. Again and again. Repeatedly. Where did you get the diamorphine from? We will come back tomorrow after breakfast and a good night's sleep and start asking the same question. Again and again. If we don't get an answer we'll get an extension from a judge, who, based on the evidence we have, will grant it, and so for a further seventy-two hours you will be asked the same one question over and over again. Wouldn't it be easier just to answer it now, not be arrested and leave in twenty minutes?' Ottey said, practically in a single breath.

'You're saying I can leave in twenty minutes?' he asked, making sure he'd heard her correctly.

'I am.' She smiled as if to show him how ready she was to let him go and how easy all of this could be.

It transpired that Simon had obtained his diamorphine from a dealer named 'Thatch' who was currently in prison. Cross found himself wondering whether this was a reference to the former prime minister or the man's hair or lack of, but he didn't ask. What they discovered was that prescribed drugs that were no longer needed by people – mostly the relatives of a recently deceased person – were often taken back to a pharmacy to be destroyed. Even brand-new unopened packets couldn't be passed onto other people in need. Cross thought this was a terrible waste, particularly as the National Health Service was always struggling financially. No record was ever made of these returned drugs. The pharmacists would then utilise the services of a pharmaceutical waste company to dispose of them. Thatch had a good line of business going with an unscrupulous pharmacist in Bristol who sold him diamorphine and other opioids, instead of having them destroyed.

As promised, they let Simon go. He went back to Hopewell. From Simon's expression as he re-joined his parents, Ottey wondered whether he was thinking that seventy-two hours in a cell might have been preferable to enduring the journey back to the clinic with them.

'How did he seem to you?' Ottey asked Cross as they made themselves coffee. They each made their own. She had given up offering to make his several months ago as he never seemed satisfied with her efforts, always leaving his cup untouched on the desk.

'His behaviour wasn't such that I thought he might be concealing something,' Cross replied.

In the interview Simon had repeatedly asked them how they thought he would've been able to inject Flick. What possible scenario ended in that way? They'd never injected together before, so how, on what pretext, would he have been able to persuade her to let him put a needle in her arm, even more so, now that she was clean and sober?

Cross had made no comment but thought it was a very

valid point, and not just for Simon. It applied to anyone they brought in. The blow to the head had to be material. She was struck on the head then injected and placed back in the chair. Ottey wasn't sure that Simon was capable of such violence against Flick, but Cross made the point that he could've been so high he just lost control.

Ottey said that, for what it was worth, she didn't think Simon killed Flick. Cross inevitably pointed out that what she thought was irrelevant unless she had evidence to back it up. At times like this she found his pedantry irritating. Hadn't he just said in as many words that he thought Simon hadn't done it?

'I said he didn't behave like he was hiding something,' Cross replied. 'An entirely different thing.'

Chapter 22

That weekend came as a natural break in the investigation for Cross. He would go back to it full throttle on Monday. Early in his career he had been unable to do this – switch off from a case when not at work; he found he couldn't settle when a case was outstanding, incomplete. He felt uncomfortable, guilty, if he wasn't working twenty-four-seven to put right whatever injustice had been committed.

One of the few senior officers who could see beyond his, then undiagnosed, condition had told him that, as a policeman, there would always be an ongoing unsolved case in his in-box. Once Cross had got past the confusion that he didn't have an actual in-box, as such, to put his cases in, he listened as he was told that the rest of his career would be like this, and if he carried on working the way he was – all weekends and well into the night every night – he would either burn out or break down. He owed it to the victims to be in the best condition both mentally and physically to try and get them justice.

Cross could see the logic of this, and although the change in his working methods that followed was slow, he eventually managed to force himself to take regular breaks and stand back. Obviously there were times when an investigation gained a momentum of its own, and sometimes as they got close to a breakthrough the hours would become long, but on the whole he regulated his time. This weekend was one of those regulated mental breaks for him.

He spent the Saturday embarking on the monumental task of trying to sort through his father's stuff and clear out the flat. He threw out things he felt were useless and worthless, but tried to do it through the lens of his father's obsession. When he was unsure of an object's value, both practical and financial, he would err on his father's side and keep hold of it.

He did apply a logic to the process, though, which was that the nearer to the bottom of any pile he found an object, the less likely it was to survive the cull. He then tried to apply a dust rule to demonstrate that something hadn't been moved or used for years and could therefore be disposed of without guilt. The trouble was that the majority of the flat was covered in a layer of dust, which made differentiation all the more difficult. Some of the dust was so thick, it was as if removal men had come in and surrounded the objects in a form of protective felt prior to moving them out.

He started in the hall, and by the end of the day had twenty-three large plastic bin bags filled with the rubbish. The process was made all the more unpleasant in that the bags had a smell of cheap rubber that he found quite nauseating. It was like being on a train with faulty brakes that, when they burned, filled your nasal passages with an acrid stench. There were several clear plastic storage boxes filled with things that had made the cut and survived. A man with a van arrived late in the afternoon and took the rubbish away with him.

As Cross left and looked at the clear hall – except for the storage boxes piled up along one wall – he realised that working this way was going to take him too long. The trouble was that he knew he needed to be in charge and monitor the whole thing. He'd have to work something out – a more efficient system. On the bike ride home he thought that Mackenzie might be a source of plentiful, young, pliant, able-bodied helpers in need of some cash. He would speak to her on Monday.

On the Sunday, Cross went to the care home to visit his father, timing his visit for after lunch. He often found the smell of any kind of institutional catering quite sickening. Also the idea of witnessing several elderly people struggling to eat their food was anathema to him. It wasn't just that he found others' eating habits generally intolerable, it was the image of these people eating only the food that was offered to them, and having no real choice, that profoundly depressed him. It was such an evocative example of their lately surrendered independence.

Even though the home was an upscale establishment with, he imagined, catering far superior to most, there was something pitiable to him in these people, summoned together at regimented times, not of their choosing, to eat food also not of their choosing. But he was pleasantly surprised when he arrived to find that there was no residual odour of lunch in the air. He looked for Raymond in his room, but it was empty. He went into the sitting room, where several residents were sleeping in their chairs around the walls. A couple played cards at a table in the centre of the room. The familiarity of their gestures to each other – unspoken signals learnt over decades – and the amenable, habitual silence that enveloped them, told Cross they were married. He imagined that if one of them passed away there – which unless they moved homes was inevitable – the other one wouldn't hang around for too long before following.

There was a small collection of empty wheelchairs at one end of the room, crammed together awkwardly as if something was going on over there that they all wanted to see. Another group of residents were watching the television. A woman called out to him.

'Are you looking for Raymond?' she asked.

'I am,' he replied.

'He's over there.' She pointed to the party of wheelchairs.

On closer inspection, Cross could see Raymond's bald head protruding over one of the chairs. He walked over.

'Dad?'

'Hello, son,' Raymond said, without looking up from the job in hand. He took the wheel off one of the wheelchairs and began oiling the axle.

'What are you doing?'

'A couple of repairs, but mostly routine servicing. Bit of oil. Cleaning out a load of gunge. Replacing the odd part. It's amazing how much wear they develop, although we shouldn't really be surprised, I suppose.'

It was typical of Raymond, thought Cross, to find something practical to fill his time. It obviously made him happy and kept him occupied.

'Are they paying you?' Cross asked.

'Certainly not. The very thought,' replied Raymond. 'Though I have been the glad recipient of some rather delicious home-made cakes.' He said this with a knowing smile and carried on with his work. He knew better than to offer his son any refreshments, as he would simply refuse – probably with a lengthy discourse on his reasoning and suppositions about how the tea or coffee was incorrectly made.

Cross had decided to tell his father about 'operation clear-up' on his way over, in the full knowledge that no meaningful conversation about it would be forthcoming. However, he felt it only right that his father should be kept informed.

'So I went to your flat yesterday,' he said.

'Could you pass me that spanner?' Raymond replied.

'I made a start on clearing out the hall,' Cross went on.

'Really fiddly, this wheel assembly, but if you think about it, it has to do a lot of load-bearing on a daily basis. Multiply that over the years...' Raymond said, ignoring him.

'I got a man in a van to come and help,' Cross persisted.

'There, looks much better.' Raymond held the wheelchair away from him. He then looked at his son. 'We agreed you could "clear out" the flat, as you call it, but we never agreed to discuss it.'

'We didn't in point of fact agree to anything. You have been forced into accepting the situation as the only possible way of your ever seeing the inside of your flat again, and not ending up in a place such as this to see out the rest of your days,' said Cross, not unreasonably, he thought.

'Don't be pedantic,' said his father.

'I'm merely being factual. But if you don't wish to discuss it, that is more than acceptable.'

Raymond started on another wheelchair. After a few minutes he broke the silence.

'There's a lady in here. Celia over there.' He pointed to an elderly woman sleeping in one of the armchairs. 'She's a wonderful woman. A nurse all her life. Devoted herself to others. She's ninety-four today.'

'And your point is?'

'She loves Cole Porter. Could you play some for her? It'd be such a treat for the old dear,' Raymond replied.

'I don't know any Cole Porter,' Cross said.

'There's some sheet music in the piano stool. I checked.' Raymond smiled exaggeratedly. It was one of the 'tells' his son knew so well – it meant that he was lying. Cross thought it was likely that his father had bought the sheet music on the internet. The coincidence was too much.

A skill that Cross had developed as a child was the ability to sight read music and play the piano. Raymond thought at the time that it was a reflection of the way his mind worked – being able to analyse patterns and interpret them with ease.

'She's asleep,' Cross reasoned, as a suitable excuse to get out of it.

'Who better to wake her up on her birthday than Cole?' his father said, eyes twinkling.

'Impossible. He's dead.'

'Go on. Please? You'll be interested in the piano. It was donated by the family of a former resident who had been a concert pianist,' said Raymond.

He knew his son well. This little piece of historical anecdotalism immediately intrigued Cross. He walked across the room like a shy child who had been asked to play by his parents after Christmas dinner for all the relatives he barely knew. He tried to come across as less awkward to the residents – none of whom were actually looking at him – by pretending he was going over simply to inspect the instrument.

It was in fact a Steinway baby grand, which both surprised

and pleased him. It had been placed by the French windows, as if to say that a piano of its stature and from this particular manufacturer required a garden backdrop. The family who'd donated it must've been grateful indeed to the home to leave behind such an elegant and generous gift.

Cross noticed a small brass plaque naming the concert pianist and noted her dates. The plaque went on to say that this was her practice piano which she kept at home. There was also a black and white photograph of her giving a recital at the Wigmore Hall in London. Cross later discovered that she had suffered from dementia, and when the disease had progressed to its very worst stage, and she was unable to understand or communicate, she was still able to play certain complicated classical pieces flawlessly. The family had moved the piano into her room at the care home and then left it there, as a gift, when she passed away.

Cross found the suspiciously brand new book of Cole Porter sheet music at the top of the pile in the piano stool. He opened it at the appropriate page and scanned it briefly. He then tested the keys quietly. He had suspected that the piano would be out of tune, in which case he would've declined to play – he simply couldn't tolerate the sound of untuned instruments. To his surprise, the piano was perfectly tuned. The home obviously looked after its musical bequest.

Cross started to play 'Night and Day'. He played a little hesitantly at first but then found his stride. Raymond looked on with a smidgeon of paternal pride from the other side of the room. The rare occasions on which Cross allowed others to witness his many gifts pleased his father hugely. Cross was on the second verse when he became aware of some voices singing along quietly. He looked up to see many of the residents, now all wide awake, singing along. Celia was also awake and beaming from ear to ear.

He played for over an hour. Residents appeared from their rooms, some wheeled in by staff. A group of the stronger voices gathered around the piano, belting out the songs with admirable gusto. Cross himself was actually really enjoying it. He liked to learn new music – he would remember these tunes by heart and would be able to perform them without music from now on, after playing them just the once – but he was also aware that he was providing these people with a welcome diversion on an anonymous Sunday afternoon – their being at an age where one day rolled inexorably and indeterminately into another. A couple of visitors arrived and were politely asked to 'Sssh!' by the relatives they'd come to see. They then obediently pulled up a chair and sat down to listen.

Towards the end of the hour a member of staff, possibly sensing that the spontaneous concert was about to come to an end, came over and whispered into Cross's ear. He listened intently as he continued to play 'I Get a Kick Out of You', then nodded to show he'd understood the message. At the end of the number, as everyone joined in the applause for the pianist and, Cross suspected, themselves, the lights faded in the room and a member of staff entered carrying a birthday cake resplendent with lit candles and sparklers. On cue Cross broke into a rendition of 'Happy Birthday', which everyone then began to sing.

After the staff member had blown out the candles for Celia, Cross closed the lid of the piano carefully and respectfully. He had felt really refreshed by this unexpected interlude. He hadn't thought about Flick's case since he arrived. He was in such a state of post-performance euphoria that he completely forgot to say goodbye to his father on his way out. Raymond didn't notice, as he was happily engrossed in another wheelchair repair. As Cross walked through reception he heard a voice call out to him.

'DS Cross?'

'Yes,' he replied, turning to see a lady with a walking frame moving towards him. She must've been in her late eighties, with her white hair cropped closely to her head in a practical yet elegant kind of way.

'I wonder if you could spare me five minutes?' she said politely. He looked unsure, which this woman seemed to pick up on immediately. 'My name's Moffatt, Esther Moffatt. Former DCI Esther Moffatt.'

'Hello, ma'am,' he said.

She smiled at his politeness.

'I wondered if you could entertain an old policewoman for a few minutes and tell me what you are working at the moment,' she said.

Cross paused, saw that he had been leaving seventeen minutes before the time he had allotted for the visit to his father, and so agreed.

He sat in a chair opposite her. She told him that she'd known him by name before she'd retired and it was a real pleasure to meet him in person. Cross was a sucker for approbation at the best of times and so replayed her the details of Flick's case, sparing none. He often did this in the office – going over what they knew and didn't know on a case at any given time. It helped him get a detached view of it all, and DCI Moffatt was an excellent, attentive audience. She listened intently as he told her about Sandra, Flick and

Daisy, her missing journal, the missing diamorphine phial; the other girls, Dr Sutton, Brian and Simon and finally Danny Stokes and his father. He didn't hold back on any detail, including everything that had now been declared irrelevant to the investigation.

When he finished she sat back in her chair and processed what he'd just told her.

'I know Gerry Stokes,' she said.

'In what context? A case?'

'No, he owned a home I was in for respite care once after a hip replacement.'

'Did you form an opinion of him?'

'He's one of those businessmen who seems to have his fingers in lots of pies. Quite diverse businesses but not without a kind of internal synergy. The laundry bill for his care homes – he owns three that I'm aware of – would keep his dry cleaning business afloat on its own. But I always thought he looked a little shifty. As if he was hiding something. From what you've said it sounds like his son's behaviour must be concerning to him if only for its potential effect on his business. Was Miss Wilson a problem of his son's creation that Gerry needed to solve?'

Cross liked the way she referred to Flick with a respectful formality.

'It had to be someone she knew,' she added.

'Correct,' he answered, checking his watch and seeing he had three minutes left of his scheduled time.

'I see you're in a hurry. Do you have a card?' she asked.

'I do.'

'Might I have it?'

'Why?'

'In case I come up with anything,' she said, as if it was obvious.

Cross was about to reply that he thought it highly unlikely that she would, when he thought of Ottey and what she would do in this situation. He knew the answer and so he indulged the old policewoman by handing over his card. Then, with an imperceptible bow and a whispered 'Ma'am', he backed out of the home and walked to his bike. He checked his watch. One minute to spare. 'Excellent,' he thought.

Chapter 23

Since partnering with Cross, Ottey had been trying to put a stop to his habit of continuing out loud a conversation he'd been having in his head, often mid-sentence. Another useful social tip she'd tried to impart to him was the notion of softening people up when he wanted them to do something for him; rather than just going straight to the point and making them feel like they'd been on the end of a command rather than a polite request.

He had been practising this last technique a lot with Mackenzie of late. So it was with this in mind, and having rehearsed what he was going to say several times in the privacy of his office, that he arrived at her desk the next morning with a coffee for her. She had learnt by now that the presentation of an unsolicited coffee by Cross was a prelude to his asking something of her, which he thought she might be reluctant to do and a coffee might pave the way for.

'I have to say I do think you've done well to achieve employment here with the economy being as it is and job prospects for people of your age not being what they were,' he began.

'Thank you, boss,' she said, then waited for the underlying truth behind the coffee gesture to surface.

'I imagine many of your friends may not have been so lucky,' he continued.

'True.'

'Particularly those starting out in the arts. A difficult career to break into at the best of times for writers, actors, comedians and the like.'

'Yes, I suppose so,' she agreed.

'Things must be tough for them financially,' he said.

'Just ask her whatever it is you need, George,' Ottey said from her desk, unable to witness this awkward mating ritual any further. 'Good preamble, though. Full marks.'

'Thank you,' said Cross, who then turned back to Mackenzie.

'I would like to offer some of your friends, say maximum four, some short-term gainful employment, helping clear out and sort my father's belongings in his flat, to enable his return from the care home,' he said.

'I can ask around,' she replied.

'Thank you,' he said, not moving from her desk.

He waited patiently until she looked up.

'Aren't you going to make any calls?' he asked, assuming, as he always did, that when he asked someone to do something, they would drop everything and get on with it.

'Oh right. Yes, of course. I'll have to wait till my lunch break, though. Unless you want me to do it on police time?' she said a little wickedly.

'No, of course not. Quite right. They need to be hard-working, honest and trustworthy and, if you can, it's probably best to make it as diverse a group as possible,' he went on.

She looked at him for a second and realised he wasn't being sarcastic.

'Is that a problem?' he asked.

'No, I was just thinking how refreshingly modern and liberal that was, George.'

'I believe the correct term is "woke". It goes without saying, no one with a criminal conviction of any kind or proceedings pending,' he said, then, satisfied he'd covered everything, went back to his office and closed the door.

After a moment he reappeared and said to Ottey, 'Do you think I should interview them?'

'No, George. It's just moving a few boxes,' she said.

'You simply have no idea of the scale of the task ahead of them.' He turned back to Mackenzie. 'Will I need to cater? If so, I suppose I'll need any special dietary requirements from them. Oh, and any allergies,' he said, suddenly worried about the scale of the undertaking.

'No, George, they'll be fine. They can look after themselves food-wise,' she said.

'Oh good, that's a relief.'

Chapter 24

Cross paid another visit to Danny's Dry Cleaner's later that day. He took with him a few shirts that needed laundering and pressing. He cycled there as he wanted to go on his own, arriving late afternoon. He was immediately allotted a service point. Karen saw him and quickly came to the counter.

'I have four shirts to be laundered,' he said, handing them over.

'Pressed or just folded?' she asked.

'Oh, most definitely pressed,' he replied, looking over at the shirt pressing with an expression which could be described as one of longing.

'There's a "five for the price of four" on the shirts at the moment,' said Karen.

'Is there?' Cross thought for a second. 'Do you have a customer lavatory?' he asked.

Karen disappeared then returned with a key on a large wooden fob. She watched as he headed off into the restroom. He went into a cubicle and took off his jacket, V-neck sweater, shirt and tie. He then put his sweater and jacket back on, put his tie in his pocket and walked back to the counter where Karen was waiting. She smiled as he handed her the lavatory key and his shirt.

'Number five,' he proclaimed.

Danny appeared, running down the stairs from his office.

'Now that's what I like to see!' he shouted. 'A man who appreciates a bargain. Inspector.' He held out his hand, which Cross ignored.

'It's "sergeant", actually,' said Cross.

'Well that's a travesty. Who do I call about that?' Danny didn't wait for an answer, but turned to Karen. 'Give the sergeant the staff discount,' he said.

'No,' said Cross.

'Ah! A stickler for the rules. You cannot accept favourable treatment,' said Danny.

'Correct.'

'Would you like to come up to my office?' Danny suggested.

'What for?' asked Cross.

'Well, it's quiet and more private.'

'Oh, I understand. That won't be necessary. I just came here to have my shirts laundered.' Cross picked up his ticket as he left.

Stokes shouted after him. 'Did DS Ottey tell you about the shirt service I suggested for your office?'

But Cross ignored him and walked over to a café next to a pharmacy in a parade of shops opposite. He ordered a bottle of water. He'd rather have had a cup of tea but having observed the milky contents of various customers' mugs, he decided on balance that the risk was too great.

He sat in the window and checked his phone for any emails and texts. There was one from Ottey asking where he was, which he ignored.

After about an hour Stokes senior appeared out of the dry

cleaner's, walked to a bus stop and took a seat. Shoulders slumped, he walked with a careworn shuffle, wearing his widower's grief like a lead overcoat. Cross got up and left the café. He'd read this about the shy multimillionaire Gerry Stokes. He was a no-frills man. Took public transport. Didn't own a car. Still lived in the same modest house he and his wife had bought when they were first married.

As Cross approached the bus stop he looked at the old man's deep jowls folding from his jaw, drawn down by years of hard work, loss, and was it disappointment? But he was ostensibly so successful. What did he have to be so disappointed about? Cross was fairly sure he knew the answer.

'Detective Sergeant Cross. How can I help you?' Gerry asked.

Cross was always relieved when someone dispensed with the need for small talk. It took so much effort on his part, and his inability to conduct it successfully often had a detrimental effect on the ensuing conversation and the amount of information he was able to extract from it.

'Why do you let your son tell complete strangers that he has done so well he's bought you out of your business?' Cross asked.

Gerry didn't answer.

'He claims to have turned the business round, and all that stuff about Milt & Edie's in Burbank is nonsense, isn't it?' Cross went on. 'There's an old picture of you and your wife hanging up by your work station, taken outside Milt & Edie's with a young child, about eight years old, probably in the eighties, judging by the cars.'

'He was seven when we took him,' said Gerry.

'So all he did was paint the premises pink?'

'No, that was Betty. It faded so Danny had it redone a couple of years ago,' said Gerry.

'Betty, your late wife?'

'Yes,' he replied dolefully.

At this point Cross remembered what Ottey had told him about these situations.

'My condolences. I understand she passed away last year.'

'Yes, cancer,' Gerry replied quietly.

'Do you have other children?'

'No, just Danny. He was fantastic with her towards the end. Began sleeping over at our house again. Getting up every couple of hours to turn her so she didn't get bed sores. The visiting hospice team couldn't believe the condition she was in. So well cared for, they said.'

'I detect an element of surprise in your voice,' said Cross.

Gerry looked at him for a moment as if affronted.

'It wasn't what I expected, if I'm honest. It was a bit of a surprise. There you have it. He's far from perfect. All of us are.'

'This tribunal business. It must have been very upsetting for you.'

'If she had a case,' replied Gerry.

'Oh,' said Cross, surprised. 'You don't think she did?'

But the old man didn't answer. He didn't seem to be at all sure that Cross wasn't taking the piss. He wasn't. He was genuinely interested to know if this was the case. But the old dry cleaner clammed up.

'Complicated things, relationships between sons and their fathers,' Cross began. He then went on to tell Gerry of his present situation with his father. He talked to Gerry like he was talking to a friend whose opinion and experience he valued. The fact of the matter was that Cross was just pleased to be talking to someone about it. How Raymond had ended up in hospital. His hoarding habit and how, to avoid moving in with his son, he had agreed to go to a home that mainly dealt with dementia. Cross had now found him a different home but still wondered whether moving him into his flat had not been the better option all long.

'Nonsense,' Gerry said.

'What do you mean by that?'

'Do you have money?' Gerry asked.

'Enough, yes,' Cross replied.

'So leave him in the home for a few weeks while you sort out his flat. He may not say so, but he will be grateful and you'll avoid all the unnecessary arguing.'

'Do you think so?'

'I do, and something tells me you're not the easiest person to live with,' Gerry replied.

If Cross hadn't thought this was true he would've objected to it, but he found himself thinking how astute this man was. 'How have you come to that conclusion?' he asked.

'I've spent my life watching people bring me their dirty laundry, both literally and metaphorically. Families, single people, couples – you can tell a lot from people when they get you to do their washing.'

'You can really tell that much from just watching people across a counter?' Cross asked.

'It's a very intimate business doing people's laundry, and they know that. They tell you things. I'm a people watcher. Bit like you. Here's my bus.' Gerry got up. As he boarded the bus Cross made another observation.

'I didn't expect to see you at the funeral. What were you doing there?' Cross asked.

'What does anyone do at a funeral, Sergeant? Paying my respects,' said Gerry.

'Why?'

'Because she was a former employee. It's the done thing.'

'A former employee taking her former boss to a tribunal,' Cross pointed out.

'That had nothing to do with me.'

'But you feel a sense of responsibility?' said Cross.

'Is that a question?'

'I can understand the confusion. Let me put it more succinctly. Did you?' Cross said.

'What for?'

'For her. For what happened to her. Here,' Cross said.

'Look, she worked for us and she died. It was no more than that. I would do it for anyone associated with the business. Customers, suppliers, former employees.'

The bus doors closed bringing the conversation to an end. Cross thought Gerry's reasoning was plausible but he couldn't determine whether there was more at play. Was his presence at the funeral an apology for his son's past behaviour? Was he conceding that his son was at fault, and if so, at fault for what exactly? Was it more than just Flick's treatment at work?

Chapter 25

Cross arrived at work the next morning, took off his coat, put his bicycle paraphernalia in the corner and before he sat at his desk was aware of Ottey approaching purposefully. She walked straight into his office without knocking, which he now knew meant he had irritated her in some way. Often this was confusing but in this instance he knew what it was. He hadn't told her he was going to the dry cleaner's the day before.

'I couldn't find you yesterday afternoon,' she began.

'That's because I didn't tell you where I was going,' he replied.

'Which was where?'

'I had a domestic chore to do.'

'On police time?' she asked disingenuously.

'It wasn't unrelated.'

'Well, in that case why don't you share?'

He was unsure what this meant momentarily, then understood and answered. 'I needed to get some shirts laundered.'

'At Danny's?' she asked, knowing the answer full well. 'I thought you did your own laundry. In fact I'm pretty sure you told me it was something you enjoyed and did with pride.'

'Correct on both points. I was impressed by their shirt-pressing machines. I wanted to compare the results.'

'Well I hope you'll report back on your findings.'

'If it's something that interests you, then certainly,' he replied.

'And did you speak to Stokes?'

'Briefly, but I wasn't there to talk to him. I wanted to speak with the father.'

This interested her. Cross often did this kind of thing, with astonishing results. He would hover around people on the periphery of a case, talking to them about all manner of things, often seemingly irrelevant. He took great interest in their jobs or other aspects of their lives. He came across as genuinely interested in things he had no knowledge of, asking what appeared to be naive questions. People under suspicion sometimes thought it was an act. They were wrong, of course, but they were right to be wary. Cross's persistent, relentless curiosity and questioning of things that had no apparent relevance to the case often had results that were completely unexpected. Ottey thought it was like a sixth sense, but Cross of course didn't tolerate such notions.

'What did you make of him?' she asked.

'He's embarrassed by his son but doesn't have the appetite to fight. He tolerates his behaviour at work but Karen says they argue. He seems quite a quiet man who is still grieving the loss of his wife a year on.'

'I've been doing some digging into the business,' said Ottey. 'As you know, the dad is still very much in charge despite his son's antics. Danny has said in the local press that he wanted to expand the business in the south-west. But it was the father's blueprint and he's invested quite a lot of dosh into the project. Buying some sites, taking out leases on others, but they needed a financial injection. It was coming from the bank until the Flick dispute became public. The loans dried up as word got out about Stokes Junior's behaviour to other women he employed.'

Cross thought about this for a moment.

'Did he tell his son to sort out the Flick situation? Make it go away, do you think?' Ottey asked.

Cross didn't reply. Her instinct was the same as Moffatt's. He himself refused to indulge in hypotheticals but no longer minded Ottey doing just that. He realised that everyone had their process, and as vexing as he found it, he knew there was nothing to be gained from criticising her.

She left the office amazed that he hadn't rebuked her. Were things looking up or was he maybe feeling just a tiny bit guilty about his illicit trip to the dry cleaner's? Then she remembered he didn't do guilt.

Chapter 26

'George! Come in!' said the super, as if welcoming an old friend he hadn't seen for years into his home for dinner.

Chief Superintendent Christopher Ellis was someone who found Cross perplexing, vexing and infuriating at the best of times. But being a numbers man and someone who was acutely aware of the need for the police to be perceived by the public, as well as by his superiors, as getting results, he appreciated that Cross was an invaluable asset who needed handling with care. His effusive politeness in this instance was familiar to Cross and indicated that the super was about to ask him to do something which, he already knew, Cross would be reluctant to do.

Carson was also in the meeting. Ellis never had meetings on his own since his recent promotion, Cross had noticed. He wondered whether having subordinate officers in the room was intended to remind everyone of Ellis's superior rank or whether he just wanted witnesses to bear testimony at a later date to his version of what had taken place in the meeting. Ellis was a classic 'cover your back, cc everyone on any email, create an electronic paper trail' kind of operator. He spent so much time managing everyone's perception of himself that Cross wondered how he ever had any time to do any actual police work.

'So, this Campbell business. Do we really need this right now, at a point when the department is stretched badly enough as it is, I find myself asking?' Ellis began.

'Isn't that a question you should be putting to DI Campbell?' Cross asked.

'Yes, but I thought I'd speak to you first. Wouldn't it be best if this complaint wasn't made at all?' Ellis went on.

'Again. Isn't that something you should be putting to DI Campbell?' Cross repeated.

'We have and his position is that he is willing to withdraw the complaint.'

'If the purpose of this meeting was to communicate that to me, surely it could have been done on the phone?' Cross said.

'It's actually slightly more complicated than that. In order for Campbell to drop the complaint he needs an apology. From you.'

'Then let him make the complaint. I have no intention of apologising for having to make up for the numerous shortfalls and mistakes in his investigations. Although to describe them as such is to push the dictionary definition of "investigation" into uncharted waters.'

'You see, this is the problem. Your attitude, George,' said Ellis.

'The problem is his ineptitude, not my attitude,' replied Cross.

'He finds your tone disrespectful and rude.'

'If he finds my tone disrespectful and rude he might care to remember how he and his colleagues treated me when we were junior officers together. Their treatment of me was more than disrespectful and rude, it was blatant abuse. Yet I never saw fit to complain.'

'Those were different times,' said Carson.

'Which, as we know, is no excuse,' said Cross.

'No, of course not,' said Ellis.

'I will not apologise. He is a classic ipse-dixitist,' said Cross.

Ellis laughed. 'What is that when it's at home?'

'Someone prone to ipse-dixitism, whether at home or elsewhere,' said Cross. He then realised from the ensuing silence that further elaboration was required. 'It's someone who is prone to making assertions without any factual evidence to support them,' he added.

'Well, thank you for the English lesson,' said Ellis.

'You're welcome,' Cross replied. 'As for the complaint, I welcome it. The chances of it being upheld are minimal.'

'The panel might not see it that way, and there's always the question of how you'll come across to them,' said Ellis.

'That won't be a problem,' Cross assured him.

'How can you be so certain? Some people, well, Campbell being a prime example, find you difficult to read,' said Ellis, as diplomatically as he could.

'Because I won't be attending the panel,' said Cross, getting up.

'Then you will be in breach of a direct order,' said Ellis.

'For which I'm sure I will be accorded the appropriate censure, which will, unlike this complaint, be fully justified, and which I will therefore happily accept.' So saying, Cross left.

Ellis turned to Carson. 'Did I actually dismiss him?'

'You didn't, sir,' Carson replied.

Cross now reappeared at the door.

'On another matter, sir, did you know a DCI Moffatt?' Cross asked.

'Esther Moffatt? Gosh, that's going back a bit. Yes, I did. Why?' Ellis asked.

'I met her at the weekend.'

'I didn't know she was still alive,' said the super.

'She is,' replied Cross, then, thinking about it, added, 'Well, she was yesterday. Was she "good police"? I believe that is the expression.'

'She was. "Little Miss Moffatt" she was called, inevitably, when she first joined. She was quiet. But then she proved a force to be reckoned with. You'd have liked her, George. "Esther the arrester", she became known as. People thought she might be our first female chief constable, but she wasn't interested in the politics of it all. Preferred to be on the ground,' said Ellis, prompting Cross to turn and leave without a word.

Ellis turned to Carson.

'You have to say, as far as his manners are concerned, that Campbell might have a point,' Carson said.

'Frankly, I think Campbell is the last person we should be taking any guidance from on what makes good manners. This is the police force, for God's sake. When did we ever have to worry about good manners?'

And therein may lie the public's perception of us, Carson found himself thinking.

Chapter 27

On the Thursday Cross was at his father's flat awaiting his small, diverse, trustworthy workforce to arrive. He'd taken advantage of the lull in the case and taken the rest of the week off. He had with him a few rolls of black bin bags and had just taken delivery of fifty more clear plastic storage boxes. He was also equipped with labels and indelible markers.

A car horn sounded, and as he looked out of the window, he saw Mackenzie's car pull up. Four of her friends then piled out of the car. Cross was aware, particularly thanks to the nature of his job, that you shouldn't judge people by their appearances, but he wasn't hopeful. Two of the boys, he was fairly certain, were still asleep as they walked towards the building.

'Why aren't you at work?' Cross said to Mackenzie as he opened the door.

'I've taken a couple of days off to help,' she replied.

'You didn't have to do that.'

'I wanted to.'

'I see. But I haven't budgeted for you,' he said, a little worried.

'That's all right. I wasn't expecting to be paid.' She smiled and tried to go past him into the house. But he moved fractionally, making it impossible for her.

'You have to be paid,' he said.

'Why?'

'Because otherwise it would be an exploitation of our friendship.'

'Well,' she replied. 'Firstly, I'm flattered that you consider me to be a friend, and secondly, if you look up "exploitation of friendship" in Brewers you'll find it means "favour".'

'I don't think so,' Cross said, racking his brain.

Mackenzie decided that it was time to move things along. 'Right, well, this is Roxy, Aidan, Harry and Sanjeev.'

'Just wait there a moment,' Cross said, and disappeared back into the flat.

The truth was that Mackenzie had come because she wasn't entirely sure how long her friends would put up with Cross without her being there. He was bound to offend them unintentionally, or just freak them out in one way or another. So she was there as a moderator, interpreter and general peacekeeper.

What happened next confirmed to her that taking time off was definitely the right thing to have done. Cross appeared with a clipboard, on which he had forms he'd printed up for them all to fill in. Contact details, national insurance number, agreement of fees, an indemnity and a disclaimer in case of injury.

Mackenzie laughed. 'George, stop it. You don't need all this.'

'I can assure you, as an employer, I most certainly do,' he said.

'It's fine,' said Roxy.

'Yeah, it's totally fine,' said Harry.

So they all filled out the form as best they could – none

of them had their NI numbers but promised to bring them the next day. They then had a brief discussion as to how to proceed with the job. Cross initially suggested they each take a room, but eventually they all agreed it would be more efficient if they cleared a room at a time together. So this is what they did.

By the end of the day they had made good progress. The kitchen was completely cleared. Most of it was rubbish. There were also the ubiquitous piles of magazines and four microwaves which Cross decided to chuck. The next day a skip appeared, which Cross had hired on Sanjeev's advice from his father's building company at a good rate – Mackenzie had convinced him that a discount was perfectly acceptable as he wasn't using his position as a policeman to obtain it. It was because of his new friendship with Sanjeev. He found this reasoning perfectly acceptable. Cross was impressed by all of them; they were hard workers and didn't complain.

His patience was stretched a little on the second day when Harry appeared at noon. He made a note of the time and called Mackenzie – who had returned to work – telling her of his intention to deduct the requisite amount of money from Harry's pay packet that night (he had gone out and bought some brown wage envelopes for their daily pay).

She told him he would do no such thing and, much to her surprise, instead of embarking on a twenty-minute lecture about the virtues of punctuality, he just agreed not to. She was flattered by this as it meant he was beginning to trust her. When he discovered that, after finishing at the flat the day before, Harry had worked as a waiter at a gastropub till one a.m., he was glad he hadn't said anything.

It was in the spare room that Cross came across something

that stopped him in his tracks: an old wooden roll-top bureau. It was Edwardian and he hadn't seen it for years, but as soon as Aidan had revealed it from under dozens of boxes and piles of papers, Cross remembered it at once. It had been the centre of his father's administration of their lives when he was a child. All the bills were paid from this bureau in a weekly session, with a cheque written and placed in an addressed envelope. Then the corresponding amounts were entered into a ledger and the appropriate bill was stamped with a big red stamp that proudly proclaimed 'PAID'.

Cross could still remember the smell of the ink, and could hear the two stamping sounds now, the first softer one on the ink pad followed by a harder, louder, satisfied stamp on the bill. This bureau hadn't seen the light of day for decades. The roll-top was locked. Cross remembered his father reaching under the desk into the leg well, where he'd attached the key with sellotape to the underside, and opening the desk. Cross reached under and felt remnants of sellotape now hardened, but no key. The leg well was filled with piles of books, which he removed. He then found the key on the carpet.

The inside of the bureau, with its small compartments and drawers, was much more organised than the chaos surrounding it. His father obviously hadn't always been a hoarder, but Cross couldn't recall exactly when it started. He always remembered it being this way. He found the 'paid' stamp and the ink pad for it, and boxes of transparencies. He looked at a couple. They were of his dad and best mate Phil – 'Uncle Phil' to George. In the centre of the leather inlay of the desk was a letter addressed to his father. The postmark was 1972. He realised it was from his mother. Cross had never read anything written by his mother. He couldn't even remember the sound of her voice, he'd realised one day. She had formed no part of his life since she left when he was five.

He read the letter carefully, as his gang of helpers cleared up around him. They continued asking questions about what they'd found, but realised quite quickly that he was engrossed in whatever it was that he was reading, so they stopped bothering him. Anything they had doubts about, they put to one side. But they were getting pretty adept at sorting the chaff from the wheat anyway. Cross had insisted day one on giving his opinion about everything they found, but soon realised this was time-consuming and inefficient, so now they were good at discerning what was crap to be thrown out and what was crap that an old bugger of seventy-two would think of as indispensable. To their young eyes it was all crap.

From what he could tell, this was possibly the last letter Cross's mother had sent to his father. The fact that it had been left out on the desk made Cross think that his father had probably read it and then left it there, locking up the desk that moment and never reopening it. As if that part of their life was now closed. But it was the last few sentences of the letter that Cross kept reading.

I can't live with things like this. I cannot accept him the way that you want me to. He's driven a wedge between us and we now live a life I no longer recognise. It is so far away from what I dreamt of when we first met. I hope you can see that. If when little George has grown up he wants to find me, let him know I would welcome it. But for now things will have to be this way. Christine.

So there it was in black and white. What he'd assumed all his life. What his father had never told him, doubtless to protect him. That his mother left because she couldn't cope with him as a child. This was way before his diagnosis and he thought she probably just found him uncommunicative, recalcitrant, possibly rude and unloving. But the fact of the matter was that he'd wrecked his parents' marriage. He wasn't upset by this discovery but relieved, perhaps, that he finally knew the truth, as it was a topic of conversation his father had tried to avoid his entire life. He put the letter in his pocket, locked the bureau, found some fresh sellotape and put the key back in its proper place.

After four days the flat was clear, except for the furniture that was staying put. Mackenzie's friends had done a terrific job. In many ways they had made the whole process almost enjoyable. Whenever they found something curious or odd, he would tell them stories of how his father had come across it and how he justified holding onto it, often with the most tenuous and outrageously funny reasoning. The young people ate their lunch together every day, and every lunchtime he refused their invitations to join them. That was a step too far for him. On the last day, as he paid them and they surveyed the empty space in front of them, he commented that all he needed to do now was get someone in to deep-clean the place and maybe give it a lick of paint.

'We could do that for you,' said Sanjeev.

'Really?' Cross asked.

'Of course. We'd be a lot cheaper than getting professionals in,' said Harry.

'And probably a lot less professional too,' Cross pointed out.

There was a pause and then the four kids laughed. Sanjeev could borrow the equipment off his dad's firm and also get all the materials at trade prices. They could have it finished in a week.

Cross had to agree that anything they did would be an improvement on the current state of the place and, what was more, they were keen to do it and needed the money. But he had to be back at work the following week so they would be on their own.

Initially this was a stumbling block for him. Then Sanjeev's father agreed to drop in every evening and inspect their work. It didn't occur to Cross, but Mackenzie made a passing comment to Ottey about the effect he sometimes had on people who saw beyond the eccentric exterior – people would often go out of their way to help him, in any way they could.

Chapter 28

Two things were on Cross's mind when he returned to work that Monday. Flick's case, of course, and his mother's letter. He had made the decision to track her down. Not because of any emotional need for connection – he was just curious, he told himself. In truth, though, he did have a need to find her. He needed to show her that he had turned out well. He was all right. Different, yes, but fine. He had a job, one he was extremely good at, in no small measure because of *how* he was. He looked after his father; took responsibility for him. In short, he needed to prove her wrong.

Her leaving them because of him had had a huge effect on their lives. It had been a dreadful, selfish thing to have done to his father, now that he thought about it. His need to show her this was, in a funny way, born of the same compulsion that drove him to work at investigations the way he did. He couldn't bear injustice. He had to put it right whenever he came across it, and if that wasn't possible, at least alert others to its existence. This was what he wanted to do with his mother – point it out, that was all. He didn't want her in his life and she probably didn't want him in hers. But he needed her to know that she'd been wrong.

'So Raymond settled in at the home?' Ottey asked as they had coffee, ruminating about their progress, or lack of, in the case.

'I think so. He seems to have set up a small business in there,' Cross replied.

'How do you mean?'

'He's offering a wheelchair repair service to all the other residents.'

She laughed.

'Why is that amusing?' he asked.

'It's just so sweet and typical of him,' she said.

'You know him well enough to make that judgement, do you?'

'I hope he's charging them,' she said, ignoring the question.

'That's what I said. He's being paid in kind.'

'I beg your pardon? What exactly do you mean by that?'

'Cake. He's getting a lot of cake,' he explained.

'Oh, okay. That's a relief. I must go and see him. Take the girls,' she said.

'I'd go quickly, as I'm not sure how long they'll last,' he replied.

'What?' she asked.

'The cakes.'

'I'm not going for the cakes,' she replied.

'I met an old DCI there. Moffatt. Esther Moffatt.'

'Don't know her.'

There was a momentary silence. Ottey found herself thinking about Flick.

'Could we be wrong about this case? Could she have killed

herself? Suicide is such a weird act, but who knows what was going on in her head?'

'Maybe we should ask the man who's supposed to know exactly that,' said Cross.

'Dr Sutton? Good idea.'

'I'll go on my own.'

'Why?'

'Because he's made various assumptions about me, because of the way I am, and so thinks he has the upper hand.'

'Why would he feel the need to have the upper hand?'

'Firstly because I'm a policeman and secondly because that's how he operates, whoever you are.'

'Well, more fool him. Take Mackenzie with you,' Ottey suggested.

'I would ask you why but it occurs to me that it would be convenient to be driven.'

'Do you think he could involved?' Mackenzie couldn't help but ask as she drove them to Sutton's office. Cross was about to call her out on this when she stopped him. 'I know. Stupid thing to ask. No evidence. No facts. No reason to think anything.'

Cross was happy with this. He thought she was learning, and anyway he didn't want to correct her and possibly upset her because she'd been very useful getting her friends to help with his father's flat.

They arrived at a Georgian building in the middle of Bristol. As they entered, Mackenzie noted the brass plates by the front door with names of various doctors on them – Sutton's office was on the first floor. They walked into a very well-furnished reception with a couple of sofas and armchairs. Cross walked up to the receptionist. She was busy organising things on her desk, and as Cross began to speak she held up her hand to stop him. As she was finishing he noticed how immaculately tidy her desk and the shelves behind her were. She was immensely organised. He was impressed.

She finally looked up, in her early forties, Cross estimated, but dressed like someone twice her age, conservatively and in muted colours. She wore a tweed skirt with a silk shirt and cardigan. She had horn-rimmed glasses on a chain around her neck that looked like they might have been passed on to her by her grandmother.

'Can I help you?' she asked Cross.

'We'd like to see Dr Sutton,' he replied.

'You don't have an appointment.'

'I don't.'

'Do you have a doctor's referral?' she asked.

'I do not,' he said. 'I'm a detective from the Avon and Somerset police force,' he went on, displaying his warrant card.

At this point Dr Sutton opened the other door in the office and appeared.

'It's okay, Diana. I'll see them, thank you,' he said, disappearing back into his office.

Cross was about to follow when Diana held up her hand and said commandingly, 'Wait!' He did so and she pushed a book towards him, with a biro. 'Please fill out your details, including your warrant card number.'

He complied and was about to walk into Sutton's office when again she said, 'Wait!'

He stopped obediently while she tore out the strip he'd

written his details on, put it into a plastic badge holder and gave it to him. 'Clip it onto your lapel please. Are you going in as well?' she asked Mackenzie.

'She is,' Cross replied for her.

'Name?' she asked as she started to fill out another strip.

He looked at her for a moment, put the badge on nevertheless and walked into Sutton's office. Mackenzie followed. The room had a comforting smell of Sutton's aftershave and leather seats, whose odour may well have been enhanced by the past tears of many a patient. The room was old-fashioned in its decor – light-panelled walls and framed prints. Sutton sat behind a large wooden desk with a leather inset which wouldn't have looked out of place in a Dickensian bank. Cross was conscious that Sutton's chair was higher than his, making Sutton look down over the desk at him; an obvious ploy to give him an air of superiority.

'DS Cross, a pleasure to see you,' he said. 'I'm sorry about Di— Miss Coogan. She does have her little peccadilloes.'

'Interesting choice of word,' Cross commented.

'In what sense?'

'In the sense that it is applied to me with irritating frequency at work when people are trying to be polite about what they find most annoying about me,' Cross replied.

'I see. Then I apologise to you both. The thing is with Di, I think she's probably on the spectrum.' If Sutton was expecting this to elicit some sort of acknowledgement from Cross he would've been disappointed. 'She has her routine and systems and nothing will sway her away from them. It seems pedantic and at times unnecessary, but on occasions it does pay dividends. I suppose you could say there's method in her madness.'

'She didn't strike me as mad,' said Cross.

'No, I didn't mean that. I don't actually know what I'd do without her,' said Sutton.

'There's no need to apologise. I can certainly see the logic of her system.'

'Well, I have an appointment with a patient at four thirty, Sergeant, so perhaps we should get straight to the point,' he said.

'I'd like to ask you more about Flick. You seem to have had a profound effect, or, it may be more accurate to say, important effect on her life, recently,' Cross went on.

'I would hope I have such an effect on all of my clients,' Sutton purred.

'Tell me. In your opinion, was she happy?'

'That's not the sort of question a psychotherapist finds easy to give a straightforward answer to.'

'And why is that?' asked Cross.

'Because of its generality. Happiness is a complex issue. How do we define it? Was Flick happy? The only thing I can say is that, at times, she was; at other times, she was not,' Sutton said, choosing his words carefully.

'So she did have periods of unhappiness?' Cross asked.

'Don't we all? I'm sorry, I don't mean to be glib. To answer your question, yes, she did.'

'And was there a particular area of her life that made her prone to these periods of sadness? Or do you call them triggers?' Cross asked.

'Yes, there were,' Sutton replied, giving nothing away.

'What were those, exactly?'

Sutton rested his lips on the tips of his fingers as if in prayer.

'I fear we're moving into areas of patient confidentiality here, Sergeant,' he said and smiled.

Cross said nothing for a moment, and merely looked back at Sutton. He was trying to gauge whether the therapist genuinely felt this, or whether it was something he was hiding behind.

'So would you say that doctors, therapists, lawyers, any profession bound by ethical concerns are ipso facto of no use to the police in a murder enquiry?' Cross asked.

'Interesting question, Sergeant.'

'Your answer would be more interesting, Doctor,' replied Cross.

Sutton now demonstrated that he had as much prowess as Cross in being silent when it suited him. Cross turned to Mackenzie. She reached into her jacket pocket and produced a piece of paper. She held it out for Cross who looked away from her to the doctor. She then held it out for Sutton.

'A warrant for any medical records you possess pertaining to Felicity Wilson,' she said.

Sutton examined it and smiled.

'Thank you.' He went over to a filing cabinet and pulled out a file, then flicked an intercom button on his phone. Diana appeared promptly.

'Could you please make a copy of these, Di?' he said, then turned back to Cross. 'I assume you'd rather spend the rest of our appointment discussing Flick than poring over her file, which you could look at in your own time if you had a copy?'

'That would certainly make more sense,' Cross replied.

But although she had the file in her hands, Diana remained rooted to the spot. Sutton looked at her for a second and then realised what she wanted.

'Oh yes, he does have a warrant. Here you are,' he said, handing it to her. She looked at it quickly and left.

'A little by the book, our Diana,' said Sutton.

'If only more people were like that,' replied Cross. 'I'm assuming you're now happy to discuss Flick?'

'I am. You can understand my need for legal enforcement,' said Sutton.

'I can see your need for it, but in the circumstances, I can't claim to understand it,' Cross replied. 'What were Flick's periods of unhappiness related to?'

'Firstly, I'm not sure I would categorise them as periods. It would be more accurate to describe them as moments,' said Sutton.

Cross made a note of this, then looked up. Sutton said nothing. Neither did Cross, who just waited for an answer. After all, Sutton had merely made a distinction in the terms of his question.

'Do you need me to repeat the question?' Cross asked.

'No. I'm sorry, of course not. Um, she regretted her past drug use. Was worried that she was always vulnerable to it, which upset her. She had residual guilt about Daisy's ill-health at birth. Simon was also a major factor in making her miserable, insecure, anxious, worried.'

'"Vulnerable to it"?' Cross said, quoting Sutton. 'Her addiction, presumably?'

'Yes.'

'Would you describe her as an addictive person?' Cross asked.

'Excellent question, Sergeant Cross. No, I wouldn't. She may have spiralled into drug addiction at one point in her life, but she didn't have an addictive personality.'

'Wouldn't you say recovery itself can sometimes be addictive?' Cross asked.

'For some perhaps, yes, but a better addiction. I wouldn't confuse determination with addiction.'

'Why did she give up alcohol as well then? She didn't have an alcohol problem, as far as I'm aware.'

'No, she didn't, but people in her situation often do. Give up alcohol,' said Sutton. 'People in recovery often avoid things like alcohol because it lowers their defences, leaving them vulnerable to a relapse.'

'That's the second time you've used the word vulnerable,' Cross noted. 'Was Flick vulnerable to a relapse, in your opinion?'

'Everyone in her situation, in recovery, is vulnerable to a relapse. Recognising that is part of being able to stay clean,' Sutton explained.

'But you've said before that Flick relapsing was out of the question,' Cross commented.

'I think I said it was unlikely in her case, but now that you're phrasing it in that way, let me say categorically that, in my opinion, it was out of the question – her relapsing.' Sutton again gave Cross the level-eye.

'How can you be so sure?'

'I can't. You asked for my opinion, which I'm giving you,' he replied firmly.

'So you think it's more likely that she killed herself?'

'More likely than what?' Sutton asked.

'Than that she relapsed and accidentally overdosed,' Cross said.

'I think either scenario is highly unlikely, Sergeant. I agree with you. Someone killed her,' the therapist stated emphatically.

Chapter 29

Cross dropped in to Danny's Dry Cleaner's on his way home that night to pick up his shirts; Karen was quick to serve him before anyone else. He thought she was looking a little stronger in herself. There was less of an air of defeat about her. She seemed pleased to see him, giving him a rare, welcoming smile. She was eager to show him the crisp creases on his shirts, pulling up the polythene covering so he could see properly.

'I did them myself,' she said with pride.

'Is that so?' said Cross.

'I wanted to make sure they were done just right for you.'

'They look very good,' said Cross. 'Expertly pressed.'

'Thanks,' she said. 'Are you on your bike?'

'I am.'

'I'll fold them then,' she said. 'You don't want to crumple them before you've even got home.'

Cross looked up at the mirrored glass of Danny Stokes's office and wondered whether he was being watched. He then saw Gerry Stokes heading back to his workstation with a cup of coffee. Cross walked over.

'DS Cross, have you managed to sort your father out?' Gerry asked.

'I have, thank you. You didn't mention that you were in the care home business yourself.'

'I'm not one to tout for business, Detective. You were asking for my advice about care homes. I thought it a little distasteful to recommend one of mine. However, if you have any further problems I would be more than happy to see what I can do.'

'I met an old customer of yours. DCI Esther Moffatt,' Cross went on.

'The name doesn't ring a bell.'

Cross observed Gerry as he went back to work on his sewing machine. It wasn't an indication that the conversation was over, simply that he was busy.

When Cross took his carefully wrapped shirts from Karen she also passed him a note. He read it when he got to his bike outside. It stated that Angie, the addict who used to work at the dry cleaner's, had turned up that afternoon and was waiting for him in the café opposite. Karen thought he'd come in for his shirts today, she said, as he didn't look like he owned too many and so would probably need them for work; so she'd told Angie to wait. Cross thought this was an accurate observation and that if circumstances had been different she might have made a good police officer.

He wheeled his bike over the road and went into the café. But it was empty. A girl had been in there earlier, the owner told him, but she'd left. Karen was apologetic when he told her, while at the same time being unsurprised. She couldn't give Cross Angie's number because she didn't have a phone at the moment. She had one now and then but usually ended up selling it when she needed cash for a score.

Chapter 30

The next weekend Mackenzie's friends completed the refurbishment of Raymond's flat. The original idea had been for them to finish on Saturday morning and for Cross to do an inspection before collecting his father on the Sunday morning. But they had fallen behind, not from a lack of hard work, but due to an overly ambitious schedule. They actually finished at four in the morning on Sunday. Social services had been round earlier in the week to inspect it and were happy that the flat was being made safe for Raymond's return.

'Made safe?' Raymond was heard to exclaim. 'It wasn't a bleeding bomb!'

Cross hadn't seen the flat when he went to pick his father up on the Sunday morning, as Mackenzie had persuaded him that it would be nicer for her friends if he could see it in all its completed grandeur with his dad. He and Mackenzie – she wouldn't hear of him taking a taxi, so had driven him – arrived at the home earlier than the appointed time to pick up Raymond, because Cross had wanted to say goodbye to DCI Moffatt.

Mackenzie insisted on going with him, and on the way to the room he explained who she was.

She was tired and her voice was faint, but she was pleased to see Cross and, even more so, a young staff officer.

They sat on either side of the bed. Esther's skin and eyes were now a sallow yellow. Cross noticed how Mackenzie instinctively took hold of one of the old woman's hands, as if it was the most natural thing in the world to immediately want to comfort someone she'd never met before. A complete stranger.

'How's the case going, DS Cross?'

'It's slow. Nothing more to add than the last time I was here.'

'It'll come to you, one way or another,' she said.

'Gosh, your hands are dry, ma'am,' said Mackenzie. 'Ma'am' – good for you, thought Cross. 'I think I have some hand cream in my bag. Would you like me to moisturise your hands for you?' she asked.

'That would be nice,' Esther said weakly.

Cross took this opportunity to go and make sure Raymond was ready to leave.

Mackenzie stayed with Esther, who fell asleep but then woke up a few minutes later. Initially she was confused as to who the young woman was, holding her hand at the side of her bed. Then she remembered and smiled. They spent the next ten minutes talking about Esther's career in the police force and some of her cases. She talked fondly about the old unit and her former colleagues, most of whom had passed away, and it got Mackenzie thinking.

Raymond and Cross appeared at the door, ready to leave. Esther was asleep again. Raymond had said his goodbyes to her the night before. Cross noticed, though, his father's eyes fill with sadness as he took the old woman's hand and said goodbye again. Mackenzie stroked Raymond's arm comfortingly. He turned to her.

'Are you my Uber?' he said, making a joke.

'I am,' she replied.

'Oh good.' He smiled.

And so they left Esther's room with Raymond navigating his way on his crutches uncertainly, like a child on stilts for the first time.

'Do you know what the statistics are for elderly men post-operative or post-fracture using crutches and having a fall which breaks their hip?' he asked Mackenzie.

'No. I do not.'

'Neither do I!' he laughed.

As Raymond said goodbye to the manager and the lady at the desk, several other staff members appeared to bid him farewell. Some residents waved from the sitting room. Raymond had obviously made quite the impression during his stay there.

'Look after yourself, Raymond,' said the manager.

'I will.'

'And we'll see you in two months,' she went on.

'You will!' he replied with a breezy laugh.

As they walked to Mackenzie's car, Cross asked his father, 'Why will you see them again in a couple of months?'

'I've booked myself in for a week,' Raymond replied.

'What for?'

'Respite care.'

'What are you talking about? Respite from what? Respite care is to give family carers a break – that's why it's called respite,' said Cross.

'That is one way of looking at it, I suppose.'

Chapter 31

They arrived at Raymond's flat to find the three bleary-eyed young decorators waiting for them outside – Aidan had managed to secure himself an internship. They were all covered in paint, but smiling from ear to ear. Mackenzie laughed as she saw they'd put a large ribbon across the front door. Roxy was holding a pair of scissors. As Raymond hobbled towards them she held out the scissors and said, 'Would you do the honours?'

'A grand opening!' said Raymond, laughing. 'We should've got the mayor or something!'

He manoeuvred himself into position on his crutches, got hold of the scissors and cut the ribbon. They all cheered and clapped – all except for Cross, who stood waiting patiently with his father's suitcase. But the joy was short-lived, as Raymond's face fell when they walked into his unrecognisable flat. The gang had done a wonderful job. The place was clean, and furnished with pieces they'd found in the various piles. It had that smell of new paint, the smell of promise and life to come. It was like the smell of a brand-new car interior – transient, indescribable and non-replicable, like all the best things in life. But Raymond was crestfallen as he looked around.

'Where's all my stuff?' he asked plaintively.

'We discussed this, Dad. It had to go, to facilitate your return,' said Cross.

'But all of it?' Raymond asked.

'There's plenty still here. Look at all your books and records, pictures on the wall. Furniture you've probably even forgotten you owned,' Cross pointed out.

'I didn't think you'd throw it all out,' Raymond protested.

'And you were right. We didn't,' said Cross. Raymond looked deeply upset, something his son seemed oblivious to, so Mackenzie stepped forward.

'Why don't you sit down, Raymond? Boss, why don't you make us all tea?'

'I can do that,' said Roxy breezily.

'I doubt it,' said Cross, as he left for the kitchen.

Roxy looked at Mackenzie in disbelief, then burst out laughing. Forewarned was forearmed when it came to dealing with Cross, Mackenzie thought. She sat down next to Raymond at the table. He was sweeping its surface with his hands. It was quite a novelty for it to be clear.

'Did you rub it down at all?' he asked.

'No,' said Sanjeev. 'Just cleaned it, then used beeswax polish.'

'Beeswax? Good for you. It's come up lovely,' Raymond said.

'My dad told me to use it,' said Sanjeev.

Raymond nodded approvingly. 'Well, he knows what he's doing.'

'He's a builder,' said Roxy.

'Lent us the wallpaper stripper,' said Harry.

'Did he? Was it steam?' Raymond asked.

'Yeah. It was amazing. Proper industrial it was,' Harry went on.

'You still got it?' Raymond asked.

Sanjeev nodded. 'Yeah, it's in the hall.'

'Can I have a look?'

'Sure,' Sanjeev said, immediately disappearing to find it.

'Raymond,' said Mackenzie, getting his attention as she opened up the photos app on her phone. 'You know the self-storage place down the road?'

'Yes.'

'Well, George has rented two units there and put all your stuff in them,' she said, showing him pictures of two large storage spaces, lined with ordered rows of boxes, piled on top of each other. It was a bit like an archive warehouse. 'George has labelled each box with its contents. There are over a hundred and fifty of them.'

'A hundred and fifty?'

'Yes, and he's written everything down in this ledger.' She produced a small notebook.

Raymond opened it and saw page after page of entries in Cross's handwriting. Each box was numbered with details of its contents, then a number telling him where in the unit it was – U1BRWR3L4, for example, meaning 'unit one, back right wall, row three, level 4'. This format had been formulated after a long, complex conversation with Edwin at work.

'Storage,' he'd said thoughtfully after Cross had approached him at the end of a working day, so as not to encroach on his police time. 'You need to concentrate on geography rather than content in the labelling. Otherwise Raymond is going to be spending all his time walking up and down the unit trying to locate contents,' Edwin explained. 'He needs to concern himself with just finding out the location of the box already knowing what its content is. So we should index the contents in a notebook for him – I'd make a copy if I were you.'

'Of course,' replied Cross.

'The index will relate the contents to the label of the box which in itself locates said box.'

'Very effective,' said Cross as he thought it through.

'The simplest solutions are often the most efficient.'

'Quite so,' agreed Cross. Unbeknownst to them this conversation had made the rest of the unit's day. Ottey had later bought a bottle of whisky and instructed a confused Cross to give it to Edwin as a gesture of thanks. A gesture which Cross thought was completely unnecessary. He was however a little puzzled when he gave it to Edwin who then promptly thanked Ottey.

Raymond looked at the notebook and then back at the photos of the units. Then he looked over at his son in the kitchen, making tea.

'It must've taken him hours,' he said.

'It did,' she replied. 'And it's within walking distance, so whenever you need something you just pop down there and get it.'

'And you all helped?' He looked at the gang with a smile.

'We did,' said Mackenzie.

Raymond was quite lost for words. It wasn't just the generosity of these young, well, let's face it, strangers, but the fact that his son had managed to see the situation from his father's perspective, not his own, and find a solution that would make his father, not him, happy. He'd actually put himself in someone else's shoes for once and thought about what their feelings and views would be. This was an extraordinary step for his son and not something Raymond had ever been aware of him doing before.

Having said that, it was strange to think that Cross had always managed to use this skill when it came to work and investigating a case. He would often try and imagine what a suspect was doing or thinking in any given set of circumstances. Yet up till this point he'd never been able to do it when it came to real life.

Raymond was completely taken aback by this development in his son and wondered where it had come from. He was unable to demonstrate his gratitude in an emotional way, because Cross wouldn't like it; he wouldn't understand it. Raymond was sure his attitude would just be: problem solved. So when Cross returned carrying a Concorde commemorative tray with cups of tea, Raymond simply said, 'Thank you for storing my things, George, and cataloguing them.'

'It seemed the most logical solution,' Cross replied.

Raymond smiled broadly.

'What is it, Raymond?' Mackenzie asked, hoping for some grand acknowledgement of their efforts.

'I'm just so happy he didn't throw out my Concorde tray,' he replied.

At lunchtime, Mackenzie ordered some beer and pizza for everyone. The six of them sat around talking well into the afternoon. Raymond wanted to know all about the renovation. He was keen to examine the wallpaper stripper. They told him of all the amazing things they'd found squirrelled away that had really intrigued them. He regaled them with stories of where he'd got hold of them and the improbable plans he had for their future use.

Harry had found an old Philips radiogram from the 1950s. His grandfather had had one. It was a great big rectangular box, encased in a box of walnut veneer. Across the front was a long dial with the names of radio stations printed along it, and it had huge plastic knobs. The front section was made from a beige fabric that concealed a large speaker behind it. On top was a turntable which you accessed by lifting a panel. It was like the bonnet of a car – it even had a metal stay to hold the top open.

Harry had cleaned it up and was excited to see that it was still in working order. They played jazz records from Raymond's vinyl collection, which was now in pride of place on one of the bookshelves. Raymond then extolled the virtues of listening to vinyl records rather than digital. Its warmth and immediacy. How each scratch – though they wouldn't find many on his collection, he proclaimed with pride – told a story of when and how it happened. He was thrilled when Roxy told him there was a vinyl revival going on with lots of young people buying records and turntables.

Mackenzie was talking to Cross at one point.

'The storage unit was an inspired idea,' she said.

'I was just thinking the same thing,' he replied.

'Were you now?' She smiled.

'And how it would've been a lot cheaper and easier to have photographed the interior of someone else's storage unit, told him it was his stuff and thrown his all away. He would never have known,' he said.

'Rubbish. He'd have found out at some point.'

Cross shook his head. 'On the contrary; he'll never go

there. He just needs to know it's there.'

'How do you know that?' she asked.

'Because he'll be too busy starting a new collection here.'

'Well, there's a job for you – to make sure he doesn't,' she said.

'Easier said than done. He's a difficult, recalcitrant old bugger, that one,' he said, without a hint of self-awareness.

'Like father like son, if you ask me,' she said, and left before he could offer a retort.

After a couple of hours, Raymond was tired and needed a nap.

'At least you'll be able to find the bed,' Harry joked.

Raymond swung round and gave him a deeply offended look. 'What on earth do you mean by that, young man?'

Harry looked mortified, realising he'd overstepped the mark. His friends gave him a withering look.

'I'm so sorry, Raymond—' he began, but was cut off by a loud cackle of laughter bursting forth from the old man.

'Ha! Got you!' he said. 'All of you!' and he disappeared into his bedroom.

When it came to saying goodbye, the gang weren't at all surprised, or offended, by the lack of warmth in Cross's thanks. It was brief and perfunctory. What did surprise them, though, was when Cross handed them each an envelope containing one thousand five hundred pounds.

'We can't take this, George. It's way too much,' said Sanjeev.

'How much is it?' asked Mackenzie.

'Fifteen hundred pounds each,' said Cross.

'George, mate. We can't.' Harry offered his envelope back.

Cross winced at being called 'mate' by this young man, but ignored his discomfort and said, 'Nonsense. I made some enquiries from other tradesmen, and quotes for the work were all around seven thousand. So I took a small percentage off for your lack of experience and the fact that you obviously had no intention of paying tax, and came up with this. The correct figure.'

'Thanks,' said Roxy, who immediately lunged forward to hug Cross.

But he was too quick for her and stepped to one side. 'You did an excellent job,' he said. 'Quite as good as I would've expected from a professional, in point of fact.'

'Oh George, that's so nice,' said Mackenzie.

'Not as good as a top-of-the-rung decorator, obviously,' he said, 'but certainly one of average talent, which was all I could afford, and certainly more than adequate for the job. I'll see you tomorrow, Alice.'

Relieved all the social niceties were over, he marched down the path to find his bike. Except that he hadn't brought it with him. He'd forgotten that he had come with Mackenzie. He stopped at the end of the path as this dawned on him and turned back to the young people, who were still watching him.

'Would you like a lift?' asked Mackenzie.

Chapter 32

Angie finally surfaced later that week, on the Thursday, at the dry cleaner's. Karen called Cross. Angie was in the café opposite. This time she'd promised to wait for Cross. She was, like Karen, a skinny young woman in her early twenties. But Karen looked like a beacon of health in comparison. Angie's hair was a mix of different faded colours from past experiments with dye. She was nervy and suspicious.

'I thought you'd never come. I've been here ages,' she started by saying.

Cross said nothing, just sat opposite her. She was fiddling with a rolled-up cigarette in her fingers. She had obviously been about to go out for a smoke, or perhaps it was a source of comfort – the fact that the next fag wasn't too far away.

'Karen said you wanted to see me.'

'I do,' Cross replied.

'So are you going to buy me a tea or what?' she asked.

'If that's what you want. How do you like it?' he asked, getting up.

'Milky, three sugars.' Cross grimaced at the very idea of it.

'What's wrong with that?' she asked indignantly.

'It almost seems like a waste of a tea bag,' he replied and walked over to the counter.

He ordered the tea then looked at the young woman's reflection in the window. Her face was the colour of a grey, dull sky in the middle of winter. She looked wretched, he thought. An adjective he felt was evocatively ideophonic on this occasion. 'Wretched'. He went back over to the table.

'Would you like some food?' he asked.

'I'd rather have some dosh.'

'That may well be the case, but it's not on offer. Would you like something to eat?' he asked again.

'Bacon sarnie.'

'On brown or white?'

'Proper little waiter, aren't you?' she snarled.

'Very well, just tea then,' said Cross, turning away.

'All right, all right. White with brown sauce,' she said quickly before he changed his mind.

They had already started talking when her sandwich was delivered to the table. She devoured it greedily. Brown sauce spilled out of the sides, down her chin and over her hands, but she was oblivious. Cross got up, went over to the counter and grabbed some paper napkins. He gave them to her and indicated her chin.

'You not having anything?' she asked with her mouth full, much to his discomfort.

'No. Tell me about Flick,' he said.

'What about her? He done her in, most likely.'

'Who?'

'Stokes,' she said, as if it should have been obvious to him.

'What makes you say that?' said Cross.

'Because he's a prick.'

'You didn't join Flick's action against him. Why?'

'Her lawyer said I was no use,' she said sulkily.

'But you've been clean, haven't you?' he asked.

'Yeah. That's where I met Flick. At Hopewell. They didn't know, I reckon,' she said.

'Didn't know what?'

'That they were sending girls there just for him to try and fuck them any way he could.'

'Karen said you're using again because of Danny Stokes,' he said.

She didn't answer.

'What did he do to you?'

'Nothing.'

'Nothing?'

'No. It was the other girls. Guess I was too rough for him.'

'I don't think you're telling me the truth.'

'You calling me a liar?'

'I don't think you're telling me everything. Would you prefer to talk to a female officer?'

'I'd prefer not to talk to any of you, truth be told. We done here?'

'Why did you agree to meet?'

'Why d'you think? Thought there might be some cash in it for me. Why else?'

Cross got up without a word.

'Is that it then?' she asked.

Ignoring her he went up to the counter and gave the owner of the café thirty pounds to pay for food and tea for Angie for the next few occasions. Not for anyone else. Nor was he to give her the money. The owner agreed, putting the money in the till. Cross then wrote something on the back of his contact card and gave it to the owner. Angie watched Cross as he walked past her without a word and left the café. Then, once properly attired in his dayglo safety gear, he cycled off.

'Well weird,' Angie commented to herself, before venturing into the night to find out what dubious delights it held for her.

Chapter 33

Cross had been declining calls from an unknown number on his phone for the past couple of hours. When he got back to the office it rang again. Again he ignored it. It rang again. Whoever it was, was persistent. He decided to answer it.

'Cross.'

'DS Cross, it's Moffatt. Are you able to come and see me?'

A little later he sat beside Esther's bed at the appointed time. She had been very specific. She seemed to have sunk further into the bed since the last time he'd seen her. Her face was more drawn, the little skin left on it pulled tight around her eye sockets. She had noticed in the paper that there was a documentary on TV that night about a local woman who had decided to end her life, after a diagnosis of early onset dementia. She was going to the Dignitas clinic in Switzerland with her family. What had interested Esther, though, was that the doctor, well, more accurately her therapist, who had accompanied the family and witnessed her death was Dr Benedict Sutton. She thought they should watch it together, which Cross had agreed to.

The journey to Switzerland was poignant, filled with laughter and tears of joy and sadness. They were a family of four – father, mother, adult son and daughter.

'They look like a close family,' observed Esther.

The children, even though adults, felt they were being abandoned by their mother, and said so. They then expressed awful guilt about having such feelings. The mother's view was that dementia would take her away from them anyway – they would be abandoned whichever way you looked at it.

'How dreadful for them,' commented Esther.

The day after the family's arrival in Switzerland, they travelled to a nondescript, modern house on a bleak industrial estate, where the mother took the poison prepared by the doctor for her. Her last words were a whispered, 'My throat is so dry. Can I have some water?' The doctor declined politely and quietly. Apparently there was a danger that the patient could choke.

Sutton had argued in the film against his being present, but the family insisted. As she died quietly, the camera focused on him. Cross assumed this was to give the family a moment of privacy at such a devastating moment. Sutton's face gave nothing away, but as the family comforted each other, he slipped out of the room. The film crew followed him and then filmed him outside comforting the young director, who had broken down in tears.

'Do you believe him?' asked Esther.

'Believe what exactly?' Cross asked.

'That he didn't want to be there at the end. That it was a private moment for the family?'

'I see no reason not to.'

'I think he was acting a little.'

'Possibly to conceal his own emotions. A voluntary death has just been administered in front of him. That's a lot even for a medical practitioner to take in. A person taking someone else's life right in front of him.'

'True. I wonder if the family will face prosecution now this has been aired?'

'The police are obliged to investigate,' Cross said, knowing he was telling her something she was well aware of.

'That would be one thing I wouldn't want in my in-tray.'

'I take it you approve of assisted dying then?' said Cross.

'In certain circumstances, yes.'

'Would you be willing to go to Switzerland to die?' Cross asked.

She smiled ruefully. 'Oh, that won't be necessary, George.' It was the first time she had called him by his Christian name. He had no feelings about it either way.

'I don't understand.'

'I have late stage pancreatic cancer. I'm dying quite successfully on my own. No help necessary,' she replied.

'I see.'

At the end of the film Sutton talked about how dreadful it was that the family had to travel so far to find a solution and risk possible prosecution when they got home. He felt that she should have had the opportunity to die in her home, without the additional emotional turmoil and stress.

'I think Sutton is worth looking at,' Esther said, almost in a whisper. Cross sensed that his visit and watching the programme had tired her out.

'Everyone is worth looking at.'

'The daughter seemed the most conflicted of the kids,' Esther reflected.

'She did.'

'Worth a visit?' Esther enquired.

'Indubitably.'

'Thanks for indulging an old woman.'

He had no idea what she meant by this, so said 'Goodbye' and left.

As Cross left the care home he bumped into Mackenzie in reception.

'You're too late,' he said.

'Oh my God what's happened?' she asked.

'It's over.'

'But that was so sudden.'

'I don't know what you mean. I think it finished at the scheduled time.'

'What *are* you talking about?'

'The documentary DCI Moffatt wanted to watch. What are you doing here?'

She held up a chemist's carrier bag. 'I'm going to do her nails.'

'Why?'

'Because I thought it would be nice for her.'

'I see. Well then, I'll leave you to it,' and so saying he spun on his heels and left.

Chapter 34

Back at his flat Cross looked at his mother's letter to his father again, not to reread the contents, which he pretty much knew by heart now, but to double-check the address. It was in Gloucester, where he was going the next day. Ottey and Mackenzie were going to visit Sandra. He was fairly sure the address he had was where his grandparents had lived. He knew they'd lived in Gloucester but they had ceased contact with him and Raymond at the same time as their daughter. He knew it was unlikely that she would still be there after all these years, but it was the only starting point he had. He had checked social media for her in her married and maiden names, but hadn't come across anything. It was quite possible, probable even, that she had remarried and had a different name. But it was also possible that she, like him, chose not to make her life publicly accessible on the various social media platforms.

If Cross needed to travel any distance on a case he would always take the train, with his bicycle in the carriage with him or in the guard's van, depending on the type of train. He loved trains; always had done. He loved their predictability and hated it if they were late. He felt modern trains had lost something, though. The new carriages were soulless affairs.

He liked the older trains, particularly if they had small compartments. He liked it when the cushioned seats were covered with thick, almost velvety moquette.

He vividly remembered whiling away time on a tedious journey with his father to visit some piece of Brunel engineering somewhere, by making patterns in the seat material. He would do this by brushing the fabric against the pile, making it go darker, then brushing with the pile to make it smooth and light. With a sweep of his hand he could then erase the pattern permanently, leaving no trace of his artistic endeavours. He remembered to this day the names of some of the designs used by the railways in his childhood and teens. There was Trojan, his favourite Red Candy Stripe, and then in later years the Inter City Dogger Red.

The seats also had two very distinct seasonal smells. When it was raining and the seats got wet from people sitting on them or inconsiderately placed umbrellas, they had a smell of damp autumnal rot. It wasn't altogether unpleasant, as it had an association of being recently sheltered from the rain outside. In the summer they had a musty smell of roasted dust, which seemed to impart the joy of journeying to an eagerly anticipated destination, which promised familiar treats like pier amusements and ice cream. There was something comforting and familiar about those smells. Now the seats offered no sensory additions to a journey. They were functional, bland and without personality. Like much of modern life, Cross thought.

Mackenzie had found contact details for Melissa Conrad, the daughter in the documentary, from the production company who had made it. They informed her that Melissa was happy for Cross to contact her. He had called and made an appointment for that afternoon. He had forewarned her that he wanted to talk to her about the documentary and specifically Sutton. He hoped this might give her time to think and formulate her thoughts about the doctor and the film. This way he thought he might get a more cogent and considered reaction from her, rather than just arriving cold.

Melissa Conrad lived in the small town of Quedgeley, outside Gloucester. It had an interesting-sounding name for such a dull, modern place. She was married now, and a new mother, at home with her six-month-old daughter. She greeted Cross at the door with a muslin cloth over one shoulder and the baby over the other.

'Sorry, I was just feeding her,' she said, apologising for the slight delay in answering the door.

'Breast or bottle?' asked Cross.

'What?' She was taken aback by such a direct, personal question. 'Um, breast.'

'In that case, would you like me to return?' he said.

'Oh I see. No, not at all. Come in,' she said, holding the door open for him.

They walked into the small house. It was on a bland modern estate built in the eighties.

'Can I offer you a cup of tea?' Melissa said.

Cross would normally have said no to this, but he'd seen a teapot and a box of loose tea on the kitchen counter top as soon as he walked in, which he immediately thought upped the chances of getting a half-decent cup of tea. So it might be worth the risk. In his experience, people who made tea with loose leaves were generally far more interested in the quality of the beverage than those who just chucked a tea bag into a cup. Some even threw the tea bag in with the cold milk before the hot water, to his horror, before squeezing the bag against the side of the cup before fishing it out. So he acceded.

'Let me just deal with this,' said Melissa, referring to the baby.

This was when he spotted the opportunity to ensure the tea would be to his exacting standards. 'Why don't I make it?' he volunteered.

'Are you sure?'

'Of course,' he replied, and set about making a pot for them while she finished feeding the infant. He enquired how she preferred her tea, then brought the pot, two cups and a jug of milk through.

'What a treat,' she said as he set the tea down. 'Thank you.' She settled the baby in a Moses basket. 'So, Benedict Sutton; what do you need to know?'

'How did you find him?' Cross asked.

'I didn't. My mother did.' Her tone implied that she would never have gone looking for him.

'What I meant was – how did you find him personally? What did you make of him?' Cross asked.

'Can I ask why you're here?'

'It's not relevant to your view of him.' Cross didn't want the reason for his visit to affect what she might have to say.

'I see. Well, I didn't like him. I was unhappy about the whole thing,' she replied.

'The documentary or your mother's ending her own life?'

'Both,' she said. 'He was, is, a big advocate of assisted dying, as you probably know. My mother got in touch with him, initially, to discuss it. He seemed to be the only person around in a position of knowledge.'

'Are you saying he'd been to Switzerland with patients before?'

'Yes, three to my certain knowledge.'

'That I didn't know,' he replied.

'Anyway, over time he became more and more involved in my mother's life and so more involved in ours. It was "Benedict this, Ben that".'

'Whose idea was it for her to end her life abroad, when it came to it?' Cross asked.

'Well, to be fair, it was mostly hers. I mean, that's why she got hold of him in the first place. But then he kind of took over. It was happening. She was going. End of discussion.'

'But you discussed it quite a lot in the film,' Cross pointed out.

'It was restaged for the film. We'd done our talking in private away from the cameras. They asked us to do it again. It was awful.'

'How did you feel about your mother wanting the whole thing documented in that way?'

'Oh, it wasn't her idea,' she replied.

'But again – it's in the film,' Cross said.

'It's a much better story if she'd decided to have it recorded for posterity than being persuaded to do it by her doctor. He pushed her into it. Pushed us all into it.'

'How did he come to have such an influence over you?'

'He had a secret weapon. Her. None of us wanted to upset her. We wanted things to be the best possible version of themselves towards the end of her life. We loved her. He used that against us. Can you believe that? He used a family's love against them. He's very patient. That's his killer skill, if you'll excuse the pun. He takes his time, inveigling his way

in, till he's suddenly everywhere and completely in charge.
He was indispensable to my mother by the end. It was really
insidious.'

'You didn't like him?'

'Have you met him?' she enquired.

'I have.'

'Then you'll know he's not someone it's easy to warm to.'

'I understand.'

'You make a mean cup of tea,' she said, taking a sip.

'I'm sorry, do you not like it?' he asked.

'Yes, it's excellent.'

'Yes, I thought so too.'

'Like I've said before,' she went on, 'it was a bit like joining
a cult with this charismatic leader with followers adoring him
devotedly and hanging on his every word, however crazy.
They'd do absolutely anything he said. Anything.'

'Like killing themselves?'

'In this instance. Yes,' she said emphatically.

'Have you kept in touch?' asked Cross.

'No. He tried to. My brother spoke to him. He said he
wanted to include us in his follow-up research. I didn't want
anything to do with it. My mother wasn't just some example to
illustrate an academic thesis. She was my mother, not a statistic. I
hadn't wanted her to go through with what she did but in the end
she listened to him more than she listened to us. Have you any
idea what that's like? She was more willing to listen to a complete
stranger than her own daughter; and about something like that.
Something so final. She would've seen and met my daughter,
Chloe. She had vascular dementia and it wasn't progressing
as fast as they initially thought. It's often much slower than
Alzheimer's, but she wouldn't listen to us once she'd met him.'

'Do you blame Sutton?' said Cross.

'I don't blame him, but I hold him partially responsible. After all, it's what she wanted. I resent his encouragement. He's like a Svengali; completely controlling.'

Cross realised that was the second time someone had described him that way.

'And then, right at the end, there he was with his bloody film crew. What was a sad, tragic end to a life which should've been private and sacred, if you like, but became a piece of public property. Propaganda,' she said.

'The film made it seem like he'd been unwilling to attend and your mother had insisted,' said Cross.

'Completely untrue. He persuaded my mother he should be there "for her", to give her strength. He described the film as her legacy. It was more of a monument to his ego, though,' she said bitterly. Cross processed this. 'So now can you explain your interest in him?' she asked.

Cross did so. She was taken aback and thought for a bit about the implications of what he'd said.

'Do you think he did it?' she asked.

'I don't as yet think anything.'

'It seems unlikely, doesn't it?' she asked. 'Even I find that a bit of a stretch, and as you know I'm not his biggest fan. Unless…'

'Unless what?'

'Unless he's completely lost the plot.'

'What exactly do you mean by that?'

'That he's gone mad with it all. He's always had a bit of a god complex about him. What if now he actually believes it?'

★

Cross cycled back into Gloucester to what he presumed was his maternal grandparents' house. His first instinct, out of habit, was to reach for his warrant card, but he remembered that he wasn't there on police business, so not only was it unnecessary, but it would've been against regulations for a private matter. The current residents weren't familiar with his grandparents' surname. They'd bought the house seven years before. But they did recall the previous owner saying he'd bought it from a family who'd owned it for over forty years. That had to be his grandparents. They were more than happy to go and look, while he waited in the hall, for the forwarding address they had for the previous owner, but reminded him that it was from seven years before so might well be out of date. Cross was just impressed that they were organised enough to be able to put their hands on it so quickly.

Chapter 35

Cross spent the next few days taking a closer look at Flick's therapist, Benedict Sutton. It wasn't so much that he suspected him of killing Flick, but it was the only other avenue available to him to wander down at this point in time, while they waited for something pertinent to advance their case against Danny Stokes. The path might lead nowhere, but who knew what or who he might encounter on that particular stroll, and the documentary had interested him.

He started, as he always did in these situations, with a general search. During this time Ottey left him well alone and got on with other casework. Carson, though, hovered outside Cross's door occasionally, hesitating and wondering whether to knock. Then, thinking better of it, he would walk away, congratulating himself on his restraint. Cross was often aware, out of the corner of his eye, of his boss's presence outside his door – it had a glass panel – but didn't look up, as he knew any acknowledgement of Carson would be interpreted as an invitation to come in.

A basic Google search showed that Sutton had quite a lot to say for himself. There were interviews in magazines and papers, video clips from local news and soundbites from radio. They were mainly about substance abuse and recovery, but he also spoke a lot about bereavement and grief counselling. For one journalist in the *BBC Points West* newsroom, though, he had become a reliable source for a quote or point of view on anything medical. He had also been married but his wife had died a number of years earlier. They had no children.

One topic stuck out and seemed to have become something of a theme. Sutton had made some quite controversial comments along the way about legalising assisted dying, not only for medical reasons, but also for mental health issues. This had caused a lot of heated debate at times. He had argued that people suffering from long-term, seemingly incurable mental health problems should be able to choose to die, as they could in the Netherlands. There, if a doctor was satisfied a patient's suffering was 'unbearable with no prospect of improvement', and if there was 'no reasonable alternative in the patient's situation', euthanasia was legal.

This was, of course, hugely contentious in the UK. Sutton's argument was that many people with such issues often took it upon themselves to end their lives, but not always successfully, and often in the most unpleasant of ways. This argument had placed him at odds with several other medical practitioners, religious leaders and members of Parliament. The general consensus was that the very fact that these people were suffering from mental illnesses meant they weren't competent enough to make such a decision in the first place. The argument against was also based on the innumerable ethical considerations applied to the idea of state-sanctioned euthanasia. Over time, Sutton seemed to have warmed to his thesis.

Sutton also appeared to have a nemesis in the form of another media-loving doctor in Bath. He was a GP who had a health advice slot on an afternoon TV lifestyle show. His name was Marcus Todd, and he had been asked in passing about Sutton's views. He rounded on both Sutton and his views, criticising them as socially irresponsible and ill-considered. Sutton had replied robustly in a tweet. The gripe between the two of them had then grown exponentially. If Sutton was on a radio talk show, Todd would often be asked to give the opposing view. Cross thought, looking through the various interchanges, that their public debate had become more and more personal.

Chapter 36

Dr Marcus Todd wasn't at all like his colleague, Benedict Sutton. Cross had arranged to meet Sutton's media sparring partner, suspecting that there was more to his constant opposition to Sutton's views whenever and wherever the opportunity presented itself. He wanted to find out what it was.

Todd was genial and welcoming, with none of the airs or sartorial flair of Sutton. He was a down-to-earth, bearded GP of the old school, roughly the same age as Sutton. His breath smelt of recently drunk coffee – instant, Cross surmised. There was a hint of dandruff on the shoulders of his avuncular woollen cardigan. He looked like he might've been better suited to being a country doctor back in the post-war early fifties, with a pipe as a permanent smoking protuberance from his mouth.

Relationships with doctors had changed during Cross's lifetime. You never knew which doctor you were going to see when you made an appointment these days. The best doctors, and by that he meant the most communicative and interested in their patients, were always fully booked. If that was the case, you were asked to call back on a Monday morning at eight a.m. when new bookings would be taken. So, of course, every patient wanting an appointment duly called back and was placed in an automatic queue of indefinite length. For Cross there was only so much tinny recorded ABBA he could take down the phone so early on a Monday morning. By the time he called back in the afternoon, all the appointments for the new booking period were, of course, gone and he would be offered a telephone consultation – which he much preferred anyway – two weeks hence.

Todd was immediately curious as to why a policeman, and a murder detective at that, should be interested in Sutton.

'Is he a person of interest in the case?'

'He is not.'

'Then why are you here exactly?'

'I've listened to a number of your discussions with Dr Sutton and you seem to be at loggerheads in your views.'

'He's too fond of the media and maintaining his presence on it. It jars,' Todd said.

'Did you not have your own slot, I believe they call it, on an afternoon television programme for some time?' Cross asked, puzzled by the apparent contradiction.

'I still do,' the doctor replied. 'But I prefer to see it as an extended surgery. I deal with patients' problems and give them advice. I don't have a morally dubious cause to espouse.'

'Do you doubt the veracity of his beliefs?' Cross asked.

'I'll be honest with you. There is something I just dislike about the man. I don't trust him. I don't trust his motives. I think he says a lot of what he says just to get the attention that will inevitably come with it. The man is vain, interested almost solely in notoriety.'

'You didn't, in fact, answer my question,' said Cross.

'I'm not sure I believe him, no. For the reasons I just gave, Sergeant.'

'Ah, I see. Now I understand.'

Todd frowned. 'I don't think that man should have anything to do with the provision of care for the mentally vulnerable. It's always about him. He's his first priority in any given situation.'

'Hearing you speak like this makes me wonder whether you don't have some personal experience with him,' said Cross.

Todd considered this for a moment. Was this, Cross wondered, because what he was about to impart was confidential, or because it didn't reflect well on him?

'I had a patient,' Todd began. 'A young woman. Complicated. A difficult upbringing. Classic case of in and out of foster homes. She had a history of mental health issues, which is why she was moved around so many times. As a young adult she developed a dependence on various drugs and alcohol. Sutton had just stopped his medical practice and was concentrating on being a substance abuse and recovery therapist. He had a good reputation. People liked him. So I referred her to him. Six months later, under his care, she committed suicide.'

'Which presumably wasn't a complete shock, in her case?' Cross asked.

'I didn't feel she was a suicide risk when I referred her. I was shocked and profoundly upset,' Todd said.

'Did you talk to Sutton?'

'Of course.'

'And what was his reaction to her death?' said Cross.

'He said he was puzzled. It was unexpected,' replied Todd.

'Anything else?'

'No. That was all.'

Cross felt that Todd had more to say, but that the conversation had reached an inertial lull. So he did what he habitually did in these situations, and left. He could, if necessary, always come back. He also thought that Todd's reliability might be a little suspect as he seemed to have an axe to grind. Cross needed to make sure the information the doctor had given him hadn't been interpreted or tailored in a way to suit Todd's agenda.

Chapter 37

A few days later Mackenzie received a call from the care home. Esther had taken a turn for the worse, which wasn't entirely unexpected in the circumstances, but it had come to the point where she obviously had just a few hours left. They thought she'd like to know. It was four in the afternoon; not the end of her working day, but she decided to leave anyway. She grabbed her things and got up.

'Where are you off to?' asked Ottey.

'It's DCI Moffatt. She's dying,' Alice replied.

'I had no idea she was that ill,' said Ottey.

'Yeah. I thought I'd go over. She hasn't got anyone.'

Ottey thought for a moment.

'Give me a second,' she said, getting up and going over to Cross's office.

Esther was unconscious when they arrived. The manager was sitting at her bedside, holding her hand, which impressed Ottey. She got up as Mackenzie, Cross, Ottey and Stephen entered the room. Cross had insisted on picking the priest up on their way there. Esther had said to him that she was a lapsed Catholic, and he thought it might be of some comfort for her to see a priest.

'It won't be long now,' said the manager. 'You can talk to her if you want. She may be able to hear. She's on a morphine pump, so she's completely comfortable. And she's had a wonderful week this last week, thanks to Alice.' She left.

'I didn't realise she was unconscious,' said Cross. 'I'm sorry to have wasted your time, Stephen.'

'Not at all.' Stephen moved forward and took Esther's hand. 'Would anyone object if I gave her the last rites?' he asked.

'I think she'd like that,' said Mackenzie.

Stephen then draped a purple stole over his shoulders. When Cross had told him how ill Esther was – that she was close to death – he'd put on his full-length cassock and grabbed his Bible and rosary. He held Esther's hand and gently read her the last rites. As he finished he closed his eyes for a few moments in silent prayer, then looked up and quietly said goodbye to the three of them. He refused a lift back to his church from the now tearful Mackenzie.

'What a lovely man, George,' she said. 'How nice of him to drop everything, and he did it so beautifully. Lucky you to have such a good friend.'

'Oh, he's not a friend,' said Cross. 'I just play his organ.'

There was a moment's pause, but when Ottey and Mackenzie looked at each other they completely lost it. Cross just looked on disapprovingly.

Mackenzie sat down and took Esther's hand. Ottey stepped forward and spoke even though the old woman was unconscious.

'DS Ottey, ma'am. I'm sorry we haven't met before, but I've heard a lot about you.'

Cross then turned to Mackenzie.

'What did the manager mean about DCI Moffatt's last week being so wonderful, thanks to you?' he asked.

It turned out that Mackenzie had done a little digging and tracked down a few of Esther's former colleagues. When they heard she was dying, they came in and visited. She'd basked in the company of old friends she hadn't seen in many years, as they reminisced about the old days in the force and some of the more memorable cases they'd worked together. Mackenzie was struck by their immediate familiarity. Esther suddenly became a woman with a story, rather than just a sick, elderly body occupying a bed temporarily in a care home, before she passed away and was forgotten.

'That was such a great thing to do, Alice. I'm really impressed. Really touched,' said Ottey.

'Yeah, well, it didn't take much effort and they were more than happy to come in,' Mackenzie replied. 'She was very popular – respected as a great detective. Sounded a bit like DS Cross, if I'm honest. Never gave up. Their only regret they had was falling out of touch after they were finished on the job.'

'And therein lies a lesson for all of us, George,' said Ottey.

He looked at her, not having a clue what she was talking about, but thought the best course of action in the circumstances was just to nod in agreement.

They sat there for a couple of hours and then the two women left, Ottey to get back to her children and Mackenzie because she had been there every night that week after work and was tired. She offered Cross a lift, which he declined. He was going to stay.

*

Early the next morning, at around two, the night manager was doing his rounds when he stopped outside Esther's room and listened. He could hear a man talking softly. The manager smiled a little mournfully and walked on. Inside, Cross was talking the still unconscious Esther Moffatt through the Flick case. He was reciting the facts as he knew them out loud – something he normally did in his head. He told her that Flick's journal was still missing. It was conceivable that the killer had taken it and destroyed it, lending all the more credence to the fact that it was someone who knew her well. Then he surprised himself by saying, 'I wish you were able to hear all of this. I'd be very interested to know what you thought about it.'

Half an hour later Esther opened her eyes slowly. She took a while to focus, then she saw Cross. She squeezed his hand, and he squeezed hers back gently. She seemed to be mouthing something. He leant forward and she whispered, 'How did the killer get her consent... to inject her?'

'Yes, indeed. That is a pertinent question,' Cross replied quietly.

'No,' she whispered back. 'It's *the* question, George.' She closed her eyes again and drifted off.

At four in the morning, Esther's breathing became shallower and shallower, and she finally slipped away. After a couple of seconds she let out a loud involuntary gasp and then there was no more.

Cross was actually quite shocked in the moment of death. He'd seen many dead bodies throughout his career, but this was the first time he'd seen anyone actually die. He was moved by the finality of it. There was an inexplicable power. He'd never believed in the notion of a soul leaving a body before, but now he had an understanding of where such a thought might have originated, having witnessed what he could only think of as Esther's life leaving her body in that last sigh. It was a deeply profound moment to witness. But what he also found himself thinking was whether someone could become drawn irrevocably to such moments. It gave him pause to think about Sutton in a fresh, sinister light.

He found the night manager and informed him of Esther's death. He then walked home. It was a good hour's walk, but he enjoyed the clarity of thought the fresh air and empty streets seemed to afford him. When he arrived at his flat he saw that Tony was opening the café up. It was six in the morning. He went in. What he didn't realise was that he was in need of company as well as an early breakfast.

Tony was surprised to see him. 'Pulled an all-nighter, George?' he asked as he brought him his tea.

'I beg your pardon?'

'Have you been working all night?'

'No, I've been with a friend,' Cross said quietly.

'George! You old dog, you!'

'She died,' said Cross.

'Oh, George, I do apologise. I'm sorry for your loss. I really am. You'll be needing something to eat. Just give me ten minutes.' Tony disappeared into the back.

Cross sat there, wondering whether his presence had made any difference to Esther in her final hours. It had to have done. She knew he was there. She spoke to him, and what a surprising thing to say. A true detective to the end. He wasn't sure, but what he did realise was that it had made an enormous difference to him. He was pleased to have been there. He felt almost privileged to have shared that moment with her, and he found himself thinking that the chances were that he would die on his own, which was a little disappointing.

Mackenzie wasn't able to get Esther Moffatt out of her mind back at work – her smile and the slightly pathetic gratitude she had shown to Mackenzie for tracking down her colleagues. This little wizened old thing with a plethora of tiny, vertical lines around her lips from years of smoking, beaming with her ill-fitting dentures, just didn't fit the descriptions of the dynamic young policewoman who had fought to be treated equally – 'not like one of the boys,' she had told her; that was quite different. Just 'equally'. Mackenzie could imagine her rocking a leather jacket and pair of flared denims, charging through kicked-down doors. You simply wouldn't know if you'd only met her like this, curled up in bed, her feet encased in thick pink woollen socks, with little anti-slip pads on the soles, over surgical stockings. And now she was dead.

It appeared that her nickname 'Little Miss Moffatt' soon took on an ironic meaning as her career progressed – she was anything but. Mackenzie was glad to have made a difference to this woman's final days. She realised that time was a fickle mistress and how quickly people could be forgotten and cast aside. She was also glad that Esther hadn't died alone; that Cross had been at her side.

She found herself thinking she'd like to go to Esther's funeral. She called the management at the home, who were glad to hear from her. They imagined that Esther's funeral would be a tiny affair – just a quick cremation at Canford with a couple of staff and any residents who were up to it. Mackenzie was really saddened by this, but they promised to call her when they'd finalised the arrangements, such as they were, with the undertakers.

But as she ended the call she felt a distinct sense of unease. On impulse she called the care home straight back and asked if she could take charge of Esther's funeral arrangements. They were bemused by the request at first, but then agreed and told her the amount of money that Esther had left for her final arrangements. It wasn't much, but having said that, Mackenzie was determined to send DCI Moffatt off in proper fashion.

That night she set about the task with fervour. Her first call was to the delightful priest who had given Esther her last rites. Stephen said he would be honoured to conduct a service for Esther at his church, and they decided on a date. He then asked her to email him with any information she had about Esther so he knew a bit about her for the service.

Mackenzie had persuaded Ottey to get hold of Esther's personnel file from Human Resources when she was looking for former colleagues to visit her in the home. She had contact details for some of these, so started calling them and letting them know about the funeral. But she could still count the number of attendees on one hand. Esther had to have had some relatives, surely.

So she made a Facebook page – an In Memoriam page for Esther, detailing her life and dates and asking any family or old friends to get in touch. She then got her friends to share the page as widely as they could. She gave an account of a couple of famous cases Esther had been involved in over the years, including a foiled bank robbery back in the seventies that had a lot of notoriety about it. She then sat back and let the internet do its thing. She would, of course, do an email in the department and ask anyone who was free on the day to come and make up the numbers.

Chapter 38

As happened so often with murder cases where there wasn't an obvious suspect to investigate then arrest, there followed a period of frustrating inaction. In this case it lasted a few weeks. The evidence available to them simply wasn't pointing to anyone specifically.

'We need a little luck,' said Mackenzie one day. Ottey winced as it was within Cross's earshot but his response was unexpected.

'I think you may be right,' he replied.

'I thought you didn't believe in luck when it came to solving cases,' Ottey objected.

'I don't but sometimes a little luck is needed to prod you in the right direction.'

It wasn't luck in this case that finally moved them on but something Cross had put in place the previous month. He received a call from the café owner, who wasn't exactly happy. He'd called Cross every time that Angie had come to the café to eat. Cross had shown no interest in going to meet her until now. The money he'd left behind the counter had run out and Angie was back at the café demanding food and was 'totally strung out' as the owner had described her. This was the moment Cross had been waiting for, when she might be inclined to barter some information with them. He grabbed Mackenzie and they headed out.

Angie was picking butts out of a wall-mounted cigarette bin near the café as Mackenzie parked up.

'Angie, don't do that, it's disgusting,' said Mackenzie as she approached her.

'And who the fuck are you?' came the reply.

'The mug who's going to buy you something to eat. Now come on,' Mackenzie said, taking her by the arm.

'Oh, there he is! Weird bastard!' she yelled at Cross. 'Mr Bean in a police uniform.' Mackenzie couldn't help but grin at this description.

'I'm not in uniform,' he pointed out.

'See? Weird. Are you with him?' she asked Mackenzie.

'Well, are you buying me some food or what?' she asked unceremoniously and loudly as they sat at a table in the café. The owner looked on warily.

'Sure. What do you want?' asked Mackenzie.

'Bacon sandwich.' Mackenzie got up.

'Sit down,' Cross instructed Mackenzie. 'We'll get you something to eat when and if you have something of value to tell us.'

'I told you. I don't have anything to say.'

'Then you need to leave and not bother this gentleman anymore.'

'He stole my money. Your money. There's none left.'

'What makes you think he stole it?'

'Are you stupid or what? There's none left!' she shouted.

'I'm sorry but you're going to have to leave. You're upsetting the other customers,' said the owner, a little desperately as they were actually the only people in the café.

'Seriously?' Mackenzie asked incredulously.

Cross got up. 'We're leaving. Come on.'

'Angie, you look terrible. You need to eat something before you become really ill,' said Mackenzie.

'Then buy me something!' she shouted.

'First you need to stop shouting. Would you like some tea? With sugar, a bacon sarnie, bar of chocolate?' asked Mackenzie quietly.

'Yes please,' Angie said pitifully. Mackenzie looked up at Cross, who didn't move.

'Are you willing to tell us what happened to you, Angie? With Stokes?' he asked. She thought about it for a moment. She really didn't want to but had a more pressing problem than her intuitive reluctance. Hunger.

They let her eat, drink and get herself together. Cross then looked at Mackenzie which she took as her cue to talk.

'Are you using again, Angie?'

'What do you think?'

'Karen says it's because of Danny Stokes.'

'Yeah, but it takes two to tango, if you know what I mean.'

'I don't,' Cross said.

'It's like what they say at Hopewell. You've got to take responsibility. Yeah, it was his fault, but I didn't have to do it. I'm just a sorry loser.'

'Tell us what happened,' pushed Mackenzie.

Angie relayed her story. It contained much the same pattern of behaviour as the other girls. Harassment, suggestive texts, exposing himself. Then one night he asked her to take some of his clean laundry round to his flat in the docks. He was completely charming. Very different to how he was at work. They talked for a while. He feigned an interest in her life and what plans she had for the future. Then he offered her drugs. He was so persuasive – made out that they would take them together. So she did, but of course he didn't. Then he took her to bed. She didn't remember much about it.

'I did make him wear a condom, though. I'm not stupid,' she said with pride.

'What did he give you? Heroin, cocaine?'

'No, it was the real deal,' she replied. 'Bastard.'

'What's the "real deal"?' Cross asked.

'Hospital stuff. Proper morphine.'

'Diamorphine?'

'Yeah, that's it,' she said.

'Have you injected before?'

'Yeah, but I was well out of practice. He did it for me. Should've been a nurse!' she joked.

Mackenzie looked at her superior officer but he gave nothing away. Cross simply took this information in and logged it. For many of his colleagues the alarm bells would've rung, telling them that they had their man, sending them sprinting across the road to arrest Danny Stokes. But not for Cross. For him it was more like a note pushed gently under a door to tell him something of possible interest. He got up to leave without a word.

'Is that it then?' Angie said, surprised.

'For now,' he replied.

'You're welcome. Bloody hell,' she said.

Cross thought for a second. Definitely sarcasm, he decided

from the expression on her face. What had he left out? Oh yes.

'That was very helpful, Angie. Thank you,' he said as if reciting a script.

Mackenzie wanted to give Angie some money but knew this wasn't a good idea. She left with a huge pang, though.

Chapter 39

'Diamorphine!' exclaimed Carson. 'When did you find this out?'

'Last night,' Cross answered.

'Last night! Then why on earth haven't you got him in custody? He's obviously our man.'

'He's no such thing,' said Cross.

'Oh come on, George, give me a break. This is a game changer. Great work,' Carson went on.

'We'll need a search warrant for his flat,' said Cross.

'Sure. What for?' Carson asked.

'To see if the drugs are still there,' said Ottey.

'Is this girl willing to testify to Stokes injecting her?' Carson asked.

'Yes, but I think it might be an idea to get her some help,' said Ottey.

'Josie, how many times do I have to keep telling you? We're not social services,' said Carson.

'It would add to her credibility in court,' Ottey sighed.

Carson nodded. 'Good point.'

'I'll get Mackenzie on to it,' Ottey said.

'No. I'll do it,' said Cross.

'Okay,' said Ottey, knowing that her partner had to have his reasons.

Danny's Dry Cleaner's smelt of freshly pressed laundry that morning. Cross remembered, as a child, his father taking his suits to the dry cleaner's, which always seemed to have an overpowering, but quite pleasant nevertheless, smell of chemicals. But not so here. They asked for Danny Stokes and were told to go up to his office. But they declined and asked him to come down. Ottey wanted to do this in public. Gerry Stokes stopped working and came over.

'Sergeants... can I help?' he asked.

'No thanks. We're here to see your son,' said Ottey.

Cross had noticed that she had her handcuffs in her hand, not discreetly on her belt underneath her jacket. He wondered what had made her take them out early. Maybe to demonstrate from the get-go that she meant business?

Danny came down the stairs, two at a time, smiling broadly as if to impart a carefree, insouciant confidence.

'Detectives. How can I help?' he asked breezily.

'Danny Stokes, I'm arresting you on suspicion of the murder of Felicity Wilson...' said Ottey.

There was an audible gasp from some of the laundry workers as she read him his rights and cuffed him. Karen burst into tears. Cross looked at her. Possibly she was thinking how close she might have come to death, if he was the killer.

'Is this a joke?' Danny asked.

'Yes, we always go round pretending to arrest people,' said Ottey. 'It's a sideline we have going on, like kiss-a-grams.

You know how poorly we're paid these days. Isn't that right, DS Cross?'

'No! That would be completely improper,' said Cross, a little startled.

Ottey turned to the transfixed laundry workers. 'Come on. Own up. Who booked us?' she shouted.

Cross was now completely perplexed. He had no idea what she was talking about. But Ottey had decided she hadn't been having enough fun on the job recently; well, specifically since partnering with Cross. So she was going to find amusement wherever she could, no matter what the effect was on her partner.

'Look, we can sort this out really quickly,' said Danny. 'This is completely unnecessary.'

Ottey started to guide him out.

'Wait a second. I have an alibi. I was with my father that night. We were having dinner.'

'You told us previously you were at home.' Ottey stopped and they both turned to face Gerry, who said nothing.

'Well I was wrong. Dad?' said Danny confidently.

'The night Flick died?' Gerry asked.

'Yes. We had dinner. Remember?' said Danny.

'No. No, we didn't. I remember very clearly. I was on my own. Not unusual,' he said, turning to Cross.

'What?' asked his son. 'How can you be so sure?'

'Because I remember discussing her death with you the next day and you making a terrible comment about a problem being solved. I hadn't seen you the night before,' said Gerry.

Ottey looked at Cross. What was the old man up to?

'Dad, why are you doing this?' asked Danny.

'Because it's the truth, son,' replied Gerry.

'Dad!' pleaded Danny as Ottey started to lead him out again.

'Answer me one question, Danny,' said Gerry. 'Did you kill that girl?'

'No, I didn't,' answered Danny. 'How could you even think that?'

'I don't, as it happens. I believe you, which is why there's no point in starting to lie and create false alibis. It's not going to help anyone. DS Cross here will get to the truth, I'm sure of it.'

As Ottey led a disbelieving Danny Stokes out into the car park, Stokes senior took hold of Cross's elbow gently. 'No need for a duty solicitor,' he said. 'I'll find a lawyer and send him down.'

'Very well,' Cross said.

Chapter 40

While they waited for Danny to be processed and for his lawyer to arrive, Cross sat in his office and wrote out his 'script'. This was essentially his structure for the interview with Danny, based on the evidence they had thus far. It was his way of ensuring he asked all the questions he intended, in the right order for the narrative to develop. If Danny was guilty, it would give him enough opportunities to slip up, prior to their revealing their evidence, which would contradict his denial and version of events. It also provided Cross with something to fall back on when the interview went in an unexpected direction. It would be his way of getting back on track.

As there was still no sign of the lawyer a couple of hours later, they decided to exercise their warrant and search Danny's flat. Cross wasn't worried about the lawyer's tardiness because Danny would be his only client, and he wouldn't be going off to see other suspects being held in the custody suite as the duty solicitor was wont to do. It also gave them the chance to get evidence, hopefully from the flat, something he would've liked to have done before the arrest. But such was Carson's urgent need to make an arrest that things had got out of their proper sequence. That is to say, Cross's sequential order.

Danny provided them with his keys when he saw the

warrant. An officer took his fingerprints and now set about seeing if they matched any of the prints found in Flick's flat. Sandra, Simon and Brian had already given theirs and been excluded. Simon was still a person of interest and hadn't yet been ruled out of the investigation, although Cross was fairly persuaded by the sincerity of Simon's persistent question, 'How could I have injected her?' There was still the blow to the head, but he couldn't persuade himself that Simon was capable of such violence against Flick, however high he was. The fact that Danny had injected Angie and therefore had the wherewithal to do it also changed things.

Danny's apartment was in a harbour-side conversion of an old warehouse. He had one of a pair of penthouses with its own terrace, all concrete with wooden ceilings. Ottey thought that maybe Danny had bought it furnished, as it was in the brochure, and just moved straight in. There was a large mid-century-style L-shaped sofa in the main room. In a corner of the same room the kitchen looked barely used, with black work surfaces and a huge American-style double-doored aluminium fridge with an ice dispenser. There was also a wine fridge built into the units. It was filled with champagne. The lights over the island hung from long cables and had large bare bulbs with oversized dimmed yellow filaments in them. There was a large pink neon sign above a bar in a corner of the room saying 'Danny's Den' – hardly original, thought Ottey. In another corner was a deconstructed gym, which looked in as pristine a condition as the kitchen. It had weights, a punch bag suspended from the ceiling and an exercise bike. This immediately took Cross's interest.

'A Peloton bike. I've been thinking about getting one of these,' he said.

'What's so special about it?' Ottey asked.

'It connects you to a class by the internet. Gives you more competitive motivation, without actually having to be with the other people.'

'Sounds perfect for you.'

'I thought so too,' said Cross. He got on it and cycled for a little bit.

'Shall I search the bathroom?' she asked, trying to remind him politely why they were there.

'No,' he replied, getting off the bike. He walked over to the large fridge and opened it. It was filled mostly with ready meals. He looked around, then opened the salad drawer. In amongst the bags of leaves he found what he was looking for. Five bottles of diamorphine, together with hypodermics sealed in packs. The labels on the bottles said they'd been prescribed to Danny's mother.

They took his laptop, and having done a cursory search of the rest of the apartment, they left. If things progressed, a proper forensic search would be carried out at a later date.

Chapter 41

Cross came into the interview room with Ottey close behind. Danny was sitting next to his lawyer. Cross wondered whether criminal law wasn't this lawyer's usual field, as the air of disdain for the proceedings was stronger than the cloud of aftershave he seemed to inhabit. For some of the modern legal profession this was the equivalent of the Victorian ladies' floral posy used to ward off noxious smells. Lawyers, Cross had noticed, often drowned themselves in scent when they felt that their client's personal hygiene was likely to be suspect and they would have to endure sitting in a pervasive microclimate of pungent body odour for the following few hours. Cross had seen many a client conference called by a lawyer, in the middle of an interview, for the sole purpose of being able to get out of the room briefly for some fresh air.

It was also possible that this man was the family lawyer and simply didn't like Danny Stokes.

Cross placed his file on the table, making sure it was equidistant from two sides, then opened it. Inside was his list of questions and a police file on Danny. He looked up as if he was about to speak, but it was Ottey who started.

'So, let's begin with the obvious question. Why did you lie about your whereabouts on the night of June the seventeenth?'

'I didn't,' he replied.

'You said you were with your father,' she went on.

'I was,' he insisted.

'As you are aware, he says you weren't.'

'He gets confused. He's getting on and can't remember things,' Danny said.

'Oh yes he can, and he's adamant you weren't with him, so where were you?' she asked.

'I was at home. At my flat,' he said after a pause.

'Can anyone verify that?' she asked.

'No.'

'Nice pad,' she went on.

'Thanks.'

'Do you rent?'

'No. I own it,' he said.

'Really?' she replied, then made a show of looking through her notes.

'The leasehold is in your father's name,' she said.

He made no reply.

'So you don't own it,' she went on. 'In the same way that you don't own the laundry business. Your father does. Quite the success, your dad. Not that you would know. He seems to keep it to himself. Why do you lie about it all?'

Again, he made no reply.

'What's really interesting is how he lets you get away with it. What's that all about?' she asked.

Again, no reply. Cross was just staring at Danny who had noticed and looked like he was trying not to let it bother him. Finally he cracked.

'Do you have to do that?' he asked Cross, who didn't answer. 'Does he have to do that?' he asked Ottey.

'Do what?' she said.

'Stare at me like some lunatic.'

'He's not staring. Just observing. Do you get on with your dad?' she asked.

'I did before,' he scoffed.

'Before he refused to lie for you, you mean?' she asked.

Of course he didn't answer.

'What did you do at your flat, on your own, on the night of June the seventeenth?'

'Cooked for myself. Watched the TV.'

'Are you a good cook?' she asked.

'I like to think so.'

'Again, not really true, is it?' she asked teasingly, almost like a friend she was making fun of.

'What do you mean?'

'Well, your fridge is filled with ready meals. I mean, cooking isn't putting things in the microwave, is it? Why do you lie about everything?'

'I do cook. I've just been busy recently,' he said.

'What did you watch on TV that night?' Ottey asked.

'I don't know. I have no idea. I couldn't tell you what I watched last night. Some crap. There's nothing decent on the TV anymore. All quiz shows and reality shows with wannabes.'

Cross thought this was interesting. People who had committed a crime or had something to lie about normally perfected their story. They would have had the name of a TV programme or film up their sleeves to say they'd watched it. Danny hadn't bothered.

'Tell me about your mother,' Ottey asked.

'She was a good woman,' he said.

'Your father said you really stepped up when she was ill,' she said.

'Yep.'

'No need to lie about that,' she commented.

'No need to harass my client,' said the lawyer, speaking for the first time.

'Got up with her in the middle of the night, took her to the loo, managed her pain meds,' she said, looking at Danny for a reaction.

There was none.

'You told your dad you'd get rid of all her meds after she died.'

'Yep.'

'But you didn't.'

'Just hadn't got round to it. Like I said, I've been busy recently.'

'Then why were they in the salad compartment of your fridge?' Cross asked.

'You're supposed to keep them in the fridge. Everyone knows that,' Danny said.

'Only if you're going to use them,' Cross replied. 'Not if you intend destroying them. But you had no intention of destroying them, did you?'

'Tell me about Flick,' Ottey asked, changing the subject. This was part of their agreed plan that day: just to unsettle him with something, like the drugs, then not pursue it, knowing it would linger in the back of his mind.

'What about her?'

'How did she come to work for you?' she asked.

'You know all this,' he protested.

'Just answer the question,' she said firmly.

'She was at Hopewell.'

'The rehab facility?' she confirmed.

'That's right.'

'You take a lot of girls from there.' He made no comment. 'Why is that?' she asked.

'I'm on the board. I'm putting my money where my mouth is. Giving them a chance to get back on their feet,' he said.

'You *were* on the board. You took your father's place when he stepped down,' she said. 'Why aren't you on the board anymore?'

'No comment,' he replied.

'Isn't it because of the allegations made by a number of your former employees? Fourteen, in point of fact,' Ottey said.

'No comment.'

'And of those fourteen, twelve had come to you from Hopewell,' she said. 'Sexual harassment is the common theme.'

'No comment.'

'She didn't ask you a question. You don't have to say "no comment" if you're not asked a question,' Cross pointed out.

'You were given a police caution when you were fifteen. Do you want to talk about that?' Ottey asked.

'No comment,' came the reply.

'You exposed yourself to your father's secretary at work. Is that correct?' she went on.

'No comment.'

'What puzzled me was that she'd been his secretary for twelve years,' Ottey said. 'Known you since you were a baby.

Why didn't she just put it down to a case of excess teenage testosterone? Not that I'm excusing it. She went to the police. Then I read that it was one of dozens of such instances. You were even discovered pleasuring yourself in the cubicle next to her in the ladies' lavatory. She felt she had to leave your father's employ after all those years. What did your dad say to you?'

'No comment.'

'And here you are, thirty-five years later, accused of doing pretty much the same thing,' she observed.

'Do you actually have a question for my client?' asked the lawyer.

'I think I've asked several, haven't I, DS Cross?' she said.

'Twenty-four, in point of fact,' Cross replied, without even having to consult his notes.

'These women are all addicts,' Danny began.

'Recovering addicts,' Cross corrected him.

'Whatever. They're not to be trusted. It's all lies,' said Danny.

'Interesting that someone who makes out that he has these women's best interests at heart, giving them a second chance to "get back on their feet", as I think you put it, should dismiss them in exactly the kind of judgemental way he's supposed to be protecting them from,' said Cross.

'And that's what really pisses me off. I have given them a chance and this is how they repay me,' he said.

'Were you expecting some form of repayment?' asked Cross.

'Not as such.'

'In kind then,' said Cross.

'I didn't say that. You're twisting my words.'

'You expected them to repay you by granting you sexual favours,' Cross went on.

'No comment.'

'But they all say the same thing. Give exactly the same accounts of what you did,' Ottey pointed out.

'Exactly. It's rehearsed. Scripted. I've been saying this all along. It's one big scripted lie,' Danny said.

'Possibly,' replied Ottey. 'Or it's a pattern. A pattern of abuse from a small man who finds it impossible to get sexual satisfaction from women in a normal way and so subjects them to this abuse. Because that's the only way you get off, isn't it? To be the dominant one with a reluctant partner. Need to know they're powerless, because that's what they are, aren't they? In danger of losing their jobs if they don't go along with it or if they tell anyone. And who would believe them? It's perfect for a predator such as yourself. A steady supply of vulnerable women under the pretext of a charitable act. Is that about right?'

'I didn't abuse any of them. With one of them maybe I misread the signals and I'm sorry for that,' he said.

'I can understand that. Like you said, they're grateful and maybe give out the wrong signals, as you put it,' said Ottey.

'Exactly.' He sounded relieved that finally someone understood him.

'I can see that.' Ottey turned to Cross. 'It's like he's caught in the emotional crossfire. He's collateral damage.'

'Then why sack them all?' Cross asked.

'Because they started lying,' said Ottey, before Danny had a chance. 'These girls will do anything to get what they want. Money, affection, drugs – I bet they asked you for drugs.'

'They did!' Danny replied. 'They begged me. I tried to persuade them not to.'

'Is that what Flick did the night she died? Begged you for a fix?' Ottey said.

'No!' Danny protested.

Chapter 42

They had found no forensic trace of Danny in Flick's flat which meant he couldn't be placed at the scene. This didn't mean he wasn't there, just that they couldn't prove it. Cross thought they should give him a few hours to stew then go in and ask him about injecting Angie with the diamorphine – something he currently wasn't aware they knew. They would often do this: come up against a brick wall in their questioning and leave the suspect under the impression that he or she was winning the battle against his or her interrogators. They would then go back in and unsettle the suspect with further evidence. Carson was also fairly sure that with the evidence they had – even though entirely circumstantial – they would be able to get an extension from a judge to keep Danny in custody for another forty-eight hours.

Cross received a text from the café owner opposite the dry cleaner's saying that Angie was in again. He and Mackenzie set off. The aim of this visit was probably going to be as difficult to achieve as the last, when they persuaded her to talk about Danny Stokes. This time their task was to try and get Angie some help with her addiction, so that if the Stokes case came to trial she would be a more reliable witness. Cross explained all of this to Mackenzie in the car. For a moment she had thought they might be doing it for an altruistic reason, but then she remembered firstly that they were the police and secondly that she wasn't entirely sure it was in Cross's nature to do something like that.

When they got to the café, Angie was eating some scrambled eggs and had a mug of tea.

'Thanks,' she said.

'What for?' asked Mackenzie.

'He told the bloke he'd pay again.'

'Angie, do you want to get clean?' Cross asked as he sat down opposite her.

Angie thought about this for a moment.

'Why?' she asked suspiciously.

'Because I think we can help you. But only if you want us to,' said Cross.

This wasn't so much Cross going along with the view that an addict had to want to get clean before they could benefit from any kind of rehab programme, but because her testimony would be undermined if, under cross-examination at trial, she said that she went along to rehab because the police forced her to.

After a long, protracted conversation, in which Mackenzie eventually took the lead, Angie agreed to go with them. She didn't know where, and nor did Mackenzie for that matter.

'You've brought someone with you who you'd like me to see, I assume,' said Sutton in his office as Cross refused the offer of a seat. Mackenzie and Angie were sitting in the outer office under the watchful gaze of Miss Coogan.

'I have. Angie. A friend of Flick's,' Cross replied.

'The thing is, Sergeant, it doesn't actually work this way. She'll need a GP referral.' Sutton smiled, as if to sweeten the message.

'She doesn't actually have a doctor,' Cross replied, repeating 'actually' with deliberate emphasis.

Sutton thought for a moment.

'Is this relevant to Flick's case?'

'I'm a detective, not a social worker, so it is, yes,' Cross pointed out, echoing Carson's words.

'Of course. Why don't you tell me the details?'

Cross then briefed him on Angie's situation. Her trouble with Stokes. His drugging her, sacking her and how she was basically back on the streets. Sutton listened with his hands in front of his face, fingertip to fingertip, eyes gazing at Cross over this judgemental pyramid.

'She turns up at her former place of employment regularly to harangue her former boss for his treatment of her. He has on occasion called the police, and now that he has been arrested on suspicion of murder…' Cross said.

'You've arrested him?' asked Sutton. 'You could've led with that. Do you think he did it?'

'I don't think anything. But the evidence would suggest it's a possibility.'

'Why?'

'When he drugged Angie, he used diamorphine,' said Cross.

Sutton digested this for a moment.

'But where on earth did he get it from?' he asked slowly.

'His mother died from cancer last year. The drugs had been prescribed to her.'

'So do you think he killed her accidentally?'

'I have no idea.'

'Or was it to stop the case going to the tribunal?'

'Again, I have no idea.'

Sutton shook his head slowly. 'Son of a bitch,' he muttered. He looked back up decisively. 'Well, these are exceptional circumstances, so leave... Angie, was it?... with me and I'll make the necessary arrangements for a residential facility.' Sutton sounded as if he was granting the world a favour of extraordinary generosity. 'I think it's what Flick would have expected of me, which gives me some comfort.'

Cross got up and turned to leave without a word.

They went into the waiting room, where Mackenzie and Angie sat, each boasting the obligatory visitor's badge as furnished them by Diana.

'Angie, this is Dr Sutton. He's a psychotherapist who specialises in addiction and substance abuse,' said Cross.

'As well as bereavement and grief,' Sutton added unnecessarily.

'He will get you into the most suitable establishment,' Cross went on.

She looked unsure.

'He was Flick's doctor,' Mackenzie said, which seemed to reassure her. 'We'll be in touch just as soon as we know where you are.'

Sutton took Angie into his office. She gave Mackenzie one final look, which seemed to be asking for further reassurance. Mackenzie supplied it with a comforting smile. She and Cross then turned to leave.

'Wait!' came the formidable command from behind them.

They turned to see Diana standing behind her desk with one arm outstretched.

'Passes,' she said.

They both took them off, handed them back and looked on as she checked her watch and entered the exact time in the appropriate slot in her visitors' book.

Chapter 43

'So we know he has the means – the diamorphine. We know he has form – Angie. But we can't place him at the scene although he has no alibi,' said Carson to Ottey and Cross in his office.

'That's the long and the short of it,' replied Ottey.

'George?' Carson asked.

'That is an accurate summary of our position,' said Cross.

'But we're sure he's our man?' asked Carson.

Cross sighed and needed to say no more.

'Well, you'd better see if you can get him to crack with what we have,' said Carson.

They went back into the interview room. Danny was more animated than before; angry at his incarceration. Was this genuine because he was innocent or just more posturing? Cross wasn't sure.

'Why did you keep your mother's medication?' Cross began.

'Like I said, I was going to destroy it,' Danny replied.

'But you didn't.'

'No.'

'And you kept it in the fridge,' Cross went on.

'Again. I thought that's what you did.'

'If you intended it for use, then yes, perhaps,' said Cross.

Danny said nothing.

'And you not only intended to use it illicitly, you actually did,' said Cross.

'I don't know what you're talking about.'

'I'm talking about Angie,' replied Cross, looking him straight in the eye.

Danny looked worried for a moment.

'She's a junkie. You can't believe a word she says,' he scoffed.

'And whose fault is that?' asked Ottey.

'Certainly not mine. She was clean when she came to me, then six months later she was using again.'

'And why do you think that was?' Ottey asked.

'I have no idea. I don't know how these people behave or think,' he said.

'Did you ask her to bring some laundry to your flat in February of this year?' Cross asked.

'I might've done. I don't remember,' Danny replied.

'Really? Do lots of your employees run errands for you like that?' Cross asked.

'Yes. Occasionally.'

'Do you sleep with all of them?' Cross asked.

'You what?' said Danny, in an attempt at disbelief.

'You heard him,' said Ottey.

'No, I don't,' replied Danny.

'Despite all the claims against you,' said Cross.

'Like I said; they're all fabrications.'

'Then let's talk about one specifically. Angie,' said Cross.

'What about her?'

'Did you have sex with her?' said Cross.

'No,' came the terse reply.

'Well, she says you did,' said Cross.

'And whose word are you or any jury in this country going to take?'

'What has a jury got to do with any of this, Mr Stokes?' asked Cross, a little surprised.

Danny made no reply as his solicitor shot him a look.

'Why would you think a jury would be asked to believe anything either of you said? I'm curious,' Cross went on.

'It's a turn of phrase,' said Danny.

'An interesting choice in the circumstances,' Cross observed. 'Angie maintains you drugged her at the apartment and then proceeded to have sex with her.'

'I did no such thing. She's making it up.'

'So, what I have difficulty in understanding here, is the logic of it all. She said you drugged her with,' Cross checked his notes in his file, 'the "real stuff". Diamorphine, in point of fact. How would she know you had your mother's diamorphine?'

'I don't know.'

'Did you tell her? Did you say in passing, "Oh here's a thing. I have my late mother's morphine which I have to destroy, but why don't you have some?" A little unwise, though, with a recovering addict. Because, of course, she was still in recovery at this point,' said Cross.

'She must've looked in the fridge,' said Danny.

'All right, so let's go back a couple of steps. You asked her into the flat?' said Cross.

'Yes.'

'Why?' asked Cross.

'I don't know. Probably to offer her a glass of water.'

'Which was why she was in the fridge,' said Cross, as if it now made complete sense to him and had cleared this issue up.

'Yes!' said Danny, taken in a little.

'So why was she looking in the salad drawer, which is where you kept the drugs and so was the only place she could've seen them in the fridge? Did you tell her that was where she'd find the drugs or do you keep your water in the salad drawer?' asked Cross.

'No comment.'

'You drugged Angie so you could then take advantage of her,' Cross said. 'You even injected her yourself. The same drug which someone injected into Flick and killed her. You have a litany of allegations of sexual harassment hanging over you. Going back to your own question – what do you think a jury is going to believe if that set of circumstances is put in front of them?'

'You said it yourself, Sergeant. It's all circumstantial. You cannot place him at the scene and you have no definitive proof whatsoever,' said Danny's solicitor.

'Ah yes, but funny things, juries. Unpredictable, don't you find?' said Cross.

'I'd like to speak with my client,' replied the lawyer.

Chapter 44

The next day, with Danny safely in custody and everyone fairly sure they had their man, Cross now did something that was so counterintuitive it always drove his colleagues crazy. Whenever they reached a point in a case like this – namely a suspect with no alibi, but with all the available evidence pointing in his direction and who was denying the charge – Cross would do his best to find an alibi for them. That is to say he would try and determine if the suspect had a legitimate alibi that they couldn't, as yet, prove.

Cross did this because, on the one hand, if they weren't guilty of the crime, it was important to rule them out so that the real culprit could be found and apprehended, but also because, in trying to find an alibi, Cross would often come across a crucial piece of evidence confirming the suspect's guilt. Many a junior officer had complained when asked to do this, saying their job was to find evidence against the suspect, surely. No, Cross would reply. Their job was to find out who committed the crime, and if it involved excluding someone they 'thought' was guilty, that in itself was progress.

Those who took his advice on board benefitted hugely in their career from this single observation. The ones who didn't, wasted a lot of their time trying to find evidence to fit the suspect, rather than the other way round, and ended up either without a charge in the first place, or with the case falling apart in court. This meant that, either way, the real culprit was still out there months later.

Mackenzie had been tasked with looking through Danny's social media, along with his bank and credit card statements. Another member of the team was trying to track his mobile phone pinging off any masts on the night in question. Catherine in CCTV was now asked to check his building's CCTV. It had cameras at the entrance, covering the corridors and in the lifts. The problem was that the footage was erased every month and so no footage existed of the night Flick died. This meant she had to try and piece together his movements from the dry cleaner's to wherever he was going. She would have to find and look at all the street cameras and any on buildings in the surrounding area. Cross told her to work on the assumption that Danny was telling the truth. This would save her time.

While they interviewed Danny, uniform had returned to the area surrounding Flick's flat and were canvassing the neighbours again. They wanted to see if anyone could place him at the scene. This time, the two uniformed officers had a photograph of Danny Stokes and were trying to ascertain whether he'd been seen in the vicinity of Flick's flat at all. It was mostly inconclusive until one of them went into the minimarket. The shop was still clad in scaffolding with a couple of butt-crack-exposing builders on the roof. The woman behind the counter, Sunetra, who owned the shop with her husband, studied the photograph. Yes, he had gone to Flick's flat on the day of her death. She was sure of it. The curious thing, though, was that it was the wrong Stokes. The photograph was of Danny with his father Gerry. She had picked out the father.

Cross phoned the shop to make sure she hadn't made a mistake. But she said she was sure. During the earlier canvass she'd mentioned to a uniformed officer that a man had been to the flat on the day of the murder. Cross checked and found that uniform had recorded Sunetra as saying she'd seen the boyfriend go into the flat. Uniform had made a mistake, as a further call to her led to her confirming she'd said no such thing.

'How could a mistake like this have happened?' Cross asked Ottey.

'Don't fret, George. It would've surfaced eventually. I mean it has – we're discussing it now,' she said.

'It's the principle, and it's our job to educate new officers,' said Cross, as it had been a rookie who'd made this mistake.

The hapless young man was called up to Carson's office. Cross was instructed to go easy on him because he was a new recruit.

'I assumed it was the boyfriend because she'd just been talking about him sleeping in her doorway,' he said, checking his notebook.

'What does your notebook say?' Ottey asked.

'"Victim's bf slept in doorway." Then, I'm not sure what that is, but then – "seen going to the flat",' he said.

'Could it be "man"?' Cross asked.

The PC looked at it again. 'Yes,' he replied. 'I just assumed it was the same man.'

'Two lessons to be learnt here. One – write legibly.

"Man seen going to flat" is quite different to "bf slept in doorway... seen going into flat". Secondly, never make assumptions. We deal in facts. The evidence in front of us. Don't make assumptions about those facts. Facts back up facts – not assumptions, not theories, not hypotheses. Assumptions lead to a huge waste of time in investigations. So don't make them.'

With that Cross left, followed by Ottey.

Carson looked at the PC. 'You'd do well to remember what DS Cross just told you,' he said – the man who, on a daily basis, made more assumptions than the entire department put together.

Chapter 45

Gerry Stokes was manning the operation when they got to the dry cleaner's. No longer huddled over his workstation like a Dickensian haberdasher, he was serving a customer when Cross and Ottey arrived. He was dressed differently, wearing the trousers and waistcoat of a three-piece suit and a smart shirt and tie – but still with the green editor's visor. The customer he was dealing with was chatting happily away to him, long after she'd been given her dry cleaning. Gerry kept smiling indulgently at the customer and nodding his head understandingly, with the occasional apologetic glance towards the waiting detectives. Finally she left and Cross and Ottey walked over.

'Sergeants, good afternoon,' he said cheerily.

Cross thought he looked different. He was standing taller. He appeared to be happier, which struck Cross as slightly odd, bearing in mind the man's son was in police custody on suspicion of murder. Perhaps he was just fulfilled. Was it because he was back to doing what he loved – running his business? Or was it simply the relief of his son not being there, parading around?

Gerry smiled ruefully when told of Sunetra's identifying him on the day of Flick's death.

'I should have mentioned this earlier,' he said.

'Yes. You should've,' agreed Ottey.

'I just thought it might confuse things.'

'Well, it certainly has us confused now. So perhaps you'd like to clear it up for us at the MCU.'

'I don't think that'll be necessary,' he said.

'Really?' Ottey replied.

'I was there that day in a last-ditch attempt to see if we could settle the wretched tribunal business once and for all.'

'Someone certainly did that,' said Cross. 'Very much finished it, once and for all.'

'How were you going to achieve that? Offer her more money?' Ottey asked.

'No, no, Sergeant. Please don't confuse me with my son. I offered her restitution, obviously, and I promised that Danny would make a public apology. It wouldn't be brushed under the carpet. He would have to acknowledge his wrongs. That the other girls who had been willing to join her in the action would be compensated and, where possible, offered employment. I also guaranteed that Danny would never behave in such a way again.'

'How could you guarantee that?' asked Cross.

'By making sure he wasn't in a position to do so,' Gerry replied.

'Meaning?' Cross persisted.

'I was going to take him out of the front-of-house part of the business. He would manage my other commercial interests, but from behind a desk. Mostly property where he would have no contact with vulnerable young women. I was also going to make arrangements for the laundry to be put in trust for Hopewell House, as a kind of employment halfway-house for their clients, when they first leave rehab. Male or female,' he said proudly.

'Was he happy with that?' Ottey asked.

'No, the truth is he was furious, and, in saying that, I'm well aware that it could look like I'm giving you motive, but I do so in the confidence that he didn't kill Flick.'

'Confidence is one thing. Proof is another,' Cross commented.

'He doesn't have it in him, Sergeant,' Gerry said.

'Maybe he doesn't. Do you?' Cross asked.

'I didn't kill her. She liked me and I liked her. I'd go as far as to say she was fond of me, in an avuncular sort of way. I think she also felt a little sorry for me. The way Danny behaved – she knew it was difficult for me.'

'Why do you let him get away with it?' Ottey asked.

'Danny has been through quite a lot. He's adopted and has a lot of emotional issues tied up with all of that. In his case rejection, an inability to form long-lasting relationships. I'm not excusing him. I don't think he helps himself at all. It's why we got involved in Hopewell, Betty and I. Danny's birth mother was a drug addict and put him up for adoption. Betty had more control of him but even she struggled.'

Cross noticed that lots of the workers had stopped and were listening to Gerry. This was news to them, obviously.

'So maybe I do make excuses for him because I know it hasn't been easy for him. But we reached the point with Flick and the others where it had to stop,' Gerry said.

'The issue here, Mr Stokes, is that we have a witness placing you at Flick's flat the night of her death,' said Cross.

'Ah, okay. Well, I didn't kill her and I have someone who can actually prove that.'

'Who?' asked Ottey.

'Flick,' he replied.

'I beg your pardon?' said Ottey.

'She was smart, worldly-wise, that girl. She was pleased to see me. After all, she asked me into the flat. But she insisted on recording the entire meeting on her phone. Do you have her phone?' he asked.

'We do,' Ottey answered. 'It's being examined at the moment.'

'Well, it's in there somewhere. The entire meeting, and I don't believe she switched it off before I left.'

On her way out Ottey saw Karen who waved half-heartedly, almost embarrassed. But it was enough for Ottey to go over. She handed Karen a card.

'This has my mobile number on it. Call me if you want.'

'Do you think he did it? Killed Flick?' She sounded frightened.

'I don't know as yet. But, Karen, I think you have something you want to tell us. So when you're ready, give me a call. Okay?'

Chapter 46

Going through someone's smartphone when you don't know what you're looking for could take weeks, Cross had discovered. There was so much data, so many photos, emails, texts, call records, browser records. But if you knew what you were looking for, it could be found in minutes, so by the time they were back at the MCU the voice memo recording of the meeting on Flick's phone had been tracked down. They sat in the office and listened. It was always odd hearing a deceased victim's voice for the first time. Disconcerting but also incentivising at the same time.

'I'm recording this, do you mind, Gerry?' Flick asked. Her voice was lighter than Ottey had expected.

'No, of course I don't. Is that a bruise? On your forehead?'

'Yes. I tripped over one of Daisy's toys. I fell awkwardly because I had her in my arms,' Flick replied.

'It looks painful. Have you had it looked at?'

'No. Haven't had time. I think it looks worse than it is. Would you like a coffee?'

'That would be lovely, thank you.' She could then be heard filling the kettle and getting out a couple of cups.

'If you're here to persuade me to drop my claim you're wasting your time,' she said nervously.

'I am, of course, and you knew that when you let me in. I just hope maybe you'll listen to me for a little and if I don't change your mind, know that you will have my full support at the tribunal.'

'Okay, but I'm not promising anything,' she replied as an invitation for him to continue.

'Well, I am, dear. I intend making full restitution to all the girls affected and where possible offer them employment.'

'They won't come back and work for Danny. No way.'

'He won't be there anymore. I'm going to move him to our head office, well out of the way. He won't be allowed back at the laundry. I'll be running that now. He will also make a full public apology and acknowledgement of his behaviour and undertake some form of therapy.'

'That could lead to the police making charges, though, couldn't it?'

'Quite possibly.'

'Then why would Danny agree to it?'

'Because he won't have a job nor a place to live if he doesn't.'

'Really?'

'Absolutely. On my honour.'

She thought about this for a moment then something discomfited her.

'I still find it hard to believe you didn't know, Gerry,' Flick said. There was a pause.

'He's my son, Flick. Maybe I didn't want to accept it.'

'And look where that's got us. I'm sorry. I'm very grateful for what you're trying to do,' Flick went on.

'You shouldn't be grateful. None of this should have happened and of course I have to take some responsibility.'

'You looked the other way,' Flick said. He didn't answer. 'You have no idea what it's like going to work feeling sick to the stomach. Not knowing what he might do that day. And the worst part was that we didn't have a choice, with our history. We were trapped.'

'I know.'

'I don't think you do, Mr Stokes. We were terrified of that man. Your son. Absolutely terrified. Some of the things he did and said. It wasn't right.' There was the sound of a young child stirring over a baby monitor.

'That's Daisy.'

'Oh, I'm glad she's woken up. I've brought something for her.'

The meeting continued pretty much exactly as Gerry had described it. Flick became more warm and friendly, having made her feelings clear. They drank their coffee. He could be heard playing with Daisy. During the meeting everything he'd laid out to them that afternoon was, indeed, said. At the end of the meeting, Flick thanked him and said that he'd given her a lot to think about and could she call him the next day? He was delighted.

To Cross it all sounded genuine. It didn't sound like she was making an excuse for it or making up a story. What it did mean, though, was that the bruise had occurred before the overdose and could be ruled out. Whoever killed her hadn't struck her in order to administer the morphine, which made things a little more complicated. It also confirmed that Gerry Stokes had told them the complete truth.

It was strange for Ottey to hear Flick's voice. Evidence of the deceased always affected her in this way. It touched her emotionally to hear the victim alive. Cross had no such feelings. He just listened to it factually, impersonally, trying to glean as much information as possible from it.

They went back into the interview room. Danny Stokes now had the look of someone who was tired and worried. Cross felt that this wasn't a sign of guilt, by any means. In circumstances like these, suspects realised that the situation wasn't just going to go away, guilty or not, and it had a grounding effect on them that could almost be heard. Cross organised his files carefully on the interview desk, as Ottey set up her laptop. They then played the entirety of his father's meeting with Flick, all twenty-five minutes of it, without interruption or comment. When it got to the end the two detectives said nothing. Danny looked up expectantly, waiting for a question. None was forthcoming. Danny caved first.

'What?' he said.

'Your father was going to sack you from the laundry business,' Cross said. There was no response. 'Compel you to make a full, public admission.'

'And put you behind a desk at head office where you could hopefully do no more damage,' Ottey added.

There was a slight scoff from Danny which seemed to imply 'as if'.

'Well, it was either that or no job at all and no penthouse flat. Or did I misunderstand?' Ottey asked. 'Not to mention the possibility of the police taking an interest.'

Danny made no reply but the shifting in his seat acknowledged the uncomfortable truth of it all.

Ottey then replayed the part of the conversation where Flick specifically said how frightened she was of Danny and what he might do. Danny said nothing. Then Cross spoke up.

'This tape provides us with motive and evidence that Flick perceived you as a threat.'

'At the risk of repeating myself, you cannot place him at the scene,' said the lawyer.

'Not as yet, no,' said Cross. 'But that isn't always necessary. Murderers have become much more adept at leaving no tracks forensically these days. So judges often take a view on whether they have to be placed at the scene for a guilty verdict. Other evidence comes into play, and the evidence we have seems to be becoming more and more compelling as we go on.'

'You can't prove I was there, because I wasn't, and that's not going to change,' said Danny.

'As my colleague says, it's possible we have enough as it is,' said Ottey. 'Perhaps now is the time to come clean and hope the judge may look favourably on that when it comes to sentencing.'

For the first time Cross thought that Danny looked genuinely concerned.

'I'd like to speak to my lawyer,' he said.

Chapter 47

'The CPS think we have enough to charge him, and now he wants to speak to his lawyer, which is always a good sign,' said Carson.

'He just needed a break. It doesn't mean a thing,' said Cross.

Carson sighed. Why did Cross always take the opposite view?

'Charge him,' he instructed them.

'We have a few more hours,' said Cross. 'What's the rush?'

'Why wait?' Carson responded.

'There's a huge difference between thinking that someone's guilty and conclusively being able to prove it,' Cross retorted.

'Well, I'm willing to take my chances with a jury on this one,' said Carson, but immediately regretted it. 'I know, George. There's no need for another lecture on the pitfalls of relying on a jury reaching the correct verdict. Although that is their very purpose.'

'And our job is to give them as much help as possible to come to that – correct – verdict,' said Cross, by way of a parting shot, as he left the office.

Carson looked at Ottey for some support.

'What is it you told me when you partnered me with him?' she asked mischievously.

'"Best conviction rate in the force", I know. It doesn't make him any less irritating, though.'

Cross was studying a recording of his interview with Stokes when Ottey walked straight into his office; something he truly hated. It invariably startled him, interrupted him in what he was doing and annoyed him. He'd made it abundantly clear that admission to his office was contingent on a firm, but polite, knock.

'You should hear this,' she said, putting her laptop on his desk. For a second his irritation was assuaged, as he thought she must have had some sort of breakthrough in the case. But it was an interview on local radio with someone who sounded unmistakably like Alice Mackenzie. She was talking about the late DCI Esther Moffatt, who had died with no known relatives and few friends. She was appealing for relations to come to the funeral in a week's time, having persuaded the funeral home to delay to give her time. It appeared that Mackenzie's Facebook posting, liberally shared by her friends, had gained traction and media attention. Local radio had been in touch. But sadly no relatives had made contact, as yet.

'Isn't it great? Fab little local news story,' Ottey said.

'Ask her to come and see me when she's back,' was all he said, inexplicably annoyed that he was sure he'd heard the name of Stephen's church being the venue for the funeral. After Ottey left he stopped to think for a moment. Why was he annoyed by Stephen's church being used? But he couldn't come up with an answer.

Half an hour later there was a knock at the door and Mackenzie appeared, having enjoyed a fair amount of ribbing and praise as she walked through the department.

'You wanted to see me?' she said to Cross.

'I still do,' he said instinctively correcting her errant tense. But he was prevented going any further by Ottey.

'It's the chief constable's office on the phone,' she announced.

'Okay, put him through,' replied Cross.

'It's for Alice,' said Ottey.

'Really? Oh shit,' muttered Mackenzie, as she quickly left the office to take the call.

Chapter 48

Cross was coming into work early every day now. He often did this when a case gathered pace. He liked the peace and quiet of the empty office. So he was surprised to find Mackenzie and Catherine waiting for him, the next morning, looking miserably businesslike.

'I've now managed to follow Danny the night of the murder,' Catherine said. 'He left the dry cleaner's just after seven in his car. Drove straight home. Drove into the underground car park of his flats and didn't emerge till the next morning just before eight. I got the CCTV footage from the building opposite.'

According to Mackenzie, once home he'd ordered in a pizza. She found it on his credit card and then got the exact time from the delivery company. It was delivered to his flat shortly after nine thirty that night. The tech guy charged with tracking his phone had drawn a blank, but they had enough.

Danny was not their man.

Carson was as disappointed as anyone else, but Ottey noticed that in these situations he always seemed to imply that Cross was to blame, although all Cross had done was find the truth. It was a paradox. She found herself wondering at times whether Carson was interested in the truth at all. His attitude, of course, went straight over Cross's head.

Danny's behaviour as he was released interested Ottey. He wasn't at all celebratory or crowing, which she thought was a little out of character. Maybe the seriousness of the situation had finally got to him. She often thought that people, when innocent of the crime they'd been charged with, had sufficient time in their cell to dwell on whether the British justice system was as good as it was cracked up to be. Whether they thought they could, on the purported evidence of the police, be convicted of a crime they hadn't committed. She was sure that lots of people, when released from the custody suite like this, might have second thoughts about the efficiency of the justice system, because it had suddenly felt like it could be a fifty-fifty situation if it went to court – despite their innocence.

Mackenzie was sitting at her desk like a sulky adolescent when Ottey came back into the open area. 'I can't believe we had to let him go.'

'It's what we do when people haven't done anything wrong,' Ottey replied.

'That man has done plenty wrong and now that Flick is dead he gets away with it.'

Ottey looked over at Cross's office. It was empty. 'Where's George?' she asked.

'I don't know,' said Mackenzie.

Ottey checked her watch. When she saw how long it had been since Danny's release she knew exactly where Cross would be. Where he always went after someone had been released, if he still thought them of interest in a case – on the back staircase to watch them leave the building and observe their behaviour.

'We don't have to give up on nailing Stokes, Alice. In fact we shouldn't,' said Ottey.

'But we've given him an alibi.'

'Which is our job, because he didn't kill Flick. But he's done enough to those girls to be put behind bars for a good stretch. We just need to get the evidence.'

Four days later the sight that presented itself to Ottey and Cross, when they arrived at the church for Esther Moffatt's funeral, silenced them both. There were dozens and dozens of police officers, male and female, of all ranks, all in uniform and wearing white gloves. Groups stood around chatting quietly. Cross secretly loved the opportunities to wear uniform when they presented themselves. He missed wearing it as a detective.

There were also hundreds of members of the public gathered, attracted by the local news story. A local TV camera crew stood at a respectful distance, picking up shots when they could. Hundreds of feet crushing wet, fallen leaves created that sweet, decaying smell of autumnal rot, which somehow seemed appropriate for such an occasion.

'This is incredible,' remarked Ottey.

'It certainly is impressive,' said Cross.

The reason for the huge police presence, with senior detectives from all parts of the Avon and Somerset police force getting out their old uniforms and dusting them off, was that the chief constable's office had become involved in Esther Moffatt's funeral. That was why he'd called the previous week. He had been alerted to the radio interview with Mackenzie and knew immediately who they were referring to. It turned out that Moffatt had been one of his training officers when he was a young constable and he remembered her with affectionate admiration. He was keen that the police recognised her service, and of course as soon as he became involved it became a bit of a three-line whip. Everyone who was available was going to attend.

Cross had been reluctantly conscripted to give an address at the service, something that had kept him awake at night. This was a man who couldn't bring himself to address a staff meeting of twenty during an investigation. The idea of addressing a congregation – however small – from a lectern, terrified him. He spent hours researching Moffatt's life and career with Mackenzie.

He then came up with an inspired plan. He called the Chief – it irritated the hell out of other officers that he had a direct line to the Chief, who had taken quite a shine to his star, if a little bizarre, detective. Cross suggested that the Chief make the address at the funeral, as he'd worked alongside DCI Moffatt, so it would not only be more personal but would give the whole occasion more authority. The public would be impressed that the police looked after their own in this way, and respect for the service Esther had given would be acknowledged right at the top of the force. What was more, Cross had added, he'd already written a eulogy which the Chief could use. The Chief thought it was a great idea, so Cross sent him his address to use as a basis. The Chief, together with his staff presumably, rewrote it and, much to Cross's surprise, sent it back to him for his comments. Cross thought it had become a little sentimental, but realised that it wasn't for him to judge. He did, however, make several syntactical and grammatical corrections which he sent back.

Esther Moffatt had a police guard and police pallbearers. Her coffin was draped in a Union Flag, together with her hat and badge. There was also a large photograph of her as a young policewoman in uniform on an easel alongside. The church was rammed. The service, moving. Cross was impressed with Stephen's personable touch; he really was skilled. It was something Cross had never witnessed before as he hadn't been to a service in the church; he just practised the organ there. The Chief made his address, which Cross thought he delivered well. The whole thing was perfect – except for the organ playing, during which Ottey noticed Cross constantly wincing.

She leant over and whispered, 'You could've played, which would've been really nice.'

He ignored her.

Among all the police officers attending there was an underlying sense of gratification that someone who had served so long ago, before some of them had even been born, should be afforded such a public display of thanks and respect.

There was a tea laid on in the church hall afterwards – paid for out of the Chief's discretionary fund. He and Mackenzie did a couple of interviews together, including one for local television news. He then came over to Cross and thanked him for the address.

'I understand you were with her all night. The night she passed. Till she died. Talking to her,' the Chief said.

'I was.'

'That's really touching, George. You didn't know her as an officer?' the Chief went on.

'I did not.'

'Well, what a wonderful thing to have done. I understand she had no family we know of.'

'Correct,' Cross answered.

The Chief then turned to include Mackenzie in the conversation. 'Congratulations to both of you. I'm extremely proud of your thoughtfulness and humanity. You should be very proud of them,' he said to Carson who, he assumed correctly from his epaulettes, was their boss.

'Oh I am, sir,' replied Carson, like an overeager puppy grateful for a treat that his owner had just popped in his mouth.

The Chief turned and walked away.

'DCI Carson,' Carson said, name-checking himself to the Chief's back to make sure the great man knew who he was and in the hope that some of the kudos his junior officers had achieved might rub off on him.

Ottey came over to Cross. 'I'm going to take Raymond home,' she said.

'Is he here?' Cross asked.

'Seriously?' Ottey asked.

'He wasn't sure whether he was coming,' Cross said, justifying his ignorance of his father's social diary. He went with Ottey and found him.

Raymond's eyes were red-rimmed. 'That was very moving,' he said.

'If you say so,' Cross replied, not because he doubted his father but because he had no idea of the emotional temperature of the service they'd just attended.

'She would've been so happy and surprised,' Raymond went on.

'I'm very happy you afforded me the opportunity to make her acquaintance,' said Cross.

'So am I,' his father replied.

'How's the flat?'

'All good, thank you. Still as tidy and uncluttered as last week. You can judge for yourself at dinner tomorrow,' Raymond said, smiling.

'Indeed I can.'

'DS Cross?' said a voice behind him which Cross didn't recognise. He turned to see a man in his late sixties, he guessed, with a thick mane of grey hair. He had a military bearing about him; the way he stood, the neatness of his suit and shirt.

'DCI Mike Brady, retired.' He held out his hand. Cross ignored it and waited for the man to continue.

'I understand Benedict Sutton was the victim's therapist in your current case.'

'That's correct. Do you know him?'

'We received information about him a few years ago which meant we looked into him briefly. I thought it might be of interest to you.'

'What kind of information?'

'It turns out he has an incredibly high mortality rate with his patients; way above the norm.'

'Surely that comes with the territory. He's dealing with drug abuse,' Cross answered.

'That's exactly what he said. But if you compare his patient suicide rate to other professionals in his field – it's at least twenty-six per cent higher.' Cross thought about this for a moment. It was clearly of some material interest.

'And what did you find out through your investigation?'

'Nothing much. I didn't like him, though. There was something about him. I just thought you should know.'

'Why would your not liking him have any bearing on my case?'

'What I meant was the high mortality rate. That might have a bearing, might it not?' said the old cop, a little irritated.

'Where did this information come from?' asked Cross.

'A concerned colleague.'

'Dr Marcus Todd?'

'Yes that's right.'

Cross wasn't sure whether this tainted the value of the information or not. But he made a note of it all the same. Todd definitely warranted another visit as Cross was sure he had more to say about Sutton.

Chapter 49

'It's a puzzle,' said Carson, a few days later.

A meeting had been convened of the small team working Flick's case. Carson was privately really annoyed. Cross had brought a case to them which seemed to have been initially resolved by the coroner, and here they were, weeks later, at a dead end with an unsolved case on their books.

'So we're convinced we've trawled through all of the victim's contacts and come up with nothing. Yet we're as convinced that it had to be someone she knew...' he said.

'Are we at a point where we should be thinking it could be someone she didn't know, but who she thought had a legitimate reason to let into her flat?' asked Mackenzie.

Cross had thought this was interesting. He had been pushing the theory that it had to be someone she knew, but this was definitely worth discussing.

'It's a perfectly valid question, and one we should deal with before dismissing it completely out of hand,' he began. 'I think the problem is the motive. Why would someone she didn't know want to gain access to her to kill her?'

'What if someone paid them to do it?' Mackenzie continued.

'I think the idea of a third party hiring someone to kill a recovering addict, single mother, with no criminal connections or past record seems a little far-fetched,' said Ottey. 'The fact that we don't have any answers at the moment doesn't mean we should start scraping the barrel. Sorry, Alice.'

'Oh, don't apologise. It was just a thought,' said Mackenzie.

Cross had decided not to alert Carson to his interest in Sutton, some weeks back, for fear of him jumping to his usual rapid conclusions and insisting on an untimely arrest. He knew he could take his time. The good doctor wasn't going anywhere.

Later that day, Cross and Ottey drove out to the New Zealand-owned coffee bar that had been ordained by Cross as the only café in Bristol capable of making a coffee good enough for him to enjoy. She thought it was a good opportunity to discuss the case away from the distractions of the office. Cross thought it was an opportunity to get a welcome cup of decently made coffee. As she got their order at the counter, Ottey thought the staff had no idea of the accolade her eccentric and fussy colleague had bestowed on them. She felt that if they knew him and how deeply held his idiosyncratic views were, they would probably advertise this endorsement in their window.

'How are you feeling?' she asked him as she sat with their coffees.

She waited as he counted out the exact change for his beverage. He hadn't, as yet, been able to embrace the idea of colleagues buying each other coffees in an alternating fashion, despite the number of times she'd tried to explain it. He just couldn't see the point. If they were to alternate in a strict fashion, they were essentially paying for their own coffee anyway, so why not just do that every time and not have the worry of trying to remember whose turn it was?

She went on to explain further that it was a social ritual that implied friendship and the idea of generosity. He had countered by saying that, as with most social rituals, it was plainly meaningless, so why bother? As he'd already pointed out, no such generosity was involved. It was a never-ending reciprocal gesture, thus rendering it neither generous in spirit nor in fact. So she'd given up and now went as far as to check that the money he'd given her was right, something he, of course, entirely approved of.

'My father was very like you,' she began.

'Really?'

'When it came to his coffee, that is.' Cross said nothing. 'This might be the point where you asked me something about my parents,' Ottey went on.

'Why?'

'So we could have a conversation. We don't just have to talk about work,' she said, trying to help. He thought about this for a moment.

'Are your parents still alive?'

'My mother is. My father died a few years ago.' Again he said nothing. It was like pulling teeth but she was determined to carry on. He knew from her expression that he needed to say something at this point, but had no idea what it was.

'You now say you're sorry to hear that – even if you're not.'

'I'm sorry to hear that,' he answered parrot fashion, before adding, 'I don't know anything about your family, aside from the existence of your daughters.'

'That's because you've never asked.'

'You know a lot about mine.'

'That would be because I did ask,' she said not unreasonably.

'Where were your parents from originally?'

'My father was from Jamaica. He was a lot older than my mother. She was born here.'

'When did your father come over?'

'With my grandparents in the seventies. They were from the Blue Mountains area of Jamaica. His whole family had worked in coffee. So he became a self-proclaimed caffeine expert. He always said he had coffee in his veins instead of blood.'

'Which is why he was so fussy.'

'Yes. I think he would've approved of this place,' she said, looking around. 'Well, maybe not the place so much, but definitely the coffee. When I was young there was a coffee roaster at the bottom of Cotham Hill where my grandfather and father insisted on getting their coffee. We'd be in there for hours. I can remember the smell even now. There was a vent in the window for the machine. The whole street smelled of roasted coffee.'

'I found a letter from my mother in my father's flat.' And so the conversation changed direction abruptly.

'Really? A recent one?'

'No, from around the time she left us.' Ottey waited for him to expand on this but it seemed that giving her this information was all he intended to do.

'What did it say?'

'She apologised for leaving. She said she couldn't cope. With me.'

'I'm sorry.'

'I visited the address when I went up to Gloucester. It was my grandparents' house. I think she must have gone back there. The new owners had a forwarding address. But whether it's for her or a subsequent owner, I don't know.'

'And?'

'I've written her a letter.'

'Wow. Have you heard back?'

'Well, obviously not.'

'Why "obviously"?'

'Because I haven't posted it.' He took it out of his pocket as if to demonstrate the point.

'You need a stamp?' She reached for her handbag.

'No.'

'Then why haven't you posted it?'

'I'm not entirely sure why I'm sending it in the first place.'

'Curiosity?'

'That would certainly seem to be the most obvious explanation.'

'Would you like me to read it?'

He looked at her, genuinely perplexed. 'Why would I want you to do that?'

'In case I have any comments or suggestions? As a mother?'

He thought for a moment. 'Interesting. That hadn't occurred to me.' He handed her the letter. She started to read then looked up.

'"Dear Mrs Cross"? Isn't that a little formal?'

'I hardly know the woman.'

'How about using her Christian name?' She continued to read then looked up, a little concerned.

'"Dear Mrs Cross, I am writing to inform you that I, your son, am a detective sergeant in the Avon and Somerset police force. So, in spite of your misgivings about me and your abandonment of myself and my father, things have worked out considerably better than your actions would suggest you thought. Yours sincerely DS George Cross (your son)."'

He nodded his approval. 'It seems to get all the pertinent information across.' He held out his hand to take the letter back.

'Can I make a couple of suggestions?'

'That won't be necessary but your offer of a stamp would in fact be most welcome.'

She rummaged through her handbag and handed him a sheet of stamps. He removed one and carefully put it on the envelope. He then concentrated on his coffee in such a way that Ottey knew this subject was closed.

'So, where are we?' she asked, referring to the case.

He looked at her, slightly puzzled, as he thought it was obvious.

'Barnaby's Roast Shack,' he replied.

'I meant in the case. That is why we've come here, isn't it? To discuss the case away from the office.'

'Yes. Proceed,' he said.

'Right, well, Danny Stokes is now out of the frame. Brian, the downstairs neighbour, was at work. What about Simon? Did he go back after his fight with Brian?' she said. Cross didn't reply.

'It seems unlikely, and he doesn't strike me as capable. There's something a little pathetic about him when it comes to Flick.'

'But as yet we cannot rule it out.'

'True. What about Angie or one of the other addicts? Or any past acquaintances we don't know that were addicts?'

'Angie doesn't know where Flick lived and I wouldn't consider her a friend. They saw each other only occasionally at the dry cleaner's. Karen was more of a friend but has been clean for some time ergo no threat to her sobriety.'

'And Sandra was adamant that as part of her recovery Flick had cut contact with any friend who was still using. Hence the problems with Simon,' she added.

'We need to find out if there are any other people she knew that Sandra hasn't told us about. Are you planning another visit?'

'I am.'

'Ask her about Sutton.'

'The shrink?' she asked.

'The psychotherapist,' he corrected her. He then told her about his conversation with Brady, the retired detective at Esther's funeral, about Sutton's high mortality rate.

'Okay, but that could just come with the territory.'

'Exactly my response.'

'But why would he want to kill her?'

'Why would anyone? Something else may turn up but in the meantime we should focus our attention on him.'

She so wanted to ask him what his gut feeling was at this point but she knew it was a pointless question which would go unanswered, together with a look of disdainful disappointment.

Chapter 50

Sandra had by now been told by the family liaison officer about Danny's release and his lack of involvement in her daughter's death. In situations like this, the families of victims often took the news as a major blow, and Ottey wanted to make sure she was all right. She also needed to push her to remember any other people in Flick's life she might have forgotten to mention. Mackenzie went with her and they were invited in for tea and a cake she'd baked.

'I have so many visitors just now,' she said, indicating the cake. 'But I'm sure it'll ease off. Anyway, I've had a think and I really don't think there's anyone I've left out.'

'What about school friends, university friends?' Ottey asked. 'There seemed to be quite a few at her funeral.'

'There were, but they'd all been out of touch,' Sandra said. 'It wasn't their fault. That's the trouble with addiction – you cast everyone aside, especially the ones that try to help. They all felt so guilty at the funeral and they had no need. One thing that occurred to me was that, had she lived, she would've probably rekindled a lot of those relationships. Sad really.'

'Sad? It's tragic,' said Mackenzie, without thinking. 'I'm sorry.'

'No, you're right. It is. Tragic. But there we are. So I'm sorry you've had a wasted trip. If there was anyone, you know I'd bring them up.'

'Tell me about Dr Sutton,' said Ottey.

'Benedict? Oh, he was marvellous. Still is. He keeps in touch. It's been so good to talk to someone who knew her so well. As you now know, there weren't many left who did.'

'What was their relationship like?' Ottey asked.

'Well, close in the way that those relationships are. Close but professional. He knew so much about her,' Sandra went on.

'What did he think of Simon?' Ottey asked.

'He encouraged her to sever all ties with him, which you can imagine didn't go down at all well with Simon. Benedict tried to get him to see one of his colleagues, but Simon wasn't having it.'

'Why didn't he just treat him?' said Ottey.

'He said it wasn't in Flick's best interests,' Sandra replied. 'She was his client first and foremost, and he wouldn't do anything that might jeopardise her recovery. He said the best way to describe it was like it was a conflict of interest.'

'Simon described him as a "Svengali",' said Ottey.

'Oh, he called him a lot worse than that, I can assure you.'

'Do you think he had that kind of influence over Flick?' Ottey asked.

'I'm sorry, but I'm not going to enter into a discussion of what Simon thinks,' Sandra replied. 'I mean, come on. He's all over the place. Benedict was her therapist and helped keep her clean, and now he helps me.'

'I was actually asking you.'

'No. I don't. He was her therapist. He didn't influence her in any way other than in ways to face her demons.'

'How does he help you?' asked Ottey.

'Well, he's like a grief counsellor for me. Not in any official way, but you know he does that kind of work. He's an extraordinary man,' she said.

'Quite the fan,' Mackenzie observed jokily. She realised immediately that this comment was completely out of sync with the tone of the meeting and regretted it.

'Well, after what he's been through, it's amazing that he does what he does,' Sandra replied.

'Could you explain?' said Ottey.

'His wife, late wife.'

'She died some time ago, yes?' Ottey replied.

'That's right. She developed mental health problems after they married, and...' She faltered for a moment, obviously considering whether it was appropriate for her to continue. 'Well, everyone knows. She became an addict over a number of years and drank. Drink was a big problem, apparently. Anyway, she finished up ending it all. The inquest said it was accidental. Benedict has a different view.'

'How do you mean?' Ottey pressed.

'He's convinced she killed herself.'

'How awful,' said Mackenzie.

'It's like a mirror situation to Flick's, when you think about it,' said Sandra.

Ottey nodded. 'Isn't it just?'

Chapter 51

Cross wanted to examine Sutton's patient records so he and Ottey went back to his office with a warrant.

'He's with a patient,' Diana informed them.

'We're not here to see Dr Sutton,' said Ottey. 'We have a warrant for his patient records.'

'All of them?' asked Diana, shocked at the prospect.

'Specifically those who are now deceased,' explained Cross.

'Well, if you come back tomorrow I'll have it organised,' she replied.

'Had we simply wanted to alert you to our need for the records we could have done so by telephone and not gone to the effort of coming here in person,' said Cross.

'Yes, that would have been preferable,' she replied.

'The fact that we're here – our physical presence in your office – surely makes it abundantly clear that we need them today. Now, in point of fact,' Cross said.

'It'll take a while to get them together,' Diana complained.

'We'll be back in an hour,' said Cross.

'I might need longer,' she replied defiantly.

'Miss Coogan, from my brief observation of you and the way you run your office, I think you are an immensely organised person,' said Cross. 'Admirably so. I like to think of myself as similarly well organised, and as we are only talking twenty patients, the names and dates of death of whom I have detailed for you, I think that an hour is more than generous.'

'Presumably you are working on the assumption that I will provide you with copies,' she asked.

'Correct.'

'Then you need to factor in time for me to photocopy them,' she said victoriously.

'Oh, I did,' he replied. 'We'll see you in an hour.'

When they returned, the files had been duly copied and placed in a folder. Diana provided them with a detailed inventory of the files she had copied, which she then insisted both detectives sign. Sutton was unavailable to see them, she informed them.

'We haven't asked to see him,' Cross pointed out.

'I know, but he's unavailable,' she repeated.

'As I said, we haven't asked to see him,' Cross reiterated.

Diana looked at him disdainfully.

'I trust you have everything you need,' she said frostily.

'We will have, if you've given us everything we requested,' said Cross.

Ottey was sorely tempted to say, 'Hey, guys, get a room!', but she was fairly sure it would be wasted on the two of them.

'How is Angie? The young woman I brought in?'

'I can't discuss patients with you, Sergeant.'

'Did you manage to find a residential place for her? Can you at least let us have that?' asked Ottey. Diana thought for a moment.

'We did,' she confirmed.

★

Cross went through Sutton's patient files over and over again. He wasn't looking for anything specific, just things that stood out as anomalies or mistakes, patterns. But nothing seemed particularly out of place. It was when Mackenzie brought him the coroner's report for Sutton's wife he'd asked for, that he found something. He read it thoroughly. Sutton had come home from work to find his wife dead. She'd taken an overdose. The verdict was accidental death, but there was something which caught Cross's eye. Sutton had said 'her last words were "thank you".' Something in the phrasing of this struck Cross as odd.

Chapter 52

'Where's Josie?' Carson asked Cross, having summoned him to his office for an update.

'She's being interviewed,' Cross replied.

'Looking for a new job?' Carson joked.

'No, she's with HR. They're interviewing her about Campbell's complaint.'

'Ah, okay. So Flick Wilson – we have a doctor, well, more of a shrink these days—' Carson began.

'He's still registered as a doctor and has his medical licence.'

'Who deals with troubled individuals,' Carson continued, as if Cross had said nothing. 'Mostly substance abusers, and is a great advocate of assisted dying.'

'Correct,' replied Cross.

'Who has taken, of late, to going a little further with his advocacy, saying that assisted dying should be available to those with mental health issues as well as terminal illnesses, which has got him into quite a lot of hot water,' Carson went on.

Cross said nothing, even though Carson was in effect just repeating what Cross had told him not five minutes before. Ottey would've had a field day with this. But funnily enough, without her there the meeting seemed to go a lot more smoothly and quickly. Cross thought this was a reflection on both her and Carson. They spent so much time needling each other in meetings. Carson was always put on edge by Ottey, which was no doubt her intention, as she found his management style obstructive and time wasting. When Cross brought this up with her later, she said she was simply holding Carson to account.

'And he has an unusually high mortality rate in his patients,' Carson continued.

'According to Dr Todd. But I haven't been able to verify it yet,' replied Cross.

'Do you think he's maybe practising what he preaches?' asked Carson. 'It's kind of compelling, don't you think?'

'I don't think anything of the sort.'

'Why ever not?'

'We have no evidence,' Cross pointed out.

'No, of course not. Should we bring him in, though, George?'

'We have no evidence,' Cross repeated. Carson was always in a predictable rush to make an arrest to appease his superiors. He did it so often that Cross began to wonder if that was what Carson thought his job was. A conduit between actual police work and 'those upstairs'? Or just to manage department politics solely, it would appear, for his own benefit.

'Okay, let's leave him for now. I don't suppose he's going anywhere. But if he is another Harold Shipman operating on our watch, we don't want to be seen to have been aware of it at a later date and have done nothing,' Carson mused.

Ottey would've doubtless jumped on this, had she been in the room, and pointed out that their job wasn't to be concerned with appearances but to make arrests when they had evidence to do so and secure a conviction. At present they didn't have a shred of credible evidence against Sutton.

Cross had a series of newspaper and magazine articles printed up for him by Mackenzie, despite her vain protestations about the planet and his responsibility to be more green in the office. He preferred some things on paper. He could collate sheets of paper into an order which made more sense to him in a physical form than merely digital on a screen. At the beginning of what Ottey had referred to as Sutton's 'media career' – which had sent Cross into a tailspin as he thought he must have missed this in his research – Sutton spoke about a range of medically related subjects. These were mostly to do with substance abuse and recovery. But, of late, assisted suicide had become a more common theme with him.

Sutton obviously wasn't afraid of saying unpopular, contentious things on the issue, but he always remained admirably detached and calm, despite the often volatile, emotive, ill-tempered nature of the discussions.

Suicide was a subject close to Sutton's own personal experience. He was convinced his wife had committed suicide and he'd written many papers on the subject, not only on the nature and causes of suicide, but also the aftermath on the surviving family. He was also at great pains to differentiate between the ideas of suicide and assisted dying. He would not countenance the use of the word 'suicide' in the context of assisted dying. They were two profoundly different concepts, in his view. It was the one area of the argument, the one point about which he got closest to being exercised and angry.

★

Later that afternoon Ottey and Cross made their way to see Billie Williams at the Hopewell Clinic. It would be an opportunity for Cross to check on Angie's progress as well. Ottey turned to him as they drove there.

'Do you want to discuss my interview with HR?' she asked.

'Wasn't it confidential?'

'Yes. Obviously,' she said.

'Then no. Obviously.'

Billie wasn't particularly happy to see the two detectives again but Cross thought she seemed like the sort of person who was probably never pleased to see anyone.

'How is Simon doing?' Ottey began.

'Still here. He's well, better in many ways but a little more troubled about Flick,' she replied.

'In what way?' said Ottey.

'Well, it makes more sense to him that she didn't take her own life, deliberately or otherwise. But he's upset by the fact that someone else did. He feels responsible.'

'Because if he'd been clean and with her it may not have happened,' Ottey said.

'He told you,' said Billie.

'Yes, last time we were here,' said Ottey.

Cross was becoming impatient. 'We'd like to talk to you about Dr Sutton.'

'What about him?' Billie asked.

'What do you think of him?' Cross replied.

'Personally or professionally?'

'Let's start with professionally,' said Cross.

'He's extremely good at his job. He's devoted to his patients,' she said.

'I sense a "but" in there somewhere,' said Ottey.

'He likes the limelight too much, does our Benedict. Being the centre of attention. But I think you've probably worked that out already.'

'He certainly seems like a bit of a rent-a-quote on medical issues here in the south-west,' said Ottey.

'Which would be okay if it was to do with his field. But it never is. Anything but,' said Billie.

'Go on,' prompted Ottey.

'Mental health is getting a lot more attention these days, which is great, but people with addictions and substance abuse issues are still way down the pecking order.'

'Aren't the two interlinked?' asked Ottey.

'To an extent, but not always, and there's still a widely held prejudice about addiction being the addict's fault. There's less sympathy for the issue. It's like they've made their bed and now they should lie in it,' Billie went on. 'Alcoholism is a disease not a choice.'

'You think Sutton could do more to shine a light on it?' said Ottey.

'I do and I've told him so, but he chooses not to,' she said. There was a pause, and then she added, 'But he has an amazing success rate with his patients on the whole.'

'By "on the whole", do you mean those that don't kill themselves?' said Cross.

'I beg your pardon?' Billie was clearly shocked.

'How many of your clients who are under his care after they leave kill themselves?' Cross asked.

'I have no idea,' she replied.

'I don't believe that,' Cross challenged her.

'What do you mean?'

'You seem to be very concerned and involved with the people in your care. I've seen it myself. I don't believe for a minute that you're not aware of how many of them have died by their own hand, "deliberately or otherwise", as you put it. I think you know how many. Exactly. Their names. The dates they died. Where they died.' He looked her squarely in the eye.

She considered him for a moment.

'Twelve. We've had twelve deaths in the last six years, I'm afraid. One of them while she was here. The others at various times after that,' she said quietly.

'I'm sorry,' said Ottey.

'Would you call that an occupational hazard?' Cross asked.

'I wouldn't put it so crassly. I'd call it an occupational statistic,' she replied firmly.

'Quite so. Thank you for the distinction. Is it?' he persisted.

'To an extent, yes.'

'Would you say your mortality rate is higher than other such places in the area dealing with this kind of thing?' asked Cross.

'I have no idea,' said Billie.

'How many of those patients were under Dr Sutton's care? How many of the twelve?' Cross asked.

'All of them,' she replied after a moment. The two detectives made no comment on this. They just left it hanging in the air uncomfortably.

'How many of his patients do you have in your care at the moment?' Cross went on.

'None,' she said.

'Really? What about Angie?' Cross asked.

'Angie isn't here. Is she back in rehab?'

'She is. Is that a conscious decision of yours? Not to have any of his patients?' asked Cross.

'No.'

'Are you still referring patients to him?' Ottey went on.

'No.'

'So, he no longer sends patients to you, and you no longer refer them to him when they leave?' said Cross.

'That's correct,' Billie said.

'Have you had a falling-out or a disagreement?' Cross asked.

'We had a difference of opinion, let's put it that way.'

'Could you elaborate?' Ottey asked.

'Look, as medical professionals...' she began.

'You're a doctor?' Cross asked.

'As healthcare professionals,' she corrected herself, with a look of irritation directed at Cross, 'we have to maintain a dispassionate, detached relationship with our patients and it's hard sometimes. It's inevitable that you get to know some of them really well.'

'Some better than others?' Cross asked.

'Yes,' she answered slowly. She seemed to be getting a little wary of Cross and his questions, not quite knowing where any of it was leading, and it made her uncomfortable. This was not something that would have bothered him in the least, had he even noticed it.

'You feel terrible when they suffer setbacks, thrilled and happy when things go well,' she went on. 'But you have to maintain a distance, to an extent, so that you can make tough and unpopular decisions in their best interests. I feel Benedict has maybe taken it too far.'

'How do you mean?' asked Ottey.

Billie now spoke as if she wanted to tell them the truth about something, while at the same time juggling the fact that she might get someone into a lot of trouble by doing so. A bit like a schoolchild who wants to name a culprit for a classroom misdemeanour to prevent the whole of the class from being punished. An unpleasant thing, but one she's willing to do for the good of the whole class.

'It was his attitude to those who had killed themselves that offended me. It was so dispassionate. So detached. Cold almost. At first I told myself it was just his way of dealing with it. But then it became a common theme and a problem for me,' she said.

'How, exactly?' Cross pushed.

'He said he felt that their problem was now solved. That they were in a better place. Were better off…' she faltered.

'Being dead,' said Cross, filling in for her.

'Exactly,' she said. 'And he has this way of saying it through those gimlet eyes of his, which makes you feel less intelligent, less sophisticated if you don't agree. I thought he might take offence when I finally brought it up with him. But he didn't. He just looked at me in that superior way of his. As if it was so predictable that I wouldn't be able to understand something on such a higher spiritual or intellectual plane.'

The two detectives didn't say a word, both feeling that she had more to say and they shouldn't interrupt.

'But I kept pushing,' she continued. 'Asking him to be more specific about what he was saying. Was death the answer? Then he said something which still gives me chills. He said it wasn't so much their death but the beauty of the manner in which they did it. He thought their committing suicide was in some way them empowering themselves. Which is absurd, as they were doing the absolute opposite.'

'Literally,' added Cross.

'Yes. Literally,' Billie agreed. 'Then one day Diana, his assistant, called to say Benedict would no longer be referring patients to us and would be grateful if we no longer referred any to him. Our views on treatment had become too divergent and therefore incompatible.'

Chapter 53

Marcus Todd cropped up again in a local newspaper discussing the recent Dignitas documentary. It prompted Cross to go back and see him as he'd been intending to for some time. Something about Todd's reaction to the film seemed quite genuine. That what Sutton was advocating by his presence in Switzerland was dangerous and that Todd, as he had said to Cross, felt Sutton's motives were self-promotional. The detective wondered whether the documentary might have been a step too far for Todd and that he might be willing to divulge whatever he had held back in their first interview. Todd was pleased to see Cross again until he learnt that Sutton had now become a person of interest in the case. He then became much more circumspect as the reality of the situation dawned on him – that what he said could have serious consequences for the therapist. It was no longer a game of media ping-pong in which accusatory soundbites were traded like verbal punches over the airwaves. Cross had noticed this about people when he revisited them to discuss someone related to an investigation. Once that individual had become an actual person of interest in a case, people behaved in one of two ways. Like Todd, they would become more reticent and less gung-ho now the situation had become serious. Or they were carried away with the fact that they always harboured suspicions about the suspect and let loose with often unhelpful conjecture and long-harboured theories. Todd was taken aback at this development. Clearly shocked that someone in his profession could be suspected of something as heinous as killing one of his patients.

'I left with the feeling at our last meeting that perhaps there was something you were reluctant to say to me,' Cross began.

'Can he really be a suspect?'

'Yes.'

'Are you sure?'

'That Dr Sutton's a suspect, yes, but at this stage no more than that.'

'I see. Then, well, I did feel reticent saying this at the time but as you say, things have changed. After my patient committed suicide he said something I found odd and hard to forget.'

'Which was?' Cross pushed.

'That after all she'd been through it might be said that she was better off where she was. That an end had been put to her suffering.'

'I see,' Cross replied.

'This was before he became such a messianic ambassador for assisted dying, or state-sanctioned murder, as it should be called,' Todd said bitterly.

'His wife committed suicide, I understand,' said Cross.

'She did. He claimed it was some sort of epiphany.'

'In what sense?'

'I don't know,' Todd replied. 'He said it presumably because he felt it was a good dramatic and enigmatic soundbite. He didn't elaborate.' Cross waited for Todd to go on. But he said nothing further.

'Dr Todd, now is not the time for having any qualms about disclosing anything you think is relevant, whether or not incriminating.'

'Well, my concern is not just the high mortality rate in Sutton's patients, which as you know I informed your colleague about a few years ago, but, more significantly in my opinion, the proportion of his patients' death certificates he actually signs.'

'Why is that odd? They were his patients.'

'Families tend to call their GPs when a loved one has died. Not the deceased's counsellor,' said Todd.

'But he is a doctor.'

'Sure, but he wasn't acting as their doctor. He was acting as their therapist. But one thing really stood out,' Todd continued. 'A lot of his patients live alone. It's quite common in recovering addicts. They come out of rehab, and some will go through a halfway house, but they will mostly end up living alone for a period of time.'

'What are you saying?' Cross asked.

'I'm sorry; lost my thread. Who called Sutton to let him know about the death? Who was there?' Todd asked.

'Presumably whoever found the body,' said Cross.

'And that's just it.' Todd was emphatic. 'Sutton was often the one who discovered his patients dead, concluding they had taken their own lives. But it happened too often. Statistically, the number is way out of the norm.'

'It doesn't fit the pattern?' said Cross.

'What do you mean?'

'The statistical pattern.'

'Exactly.' Todd nodded. 'Which takes me back to my patient, Jodie. Sutton discovered her body in her flat. It was him who called me. When I arrived, he'd already signed the death certificate and the undertakers had been to collect the body. I remember thinking it was very quick.' Something dawned on him at that moment. 'You think he might have killed her.'

Cross was puzzled by this as he thought their entire conversation was surely predicated on this possibility. But the enormity of the situation was just beginning to dawn on Todd who looked up at Cross with an expression of horror.

'Oh no. Surely not. Are you thinking he may have killed them all?'

'I cannot say, but I will say that, bearing in mind how media-friendly you appear to be, I would ask that you keep this conversation to yourself.'

'Of course.'

Cross resisted the idea of going straight to Sutton and asking him about the information Todd had given him. Obviously it was a major point of interest, but it didn't go as far, yet, as to make Sutton a person of interest in the case more than anyone else. He wanted to do more digging before meeting Sutton again, in order to be more prepared for what he anticipated would be a tricky and demanding interview.

Chapter 54

Cross was scrutinising all the information they had about Sutton on a whiteboard. The number of deaths in his care, against the average number for a therapist in the same field. The death certificates. Having reviewed everything, the doctor had now become his prime suspect. He just needed one more piece of the puzzle to convince himself to bring Sutton in for questioning. Clare, the pathologist, was confident she could conduct tests on the remains of Sutton's deceased patients and find out if diamorphine was present. Cross applied to exhume the remains of those patients who had committed suicide over the last two years. The problem with this, however, was that those patients had been cremated. When he looked into it further, he discovered that all of Sutton's deceased patients had been cremated.

'That's odd. All of them?' Ottey asked when he told her.

'All the orders were signed by him,' Cross informed her. She waited as he further examined the orders, one by one. Ten minutes later he suddenly grabbed his coat and left the office.

Ottey sighed and followed him.

'Where are we going?' she asked.

'I wasn't aware "we" were going anywhere.'

'All right, where are you going?'

'To bring Sutton in.'

'Why?'

'He signed all of the cremation orders within a couple of hours of their deaths. Does that strike you as normal? Why such speed? Such urgency?'

'Because he's covering up evidence?' she said, almost thinking out loud.

'Exactly.'

'Cremation orders need to be countersigned by another GP. There's one doctor who crops up regularly on these forms, then all of a sudden stops. I'd like to know why, Alice.'

'Sure. Maybe he's retired,' Mackenzie suggested.

'No, he's still practising.'

Ottey looked at her watch. 'You're due before the complaints' panel at two.'

'Alice, would you tell them I'm not able to attend?' said Cross.

'George, it's not voluntary,' said Ottey.

'I'm working a murder case. It can wait.' Cross continued walking.

'So can Sutton's arrest,' Ottey said.

He stopped and turned to Mackenzie. 'Alice, please inform the board that my presence may be compulsory, but it isn't necessary. Please apologise.'

He looked at Ottey, expecting her to be impressed that he had remembered this social nicety, but she wasn't.

'And tell them that I refute everything that DI Campbell has alleged, and if they cross reference his complaints with the relevant cases they'll rapidly conclude that I have no case to answer.'

*

On their way to Sutton's office, Cross found himself reflecting how Sutton was a very intelligent, articulate individual. It was a robust shield, but he knew he'd find a chink in that intellectual armour, given time, in the interview room; his vanity perhaps. Sutton was used to being the manipulator of others' thought processes in his office. He was, in effect, the interviewer. He was in control of the narrative and took it wherever he wanted to, in the same way that Cross did so effectively. But he was now going to be placed in the opposing, unfamiliar position in the interview dynamic. Cross was interested to see whether this would have an unsettling effect on the psychotherapist.

'You don't have an appointment,' said Diana emphatically.

'We don't need an appointment,' replied Ottey.

'Everyone needs an appointment to see Dr Sutton.'

'Not when they're here to arrest him,' said Cross.

'What?' she replied with some consternation.

But Ottey had already walked over to Sutton's office door and knocked.

'Come!' commanded Sutton's voice from within.

Ottey and Cross walked into the office. Sutton was sitting behind his desk writing some notes with an elegant fountain pen. His jacket was hanging immaculately over a chair nearby. He was wearing a waistcoat. His shirt had such sharp creases in it, he probably had to take extra care when putting it on not to get paper cuts.

'Detectives...' he said. If he had any idea why they were

there he didn't give it away in the moment before Ottey spoke.

'Dr Benedict Sutton, I'm arresting you on suspicion of the murder of Felicity Wilson.' She then read him his rights.

Sutton stood up and smiled in the way that someone does who has just won the lottery and been presented with a giant cheque. A smile of amazed, amused disbelief. He walked around the desk and calmly put on his jacket.

'I'm not entirely sure what to say except that this exercise is going to be an unnecessary waste of your time – not to mention mine. Having said that, though, I am curious about the whole experience, so possibly it's not a complete waste of my time. Please continue.'

To Cross it seemed like this wasn't simple feigned bravado. It came across as genuine bemusement, with no bluff or even condescension. The man was neither angry nor offended, which Cross immediately sought to change. Ottey produced her handcuffs.

'Could we dispense with the handcuffs, Sergeant? I can assure you I'm no threat, nor am I a flight risk. It's just that we are in the midst of a lot of medical practices here and I'd rather not have my reputation sullied unnecessarily,' he said charmingly.

'Very well,' said Ottey, putting her handcuffs back.

'On the contrary, I insist.' Cross immediately got out his handcuffs and walked across the room to Sutton.

The doctor looked at him for a moment, almost as if he was accepting the gauntlet that had been thrown down in front of him. Cross turned him round and cuffed his hands behind him. He was enveloped in Sutton's lemony, musky scent, which he immediately recognised as Penhaligon's Blenheim Bouquet cologne.

As they walked past the shell-shocked secretary, she said, 'What are you doing? He hasn't killed anyone. What evidence have you got? This is ridiculous!'

But the detectives walked past, in silence, with her employer.

'I don't know what to do,' she said to Ottey. 'What am I supposed to do now?'

'I'd start by cancelling all his appointments for today and tomorrow and getting hold of his lawyer,' Ottey suggested.

'But his lawyer is a media lawyer,' protested the secretary, whose authority seemed to have fled the building in a hurry in the past five minutes.

'Why doesn't that surprise me?' Ottey replied. 'Call his media lawyer, tell him the situation and ask him to get hold of a criminal lawyer.'

'Criminal?' Diana echoed in disbelief.

Ottey thought there was a renewed vigour in Cross that morning. Not determination – he was always determined – just purpose. She wondered if Esther's death was still playing on his mind. He had been very matter-of-fact when telling Ottey of her death, as was his way. But she felt sure that he was concealing something.

As she watched Cross load Sutton into the car, pushing his head down lightly so he didn't bang it on his way in, she realised that he was already working him. On the whole... no, pretty much in every arrest they had made together, she'd noticed that Cross always backed off at the point of arrest, as if he didn't want to get involved physically; get too close to it. She thought it must be an aversion to the necessary physical contact and proximity to the suspect. She'd brought it up with him once and he had said it had nothing to do with that. He just wanted to observe the suspect's reactions throughout the process, as they were often quite revealing. They also gave him the first clue as to how he should proceed in the interview room.

On this occasion Cross had pushed himself forward, right in Sutton's face, insisted on the cuffs and then led him in what the Americans called a 'perp walk'. This was going to be a really interesting interview, she realised.

In the car Sutton was as charming as he had been in their first two meetings. It was as if he hadn't been arrested. A passer-by would never have known had it not been for the handcuffs.

'These things really aren't designed for comfort in the car when they're behind your back, are they?' he laughed, indicating the cuffs and how he was having to sit sideways.

'I have a question,' he continued. 'I know the perceived wisdom is that when arrested on suspicion of a crime one shouldn't speak to the police before the arrival of one's lawyer – but don't you think it would save a good bit of time if we just got on with it and sorted this misunderstanding out?'

'That's entirely up to you,' replied Ottey.

'Okay.' He paused for a second as he thought this through. Then something else crossed his mind. 'Will you be putting me in a cell?'

'We will,' answered Cross, before Ottey had a chance.

'How marvellous! This is going to be quite the experience,' Sutton said.

'I'm glad you find it so amusing,' said Ottey.

'How else should I treat it, Sergeant? It is, after all, somewhat farcical.'

'Interesting choice of adjective,' said Cross. 'Not one that you hear applied to a murder often, let alone to the death of a young woman supposedly under your care.'

Sutton didn't react to this.

Again, in the custody suite, Cross insisted on booking Sutton in and being by his side all the time. This was something he normally, to Ottey's habitual annoyance, left her to do. But he wanted to be there. He told Sutton to remove his tie and surrender any jewellery, his pocket watch, his pocket square, his shoes. Cross also insisted on Sutton removing his jacket and waistcoat.

'Is that really necessary?' Sutton implored the desk sergeant. But the officer simply deferred to Cross.

'Jacket and waistcoat,' Cross intoned neutrally.

Cross was taking away as much of Sutton's outward appearance as he could, removing his bespoke outer shell, his identity, the comfort blanket of Sutton's pride in his appearance. He wanted him in just a shirt and trousers. No longer a curated, manicured, exterior. His cologne, the last vestige of confident self-sophistication, would soon fade and nothing would be left.

Cross wanted Sutton to know it was him who was responsible for it. That he was in control. He was in charge. What he said, went. He stood beside the camera as Sutton's mug shots were taken, front and profile. He stood at his side when his fingerprints were taken. It was Cross who took him to his cell and locked the door. Ottey was tempted to comment but didn't want to break the spell. She wanted to see how this one would pan out in the interview room.

Chapter 55

Diana appeared in reception. Mackenzie was sent to deal with her.

'When will he be freed?' Diana asked.

'I'm afraid I can't answer that question,' Mackenzie replied.

'Can I have your name please?' Diana got a notebook and biro out of her massive handbag.

'Mackenzie, Alice Mackenzie,' she answered.

'Rank?'

'I'm police staff.'

'I know that. Rank?' Diana persisted.

'I'm not a police officer,' Mackenzie replied.

'Then why am I talking to you?'

'Because I'm working on this case and have been asked by DS Ottey to deal with your enquiry,' said Mackenzie patiently.

'Well, perhaps I could speak to DS Ottey himself.'

'*She's* unavailable at the moment as *she's* busy interviewing Dr Sutton,' replied Mackenzie, instinctively riled at the woman's sexist inference.

'I see. How long do you think it'll be before they realise their mistake?' Diana asked.

'Um, well, the initial period lasts twenty-four hours and

then they can ask for an extension from a judge, if needs be,' Mackenzie explained.

'That won't be necessary,' said Diana confidently. 'They don't have any evidence.'

'Well, in that case,' said Mackenzie, who had rapidly come to the conclusion that there might be no reasoning with this woman, 'I'm sure as soon as they realise that they will release him.'

'And how am I supposed to know when that happens? Will you organise transport together with the apology?'

'If you give me your number I'll call you the second there are any developments. You'll be my first call,' Mackenzie assured her.

The woman looked at her for a couple of moments, trying to ascertain whether this was a satisfactory course of action. She then quickly scribbled her number on a piece of paper and handed it over.

'This is my private number. My mobile. Call me on that and then please destroy the number after you've made use of it. It's not for public distribution.' Diana waited for a second to make sure the young woman opposite her completely understood.

'Of course. I'll guard it with my life then eat it,' said Mackenzie mischievously.

'Now you're just being obtuse,' Diana said, before turning on her heels and leaving.

If Sutton had been put out by a couple of hours in a cell, he wasn't showing it. A lawyer had been dispatched by Diana. Neither Cross nor Ottey recognised him. He was smartly dressed and made none of the self-important initial statements some lawyers made to the police at the outset, in an attempt to impress clients they'd only met moments before.

Cross was about to sit when he noticed a coffee cup stain on the table. He immediately disappeared. Ottey sat down and said nothing. After a couple of minutes Cross returned with a roll of blue absorbent tissue paper and a spray detergent. He sprayed the table and then wiped it down thoroughly, using a clean sheet of tissue to dry the surface. He then disappeared again to take the utensils back to the janitorial cupboard.

Ottey said nothing but looked straight at Sutton, almost challenging him to say something. Cross returned and placed his files carefully on the table. He opened one of them and examined the top sheet, as if he'd never seen it before – even though it was a list of questions he had himself just written down. He looked up.

'How would you like to be addressed?' he began.

'Dr Sutton will be fine,' Sutton replied.

Cross ticked something off in his notes very deliberately.

'Dr Sutton, where were you on June the seventeenth of this year?' asked Cross.

'Haven't we already covered this?' Sutton asked.

'We need to go over all of it again, now you are under caution. It would probably be easier and less frustrating for you if you imagined we haven't had any previous conversations on this matter,' Cross replied.

'Useful advice. Thank you,' Sutton said courteously.

Cross went quickly through all the logistical questions they needed to deal with. Sutton had no alibi for the night in question. He had worked till around nine at the office and then gone home, where he ate and watched the news on TV. They then went through his timeline for the next day.

'How would you describe Flick's mental state prior to her death?' asked Cross.

'She was on a fairly even keel, in my professional opinion. Recovery is always more stressful than we'd like.'

'In what way?'

'The sense of loss. Denial. Not denial of what has happened but the denying of certain props the patient had become dependent on. But I think she was in a good place. Which is why I'm convinced she was murdered.'

'What about her employment tribunal? Wasn't that making her stressed?' asked Cross.

'Funnily enough, once she'd decided on that course of action, she was much happier. She was stressed when she felt helpless and thought there was nothing she could do about it. The tribunal gave her purpose. I believe the closer the tribunal date got, the happier she became.'

'How was your relationship with Flick?' Cross went on.

'As you would expect. Professional,' he replied.

'But you know the family, outside of your one-to-ones with her, do you not?' asked Cross.

'By that I assume you mean Sandra,' said Sutton. 'When Flick was alive, her mother had come to a couple of sessions as part of Flick's treatment – which, before you ask, is quite normal.'

This made Cross glance down and check his notes. He looked back up.

'I wasn't going to ask that.'

'I only met Sandra away from the office after Flick's death,' Sutton pointed out.

Cross now made a note of this information diligently in his file.

'Were you aware that Flick kept a journal?'

'Of course.'

'What do you mean "of course"?'

'She told me. In fact, at times, she read me extracts from it. She was very articulate on paper. Searingly honest about her feelings and about others. But you must know all this as I'm assuming you've read it.'

'Why would you assume that?' asked Ottey.

'Isn't it what you people refer to as victimology? Building up a picture of the victim. I'm sure you would've read her journal just in the same way as you'll have been scouring her social media accounts.'

'We haven't,' said Cross.

'Well, far be it for me to tell you how to do your job, Sergeant, but your time might be better spent reading it rather than wasting your time with me.'

'Why would you say that?'

'Because it obviously might contain a clue as to who killed her,' Sutton said exasperated.

'So you think she must've known whoever killed her?'

'How else would she be persuaded to ingest diamorphine? If she knew it were diamorphine.'

This actually stopped Cross in his tracks. He completely lost his train of thought. It was so obvious and he kicked himself for not having considered this. 'We don't have her journal. It's missing. Presumably destroyed.'

Ottey thought she detected a look of surprise cross Sutton's face. Was it perhaps because he was relying on something in it to exonerate him or implicate someone else?

'Let's discuss your position on assisted dying,' said Cross, changing tack. 'You advocate the case for it also to be available to those with mental illnesses.'

'My views are well known on the subject and are in the public domain.'

'Indeed. But this is a police interview and so we need to fully understand your views on the issue,' said Cross.

Sutton nodded. 'Very well. I believe that people with extreme forms of mental illness, who have mental capacity but whose condition is seemingly insoluble, incurable, call it what you will, should be afforded the right to choose to die. As I do with the terminally ill. For me there is little difference, in essence, between the two, though I understand the concept causes great alarm and distress to many. But the outraged response to the argument that it be applied to the mentally ill just falls in line with the general prejudicial attitude which exists towards the notion of mental illness. If you can't see it, it can't exist.'

'"Terminal illness for physical conditions interminable for the mental" – to quote you,' added Cross.

'Quite so. I don't see, in the case of mental illness, that if no end, or "cure" if you like, is going to be found for their suffering, why they shouldn't be given a choice. But this is a step too far in a country which still won't allow it for those suffering from the most dreadful of physical illnesses, where the process of death is known to be inevitably unpleasant, traumatic and often horrendous,' Sutton went on.

'You also apply that to mental illness,' said Cross.

'I don't follow, I'm afraid. Isn't that exactly what I just said?' asked Sutton.

'You have argued that, in the same way that the process

of death for some terminal illnesses can cause unnecessary suffering, so it is for mental illnesses also, when people attempt suicide, whether successful or not,' Cross explained.

'Oh I see. Yes. I believe suicide attempts, both successful and unsuccessful, can cause unnecessary suffering and trauma. Some successful suicides can also be achieved in the most gruesome of ways. None of it necessary, in my opinion.'

'Unless, having failed to kill themselves, they change their mind about the whole thing,' added Ottey.

'That is, of course a valid point,' Sutton conceded.

'An opportunity they wouldn't have had, if it had been an assisted death, in which case death would have been inevitable,' Ottey went on.

'A good point,' said Sutton. 'Which is why several more checks would have to be made in a case involving mental health issues. Research shows that some suicides are spur of the moment decisions, impulses that may then fade. People would have to pass certain tests. It is, as you point out, not as easy to determine as in a case of physical terminal illness. But that doesn't mean to say it shouldn't be a fundamental right.'

'So, to be clear,' said Cross. 'We are talking about assisted dying being available for those with mental health problems?'

'Yes,' said Sutton.

'Would you also apply that to those with substance abuse problems?' Cross asked.

'Not necessarily, no. Only if there are concurrent mental issues with separate causal factors. If the substance abuse has developed as a result of those issues, then probably not.'

'An ethical minefield,' said Cross, who seemed genuinely perplexed by it. 'I mean, how do you make those choices?'

'It is indeed. But they seem to manage to make them

satisfactorily in certain European countries for both physical and mental conditions. The ethical climate is changing the world over. New Zealand had a referendum and voted in favour of euthanasia. It's already become law.'

Cross considered this for a moment, then looked up at Sutton.

'Did you assist Flick Wilson to die?' Cross asked.

Sutton had piercing blue eyes that were almost hypnotic, and his aquiline nose seemed to aim his gaze with laser-guided accuracy into the soul of whoever he was looking at.

'I did not,' he replied calmly.

Chapter 56

'Suicide has played an unfortunately significant, tragic part in your life, has it not?' Cross asked.

'If you're referring to my wife, yes.'

'I was also referring to your mother,' said Cross.

There was a significant pause. Sutton averted his eyes from Cross.

'Out of interest,' Cross continued, 'given your views on assisted dying, why have you never mentioned her in all the myriad pieces you've written and the various interviews and talks?'

'Assisted dying and suicide are two entirely different things,' Sutton refuted.

'In point of fact they're not. Suicide is defined as "the act of killing yourself intentionally". Going to Dignitas is surely, therefore, an act of suicide,' Cross pointed out.

'It's a modern distinction,' said Sutton.

'So you say,' said Cross.

'I and many other respected medical practitioners.'

Cross noted the slightest change in Sutton's delivery here. He was getting a little agitated.

'Let's go back to your mother,' said Cross.

'I don't see how that's relevant,' said Sutton.

'Oh I'm sure you don't, but as your solicitor will doubtless inform you, your opinion as to what is or isn't relevant, isn't relevant,' said Cross. He looked at Sutton as if to make sure he'd got that point across before continuing.

'Was your mother ill at the time of her death?'

'She was.'

'Could you tell us what she was suffering from?'

'Motor Neurone Disease,' Sutton said.

'Was it the case that, as the disease progressed, she decided to end her life?' Cross asked.

'She did.'

Ottey looked at Cross angrily. He hadn't shared this piece of information with her. Sutton's wife *and* his mother, she was thinking.

'Why?' Cross asked bluntly.

'Because she didn't want to end her life unable to speak or swallow, move. She wanted to go before any of that happened. It's a familiar story, Sergeant,' Sutton said patronisingly. His tone again made Cross feel that progress was being made in his attempt to get behind this man's professional veneer.

During one of the breaks in the interview, as he drank a fresh brew of tea, Cross had found himself thinking that Sutton was a little like he imagined an Edwardian doctor to be: the elegant clothes, a fragrant aura of lemon, lime and musk, a superior manner and an unfamiliarity with being challenged by ordinary, lesser mortals – in other words, anyone without the deification of 'Dr' in front of their name.

'Did she manage?' asked Cross.

'What?' said Sutton.

'To die before any of that happened?'

'Only just.'

'How old were you when this happened?' Cross asked.

'Fifteen.'

'You were brought up by your mother's sister after her death, is that correct?' Cross asked.

'It is,' Sutton replied.

Ottey couldn't help but look at Cross in surprise at this information. Not because he hadn't shared it with her but because she was always amazed at how he often came up with crucial background information that helped them secure a conviction. He had spent days before the arrest looking into areas that just wouldn't occur to others.

'Why was that?' Cross continued.

'My father couldn't cope. He was overwhelmed with grief.'

'Were you? "Overwhelmed with grief"?' asked Cross.

'I was bereaved, obviously. It's a young and particularly vulnerable age at which to lose your mother. And suicide makes it that much more difficult to process. But I understood why she'd done it.'

'Unlike your father,' said Cross.

'I beg your pardon?'

'It must have been a very formative experience. Well, in your case most definitely so, wouldn't you say?' Cross went on. Sutton didn't reply. 'How were relations with your father after that?'

'My aunt was bringing me up. How do you think?' said Sutton.

'I don't know. That's why I'm asking,' said Cross.

'Not especially close,' said Sutton.

'Isn't it true you barely spoke to him?'

'Yes.'

'And that you didn't speak to him after your twenty-first birthday till his death seven years later?' Cross went on.

'*He* didn't speak to *me*,' Sutton corrected him.

'Where are you getting this information from?' asked Sutton's lawyer.

'From the coroner's report into Dr Sutton's father's death,' said Cross. He then looked up directly at Sutton. 'He gassed himself in his car. Is that not so, Dr Sutton?'

Sutton didn't answer.

'Your mother, your father and your wife,' Cross stated.

Again, no answer from Sutton. Ottey thought the lawyer was doing his best to conceal his surprise at this. He shifted uncomfortably in his seat, obviously wishing he was more familiar with his client.

'Why, exactly, were things so fraught with your father?' Cross asked.

'He never recovered from my mother's death,' Sutton said.

'But I mean with you. His fifteen-year-old son. Why did he remove you from his life? At a time when really he needed to be a father to a bereaved son?' Cross sounded as if he was at a genuine loss to understand it.

Sutton said nothing. These silences were small signs of encouragement for Cross.

'Was it because you knew and approved of your mother's intentions even at such a tender age?'

Sutton sat there, giving absolutely nothing away.

'Or was it because you helped her? "Assisted" her, as you'd rather we said?' asked Cross. There was a distinct tension in the air at this point. Cross was very firmly in charge.

'According to your mother's coroner's report, her disease had progressed rapidly in the months leading up to her death.

She was no longer even able to feed herself. Is that right?' Cross asked.

'Yes. She was fed through a tube.'

'Could she not swallow at this point?'

'Look, I'm sorry, but where is this all leading?' asked the lawyer. Cross studiously ignored him.

'Could your mother swallow at the time of her death, Dr Sutton?' Cross asked.

'With great difficulty,' Sutton replied.

'And yet she died from an overdose of barbiturates. Is that correct?'

'Yes.'

'You'd need to take quite a few of those to overdose, would you not? Quite a number of pills to swallow. No?' Cross went on.

'Correct,' said Sutton, resigned as to where this was going.

'So my question is this. How was she able to take them on her own? By herself?' Cross said. 'Did you crush them, perhaps?'

Sutton didn't answer.

'The answer is, she didn't have to, did she? It states in the report that your father found you with your mother's body. You were there when she died, because you helped her take the pills. Isn't that right?'

No answer.

'Please don't misunderstand me here. I can see it was a compassionate act. And, for a fifteen-year-old, one of considerable courage and maturity. That's how you see it, I would imagine. And in the end at some cost. You lost both your parents that day. Not just your mother but also your father. He never forgave you, did he? He disagreed with both you and your mother, but then had to face up to the fact that you'd helped her. You'd taken away the love of his life, something he would never recover from. Not even till the day he took his own life.'

They all sat there in silence. It was as if the weight of Sutton's story pressed down on all of them. Ottey couldn't help but look at Cross.

'I should point out at this juncture that we're not in the least interested in the fact that you helped your mother die. I'm just interested in building a picture of you up to the point of Flick's death,' said Cross.

'I think we should take a break here,' said the lawyer quietly. Cross said nothing but left the room.

When Ottey came back into the open area she saw that Cross's door was closed. He was sitting looking into space, a picture of concentration. He was trying to keep himself in the construct of the interview. In his mind, he was still in the room despite the break. She left him alone even though she wanted to take him to task. For her benefit, not his. It would make her feel better but would have absolutely no effect on his behaviour in the future, she suspected.

Chapter 57

'I'd like to talk to you about your wife's suicide,' Cross began, when they reconvened.

'Is this really necessary?' Sutton's lawyer practically pleaded.

'Oh, completely,' Cross replied. 'It's most unfortunate that your client has had so much experience of suicide in those close to him. But surely the relevance of that to the investigation of Flick's supposed suicide is obvious.'

The lawyer decided to take it no further.

'Your wife had substance abuse problems. Is that correct?' asked Cross.

'Sadly, yes,' Sutton replied.

'Which apparently developed after your marriage?'

'It had nothing to do with our marriage,' Sutton insisted.

'I didn't ask that,' said Cross. 'She also developed serious mental issues. Is that correct?'

'Yes, in my opinion in all probability brought on by the substance abuse.'

'You were a GP at the time,' said Cross.

'I was.'

'And didn't change specialism till after her death.'

'After and because of, yes,' said Sutton.

'You anticipated my next question, Doctor. Thank you,' said Cross gratefully, ticking a question off on his list. 'And you discovered the body. Your wife's body?'

'Correct.'

'So here's where I get a little confused. You said at the inquest that her last words were "thank you".'

'That's correct.'

'Right,' said Cross almost to himself, as if he was still trying to make sense of what confused him. 'When exactly did she say "thank you"?'

'That morning. When I went to work.'

'You said, again at the inquest, that in those days you used to go home for lunch,' said Cross.

'Yes. The surgery was just around the corner from where we lived.'

'To save a little money and check up on her?'

'Towards the end, yes. I liked to check on her as she was in a delicate stage of her recovery.'

'And on the day of her death you went back at lunchtime and discovered her body. Is that right?' asked Cross.

'Yes.'

'Except, with respect, that's not what happened at all, was it? You stated on more than one occasion that her last words were "thank you". On your way to work. After breakfast, maybe, as you were going out of the door.'

'Yes,' Sutton sighed.

'But you see, in those circumstances, had that been what happened, had she said "thank you" at that point, I would've expected you to report that "her last words *to me* were…" not "her last words were…" Do you see the distinction?'

'I don't,' he replied tersely.

'Do you, DS Ottey?' Cross asked.

'I do,' she replied.

'"Her last words were",' Cross repeated. 'Not "her last words *to me* were". The distinction is this – "her last words were" can mean only one thing, Dr Sutton. You were there. You didn't discover her body. You found her very much alive but having deliberately taken an overdose. She wanted to die. She'd had enough of what she saw as her miserable existence. She'd told you on several occasions, you said at the inquest, that she wanted to end her life. And in that moment she asked you not to help. Not to intervene. Not to call an ambulance. And you agreed. And she thanked you for that. She said "thank you" just before she died. "Thank you", and then you watched her die.'

Cross said nothing further.

Sutton just sat there. Ottey wondered whether he was picturing the scene of his wife's death.

'Is that what happened?' she asked.

'No comment,' came the reply.

A 'no comment' after all these hours meant that things were progressing, if a little slowly.

Chapter 58

Cross came back into the interview room with Ottey an hour later. He sat down and placed his file equidistant from the sides of the table and opened it. The sheets were now covered with several ticks against questions that had been asked. Sutton's demeanour seemed to have changed. He was sitting back in his chair, arms folded – even someone unversed in the intricacies of body language would have been able to tell it spelt 'defensive'.

'How do you feel about your mother's and wife's deaths all these years on?' Cross began.

'I don't understand the question,' Sutton replied.

'You were complicit in both of their suicides. How do you feel about their premature passing now?' Cross elaborated.

'Sadness, loss, relief,' said Sutton.

'Relief?'

'Yes. That they went out on their own terms. That they were spared any further suffering,' Sutton explained.

'And what about your father's death?' Cross asked.

Sutton didn't say anything. Cross held his gaze. This obviously didn't fit Sutton's thesis.

'All right, let's put that aside. What you are saying about

your mother and wife forms the basis of your present views on assisted dying. Is that a fair statement?' Cross asked.

'No. Not at all. It's part of my personal experience. Part of my personal narrative, if you like. But it doesn't form the basis of anything. Nor can it be said to prove anything. Am I happy in my role in their deaths? Yes. Can I see any alternatives to the manner of their deaths? Yes: an officially sanctioned means for them to have done it without fear and in the open. Suicide was the official verdict of their deaths, together with all the social stigma and complications that come with such a finding. But it was different. They made a rational decision. I'm sure you can see that distinction, Sergeant.'

'The verdict with your wife was "accidental death",' said Ottey.

'That may be but we all know it was suicide.'

'It surprises me that you would get the official coroner's finding wrong in your wife's case,' said Cross.

'It's not a case of my forgetting. I felt, I feel, they got it wrong. My wife committed suicide.'

'Your certainty in the matter presumably derives from your presence at her death when she thanked you,' said Cross looking directly at him. Sutton didn't flinch. He didn't give anything away. He simply returned the detective's stare equally enquiringly.

Cross made a note in his file. Then he turned over a page and placed it symmetrically in his folder.

'A substantial number of your patients over the course of your career have committed suicide, have they not?' Cross asked.

'Without wanting to sound glib, Sergeant, in my line of work it's an occupational hazard. The demographic of my patient list is by definition mentally vulnerable,' said Sutton.

'Vulnerable? To suicide?' asked Cross.

'No. Vulnerable in itself. "Prone to suicide" might be a better description.'

'Look, all mental health professionals have experience of loss in this way. Are you saying that Dr Sutton's mortality rate is disproportionately higher than others in his field?' asked the lawyer.

'I am indeed; very much so,' replied Cross. 'They are statistically much, much higher. Dr Marcus Todd first alerted me to it.'

Sutton sighed dismissively at the mention of Todd's name.

'Bit of a thorn in your side, Dr Sutton? Anyway, prompted by Dr Todd, we did our own research and discovered that your mortality rate is about twenty-six per cent higher,' Cross went on. 'Quite a significant number, I'm sure you'd agree. But on further investigation, what is even more surprising is the proportion of those deaths which are suicides.'

He stopped there, more for the lawyer's benefit than Sutton's.

'You see where we're going here?' asked Ottey. 'A large proportion of suicides in a therapist's mortality rate. A therapist who is a well-known advocate for assisted dying, not only for the terminally ill, but also for those with mental health issues.'

'Assisted dying, or suicide, as most people refer to it,' said Cross, just to annoy Sutton.

'There are three types of lies, Sergeant – lies, damn lies and statistics,' offered Sutton. 'Benjamin Disraeli,' he elaborated patronisingly.

'In point of fact that attribution appears to be mistaken and is a matter of some debate,' replied Cross.

'I have no idea of the parameters of your research; where and how you conducted it. So it is of little interest, or significance, to me,' Sutton said drily, ignoring Cross's correction.

'These are numbers, Dr Sutton. Numbers that don't lie. These are facts, not statistics, and I can assure you they are of the utmost interest and significance to the relatives of your deceased clients,' said Cross.

Sutton made no reply.

'So. Full disclosure here,' said Ottey. 'We all – you and us – believe that Flick was murdered by the administration of an overdose of diamorphine. So, bearing that in mind, we applied to have some of your late patients exhumed for the purpose of seeing if any diamorphine was present in their bodies when they died. But as you already know, we couldn't do that.'

'Why?' asked Sutton.

'Because you had them all cremated,' answered Cross.

'Some, yes; where there was no family involved,' said Sutton.

'How many, in fact?' asked Ottey.

'I have no idea,' he replied impatiently, as if it was an absurd question which she should've known better than to ask.

'Roughly,' she persisted, ignoring his attitude.

'I don't know. Five or six?' he suggested.

Cross looked at him as if ensuring that he'd heard correctly. 'Five or six, you think?'

'Correct.'

'It was, in point of fact, twenty-two of them. *All* of your clients who died by their own hand were cremated,' Cross informed him.

'Then obviously their GPs must have signed the forms. It wasn't me.'

Cross looked at Sutton for a moment as he processed this information. It could well be crucial, he thought, though he couldn't be sure. He then opened his file, taking out a sheaf of documents and pushing them across the table to Sutton.

'These are the cremation orders, and as you can see, you signed them. Every single one of them.'

Cross noted a momentary look of confusion on Sutton's face as he examined his signature on the orders – one by one. He let out an involuntary sigh and looked up.

'I suppose I must've forgotten,' he said.

Cross said nothing for a moment. He just looked at Sutton, trying to read his expression. His manner seemed put out, as if he was less sure of himself.

'Why did you sign the orders so promptly and have the remains destroyed in this way?' Cross went on.

'Just trying to be efficient,' Sutton replied.

'Unless, of course, you were trying to conceal something – had something to hide,' Cross suggested.

'I can assure you I have nothing to hide. As you've already mentioned, I have maintained from the very start that Flick Wilson was murdered. Why would I do that if, as you say, I "had something to hide"?' Sutton countered.

'Were you aware that Dr Robert James, in a neighbouring medical practice, had complained about the number of cremation orders you'd asked him to countersign?' asked Cross.

Again there was a moment in which, it seemed to him, Sutton was deliberating how to answer the question.

'I was not aware of that, no.'

'Then as soon as he'd voiced that complaint, you went elsewhere for the countersignatures. Why was that?

Because maybe you thought you were attracting too much attention?'

Sutton didn't answer. Cross looked at him; Sutton seemed perplexed.

Cross thought for a moment.

'Let's have a ten-minute break,' he suggested and left, gathering his files with him.

Chapter 59

Cross sat in his office awaiting the call. He didn't have to wait long, as he'd told Dr James's receptionist who he was and that the matter was urgent. His mobile rang.

'Cross,' he replied, answering it.

'DS Cross, this is Dr James. What can I do for you?'

'I wanted to talk to you about Dr Benedict Sutton.'

'Oh yes,' replied the doctor.

'I understand you were uncomfortable at the number of cremation orders he was asking you to sign. Is my information correct?'

'Yes, that was what I told the officer who came in the other day,' said James, referring to Mackenzie.

'She's not actually a police officer.' Cross couldn't help himself but correct the doctor.

'My mistake, I just assumed. Anyway, as I told her, I was alarmed by the number of cremation orders and I let him know.'

'That's what I wanted to ask you. Was it Dr Sutton himself who brought over the orders for your signature? Or was it someone else?' Cross asked.

'No, it wasn't Sutton. I haven't actually met the man. It was his secretary,' said the doctor.

Cross was writing things down as James spoke.

'Diana?' he asked.

'Don't know her name, I'm afraid. Very efficient, no-nonsense kind of woman.'

'Yes, that would be her. Thanks very much, Doctor. That's all I wanted to know.' Cross ended the call.

'You didn't sign most of those cremation orders, did you, Dr Sutton?' Cross asked.

'As far as I can see, my signature appears on all of them,' replied Sutton.

'Appears, indeed. Strange that you couldn't remember,' Cross said.

'I'm a busy man.'

'I'm sure you are. Too busy to sign letters at times, possibly. Cheques even, I imagine. Cremation forms, perhaps,' Cross went on.

'What are you talking about?' Sutton asked.

'Are there times when a signature may be required quickly for something when you're not in the office? Not available?'

'Occasionally, yes.'

'What happens then?'

'Diana signs them,' Sutton replied.

'As pp Dr Benedict Sutton?'

'I have no idea.'

Cross turned to Ottey. 'They're very good, these signatures. Pretty much identical, but I'm confident that if we showed them to a graphologist...' he turned to Sutton, 'that's a handwriting expert, Doctor. We often use them. So skilled.

Some can even interpret personality traits from handwriting samples. Really clever.'

'I'm aware of what a graphologist is,' Sutton replied irritably.

'Of course you are. Forgive me. It's just that we get quite a lot of murder suspects in here who aren't of your intellectual calibre. Well, almost all of them. Anyway, said graphologist, despite the similarity between all these signatures, wouldn't, I'm sure, have much difficulty in determining that they were written by two different hands. Yours and Diana's,' Cross finished.

'It's more than possible. It's just an administrative form. Nothing more. She was simply being efficient. As you know, she's quite the sergeant major when it comes to the way things are done in my office. Actually, I'll rephrase that – *her* office would be a more accurate description.' He laughed nervously.

'But why the rush?' asked Cross.

'Like I said – efficiency.'

'You rely on her enormously, is that right?'

'I do.'

'Even to destroy evidence for you?' asked Cross.

'Don't answer that,' advised the lawyer.

'All right, let's move on. We'll leave the cremation orders for now. Let's move on to the death certificates. You signed them all,' Cross said.

'Is that a question?' asked Sutton.

'Did you sign them all?' asked Cross, getting them out of his file and pushing them across the table.

Sutton examined them all, one by one.

'I did.'

'No chance of Diana doing that, as cause of death has to be

ascertained and entered,' said Cross. He paused for a while as if he was mentally asking himself the question he was about to ask Sutton. 'Here's my question. How did you manage to be there; to sign all these certificates? All the suicides of patients under your care were signed by you.'

'They were my patients. Where's the issue?'

'How did you know they were dead?' Cross asked. 'Was it because you were there?'

'No, of course not,' said Sutton, as if stating the obvious.

'Then how did you know?' persisted Cross.

'Diana called me,' said Sutton.

'Diana called you?'

'Yes.'

'But how did she know they were dead?' said Cross.

'Because she was there,' said Sutton.

'Diana? Why?'

'She does house calls to our patients. She's like my outreach resource, if you will. She helps them with administrative social security issues, unemployment benefit, housing. Putting together a CV when they're trying to get employment. Sorting out references. She's extremely good at it.'

'She must make a lot of visits doing people's CVs,' said Cross.

'She does more than that,' said Sutton. 'Diana's a nurse. As you may or may not know, I have a no-tolerance rule when it comes to my patients. They have to want to get clean. Recover. And they have to prove that on a regular basis. Diana does regular random blood tests on all of our patients as long as I'm treating them. If any of them have been using, it's the end of their treatment. They get tested about once a month.'

But Cross wasn't listening. He was thinking about the

one issue they hadn't been able to answer in this case. The last question Esther Moffatt had asked: 'How did they get her consent?' Why would someone willingly let someone else inject them with diamorphine if they were a recovering addict? And this was the answer – *if they thought they were doing a blood test.*

Cross looked at Sutton, who suddenly smiled, an appalling victory smirk, as if he knew that Cross had just worked it out and he'd enjoyed watching it.

'We need to take a break,' said Cross calmly.

'How long?' asked the lawyer.

'I'm not sure,' replied Cross, getting up to leave.

'You won't find her at the office, Sergeant,' said Sutton, who suddenly appeared confident again.

'No? And why is that?'

'She's doing a blood test at four,' replied Sutton.

Cross looked at his watch. That was in just under an hour.

'For Angie. You remember Angie – you brought her to me.' Sutton stared right at Cross as if he savoured the moment.

Chapter 60

Ottey called Sutton's office; it went straight through to voicemail. Cross called Karen. She was at work but picked up.

'It's DS Cross,' he said.

'Hi, is everything okay?' she replied.

'Do you know where Angie is?'

'I thought you said you got her into rehab,' said Karen.

'I did. Do you know where it is?'

'No.' She sounded a little puzzled.

'If she was out, do you know where she'd go?' asked Cross.

'No, sorry. I doubt she went back to her old flat. The landlord threw her out. That's why she was on the streets.'

'Are you sure, Karen? This is really urgent,' Cross insisted.

'I'm sorry. I haven't got a clue,' she replied.

Mackenzie had called Billie Williams, who gave her the numbers of other recovery centres she knew Sutton used if she was full.

'If Diana is going to give her a blood test it has to mean she's no longer in a recovery centre,' Cross reasoned.

'She might actually just be doing a blood test,' said Ottey, hopefully.

'Possibly, but it's more likely to be her last hurrah, because she saw Sutton arrested. She knows the net is drawing in. Let's go to the office anyway,' Cross suggested.

The office manager let them into Sutton's suite of offices, which was locked.

'What are we looking for?' asked Ottey.

'Her desk diary. She wrote everything down compulsively. Absolutely everything,' Cross replied.

It wasn't on her immaculately tidy desk. Ottey noticed that biros and pencils were all organised according to colour. But the desk diary wasn't there and the drawers were locked. It was now 3.35. It took them five minutes to force open the drawers. The desk diary was in the left-hand top drawer. Cross leafed through the pages, which were filled to the margins with neat, tidy writing. Deliveries, calls, appointments – everything was written down with additional notes. They came to that day's date, and there it was at four: Angie's blood test, together with an address. Cross put the diary back in the desk.

'We should get a warrant for the diary. We don't want the defence to claim it was part of an illegal search,' he said, thinking ahead in his usual methodical way to the court case and the admissibility of crucial evidence.

'It isn't an illegal search, don't be pedantic. We're here to arrest her.'

He thought for a second then took the diary back out of the desk. 'You are, of course, correct.'

Then as they were leaving he noticed something about the box files that were neatly organised on the shelves behind her desk. One of them was upside down and protruded further out from the shelf than the others. It was the kind of thing that would annoy him and he knew it was something that Diana Coogan would not be able to tolerate.

'George, we need to go, now,' Ottey said with some urgency as he walked over to the bookshelf and carefully took out the upside down box file. He searched behind it with his free hand till he found what he was looking for. Then he carefully brought out an A5 book.

It was Flick's journal.

The address was in Bedminster, not too far away from Hopewell. It was approaching rush hour and navigating the city traffic wasn't going to be easy. Cross hated it when they used the blues and twos and Ottey drove out of her skin. It was obviously completely necessary when she did, as on this occasion, but it really upset him. He'd tried closing his eyes, but that just made him car sick. So he just stared fixedly out of the windscreen, terrified, as they drove, at times on the wrong side of the road and through red lights.

Ottey was actually a great driver, as she'd taken pains to point out to him on several occasions. She had passed the advanced police driving test with flying colours. This, and the fact that she'd never had an accident while driving in this manner, seemed to be of little comfort to him. He sat there, pale, gripping onto the sides of his seat with white knuckles, barely breathing. But this time it wasn't so much to do with her driving as the nauseating realisation that he himself had inadvertently put Angie straight into the clutches of the killer.

They arrived at a large terraced house that looked like it had once been offices, and ran in. They knocked on the caretaker's door, but there was no response. It was now 4.10.

Finally a resident opened their door and told them what room the 'new girl' was in.

They burst through the door. Angie leaped out of the armchair she was sitting in, absolutely terrified. Diana was sitting opposite her.

'What the fuck?' Angie yelled, a tourniquet hanging down from her arm.

'Has she done anything to you, Angie?' said Cross.

'No, she's giving me a blood test. What's going on?'

Diana had sat there motionless, but Cross noticed her dropping something into her handbag. On the table was a needle and a blood-taking kit.

'Just stay where you are, Angie,' said Cross.

'What is going on, Detectives? This is most alarming. I was about to take a blood test,' said Diana, pointing to the kit on the table.

'Diana Coogan, I'm arresting you on suspicion of the murder of Felicity Wilson,' said Ottey, who then proceeded to read Diana her rights.

Cross noticed that Diana was expressionless. He wondered whether she was expecting this. Had she been resigned to it after Sutton's arrest? But why hadn't she run?

Ottey cuffed her and told Cross to take her out to the car.

'My handbag,' said Diana, as Cross was moving her out of the room.

'Your handbag is now evidence,' Cross informed her, and they left.

Ottey now wanted to do something that would never occur to Cross. She wanted to sit down with Angie and explain to her what had just happened. Talk her down. The events had been very dramatic and probably frightening – two police officers suddenly bursting noisily through a closed door in that way. Angie was in a vulnerable state anyway, and Ottey didn't want this to have an adverse effect on her recovery. She managed to get hold of the duty manager and explain to her what was going on, leaving Angie in her care. Ottey then bagged up Diana's handbag and the blood-taking kit.

Diana said nothing in the car. She sat there as if in a very secure Uber. Cross was reflecting on how close Angie had come to a probable death.

Chapter 61

The interview with Diana was oddly straightforward. She seemed at times to be indifferent, and at others relieved. She initially denied everything, insisting that she had visited Angie to give her a blood test. But the denial struck Cross as almost half-hearted, as if she was just going through the motions. That she knew the truth would inevitably come out at some point. Interestingly, Sutton's solicitor had declined to act for Diana, and she was provided with a duty solicitor, whose eyes almost went out on stalks when he saw the scale of the charges they were talking about.

Mackenzie was desperate to observe the interview, but Cross had her checking Diana's phone records for all the days on which the murders occurred together with the day prior to them all. He also wanted them cross-checked with the appointments logged into her desk diary. Diana's attention to detail and obsessive recording of absolutely everything was going to be an absolute gift for the prosecution.

'What was the purpose of your visit to Angie Wright this afternoon?' Cross asked.

'I told you, it was an outpatient call,' Diana said.

'Yes, but to what purpose?' Cross insisted.

'To carry out a random blood test.'

'Do you do a lot of blood tests for Dr Sutton?' he asked.

She laughed quietly at this question.

'I do them all. I'm a qualified nurse. Dr Sutton is far too busy to do something so mundane. It wouldn't be a good use of his precious time.'

'Have you always done them?' Cross asked.

She nodded. 'I have. In fact they were my idea. He was always insistent that his patients were clean, and thought he could just tell if they were using again. Which of course he could have, being an expert in his field, but I argued that random drug tests wouldn't just mean that he could be sure, but would give them an incentive to stay clean.'

'It sounds like more of a threat,' said Ottey.

'I suppose you could look at it like that,' she replied neutrally.

'Was it always your intention to kill Sutton's patients?' Cross asked.

'I have no idea what you're talking about.'

'Did the idea of killing them occur to you after you started the blood tests, or was it the very reason for them?' Cross asked.

Diana just smiled politely as if she hadn't heard the question.

'You were about to administer a fatal dose of diamorphine to Angie, were you not?' he asked.

'I was going to do no such thing,' she replied.

'We found a syringe in your handbag containing enough morphine to kill anyone, together with an empty phial,' Cross said. Again, Diana just smiled.

'That's what you've been doing for years. Killing patients. All recovering drug addicts. On the pretext of doing a blood test. It was the one thing I couldn't work out. Why would they let you inject them? It's quite ingenious,' said Cross thoughtfully.

Diana couldn't help but smile at this.

She's taking it as a compliment, thought Cross.

'Why was this hidden in your office?' asked Ottey, pushing Flick's journal across the desk. Cross noted there was a slight hesitation in Diana. She was taken by surprise and didn't know how to react. She looked up without saying anything.

'It's Flick Wilson's journal,' Ottey volunteered, a little too quickly, thought Cross.

'No comment,' Diana replied.

It was her first 'no comment' of the interview. She'd been confident and completely open up until that point. Cross wondered why this had taken her by surprise.

'Her reaction to the journal was interesting,' Cross said in Carson's office.

'She knew it was the final nail in her coffin,' Carson said crassly.

'I don't think she knew it was there,' Cross continued as if nothing had been said.

'What makes you think that?'

'Like I said; her reaction. She was surprised and didn't know what to say.'

'Why wouldn't she just say she didn't know it was there?' said Ottey, following Cross's line of thought.

'What makes you so sure she didn't know?' persisted Carson.

'The box file it was concealed behind was upside down.

That is something she absolutely would never have done. She was meticulously organised to the point of compulsion.'

Carson looked at Ottey. She begged him mentally not to say what he was obviously thinking – that it took someone obsessively ordered to notice it. He must've read the signals, as he said nothing. Ottey spoke to take any further opportunity away from him.

'We're going to leave her on ice for a couple of hours, while we gather more evidence, before we charge.'

'It's creepy,' was all Carson could offer. 'Gives me shivers.'

Cross used the time to go through Diana's diary and all the others they found chronologically filed away, year by year, in a filing cabinet in Sutton's outer office. They had left Sutton in his cell throughout Diana's arrest and first interview. They still had fourteen hours left before they either had to charge him or get an extension. But Cross was quietly becoming more and more convinced that they wouldn't be able to charge him. Cross was looking for a pattern, but unusually in this case he actually knew what he was looking for and where. It wasn't long before he found it. The dates for the scheduled blood tests for the victims were all within twenty-four hours of their deaths. This was pretty incontrovertible. He also looked at Flick's journal. Every page was crammed with large looping handwriting characteristic of someone who enjoyed writing and took great pains with it. At times pens had been used which bled through the page onto the preceding one. She would then change pens. There were notes of her meetings with Sutton and 'badge woman' as she had christened Diana. But nothing seemed untoward. There were distressingly frank descriptions of Danny Stokes's behaviour and desperate accounts of Simon's unreliability. But towards the end of the entries Cross noticed a small triangle of paper in the bottom corner of one page. It was obvious that someone had ripped a couple of pages out of the book. Was it Flick herself? he wondered. But then he was called back down to the interview room.

The diamorphine they found in Diana's handbag had been prescribed to a recently deceased patient in a local hospice. They searched Diana's flat and discovered several more phials of diamorphine in her fridge. They were all prescriptions from the same hospice, and all of the patients were now deceased. Ottey went down to the hospice with some uniformed officers. As they made their enquiries as to who was in charge of the patients' drugs, a nurse saw them and suddenly legged it through the back garden. Uniform gave chase and made the arrest.

Back at the MCU the nurse told them everything. He had no idea what Diana had been using them for. He just assumed she was rich with a drug habit. They were being thrown away, so he sold them to her for a bit of cash on the side. There was no harm done.

'Except for the twenty-two women she killed with the diamorphine,' said Cross.

'What?' exclaimed the nurse. He then threw up and they had to move to another interview room while that one was cleaned.

When they continued, he said that she paid well and they'd met when her mother had been a patient at the hospice receiving end-of-life care. The nurse knew he was going to lose his job because of all this, but he was more concerned about not being charged as an accessory to murder.

Diana had started working for Sutton just after her mother died. The first murder occurred eighteen months later. Cross decided to systematically lay out all the evidence in front of her for each of the twenty-two deaths.

'So, Diana,' he began. 'The dates of the deaths we are discussing all correlate with the dates in your diary for the supposed random drug tests. You will be charged with all twenty-two murders and, on the balance of just the evidence we have so far, it's more than likely you'll be found guilty.'

'I didn't kill anyone, Sergeant,' she replied.

'Perhaps you could explain that to me,' said Cross.

'I assisted them in their deaths. They wanted to end their suffering, put a stop to it, and I helped facilitate that,' she said quietly.

'Is that what you believe?' Cross asked, with no edge to it. No surprise or disbelief. Just a straight question.

'If we lived in a more liberal society, I wouldn't be sitting here,' she replied.

'Oh, I think if this was Holland or Sweden or anywhere where euthanasia is legal, you would still be sitting here,' said Cross.

'That's your opinion.'

'Not at all; you see, you were missing one vital thing – consent.'

She made no comment to this.

'How did it start? What made you decide to do this?' Cross sounded genuinely fascinated.

'The first was Trisha. She was desperate to die – said so all the time. Had made a few attempts. She was in such a bad place mentally. I asked her if she really wanted to end it all. She said she did. I'd seen them disposing of my mother's morphine at the hospice. I went back and offered Patrick money – made out it was for me. Then I asked Trisha if she was sure and we did it. She was so much better off.' Diana spoke as if she was picturing it in her head.

'Were they all like that in the beginning?' Cross asked.

'Yes. They asked, or were in such a terrible place, I offered. Then I had an instinct for those that were heading that way anyway. Don't forget there are hundreds of Dr Sutton's patients who just got better. I only helped the ones who had no chance. Why let them suffer so? Go through all that pain? So I began helping some of them, without actually putting them through the burden of discussing it and worrying about it. It was so peaceful. Such a tranquil, quick, humane way to go.'

'But they hadn't asked you. The majority had no idea what you were about to do,' said Ottey.

'Lucky them, don't you think?' she replied.

'Was Dr Sutton aware of what you were doing?' asked Cross.

'Oh gosh, no. I mean, he believes assisted dying for the terminally ill and those with unending mental health issues should be available, but he would never do such a thing while it was illegal.' She appeared shocked at the very idea of it.

'So you are aware that what you did was illegal?' Cross asked.

'Of course I am. I'm not stupid. It's the law which is stupid,' she replied.

'Do you expect us to believe that all the women you killed wanted to end their lives?' Cross asked.

'Yes, it's just that some hadn't reached that awful conclusion yet. I saved them that,' she said.

Cross thought she actually believed it. But of course there was a flaw in her belief.

'What about Flick?' he asked.

'What about her?'

'She most certainly didn't want to die. She had a life, a loving mother and a daughter,' Cross said.

Diana didn't answer.

'Did she ever, at any point, tell you she wanted to end her life?'

'She was going to cause trouble,' said Diana.

'For whom was she going to cause trouble?'

'For Dr Sutton. For his work,' she said.

'His work? What do you mean?'

'He's a great man, greatly misunderstood by people such as yourself, Sergeant.'

'Then perhaps you could explain it to me. I'd be very interested. What was Flick going to do?' Cross said.

'You know his views. You just don't understand them. They frighten you.'

'What was Flick going to do?' Cross persisted.

'No comment.'

This interested Cross. She'd mentioned Flick possibly causing trouble and then had clammed up. He moved on.

'You don't seem to be particularly perturbed by your arrest. You've confessed to all of these murders and it doesn't seem to worry you in the least. Is it a front or do you genuinely feel that way?' Cross said, a few hours later.

'Assisted deaths,' she insisted, again.

'Do you have any remorse?' he asked. She sighed. She

didn't appear to be tired – it was the sigh of someone who was irritated by the intellectual inferiority of the person she was talking to.

'This was always the end game, Sergeant. I should've thought that much was obvious. Why do you think I didn't bother to flee once you arrested Benedict?'

This was the first time she'd called Sutton by his first name. Cross thought she might be infatuated with him.

'Why didn't you?' he asked.

'I want people to know what I've done. Why I've done it. To provoke debate. To get the issue discussed at a national level. To get it brought up in Parliament. It had to be done to get it properly addressed.'

'And you're willing to spend the rest of your life in prison for that?' asked Cross.

'I won't be around for long,' she said. 'Trust me.'

'What does that mean?'

'I'm sure even you can figure that out, Sergeant,' she replied coldly and calmly.

'All right. Well, we're going to charge you now. But I have one further question for you. Did you always call Dr Sutton after administering the diamorphine?' he asked.

'At the beginning, yes.'

'But not always?' he went on.

'I would go back to "discover" the body, as it were, and call him to come and do the death certificate,' she said. 'But on a couple of occasions he'd decided to go round anyway and visit, which he did occasionally. So I had no need to call him.'

'Why did you forge the cremation orders?' Cross asked.

'Because I didn't want him getting suspicious.'

'I see. One last thing,' Cross said. 'Does he have a key to your desk?'

'Of course.'

She was taken off to be charged with twenty-two counts of murder. Ottey took her down, as Cross wanted to prepare for his last interview with Sutton.

Carson appeared in the custody suite as Diana was being charged and stood to one side, observing.

'What are you doing down here?' Ottey asked him.

'It's a moment of history, Josie,' he replied.

'What are you talking about?'

'This,' he said, nodding his head towards Diana. 'My first serial killer.'

'Yours?' she said in disbelief.

Chapter 62

Cross and Ottey went back in to see Sutton.

'It's my understanding you've charged someone. Presumably you're here to inform my client that he is free to go,' said the lawyer, with a resignation that implied that, had they listened to him in the first place, all this would have been over hours ago and saved them a lot of time and inconvenience. This despite the fact that his contribution to the proceedings had been virtually non-existent.

Cross finished organising his folders on the table, as if the interview wouldn't officially start till he'd done so. He was irritated now, that someone in the custody suite had opened their mouths unnecessarily about Diana Coogan. There was no need for the lawyer to know right now, and it immediately changed the way Cross would conduct the interview.

'That is correct,' he said at last. 'Which brings me to my main question. Dr Sutton, were you aware that your secretary, who we have just charged, was committing these murders?'

'I was unaware she was helping them to die,' Sutton answered.

'So you approve of her actions?' said Cross.

'Of course not. It's illegal.'

'The way you phrase it would seem to imply otherwise,' said Cross.

'I can't help how you choose to interpret my answers,' said Sutton.

'Did you tell her to kill them?' Cross went on.

'I did not.'

Cross noticed that Sutton was more relaxed in this interview, as if the charging of Diana had changed things for him.

'Encourage her then, implicitly rather than explicitly?'

'No.'

'You told us that Flick had been, to use your exact expression, "killed",' said Cross.

'Correct.'

'Do you still hold that view?' Cross asked.

There was a momentary pause.

'I do,' Sutton said.

'So what do you think happened? I mean, you've said so yourself – Flick wasn't suicidal. She had no need to be "helped to die", as you insist on putting it.'

'I have no idea. I suggest you direct that question to Diana,' said Sutton.

'Oh, I will. Rest assured. How do you feel about it now?'

'In Flick's case? I'm devastated,' said Sutton.

'You're not devastated by them all?' asked Cross, surprised.

Sutton didn't answer.

'It's just that when you say "in Flick's case", it would seem to imply that you're not devastated by all of them,' Cross pointed out.

'I think some of them were in a very dark place, from which they saw no way out,' Sutton said.

'So you do approve. In those cases.'

'I didn't say that.'

Cross looked at him as if he was trying to work something out which was really puzzling him.

'You must've known, though. Surely.'

'I did not,' said Sutton.

'You had absolutely no idea?' Cross seemed to find this implausible.

'None at all,' Sutton said again.

'You didn't notice that within a matter of hours of Diana's appointments to conduct random blood tests, your patients were dying?'

'I have hundreds of patients. I didn't notice, no,' Sutton maintained.

'I find that hard to believe. Even you must've been aware that more and more suicides were happening on your watch.'

'No, not at all. The way I viewed it was that possibly I was willing to entertain several difficult cases that my colleagues wouldn't entertain,' said Sutton.

'So you did notice it, but you had a justifiable rationale for it?'

'No,' Sutton replied firmly.

'Again, I ask you. Random blood tests, followed by death, no fewer than twenty-two times, over eight years admittedly, but still,' said Cross.

'Sergeant, I wasn't aware of the timings of Diana's blood tests. They were random. The clue is in the word,' said Sutton.

'Did they occur during office hours?' Cross went on.

'Mostly not. No. So there you are. It wasn't even as if she was leaving the office for me to be able to notice,' Sutton reasoned. 'What is more, they weren't appointments, as you keep referring to them. They were random.'

'They may have been random to your patients, but we both know they weren't random to Diana,' said Cross. 'Far from it. They were regulated in her own way. She had a system. If you look at her diaries you will quickly see there is a pattern. The intermittence, or periodicity if you will, is always the same – for all of the patients. I can show you if you like. It's quite fascinating.'

'I'll have to take your word for it. I haven't looked at them that closely.'

'So you have looked at them,' said Cross. 'Just not closely.'

Sutton didn't answer.

'You have a key to her desk drawer,' Cross went on. 'Where she keeps her desk diary.'

'That proves nothing,' said Sutton.

'Okay. So perhaps you could answer me this question. When Diana did these random blood tests, of which you had no foreknowledge, did she report back to you? I mean, she must've done hundreds, yes?'

'She did,' Sutton replied.

'How?'

'She would either text me or email.'

'Did any of them ever fail the test?' asked Cross.

'Unfortunately, yes.'

'And what happened then?'

'I no longer treated them,' Sutton answered.

'That seems a little draconian,' Cross commented.

'Deliberately so. They had to want to get clean. Otherwise it was a waste of my time. Time I could've used treating patients who actually wanted to get well.'

'And what were the results of the twenty-two blood tests?' asked Cross.

'I beg your pardon?' said Sutton.

'Were they all clean? No issues there?'

Sutton didn't reply.

'Did Diana not provide you with them?' Cross asked, confused.

'They were dead, Sergeant! What would be the point?' Sutton said.

'You weren't in the least interested? Not even professionally?'

'It never occurred to me,' said Sutton.

Cross looked at him for a while.

'Because you knew they didn't exist.'

'No.'

'The fact is that Diana does everything by the book, through to completion. She is totally regimented in the way she works. Had she taken those blood tests, she would've had to send them to you. She wouldn't be happy until that task had been ticked off. Till she'd done her job properly. It's what she lived for. How she lived. You and I both know that.'

'I'll defer to your greater knowledge of autistic behaviour, Sergeant. As I told you previously, it's my belief that she may well be on the spectrum,' said Sutton, as if it was some sort of challenge.

Again, one Cross wasn't going to rise to.

'You didn't find it odd that there were no results for those blood tests? That they didn't exist?' Cross asked.

No answer was forthcoming.

'So you weren't aware of the timings of Diana's blood tests?' asked Cross.

'How many times is he going to ask this?' Sutton said, looking at Ottey. This told both her and Cross that Cross was getting well and truly under his skin. 'No!'

'Then how did you know about Angie?' Cross asked.

'I'm sorry?'

'Yesterday. You were able to tell us the time of her blood test. How was that?' Cross asked.

'I guess it's just the exception that proves the rule,' Sutton answered.

'No. I don't think so. You see, I think you'd worked the whole thing out. Some time ago. You knew what she was up to and yet you said nothing,' said Cross.

'Which, to my certain knowledge of the law, isn't a crime, Sergeant,' said Sutton's lawyer brightly. 'If indeed it's true, which it seems isn't actually something you can prove.'

Cross didn't look at him but just carried on.

'So you maintain you weren't, at any point, aware of your secretary's blood test appointments with your patients?'

'Correct,' Sutton replied wearily.

'Except that, as we know, you were aware of Angie's appointment yesterday?' said Cross.

Sutton didn't answer.

Cross consulted his notes, though he had no need to. He just wanted Sutton to be aware that he was taking notes of absolutely everything he said. 'You knew that Diana wouldn't be in the office when we were about to go round and arrest her because she was doing a blood test for Angie at four.'

'She must've told me in passing.'

'I see,' Cross commented. 'How did you manage to sign all the death certificates for the twenty-two cases we've been discussing? What I mean by that is, how was it that you were there?' asked Cross.

'Diana called me,' said Sutton.

'To say she'd killed them? Job done,' said Ottey, who hadn't spoken for some time but was getting annoyed by Sutton.

'No, of course not. She maintained she'd discovered the bodies. I then went over to see to all the formalities. It was the least I could do for them.'

'Well, that's true,' agreed Cross. 'It certainly was the very least you could have done for them.'

'What are you suggesting I should have done?' Sutton took the bait.

'I should've thought that was obvious. Prevented their deaths in the first place. By stopping your secretary from killing them,' said Cross.

'How many times do I have to tell you? I didn't know what she was up to,' Sutton insisted.

'In the same way you weren't aware of *when* she was doing it?' Cross went on.

'Yes.'

'I'm sorry,' interjected the lawyer, 'but by my calculations you have another fifteen minutes with my client unless you intend to apply for an extension or charge him – quite what with, however, I'm not entirely sure.'

'Why do people do that?' asked Cross.

'What?' said the lawyer.

'Are you genuinely apologetic?' Cross asked him.

'Apologetic for what?' The lawyer was puzzled.

'Why say "I'm sorry", when you're clearly not?'

'It's an expression,' said the lawyer.

'Of regret. You shouldn't use it if you're not regretful. As a lawyer, I'm surprised you're not more exact in your use of the English language,' Cross said, then without waiting for a response, turned back to Sutton. 'You maintain that Diana called you when she had "discovered" the bodies, to inform you of their deaths. Correct?'

'Yes,' said Sutton.

'Except that's not entirely true, is it?' said Cross.

There was no answer from Sutton.

'You see, we've been through Diana's phone records,' he continued, extracting the phone records from his file as if to remove any doubts from across the table. 'And while she did call you on several occasions, there were some where she didn't call you at all. Five, if we include Flick.'

'That was because Sandra called me,' Sutton said quickly.

'Indeed, but let's discuss the other four. How did you know they'd died? You signed their death certificates without Diana calling you. How?' said Cross.

Sutton didn't reply.

'Because she didn't have to, did she? Because you were there already. You were there when they died, weren't you?' Cross asked.

'Don't answer that question,' Sutton's lawyer said to him.

'Why were you there? Was it the urge to see it? Or make sure? What was it?' asked Cross. It was as if he was genuinely, naively interested.

'Have you ever seen anyone die, Sergeant?' said Sutton.

'Dr Sutton...' said his lawyer, warning him.

'I have, as it happens. Quite recently,' said Cross.

'I'm sorry for your loss,' Sutton said. 'But you now know what an amazingly powerful thing it is. To see life leaving a person's body is quite extraordinary, didn't you think?'

'I did, actually,' Cross replied.

'Then you understand,' Sutton went on.

'Understand what?'

'Not only how profound it is but also how no one should do it alone,' said Sutton enthusiastically.

'Surely none of your patients actually knew you were there?' Cross pointed out.

'That I don't know. I'd like to think so.'

'Are we done here?' asked the lawyer.

'For the moment. Despite the fact that your client was aware of his secretary's actions and that he attended some of the deaths inflicted by her hand, he hasn't actually committed a crime that I'm aware of,' Cross said with some distaste.

'Well, thank you for your time,' said Sutton, smiling. 'Doubtless I will see you at Diana's trial.'

'If not before,' replied Cross. He looked Sutton straight in the eye.

The doctor appeared to be trying to figure out what Cross had meant.

Cross went on, 'I'm not entirely sure, though, why you're smiling. Perhaps it's ironic. I can never tell. But one thing I'm fairly certain of is that nothing positive will come out of this situation for you. With all the attendant publicity which will come your way during Diana's trial, I'm not at all sure your practice will have a viable future. Why would people visit a therapist seeking help for their problems when one of his solutions is to have them killed by his secretary?'

'I did no such thing,' said Sutton nervously.

'Well, the public has a very different way of looking at these things, particularly when they learn that you actually attended some of the deaths,' said Cross.

TIM SULLIVAN

'How would they ever know? That has nothing to do with Diana's trial,' said the lawyer.

'You know how it is – these things have a way of getting into the public domain,' said Cross.

'This interview with Dr Sutton—' the lawyer began, but Cross interrupted him.

'And it won't be long, I imagine, before it's back to plain old "Mr" Sutton, once the General Medical Council are made aware of the case,' Cross concluded before walking out of the room.

'Not feeling so smug now, Doctor?' said Ottey. Cross then reappeared, as if something had just occurred to him.

'You say things were okay with Flick,' he said.

'That's a very general question, Sergeant,' Sutton replied.

'In your relationship with her. In her sessions progress was being made.'

'Yes.'

'One thing puzzles me. Why would Diana say that she thought Flick was going to cause trouble for you?'

'Again. Something you should probably ask her.'

Chapter 63

Things settled down for a few days at the MCU. Carson held a triumphant press conference about Diana's arrest and her subsequently being charged with twenty-two counts of murder. This in itself was unsurprising; what was surprising was that he insisted on having Ottey at his side. Cross had declined. Ottey wasn't oblivious to the fact, of course, that the force was doing as much as it could to present itself as being diverse, and this was probably in Carson's thinking.

The case went national in both print and TV media. It also, as Diana had predicted, brought the assisted dying debate to the fore. Depending where the various media outlets sat on the issue, they either used the case to demonstrate why assisted dying should be brought into law with all the appropriate safeguards in place, or why it shouldn't, as it would be open to abuse by people like Diana and, by implication, Sutton. Carson, it had to be said, was generous in his praise of the team led by Ottey and Cross – this despite the fact that he hadn't really considered it to be a legitimate case at the outset.

This lull in things also meant that Cross could no longer avoid the Campbell enquiry. He was duly summoned for an interview. He sat before a panel of three senior officers and listened as the list of Campbell's grievances – examples of Cross's disrespect, dissent and disregard for Campbell's rank and authority – was read out. As Cross listened, he came to the conclusion that he couldn't argue with the factual basis of the complaint. It was all completely accurate. Campbell hadn't actually fabricated anything or even greatly exaggerated. His interpretation of the facts and his perceived slights could all be taken issue with, but Cross found himself curiously indifferent to arguing the case. He thought the whole exercise was a complete waste of time.

If the board looked at the results of any of the cases Campbell had cited as involving Cross's supposed malfeasance, where he had countermanded Campbell – not the least Flick's case, which had led to Cross uncovering the worst serial killer the south-west had ever had – they would see that he, Cross, was right in every instance to take the action, or say what he said to Campbell.

After he'd finished reading out the litany of complaints, the head of the board looked up at Cross.

'How do you respond, Sergeant?' he said.

'I don't,' replied Cross.

'What does that mean?' the officer asked.

'I have nothing to say.'

'Nothing at all?'

'No. The facts, as laid out, are all correct, as far as my recollection goes.'

'Do you have nothing to say in mitigation or in your defence?' the head of the board asked.

'I do not. The facts are mitigation in themselves, and the results of my actions are my defence. Was there anything else, or can I get back to work?' Cross asked.

'I really would advise you to have something on record,' another board member said.

'I believe I just did,' Cross replied, and with that it was over as he immediately left the room.

The head of the panel was perplexed, but the other two officers were quietly thinking to themselves how impressive Cross's candour was. He thought he had no case to answer and so he wasn't going to be coerced into doing so.

Chapter 64

It was several weeks later, when Cross was putting together his evidence for the Crown Prosecution Service in the Diana Coogan case, that he began to question whether they'd uncovered the full extent of Sutton's complicity in it. Diana was maniacally, devotedly obsessed with her boss and his philosophy; to the extent that she took it upon herself to put it into practice. But Cross had a constant, nagging doubt gnawing away in the back of his mind that there was more to it. This was the kind of thing that kept him awake at night and, if truth be told, made him quite irascible. He couldn't stand the fact that justice might not have been done fully. He hadn't managed to get an answer out of Diana as to why Flick was going to cause trouble for her boss and what kind of trouble it could be. Something had passed them by and he wasn't sure what it was.

He decided to have another look at the journal. Maybe he'd find a clue there. But firstly, why had it been there? If Diana hadn't put it there, had Sutton? She had claimed later in her interview to have taken it from Flick's flat and hidden it in her office. But Cross didn't believe this for two reasons – the upside down box file and the fact that she hadn't taken any 'souvenirs' from other murder scenes. She hadn't been able to explain the missing pages either. So had Flick torn them out? But he'd gone back to her flat and checked all the other journals. In some journals there were pages that had been crossed out by Flick. Either in an irritated, angry way, where the text had been completely obliterated or crossed out with the writing still legible. But no pages had been ripped out of any of them. The ripping of pages out of the journal wasn't normal.

He was looking at it one evening when something caught his eye. He examined the small triangular residue of paper in the bottom corner from the ripped page. He opened his desk and took out a large magnifying glass. Mackenzie caught sight of this from halfway up a ladder where she was hanging the department's ancient, tacky Christmas decorations and turned to Ottey.

'I don't believe it. He's gone the full Sherlock,' she joked.

Cross could make out the remnants of a 'p' and possibly half an 'e'. What he hadn't spotted before was that there was part of a faint reversed letter that had bled from the other side of the page. He then realised he'd read the page opposite before. It was about Danny Stokes and a girl who was withdrawing from the case. It was on one of the photocopied pages that Tammy, Flick's lawyer, had given him. He kicked himself for not having put it together before. He found the pages. The first page in the photocopy was indeed the first of the pages to have been ripped out. But it had been rendered pretty much indecipherable by the ink from the following page bleeding through completely. He made another couple of copies then sat down with a bottle of white ink eraser and tried blotting out the intruding ink from the overleaf page. He realised after the first attempt that blocking it out in white completely wasn't working. He was losing too much of the letters on the page he was trying to read. After an hour of painstaking work he was able to read some sections of the missing page. It was just concluding thoughts about Stokes from the page before. He decided to reverse the process and white out the top page and try and make out the reverse lettering which had bled through from the other page, which he then held up to a mirror to read.

An hour later Ottey's curiosity had got the better of her and she knocked on the door. Cross was sitting back in the chair thinking. He handed her a page he'd printed out. It was his transcript of most of the reverse of the missing page.

'What's this?' she asked.

'Flick told Sutton she no longer wanted to continue sessions with him.'

'Okay.'

'Another patient of his, someone she knew from Hopewell, Leah, had committed suicide at the end of last year. Sutton told Flick that Leah had saved herself and her family from the pain of her existence. Flick took exception. She said that suicide could never be seen as the answer to mental health issues.'

'"He's unhappy about me leaving mid-therapy but looking back on my notes of our sessions there's a lot of subliminal hinting that suicide can be an option. He wants one last session but I've said no,"' Ottey read.

'It's not enough in itself to change anything, or prove anything,' added Cross.

'Do you think Sandra knows?'

'We'll check, but she would've said something.'

'So what are you thinking?'

'What was in the rest of the pages? I think there are at least three missing. Six sides in all. Who ripped them out? Diana hadn't come up with a satisfactory answer as to why she hid it or indeed why she took it in the first place.'

'She must've taken the pages out to protect Sutton,' Ottey suggested.

'Why wouldn't she just destroy it if that was the case?' Cross looked at her, waiting for her to put the pieces together.

'Because she didn't take it.'

'Exactly.'

But there was no more Cross could do with the information. It just added weight to his growing suspicion that although Diana had obviously killed all the other victims, she hadn't killed Flick. He went back to her desk diary. Something he'd noticed in it had perplexed him. Something that was missing. There was no appointment with Flick for a blood test the day before her body was discovered. Why hadn't Diana put it in the diary? It wasn't the kind of thing she would forget; she was a slave to procedure, almost like himself. To others, this omission might have seemed incidental and inconsequential. But to Cross it was vital. To him, the omission was glaring and there could only be one explanation. It wasn't there because Diana hadn't made such an appointment. If it wasn't her, it had to be Sutton. There was no other explanation for it. He'd known what she was doing and she'd been getting away with it. He was a necromaniac – fascinated with death; suicide in particular. It had started with his mother, his father, then his wife, and Flick was the latest manifestation.

But there were problems with this. Well, one main one for

Cross. There was no evidence. Nothing tangible. A forensic team had been through Flick's flat and found nothing other than evidence of Flick, her mother, Brian and Simon. No evidence of Diana being there, which was what they had been looking for – no DNA, no hair, no clothing fibres that could put her there. But they couldn't place anyone else there either, and most importantly for Cross that included Sutton. No appointment in his secretary's desk diary, and Flick's terminating her therapy, were nowhere near enough for a jury to convict.

Chapter 65

Ottey was finishing up for the day when she received a call from Karen. She wanted to see her. Ottey needed to get home for her children but Karen's request sounded urgent, as if she had in that moment decided to talk to the police, and Ottey didn't want to procrastinate in case she changed her mind. She said she'd be straight over. She called her older daughter Carla and after some canny negotiation, Carla agreed to make her and her sister's supper. Ottey reflected that her maternal line of credit with her teenage daughter had become a little overextended of late. She took Mackenzie with her to see Karen.

When they arrived the first thing they noticed was that the name of the business had been changed to Betty's Dry Cleaner's after Gerry Stokes's late wife. Karen was nervous when they walked in.

'Gerry said we can use his office,' she said. They followed her up the stairs. It had been changed. It looked more functional than before and certainly less ostentatious. All the photographs of Danny with his 'celebrity' friends had been removed. Gerry was sitting at the desk. He rose to greet Ottey and Mackenzie.

'Detective, thanks so much for coming.' Ottey thought he

seemed happy, but there was a lingering dullness of regret behind his eyes. 'Please sit.' He gestured to the sofas.

'New furniture?' Ottey commented.

'Yes. We got rid of the old stuff. Seemed the right thing to do, all things considered,' he replied, sitting himself. Ottey didn't understand what he meant at first then the sordid truth occurred to her. Danny must've committed some of his sexual offences on the thrown-out furniture. Gerry misconstrued her expression, as she was thinking this, to signify her surprise at his staying in the room.

'Oh, Karen has asked me to stay. I said it might be better if I didn't but she's told me everything she's going to tell you anyway.'

'No worries.'

'Gerry's made me assistant manager,' said Karen with a little pride.

'Is that right? Congratulations.'

'Well, we've made a lot of changes round here recently. Just the one final thing remains unsettled. Which is why Karen asked you here,' said Stokes. He looked at Karen as if to give her an assuring prompt. She took a large intake of breath.

'Danny raped me. Here. In this office. One night after work. It started as like a joke. Then he locked the door and...' She faltered momentarily then carried on. 'Gerry asked everyone here, all the girls, last week, if anything had happened to them. So I told him. He's the one who told me to call you,' she said.

'It took some encouragement. There are also other complaints. Those girls are also willing to come forward,' said Gerry quietly. Ottey warmed to the old man even further.

'Did you tell anyone at the time?' Mackenzie asked. She had leant forward and taken Karen's hand.

'Flick. I told Flick,' replied Karen.

'She took her to a rape crisis centre. That's why we called. They did a rape kit,' Gerry explained.

'I was so frightened. I needed this job. I decided not to go to the police after all. I'm so sorry.'

'That's completely understandable. Can you give us the details of the crisis centre?'

'Yes.' Karen searched her handbag and brought out a card which she gave to Ottey.

'Do you know where Danny is now?' Ottey asked Gerry.

'I've arranged to meet him at his apartment. Obviously I have no intention of going over. But you can pick him up there now,' he said with quiet regret.

'Karen, I have to ask. Will you be willing to appear in court?' Ottey asked. Karen looked suddenly terrified, as if she thought this would be it. That it would all be over.

'I'll be with you, Karen. I'll come to court. Everything will be fine,' Gerry reassured her.

'I can't get over Gerry. Can you imagine that? Dobbing in his own son?' said Mackenzie in the car on the way over to Danny's flat.

'He's taking responsibility,' said Ottey.

'But it wasn't his fault.'

'That's obviously not the way he sees it.'

Danny was surprised to see them. Cocky at first but when Ottey informed him of the reason for his arrest the colour drained from his face. The fact that his father had instigated it seemed like a fatal blow to his confidence. Ottey remembered how shocked and sickened Mackenzie had been when they had released Danny from the MCU and so, even though she wasn't an officer, she handed her the handcuffs. It was Mackenzie's first cuffing of a suspect. It was one she would never forget.

Chapter 66

'I've been meaning to ask. Did you post that letter to your mother?' Ottey asked as she was driving Cross through Southville on another case a couple of weeks later.

'I did,' he replied, not going into any further detail.

'Have you heard back?'

'I have not, which is unsurprising in the circumstances.'

'Maybe she hasn't received it.'

'That is a possibility. I think the more likely reason is that she doesn't want to be in touch.'

'I'm surprised at you.'

'Why?'

'Because second guessing someone's actions without any supporting evidence is so unlike you,' she said, only half teasing. He turned to look out of the window; a sure sign he agreed with her but didn't want to show it.

They turned down Flick's street. There was a 'For Sale' sign outside her flat. Ottey wondered whether it was Flick's flat or whether Brian had decided to move.

As they drove past the mini-market, Cross suddenly shouted, 'Stop!'

'What?' said Ottey, immediately pulling over, her heart thumping in her chest.

Cross got out of the car and looked back. 'The shop,' he said.

'What about it?'

'Look at it. What's missing?' he asked.

'I have no idea,' she replied.

'The scaffolding. And look what was underneath it,' said Cross.

To the left of the door, just above it was a CCTV camera.

'It covers the entrance,' said Anil, the shop owner.

'The question is how far down the street it might cover,' said Cross.

'I'm not entirely sure.'

'I thought you had arrested someone,' said his wife, Sunetra.

'We have, but the more evidence we have the better,' Ottey replied.

They went into the back office and Anil settled down at his computer. The shopkeeper typed something on a keyboard and the coverage from the exterior camera appeared. And there right at the edge of the frame was Flick's doorstep.

'When did the scaffolding go up?' asked Cross.

'I don't remember. Do you?' the shopkeeper asked his wife.

'I don't. No,' Sunetra replied.

'All right. Well, was it up on the seventeenth of June?' Cross asked.

'No idea, sorry,' Sunetra said.

'That was the date of Flick's death,' Ottey explained, hoping that it might jog their memories.

'Oh, okay. No it wasn't up then. It went up a couple of weeks later,' Sunetra said.

'Do you still have the footage from then?' Cross asked.

'I don't know. The camera's more of a deterrent to be honest. I'm not even sure if it still records,' said Anil apologetically. He spent the next fifteen minutes searching the computer. Finally he found the relevant dates. It had recorded. He put the three days around Flick's death on a USB for them.

Although they could easily have looked at the footage on one of their desktop computers, Cross insisted they take it to Catherine in CCTV. He felt her experience would make it quicker, and when Ottey questioned this, he replied, 'How would you like it, if someone else started doing your job?'

'A bit like Campbell, I suppose,' she said. He looked at her. 'Joke. Honestly. I forgot.'

'Forgot what?' he persisted. 'You forgot what?'

'That you don't have a sense of humour, George.'

'I can assure you, I most certainly do. The jokes just have to fulfil one requirement,' he said.

'Which is?' she asked, immediately regretting setting herself up as the straight guy to his idiosyncratic logic.

'They need to be funny.'

'Why didn't you just look at it on your computer?' was the first thing Catherine said.

'Because George thought you might be offended,' said Ottey.

'Oh,' said Catherine, touched.

'I did not. It was simply a matter of procedure,' Cross said quickly, destroying the moment.

They studied the grainy footage, spooling through to the night of Flick's death. Nothing at all until just after 9 p.m.

'I don't believe it,' said Ottey quietly.

Chapter 67

Cross had no interest in making the arrest this time. He left it to Ottey, who took uniform with her. Sutton was surprised and disconcerted by the arrest, Ottey noticed. He must've realised they had new evidence. This was frequently the mindset of suspects on rearrest – they knew there had to be a good reason, some sort of progression in the police's case.

Cross had obtained a search warrant for Sutton's house and cycled over. He met a patrol car, which brought a battering ram to knock down the door – he was too impatient to wait and get keys and alarm codes. As he searched the house, uniform called the burglar alarm provider to shut off the alarm.

The house was entirely what Cross expected: an imposing Georgian property in one of Clifton's best terraces overlooking Clifton Down. The inside was minimalist and aesthetically pleasing from an interior design point of view. It had clearly had professional input. The living room was book-lined, and the kitchen, while clutter-free, looked like it was used a lot. The garden was geometrically designed and immaculately pruned. Cross was interested to see a number of framed pictures of Sutton and his late wife – at their wedding, on holiday, with friends.

Cross had already known from his online research that Sutton had no children, and now the presence and number of these elegantly framed photographs underlined that there was only one important relationship in Sutton's life.

There was no evidence of anyone else living in the house – in any of the bathrooms or bedrooms. There were no women's clothes in the wardrobes of the master bedroom or any other bedroom, but Cross noticed a clothes cover hanging up in one bedroom. He opened it and discovered a wedding dress. He got it out to have a proper look and saw that it was the same one as in Sutton's wedding photograph. He had kept her wedding dress.

Miss Havisham came into Cross's mind – the dress representing something that no longer existed in Sutton's life. His wife's passing had obviously had a profound effect on him, and was possibly something he hadn't been able to put behind him or recover from. Cross wondered how this all fitted in with what he was sure had happened – that Sutton had killed Flick.

'You clearly loved your wife, Dr Sutton,' said Cross. 'I've seen the photographs in your house. Her death must've hit you hard – particularly in those circumstances. I, for one, believe your letting her die, in the way you did, was a genuine act of compassion. Self-sacrifice. Have you had many relationships since her death?'

'No,' Sutton replied.

They were back in the interview room. Sutton's aura of confidence and superiority didn't seem to be much in evidence.

'Any?' Cross went on.

'Nothing significant.'

'I also understand how your mother's and wife's deaths informed your views and your campaigning for assisted dying,' said Cross.

Sutton looked at him, wondering where this was going. As was Ottey.

'So here's my question. When did everything change? Why did it change? When did the compassion you showed your wife turn into a total lack of feeling, remorse or humanity, when it came to Flick?'

'No comment,' Sutton replied.

'Was Flick happy with your relationship?' asked Cross.

'I've already answered that question.'

'Was she completely happy with her sessions?'

'Yes.'

'Did she ever talk about ending her therapy with you? Bringing it to an end?' There was no answer so Cross looked up from his file to see Sutton staring at him. He was fairly sure he was trying to calculate how much the police knew and thereby know how to answer the question.

'Had we discussed her stopping? Yes,' he replied carefully. 'But that's quite common with patients. It happens. They believe the sessions have achieved what they set out to do.'

'But that wasn't why Flick told you she wanted to stop, was it?'

'As far as I recall it was, yes.'

'She was unhappy about your dealings with another patient, wasn't she?'

Sutton didn't answer.

'Specifically Leah Sommers.' Cross looked up for a reaction. There was none. So he continued.

'Did you encourage Leah Sommers to end her life?' he asked.

Sutton thought for a second and then appeared to make a decision.

'Are you on the spectrum, Sergeant?' he asked. Cross didn't react in any way to this question.

'Did you encourage Leah Sommers to end her life?' he asked.

'I'm thinking Asperger's, probably,' Sutton went on.

'Did you encourage Leah Sommers to end her life?' Cross asked again.

'Although the view these days is to say Autistic Spectrum Disorder rather than Asperger's. Hans Asperger has been cancelled,' Sutton informed his lawyer.

'Did you encourage Leah Sommers to end her life?' Cross asked.

'Are you autistic, Sergeant?' Sutton asked.

'Did you encourage Leah Sommers to end her life?' Cross asked, as if for the first time.

'Here's my question for you. Does the fact that you are autistic affect the way your findings are perceived in court?' Sutton persisted.

'Did you encourage Leah Sommers to end her life?' Cross repeated.

'Does his condition affect the validity of this interview?' Sutton turned to his lawyer, who gave him a cautionary look. 'I suppose it can't. Interesting, though. Here we are talking about mental capacity and people's ability to make end of life decisions and one of us is mentally... different,' said Sutton.

'Did you encourage Leah Sommers to end her life?' Cross asked again.

Sutton looked at Ottey, who was giving nothing away. 'It must be quite a challenge for you, Sergeant. On a daily basis,' he commented.

'Did you encourage Leah Sommers to end her life?' Cross asked Sutton.

In an adjoining room, Mackenzie and Carson were watching this on a monitor. He turned to her.

'This is exhausting. I'm not even in there and I need a break!' he said and left.

Mackenzie was thinking how brilliant Cross was. She also knew that he could go on asking this same single question, again and again, with the same intonation, for hours, until he got an answer.

Sutton eventually blinked first. 'We discussed it, yes. I also discussed Leah's death with Flick. Did I advise Leah to end her own life? No. I never advise patients to end their lives. Even if assisted dying was legal in this country, it would be massively unethical for any medical professional to do such a thing. It would not be in the best interests of the patient. I would never encourage, persuade or advise a patient to take such a course of action.'

Cross had won the battle. The thing was that only Sutton saw it as such. To Cross, his refusal to answer the question initially was neither here nor there. He made a series of diligent notes in his file. He then produced the photocopied pages from Flick's journal and put them on the table.

'Do you recognise these?'

'No.'

'Are you sure?'

'Yes.'

'For the tape DS Cross is showing Dr Sutton photocopied pages from the victim's journal,' said Ottey.

'As my colleague says, these are pages from Flick's journal. They detail how she was intending to stop her treatment with you. But then again you know that, don't you?'

'No.'

'Because you ripped these pages from her journal before placing it on Diana's bookshelf behind the box files. Presumably in an attempt to implicate her in Flick's death.'

'Can you actually prove that?'

'Good question. The answer is no, despite the fact that we both know it's the truth.' Cross turned to Ottey.

'She'd figured Diana out. It was quite shocking but she knew you had to be involved. You had to know. Your comments on Leah's death all but confirmed it. She was going to expose Diana. You'd be ruined. Your reputation would never recover. Twenty-two patients killed by your secretary. People you were supposed to be looking after and you hadn't even noticed. Hard for the public to believe,' Ottey stated.

'And so I killed her, then attempted to frame my secretary who, according to you, I already knew was murdering my patients. It would be laughable if it wasn't so absurd,' Sutton practically spat this out.

'"Doctor Death",' Ottey announced.

'I beg your pardon?' spluttered Sutton. Even Cross was taken aback.

'I'm just visualising the front pages now. "Advocate of assisted dying goes one step too far". Your new secretary says things are very quiet since Diana's arrest. In fact, since she started working for you, you haven't had a single patient consultation,' said Ottey. There was a long pause which Cross eventually broke.

'But it was so much more than that, wasn't it? It wasn't really as mundane as my colleague is suggesting, was it?' He waited for an answer, which he knew wouldn't come. 'Over the years you've developed a taste for death. A fascination. It began with your mother's and wife's deaths, and then grew with your espousal of the assisted dying cause. But it wasn't just death, was it? It was the witnessing of your mother's and then your wife's deaths that gave you such an inexplicable thrill. One you hadn't experienced since. Then you discovered your secretary was furnishing you with such opportunities, again and again. Your practice was a death factory and you knew how to satisfy your voyeuristic need. If Diana had a blood test booked all you had to do was turn up after she'd left and witness your patient's passing. She must've known what you were doing. It was an unspoken deadly contract between the two of you. Perfect until Flick figured it out. She became a problem you needed to solve. You talked about the power of the moment of someone dying and it was a short step from voyeur to killer. You viewed it as a necessity but the truth is you just had to try it. Maybe it would have been just the once. Thankfully we'll never know. You knew Diana had been killing patients for years, without a whiff of suspicion, so what were the chances of your getting caught? Minimal, surely? You did it because you felt you had to, and felt you could. But above all you couldn't resist seeing what it was like.'

Sutton made no answer.

'For me, the most appalling thing was that you had helped

a patient, a young mother, to recover from a terrible addiction. You had given her a second chance at life, only to take it away. And you were only able to do this because she trusted you. Even though she had decided to end her treatment with you, she still trusted you. I couldn't work out how she let you do one final blood test on her. Then I read the agreement you made with your patients. Well, it's more of a contract, in truth, in which everything is agreed, including consenting to random blood tests. You insist that, at the end of treatment, whether the termination is instigated by the patient or yourself, they have one final blood test to determine whether they are leaving your treatment clean or not. Is that what happened?'

'No comment,' said Sutton.

'Trust. If only she hadn't trusted you. If only she hadn't let you into her flat. If only she hadn't let you persuade her to have one final blood test. How can you live with yourself, I wonder? One thing I am sure of is that you've set the cause of voluntary euthanasia in this country back a good ten years. Because you've broken what everyone needs to have to make that legal: trust. Trust in the medical profession. Trust that if euthanasia existed it wouldn't be abused.'

'This is all well and good in theory, Sergeant, but the truth is you have the perpetrator already in custody. You have no proof that I killed Flick despite all your amateur psychology. Diana was obsessed with me. I can see that now. In her misguided, mad way she was trying to protect me. She's a serial killer, for heaven's sake. What's one more body?'

'Where were you on Tuesday the seventeenth of June?' asked Cross.

'We've been through this. I worked late that day.'

'Did you see Flick Wilson on the seventeenth of June?'

'I did not,' sighed Sutton.

'Are you sure about that?'

'Completely.'

Cross turned to Ottey who produced an iPad and held it up for Sutton and his lawyer to see.

'Then how do you explain this?' Ottey asked as she pressed play. The screen showed footage from the shop CCTV. A man dressed in a long overcoat approached the door to Flick's flat. His face couldn't be seen as he waited for her to answer his knock. Eventually she did. Ottey still found the sight of her alive, opening the door to her killer just hours before her death, upsetting. They talked. There was still no clear view of his face. Then, as he was about to go in, the man turned towards the shop.

Ottey froze the frame. There was absolutely no doubt about it. Looking towards the camera, frozen in time, was Dr Benedict Sutton. Sutton was then shown walking out of the building two hours later, leaving Flick dead inside, with her two-year-old infant.

There was no response from Sutton.

Cross turned to Sutton's lawyer.

'I know you're not overly familiar with the details of this case, but the video you are looking at shows Dr Sutton being let into the victim's flat, on the night of the murder. The young woman you see there is now deceased.'

Cross turned back to Sutton. 'What do you say, Doctor?'

'No comment.'

'It doesn't prove anything,' said the lawyer.

'On the contrary, it puts him at the scene of the crime on the night of her murder and it proves he's been lying to us.

But I sense a need to move things on here. So why don't we do that? As I said, I went to your house today, Dr Sutton. Beautiful home.' He noted Sutton's slight reaction to this. 'Did you have an interior designer, or did your wife do it? I rather thought it was probably done some time after her death. It has a somewhat masculine, muscular angular certainty about it. Anyway, I found these.'

Cross now produced four phials of diamorphine and placed them on the table.

'Diamorphine taken from your fridge just a few hours ago. They were prescribed to a Mrs Brenda Lodge, who it turns out was the mother of a patient of yours. The terminally ill mother. You were marvellous after her death, apparently. But no surprise there. One of the things you did was take her unused diamorphine out of her daughter's reach, so that she wouldn't be tempted to use again at such a testing time. Very thoughtful of you. But you didn't destroy it, did you? You're the second person in this case to have done this. I'm beginning to think we need to look into the disposal of unused opioids and morphine after the deaths of the "prescriptee", as it were. But that's another matter.' Cross had no more to say after this, and so just left.

Chapter 68

The arrests of Diana and Sutton brought huge kudos to the Avon and Somerset police force, but along with it came a certain amount of predictable criticism, mainly along the lines of how it had been possible for Diana to get away with killing people for so long. She herself had been placed on suicide watch in prison after two unsuccessful attempts to take her own life.

Internally it also had ramifications; well, one in particular – Campbell's complaint. His summary dismissal of Flick's death as suicide and deaf ear to Sandra's concerns now looked like being a major error. Ironically, he had actually drawn attention to his mistake, which might otherwise have conveniently slipped under the radar. His complaint had initially been prompted by the fact that he was irked by Cross's insistence at looking into a case where he, Campbell, had been sure no crime had been committed. Cross, with his usual dogged approach – he had refuted Carson's assertion that he had a 'nose' for crime, asserting that he simply looked for facts and anomalies – had uncovered a serial killer on their patch. It was also a fact that in all the other cases in which Campbell had cited Cross's bad behaviour, Campbell himself had been shown to be lacking.

'Campbell's complaint has been thrown out,' Carson told Cross. He had summoned Cross to his office so he could see his face when he delivered the news. Carson was, of course, disappointed.

'I see,' replied Cross. 'Is that all?'

'Aren't you pleased?'

'Um, no. Not particularly. Should I be?'

'Are you not in the least bit interested in the outcome for Campbell?' Carson asked.

'"Outcome"? What do you mean by that? He's not in any trouble, is he?'

'Well, the complaint doesn't reflect well on him,' said Carson.

'Even so, people need to know they can make reasonable complaints without the fear of repercussion. It's essential,' reasoned Cross.

'Of course. No, Campbell isn't being punished, or sanctioned in any way. He has, however, put in a request for a transfer, which will be granted.'

'I see.'

'Well, that must be a relief to you, surely?' Carson went on.

'I have no idea whether it is or not,' Cross replied and left.

Chapter 69

Cross now only had one thing on his mind: the organ recital, which was just a few days away. He found himself surprisingly nervous when thinking about it, and constantly changed his mind about the pieces he was going to play. Stephen was trying to negotiate some festive music to be included. Cross had needed clarification as to what he meant by 'festive' music, and Stephen was insisting on a decision, as he wanted to type up a programme.

'Is that strictly necessary?' asked Cross, who imagined the audience would consist of the elderly ladies of the 'recital committee', together with a few of their friends.

'I think the audience will be interested. I'm going to do some research into the composer and the works you're playing. Then I'll write some notes for the programme,' said Stephen enthusiastically.

'No!' Cross blurted out instinctively.

'Is that a problem?' Stephen asked politely.

'Of course it is. You have no idea what you're talking about when it comes to organ music.'

'So what do you suggest we do?' Stephen asked, smiling innocently. 'I think the audience would really appreciate it.'

'How many are in this audience, exactly?'

'Currently seventy-seven.'

'What?' Cross was horrified.

'I'm expecting it to reach around a hundred, which would be nice,' said Stephen. 'The church Facebook page has had a lot of likes.'

'Facebook page?' said Cross. Then, 'I'll do the notes.'

'Oh, well, if you insist,' said Stephen.

Cross looked at this ingenuous member of the clergy, and realised that, yet again, he'd been manipulated by him. The priest had never had any intention of writing the notes. He knew Cross would insist. Not for the first time, he'd been drawn in and duped by this wily man of the cloth.

It was a cold evening when Cross cycled to the church on what Stephen had mysteriously referred to as his 'big night'. There was an atmospheric fog descending, made a sulphurous yellow by the street lighting. He had a sense that there might be snow that night as the intake of air through his nose was cold enough to make his nostrils flare. He was less nervous than he had been, now that the occasion was actually upon him. The dreaded anticipation had been the worst part of it all. He also consoled himself with the fact that at least no one he knew would be there. He hadn't even told Raymond. In his mind he was treating it like a normal practice with Stephen and a few members of his congregation; conveniently forgetting what the priest had told him about numbers and the Facebook page.

As he approached the church he saw a couple of figures walking up the path, steam puffing from their mouths like a pair of vintage trains. He immediately changed direction and headed for the side door. He padlocked his bike in the vestibule and walked into the church. He was taken aback by the sheer number of people inside – there had to be well over a hundred. But that initial shock turned into abject horror when he saw a group of familiar faces in the crowd. Ottey and her two daughters were there, talking to Raymond. In another group Carson was with Mackenzie, who seemed to have brought Sandra Wilson with her. She was still coming to terms with Sutton having killed her daughter. First there was the shock. She had trusted him so deeply, even after Flick's death. Then the guilt. That maybe it was her fault. She had after all encouraged Flick to continue seeing him. As Mackenzie assured her repeatedly – she hadn't introduced her to him and even if she had she couldn't be held responsible for his hideous actions. No one could have foreseen that.

Cross immediately panicked and swivelled on his heels to make a hasty exit, only to find his path blocked by Stephen.

'George! How are you? Nervous? This is exciting, isn't it?' said Stephen enthusiastically.

'Not the first word that comes to mind,' Cross replied stiffly.

'Are you okay to start on time?'

'Of course.' Cross found the idea of not starting anything on time completely unthinkable and so was puzzled by the priest's even asking.

'Good. One slight problem. Oliver's ill,' said Stephen. Oliver was the church organist who had kindly agreed to turn the music sheets for Cross.

'Oh no. I can't play without someone helping. He was

403

going to do some of the stops during the Widor,' said Cross, now wanting to leave even more urgently than before.

'I know. But I'll do it. Not the stops, obviously, but I can turn the pages if you tell me when.'

'I don't think so. I might as well do it myself,' replied Cross tersely.

'Hello, George. This is exciting,' said Mackenzie, who had appeared on his shoulder.

Why did people keep saying that? thought Cross. 'It's cancelled, unfortunately, due to unforeseen circumstances,' he said.

'What? Oh no, why?' asked Mackenzie, who was now used to these overdramatic statements from her boss and knew that they were often knee-jerk reactions to things his brain couldn't process in the moment.

'Oliver is ill,' Cross informed her.

'Who is Oliver?'

'The organist who was going to turn the music for me.'

'Oh, is that all? I can do that,' she said.

'I think not,' said Cross.

'Why?'

'There is an obligatory requirement to be able to read music,' he responded.

'You're looking at grade eight piano, George,' she said.

'I didn't know that,' said Cross.

'Let's be honest – there's actually an awful lot you don't know about me.'

The audience settled. In the organ loft Cross familiarised Mackenzie with the pieces and then placed the sheet music in order on the stool next to him.

THE PATIENT

'Ready?' Mackenzie asked. 'Everyone's sitting down and quiet.'

Cross looked at his watch. They were due to start at eight and it was two minutes before. He waited, then as the minute hand indicated it was exactly eight o'clock, he began to play. He played beautifully. There were a few mistakes here and there, but only he would've noticed. It was an accomplished, elegant performance; majestic and towering at certain times, at others subtle and muted.

Mackenzie almost missed a page turn at one point, so wrapped up in the music was she. She was entranced not only by Cross's skill but also his physical dexterity and coordination. His feet floated over the pedals, finding the right notes blindly, as his fingers danced over the four manuals, occasionally leaping up to change the organ stops. It was engrossing to watch.

It occurred to Mackenzie, as she looked at his face, a picture of intense concentration, that she was seeing something she'd never seen in him before: emotion. Great tides of it passed across his face – passion, vulnerability, sadness, triumph – as he interpreted the music. She'd never witnessed him being so animated. She thought that maybe she was seeing the real George Cross for the first time. It was as if playing the organ was the only way he could really express himself. Something he found impossible in normal, everyday life.

As he finished the last piece, the audience burst into spontaneous applause, led by the delighted Stephen, who was actually on his feet. Mackenzie realised that her face was sopping wet with tears. This man, this eccentric, often infuriating creature, with whom she worked on a daily basis, and who she hardly knew at all, had moved her profoundly and unexpectedly. He looked up at her.

'Is something wrong?' he asked.

'No, I'm sorry. It was just very moving, that's all. Amazing. Listen to the audience,' she said.

'I don't understand why you're upset,' he said.

'I'm not. Is there a ladies' room here?'

'Why would you expect me to know that?'

'You're right. I'll see you downstairs,' she said, disappearing.

He was slightly puzzled and then really annoyed with himself. He hadn't said 'thank you'. Ottey would be furious if she found out.

It seemed that his playing had had a similar effect on everyone in the church. They were all deeply impressed and moved. A general purr of approval filled the church from several conversations as the audience helped themselves to refreshments. Raymond looked a little lost for words.

'What's the matter, Raymond?' asked Ottey.

'Nothing,' he replied.

'It was fantastic. I had no idea,' she went on.

'Neither did I.'

'What do you mean?'

'I've never heard him play the organ before. The piano, yes, but this was different somehow,' he said quietly.

Stephen was thrilled with the way it had gone and was speaking to Carson and Sandra.

'I'm so glad I came,' Sandra said.

'Me too,' said Carson. 'He's a bit of an enigma, our George.'

'He'll be so happy to see you, I'm sure,' said Stephen.

'I haven't had the chance to thank him for...' she said, but didn't finish.

'Well, I'm sure he'll be down in a minute,' Stephen said confidently.

Had he turned round at that point, though, he would've seen the side door of the church close as Cross left the building quietly. He had taken one look at the crowd in the church and realised he couldn't cope. He knew that if he wasn't careful he might upset someone unintentionally and spoil the evening. The safest course of action was to leave. Mackenzie saw him go and was momentarily tempted to stop him, but for some reason she decided not to. She thought it best to let him go in peace.

But she wasn't alone. Another person noticed. A member of the audience who had been sitting at the back of the church for the recital and hadn't moved. She watched Cross leave, then sat there for a few more minutes. Finally, George Cross's mother picked up her handbag, put her coat on and left the church.

ACKNOWLEDGEMENTS

I'd like to thank Fiona Marsh for sharing the book with her boss, Jason Bartholomew, who is now my literary agent who set everything in motion and more. Laura Palmer for publishing *The Patient* and all her advice along the way. The team at Head of Zeus for all their work on getting the book out there. I'd never worked with a professional copy-editor and it was a revelation, so thanks to Lucy Ridout for her thoroughness and eagle-eyed support. Hayley Cox at Midas PR for her publicity expertise. Obviously thanks to my daughters Isabella and Sophia and my wife, Rachel, for putting up with having a would-be crime novelist at the top of the house for the last couple of years. Lastly to the late Roger Michell, my oldest friend, to whom this book is dedicated, and without whose encouragement George Cross wouldn't exist.

ABOUT THE AUTHOR

TIM SULLIVAN is a crime writer, screenwriter and director, whose film credits include *A Handful of Dust*, *Jack and Sarah*, and *Cold Feet*. His crime series featuring the socially awkward but brilliantly persistent DS George Cross has topped the book charts and been widely acclaimed. Tim lives in North London with his wife Rachel, the Emmy Award-winning producer of *The Barefoot Contessa* and *Pioneer Woman*. To find out more about the author, please visit TimSullivan.co.uk.